# Steplings

## a novel

C.W. SMITH

TCU Press
Fort Worth

Library of Congress Cataloging-in-Publication Data

Smith, C. W. (Charles William), 1940-
  Steplings : a novel / by C.W. Smith.
      p. cm.
  ISBN 978-0-87565-437-9 (cloth : alk. paper)
  I. Title.
  PS3569.M516S74 2011
  813'.54--dc22
                         2010046701

TCU Press
P. O. Box 298300
Fort Worth, Texas 76129
817.257.7822
http://www.prs.tcu.edu

To order books: 800.826.8911

Designed by Bill Brammer, fusion29.com

*To the memory of*
*Private First Class James Sanders*
*1984 - 2004*

# One

It would seem a wholesome American scene, an updated Rockwell portrait. Here, on a September afternoon in 2003, a young man—shirtless, tanned torso, blond ponytail, cut-off jean shorts—was mowing the lawn of a modest ranch-style home in a Dallas suburb thirty years past its prime. Hackberry roots buckled the sidewalks, a few dead vehicles hunkered on cinder blocks in driveways or beside garages, and RVs were parked in plain sight; some houses had that closed-up, neglected look that results when the inhabitants grow old and run out of energy or money to replace a torn screen, to have the trim painted, or to worry about landscaping. When it came to lawn maintenance, people on this block watered yards with sprinklers on hoses and usually cut their own grass or hired a kid like Jason to do it.

Today, though, Jason was working *gratis* for his father, Burl. (Of course, as Burl rightly and often pointed out, it was Jason's lawn, too.) Since July, Jason had been looking for a job. He had applied at several restaurants and at three stores at Town East Mall. The mall was problematic because he'd been fired last spring from a job manning a sunglasses kiosk because he kept leaving it unattended. "It made me feel like a dog on a chain," he had complained to his father. He had also filled out applications at all three Mesquite Pep Boys auto stores (the job he wanted the most) and at two Blockbusters, including one on Belt Line and Military Parkway managed by a dweeb who had once ratted Jason out for smoking in the North Mesquite High School restroom.

After a callback at the Belt Line Blockbuster, he'd gone in and talked to the assistant manager, a black girl who said she'd attended NMHS and who seemed friendly enough, but she said he'd have to talk to the manager. He'd intended to set an appointment this very morning, but before he got around to it, Burl called from work at ten to tell him he'd just gotten off the phone with their lawyer.

There was good news and bad news, Burl told Jason. The good news was that after riding the fence for these three months, Lisa's father had finally agreed to withdraw charges for unauthorized use of a motor vehicle on the Miata, and the charge of minor in possession had been dismissed for lack of evidence. Of course, the shoplifting charge was dismissed too, because Jason wasn't even in the store when somebody stole that fistful of Slim Jims, so the clerk couldn't identify him as the culprit who had provoked his 911 call.

And the charge of resisting arrest had been downgraded to failure to obey a police officer.

When Burl didn't go on, Jason said, "So what's the bad news?"

"The bad news is that the charge of assault with bodily harm is still on you, son, and we're going to court on Monday unless you make a plea bargain."

"But I just *ran into* him, Dad! He was standing in the way trying to stop me! If he fractured his freaking skull and broke his collarbone, it's not my fault! I didn't *try* to do that—I just wanted out of his way!"

"I know that, son. The lawyer said that might make a difference, and it's possible that charge will be downgraded, too. You might want to think about how you say all that, though. You might try to sound a little bit sorry." Burl sounded a little bit angry. "In the meantime we got to expect that they'll try to scare the bejesus out of us."

"They are!"

Burl's chuckle sounded like a ragged sigh. "Yeah. So maybe

in the end it will be some lesser charge, and there's hope for a probated sentence if you plead guilty."

Jason fumed in silence. Why didn't that old fucker get out of the way instead of trying to be a hero? Who makes a citizen's arrest over a half-dozen sticks of jerky?

Burl said, "What's for sure is that Mr. Crawford will be filing a civil suit against us for damages."

"Good luck with that! I'm eighteen and I don't even have a job! What's he gonna do, have them put me in indentured servitude or something?"

"No, son, since you were seventeen when this happened, they'll come after me and Lily, and maybe even Meemaw if they feel like it. They could go after Lily's mutual fund portfolio or garnishee my paychecks or go after my pension."

Jason could tell his dad was piling it on. For one thing, pitiful old Meemaw was so poor Medicaid paid for her nursing home. But he heard his dad's steely anger and knew Burl didn't like the attitude Jason had struck. He was tempted to ask what Lily had to do with anything, but, chastened by the possibilities if not by his father's tone, he said, meekly, "Then that's the worst news."

When Burl had no response and they'd both held their receivers for a good many seconds like truculent trolls with cudgels, Jason said, sighing, "I don't know what to do, Dad. I'm sorry."

Burl said, "It would help if you'd mow the lawn."

Jason had carried this news in his head all day long, and it had made his head heavier by the hour. He moped for a while after the call, then tried to work on his song for Lisa, thinking that it would take his mind off his troubles, then he went into Emily's room to use her Mac because it had the only Internet connection in the house (his Compaq was six years old, a hand-me-down from his mother, who had gotten it when her church office upgraded). He wrote Lisa a long e-mail using his Hotmail account, spilling his guts about his worries and the call from Burl and the trial coming up and how much he missed her and loved her and how lonely he felt. He said he knew that after what he'd done at her graduation party and his arrest, he wasn't welcome at their home. He could understand that, but it hurt him bad that she was so cold. He riffed on for a while, desperately flailing about, trying to snag her heart: did she remember when they were carnival king and queen in seventh grade and wore those cheesy costumes—well, his was, she was truly bride-beautiful in hers—and when he kissed her for the first time down in the woods behind her house, and did she remember how they had their first alone date at the state fair—his mom had dropped them off and her dad had picked them up—and rode the Texas Star and it was so tall she was scared and tucked under his arm in the car they had all to themselves and you could see all the lights below around them and the lights in the downtown buildings and it seemed like they were crackling electric alive in an urban wonderland and the October breeze had made her bare arms goosebump and he'd rubbed them smooth, and later he'd won that pink giraffe at the midway with the BB guns for her, the one she'd still had on her bed as of last spring, and when he got home that night before he went to bed he wrote her that note that said *I had fun I hope you did too because I want you to be my girlfriend.*

He'd left off typing and let the images flow over him: Lisa sitting beside him and his dad as "family" at his mom's funeral and holding his hand, tutoring him in algebra for the GED, coaxing him into going with her to see their pastor about his grief. He added *When you get right down to it, you're not just the world's best girlfriend but the best friend friend.* She worried about how clean his clothes were, whether he'd eaten on any particular day or not.

Left unsaid were the blissful hours gasping and wallowing in their sweat in the backseat of her car, the miraculous whole night spent in a bed at Cara's mom's lake house where they'd discovered all the ways to use lips and tongues . . . the delicate fragrance of her flesh in the crook of her neck, the tender backs of her knees, the taste of grape Kool-Aid Lip Smackers on her soft, moist mouth.

*Babe, I love you like a monkey loves its tail, like a hammer loves a nail, like a zebra loves its stripes, like a pitchman loves his hypes.*

But even censored the e-mail sounded way too whiney and needy, too full of cheap snares. He left it in his Drafts folder instead of deleting it because there was a line in it he thought he might use in a song: *In my heart the hurt and you are crammed together in the same tight space. . . .*

Whoever said writing about your pain made you feel better was full of it. Writing that e-mail had aroused his feeling of loss, not like scratching at a scab—more like when you knock a big scabby wound against a doorframe. Made him want to howl and clutch himself.

Soon after the graduation party in June, Lisa had left for a family vacation to Vail that lasted all of July, then she'd come back for only a couple weeks in August to work at Amy's Hallmark Shop in the mall before leaving for UT Austin. She'd called him the night before she left. Or, more accurately, she'd finally answered his call.

She said she still loved him. That's what she said. I'll always love you, Jason.

The Sanborns' backyard was a simple square of grass broken only by a rusting swing set and a bumpy brick patio Burl had laid years ago without sufficiently compacting the base beneath it. By three o'clock when Emily was dropped off by Mrs. Munoz, whose son Rafey went to her school, Jason had moved to the front with the mower, the electric trimmer, and the hand clippers, and he was refilling the tank on the mower when Emily came down the walk with her book bag.

"How was school?" Jason asked, then heard in his own question the age-old parental quest for not so much knowledge as contact.

"Sucked!"

She halted in the walk to watch him, and he wasn't certain if she wanted him to press for more. Was this the "sucked" he always offered his parents merely to say it was usual, it was normal, it was boring? "Fine" would do as well, but it wouldn't suggest you were miserable and needed sympathy (but weren't directly asking for it). If you did a scratch-off on Emily's "sucked" would you uncover a picture of defeat and humiliation?

He felt a little helpless in this role in the first place. Whatever she might say, he'd wager his day spent here sucked way more. Her sucky day would only be a pimple on the butt of his. And for the umpteenth time he thought of the many bad tricks God had played on him over the past two years, plopping this twerp into his life made the top ten. *Guess what, son! You're gonna have a stepsister!* Of course he'd dreamed of a girl his age, somebody cool to hang with. Somebody to explain Lisa to him and act as a go-between. But no. Supernerd, pigtails and glasses.

He smirked. "Too bad."

Before she could sass him back, he yanked the starter cord, the mower burst into roaring life, and he pushed it off toward the far corner. As he went along, he found something soothing and pleasurable about methodically mowing the two rectangles on either side of the front walk, moving clockwise around the perimeter from outside to inside at twenty-one-inch intervals and letting the mower fling the clippings onto the next new unmowed quadrangle. That way he was always mowing the cut clippings along with the uncut grass, and he'd wind up at the center of the labyrinth with a heap of damp mulch he could bag.

Pushing the mower and feeling it vibrate through his hands woke up his muscles, his ligaments and tendons, his synovial fluids. Watching the mown path slowly but steadily increase its width as he circumnavigated the yard seemed like an antidote to the disorder of the day, of his life. He could see where he was going; he could anticipate the result of his action; what he was doing produced a beneficial result. He'd always poked fun at preachers and teachers (and his mom, of course!) who professed to live their lives this way: progress toward a distant goal with patience, construct and religiously maintain a daily unbroken regimen of diet and exercise, adhere to the philosophy of deferred gratification. It meant savings accounts; it meant getting up early and doing the same thing each Monday night or Saturday morning (Mom's Bible study group, her ironing); it meant that if somebody gave Meemaw some nice linen hankies, she kept them in their original packaging in her dresser drawer for fifty years and never used them. (Maybe that was where Mom got it from.) Meemaw was more or less the model for all of that, he considered, and look where it got her. She was brain-dead. And look where it got Mom. Just plain dead.

He shivered, shook his head, dug back into his furrow, a mule in the traces. Suppose, he thought, that he went at his life the way he was presently working at the lawn, imposing this kind of order. Could he enjoy it more? Or would it at least help him bear his troubles? Could he achieve something? Could he make his mom smile up there?

The mail carrier interrupted his labor and his musings. He shut down the mower to meet her at the box, largely as an excuse for a break. She'd told him her name was Shondell. She always sweated so profusely that her glasses slithered to the end of her nose, and her mailbag slung over her shoulder was so weighty the thick strap made a valley there between bulges of flesh. But she always seemed happy. Jason wondered what she thought of her job. He'd become curious lately (and belatedly, he felt) about jobs, careers—what adults did with their time to earn a living and how they felt about it. Did she ever feel used or useless when she had to tote around so much junk mail that she knew would be tossed into the trash unread?

"Hot enough for you?" Jason asked. The words felt like a foreign food dish in his mouth; uttering such a banal adult cliché made him feel a strange mixture of pride and embarrassment.

Shondell laughed. "Oh, Lord! If it gets any hotter they'll have to suck me up with a hose."

"Would you like some water or something?"

"Oh, no thanks, hon! My truck's at the end of the block and I've got a jug of ice cold sweet tea in it!"

He took the stack of mail from her, and she hiked up the shoulder with the bag strapped to it with a shrug and went lumbering on, her white sun helmet cocked to the side. Going up the walk, he leafed through the stack. Ad flyers, pizza coupons. There was a safety newsletter from his dad's work and a brochure from the US Army. Sgt. Brookes and his recruiting partner had stopped stalking Jason since his arrest, though he'd called Jason's house more than once to ask about the disposition of his case. Man, but those dudes were dogged! You'd think that since Bush said "mission accomplished" they'd kick back and let the guys who were all gung-ho come a-knockin' now that it was a little safer to put your name but not your life on the line. Sgt. Brookes had been like a Whac-A-Mole for a while last spring, popping up when you least expected: *Hey Sanborn, dude, lemme buy you a burger and just "chew the fat,"* ha, ha, ha. As if any conversation with him wasn't going to end up with a pitch about three squares, see the world, full medical benefits, and money for college when you get out. . . .

Lily got an issue of *Psychology Today.* He'd never heard of the magazine until Lily came into their lives. She also subscribed to *Smithsonian, Southern Living, Redbook,* and *Texas Highways.* She told Jason she'd once had subscriptions to twenty magazines but had to cut back after her divorce. Jason fingered three envelopes addressed to Burl Sanborn and culled them from the stack. Bills, probably: TXU power, Chase Mastercard, SBC. Handling them gingerly, he was instantly swept back to the morning's call about the civil suit, and the bills in his hand, once harmless because he'd been utterly indifferent to them, suddenly possessed a new potency to alarm.

Although he hadn't expected one, there was a letter from Lisa. The return address was Dobie Dorm, UT Austin. His heart thundered. They'd spoken once on the phone since she'd left, and she'd been insistent on talking only about her daily routine, so he'd surrendered to that and interviewed her when he could think of a question that she hadn't already answered in her monologue. If she was still interested in him, she sure didn't show it. She hadn't asked about his court date or his job search, but she had said, sort of flinging it at him as her cell was disconnecting, "Love you!"

Then she'd sent him a couple of e-mails, but they were chatty, breezy, full of information about her classes and her new friends, things of which he had no firsthand knowledge. Little in them showed the Lisa he felt he'd known—and they only made her seem more distant.

He slipped her letter into his back pocket and carried the stack into the house, where he dropped it on the coffee table, then strode quickly down the hall past Emily's open door and didn't glance into her room for fear she might waylay him.

He shut his bedroom door behind him, slipped the letter out and stood looking at it. Could be something as innocent as a newspaper clipping, maybe. Or a picture of her—he'd asked for one. All other reasons for putting her feelings into this form rose up like menacing specters, which Jason, like a child in a dark room, tried to blink away into harmless shapes.

He shoved his guitar to the foot of his bed and sat by his pillow. He dug his pen knife from his pocket and, carefully, as if preserving an artifact, slit the envelope down the end, blew it open, drew the folded paper out pinched between his fingers. She'd written in her best salutatorian's cursive using a pen with blue ink on peach-colored personalized stationery she'd gotten as a graduation present.

*Dear Jason,*
*This is the hardest letter I've ever had to write. . . .*

Whoa! Stop right there! Jason tossed it onto his desk but a second later picked it up again. Pursuing the now predictable path of the letter was as irresistible as taking a whiff of your own crap.

*I've felt so guilty for so long because I know you care so much for me, and, believe me, I'm so deeply grateful that you have. Over all these years I've always known that you're a wonderful person with so many great qualities and abilities, and I've always been so proud to be your friend. And I've appreciated so much having you by my side on so many occasions. . . .*

Friend? So far, this was like a speech she might deliver at her honor society banquet. Come on, girl! Get real, okay?

*But like I say, I've felt guilty all this past summer because I know you've wanted more from me than you've gotten. It seems like for a long time it was just that I was busy with school and you weren't* (he knew this was her diplomatic way of referring to his dropping out) *and then there was all the planning to get me here and stuff, and it all seemed like a whirlwind caught me up and my feet weren't on the ground, you know? Then all the stuff with the car and everything happened, and Daddy really put his foot down about us and all. At first I was thinking that it wasn't fair of him to try to control me that way, you know, and I wanted to show him he couldn't, that I was too old to be treated like that. I don't know if you blame him or not for why we didn't get together more this summer, but I know that I sort of kept acting as if he was the reason I couldn't meet you or talk freely on the phone without sneaking around.*

*But I guess what I found out when I got here and was more or less out from under his thumb is that—gosh, this is really hard, Jason!—is that I guess I sort of wanted and needed him to do that so I wouldn't have to face what I really felt myself.*

*I know what you're thinking now! We've been together so long it's like I can read your mind across all these miles as you're reading this, and I know that what you're imagining is that I'm trying to toss you aside like you're so much trash or baggage from back there, and it's just not true! You've got to believe that, Jason! What you are to me and what we've always been together will always be an important and really crucial part of me, of who I am, and nothing will ever change that!!*

*But things change, circumstances do, you know?*
*I'm here, you're there. And I have to admit I love*
*being in college! **I love** going to class and living with*
*other students my age who have ideas and who talk*
*freely about them without being afraid that some-*
*body will poke fun at them. I love my Honors*
*classes and my professors, even if two of them stand*
*at the bottom of a lecture hall filled with 120 other*
*students. It's like learning on a whole other level,*
*here.*

*That really wasn't a sidetrack. It was part of why*
*I'm writing this letter. I just feel right now that our*
*lives are taking us in very different directions and*
*that we each should feel free to explore those paths*
*without feeling that the other is going to stand in the*
*way or cause a detour that wouldn't be natural or*
*beneficial. Please believe me when I say this IS NOT*
*ABOUT GOING OUT WITH OTHER PEO-*
*PLE!!!, though if you feel you need to do that as*
*part of your exploration, then I know that as much*
*as it might hurt me, I have to believe that it's what's*
*best for you. . . .*

Jason could anticipate this next sentence almost word for
word.

*And I hope you'd feel the same for me. Loving*
*somebody often means letting them go the way they*
*need to go to become their very best, to fulfill what-*
*ever's in them that lies dormant. . . .*

Jason snickered. That was like something she'd read on a
card at Amy's Hallmark, though it was way too long to fit on
a page.

*So—please please please!! DO NOT misunderstand*
*this letter! I DO want you to be part of my life,*

*Jason! I hope you CAN be! But we each need room
to grow.*

*And whatever happens, I will ALWAYS be your
friend!*

*Love,*

*Lisa.*

After Jason had read the letter ten times, he decided that all the words and phrases in the upper case were lies. That's why they needed to be capitalized. She was just trying to shout down his doubt.

————————————————————

For Burl, the long, trying day had gotten a rocky start with the attorney's call and had continued to kick its way through his equanimity by heaping exasperation upon frustration when the pipeline repair job he was supervising got bit by one gnarly snake after the other. An old dislocation of his left knee caused the joint to buckle as he foolishly jumped off the loading dock at the service center on Main rather than walking to the end and using the stairs; he'd landed wrong, with the result that his knee had been aching and throbbing since. That set him walking at an odd cant and that in turn aggravated the arthritis in his spine. The pollen count today had been 4398, much of it fungus, and that made his head feel like a basketball swollen with snot.

After work, Burl drove to Good Shepherd to check on Mrs. Larkins and to deliver her ninety-day supply of Norvasc, which he'd refilled by mail. Today he really lacked the energy and patience to visit Jason's grandmother and hoped to make a quick drop-off and getaway (surely the mere threat of his inspection would keep the staff on the up and up), but after he'd keyed himself in on the touchpad to the Alzheimer's wing, he stumbled upon Mrs. Larkins in the TV room before he found the duty nurse. Lawrence Welk was on, muted. The Lennon Sisters, clad in yellow dresses ballooned by huge petticoats, were merrily mouthing a tune while Mrs. Larkins and three others had been parked here to languish; their chairs faced the TV and their faces were bathed in flickering washes of color. Mrs. Larkins wasn't wearing her glasses or her hearing aids, and her sunken cheeks were proof her dentures were elsewhere. Her hair had been brushed, however. A flash of rage welled up in him, but he squelched it and moved quickly to her side.

"Hey, Meemaw! How are you? It's Burl, honey. Open your eyes!" He shook her shoulder gently, and the old woman's lids popped up and her dark eyes rolled wildly for a moment then settled on him.

"Hello, hello!" she crowed. She spoke as if to a neighbor whose name you didn't know who crossed your path at a supermarket.

"Where are your glasses, hon?" he asked pointlessly. "And your hearing aids?"

She frowned in confusion. Leaning closer to search her lap and the chair seat, he caught a whiff and knew she needed changing, too. Burl felt vaguely responsible for the neglect, though his discovery of it had come accidentally and in spite of his wish to avoid it. He didn't know why her glasses were missing, but they removed her hearing aids when they showered her and sometimes didn't put them back in. Her dentures were another story; now and then a patient would pick them up if they were visible on her nightstand and take off with them. More than once, the staff had been forced to do an oral line-up of patients to locate her dentures.

He found the head nurse, Casey Bergeron, in the shower room with two orderlies; the three were bent over an old fellow sitting naked on the tile floor with his back to the wall. Soon as Burl barged in, the nurse glanced up and held her hand out like a traffic cop, so he backed away and stood in the hall. When Nurse Bergeron emerged she greeted him politely but kept glancing over his shoulder as she asked if she could help him. He reported the missing items and added that Mrs. Larkins's "protective undergarment" needed changing. She led him to the lost-and-found drawer at the nurse's kiosk, which contained three hearing aids, but none was tagged or otherwise identified. Burl could eliminate an over-the-ear model. He tested the two remaining possibilities and decided that the battery was dead in one, and the other seemed too large to be hers.

"For pity's sake!" He scowled at Nurse Bergeron. Complaining to her was fruitless, as she had the hide of a rhino and generally took his occasional protests about the staff's negligence in stride. Her refusal to take them personally exasperated Burl. But he believed the nurses did the best they could under circumstances that inevitably involved being short-handed.

Though the missing hearing aids didn't turn up immediately, Burl did find her dentures and glasses in the nightstand, though he had a nagging suspicion that the dentures didn't belong to her. After delivering them to the nurse with a sour scowl, he left feeling neither the satisfaction of having made a difference nor the pleasure of having lived up to the silent vow he'd made to Sue to watch over her mother. Lily once asked him if Sue had explicitly asked him to do this. Burl had said no, but he knew that Sue hoped he would and knew him well enough to trust that he'd try.

Tonight there'd be more arguments with Jason about the hearing on Monday and an uncomfortable session with Lily about the attorney's report. He agonized about how much to tell. Should he mention the civil suit? It hadn't been filed yet, so maybe not.

Nevertheless, Burl was eager to be home and lay down his burdens. At last, after the wedding last month, they had cobbled together a place that felt right, he and Lily and Emily and Jason. Lily's moving in with Burl hadn't been easy for either spouse; each preparatory small act he'd performed to erase Sue's presence cost him a lash of guilt and sullen looks from Jason. When Lily finally arrived with her own furniture, newer and better than his and Sue's, it had only made sense to cart the old dining and living room pieces to Goodwill, along with the nightstands and side tables and such Sue had brought over from Meemaw's place when she had moved to Good Shepherd. (When Lily suggested a garage sale, Burl said he couldn't bear to see the furniture set out in the yard.)

Burl had also surrendered to Lily's notions about paint and "window treatments," as well as her preferences for what went on shelves and walls. Sue had fairly plastered the walls with photos of family and embroidered homilies or Bible verses in gilded frames (the latter inherited from Meemaw) and ready-made art that depicted kittens or flowers. Sue'd also had a weakness for refrigerator magnets, particularly those in the shapes of hearts, fruits, vegetables, animals, and characters from newspaper cartoons such as Garfield. She also had a small, beloved collection of Hummel figurines she'd displayed in a china cabinet. Lily had a word for that kind of thing, a foreign word that sounded like "kitchen." Though Burl didn't know precisely what it meant, he could guess it signified contempt, and that piqued his irritation a little because he knew for a fact that the figurines weren't cheap and that Sue had often saved to buy one. Thanks to this collection, you always knew what you could get her for her birthday. At present, the fragile little figurines were nestled in tissue inside a box at the bottom of Burl's chest of drawers.

Lily brought to their marriage an enormous stainless steel Sub-Zero refrigerator, bumping the old GE out to the garage, where it now served as an auxiliary for cold drinks and ice and sat between stacks of cartons filled with Meemaw's dishware and clothing and such. The Sub-Zero's unadorned metallic flanks and front would be the ideal backdrop for a festoon of magnetry, but Lily wouldn't allow even a tacky-backed grocery list to mar the surface. Huge framed posters from the Metropolitan Museum of Art and prints of paintings by Frenchmen went up on their walls, and since Lily didn't have collections, she preferred an empty space along the wall to a china cabinet stuffed with knick-knacks. For the sake of making them both more at ease, they traded Burl's and Sue's old queen-size four-poster for Lily's more modern king-size bed with a bookcase headboard. Lily turned out to be a person who had to read herself to sleep. She liked thrillers by Jonathan Kellerman and Patricia Cornwell, and she had a special little light that clipped to the book. It had taken him a while to get used to going to sleep alone, back turned to his mate, because he and Sue always fell asleep in each other's arms.

He'd wound up with a far better recliner—black leather—and a flat-screen 36" Sony in place of an old 19" RCA, so he couldn't complain. All these transformations and the wearing water-drip of time itself (though they'd been together in this house a little more than a month) had altered their circumstances: Sue was no longer the absent hostess and Lily merely a guest. Now it seemed that Lily lived here as the mistress of the house, and Sue was someone from his past, a relative, say, who had come to stay for a good while but who had since returned home. It was amazing sometimes how pressingly insistent the present could be in its power to wash away the past. But it was also unnerving to unexpectedly stumble on an item from that past—in the kitchen utility drawer, at the back, a nightlight with a plastic translucent angel that Sue'd gotten for Jason's room when he was a baby; in a bathroom vanity drawer, under the towels, the shower cap that she'd always joked was "lay bone sha-po"; in his sock and underwear drawer, a small muslin bag stuffed with sage she'd stripped from shrubs herself alongside I-40 outside Santa Rosa, New Mexico, one summer vacation, sage now dried to a crumbly gray powder and the scent long since leached away into the air. In all these surprises festered a pocket of pain, a wince of sadness and loss. It was a little as if Sue had been reincarnated as a pack rat who crept about at two A.M. planting these little land mines of memory.

At half past six as he was coming down their street, he experienced a familiar raw gnaw in his gut that had normally preceded supper and always aroused a further eagerness to get parked, cleaned up, and seated at the table. In the old days, Sue never left the house for her job without having a meal cooked, maybe in a Crock-Pot or a Dutch oven, put in the stove soon as she got home at three-thirty. But Lily wasn't much for cooking. Her work was more demanding, more draining; to assemble the packets of papers necessary for a proper real estate closing required a good many phone calls and juggling dates and making second and third requests of various parties to produce copies of this and that. Burl had to admit that Lily's daily routine was a good deal harder than Sue's part-time secretarial work for her church. Since Lily and Emily had come to live with him and Jason, Burl's ideas of the division of labor between husband and wife had been jostled and knocked to the ground a time or two. In all the roiling, one thing for certain had bobbed to the surface: a husband should not expect his working wife to produce a hot, home-cooked meal each night. Lily was willing to assume responsibility for their supper but made it clear everyone was to consider the meal as sustenance only, and any complaints about the quality or quantity would provoke a walk-out.

As he came closer to the house, the front lawn clarified into focus through his windshield.

"Aw, dammit to hell!"

He pulled in behind Lily's Civic, turned off his engine, dropped his forehead against the upper rim of the wheel. Shut his eyes. He counted slowly, silently, to ten. Still, though, his hands trembled with the need to grasp and squeeze, the soles of his steel-toed boots jammed to the floorboard. *God grant me the serenity to accept the things I cannot change; courage to change the things I can; and the wisdom to know the difference.*

One step of the twelve was making amends to those you'd injured. Of course, Jason had been highest on the list, along with Sue, who, even though deceased, could be considered an injured party because while Burl was on that last toot, hopefully the *very last* toot, he'd not lived up to his implicit promise to Sue to father *and* mother Jason the best he could.

Burl had made amends to Jason. But now he wondered whether Jason hadn't taken that as a blank check for flouting the rules. Something for group discussion, really: when you ask your kid's forgiveness for being a drunk and therefore a sorry parent, does that free him from your authority? Have you undermined yourself? He and Lily were in the same boat in that regard, afloat in the same sea of spirits.

Burl got out of the truck, locked the doors. The picture of

a cold quart bottle of Vladimir vodka shot about in his skull like a cannonading racquet ball and he had to blink it down. He hoped Lily wasn't in the same frame of mind.

He paused on the edge of the grass. The choice was clear but complicated. Jason had abandoned the mower mid-cut on the lawn, walked away from the gas can sitting on the walk, left the weed-eater leaning like, well, a drunk against the untrimmed variegated privet by the front steps. This constituted a cluster of violations, chief among which was ignoring Burl's request to mow the lawn. He hadn't said "half-mow" the lawn, had he? And for Christ's sake, you'd think that considering what he'd told Jason on the phone this morning about the assault charge and the probable civil suit, the kid would want to show some good will! Wouldn't you? Was it too goddamn much to ask? And Jason knew that no job was complete until the tools had been cleaned and put away. How many times over the years had Burl told him that? And why'd he wait so late to do it? It's not as if he had been busy all day doing something else for the family's benefit, was it?

So—Burl could put these tools away himself or make Jason do it. (Other choices danced fleetingly to mind—take a stick to the boy and/or drive off to a bar.) Putting them up himself meant it would be done, of course, and while doing it, there'd be the work-up, the coal stoked into the furnace, the team whipped into a frenzy by an angry coach at halftime. As he put the tools away, Burl could enjoy the sour pleasure of feeling sorry for himself and be furious at Jason for *making* Burl do it. But he hadn't spent the last year or so in group meetings without learning something, and this solution would solve nothing in the long run.

He went through the front door and heard voices from the kitchen at the back of the house, so he strode through the dining room and directly back there rather than passing Jason's bedroom in the hall. It had occurred to him that he should give Jason the benefit of the doubt: it was possible, wasn't it, that Lily had interrupted Jason's work to ask him to do something? Or maybe somebody had called about a job while he was mowing, and he was on the phone now or had gotten a ride to an interview. It was even possible, though not probable, that he'd actually scored a job earlier in the day and had been asked to report immediately. Wasn't it?

Burl hung back a moment in the dining room beside Lily's Pottery Barn trestle table to peer through the arch into the kitchen. He didn't see Jason. Lily stood at the island in the pumps, slacks, and blouse she'd worn to work and was taking cartons from a KFC sack while Emily was setting plates onto the breakfast table. Four red plastic tumblers already stood there. Before she'd arrived in residence here, Burl had presumed that Emily was still at the age to seek parental approval by being helpful. But he'd learned otherwise. She'd do chores that Lily assigned, but not without griping, and Burl believed Jason was a bad influence on her. More and more, she seemed to be mired in a teenager's sulk even though she was only eleven. He'd tried his best to be careful in dealing with her; her wounds from the divorce were still tender, he could tell, and she idolized her professor father. Lily's custody arrangement allowed her ex to have Emily on alternate holidays and for a month in the summer beginning next year. In the meantime, he was free to drive here from Austin to be with her on alternate weekends or to fly her down there.

Emily's father had yet to exercise these rights he'd sought and won in court. Despite his behavior, the poor kid seemed to feel that she'd be better off with her dad and resented Lily for being the custodial parent. Lily told Burl what Emily didn't know: her wonderful father was shacking up with his graduate student. Lily didn't feel it was her place to give Emily that particular piece of bad news, though, *Believe me,* she said, *I've been sorely tempted many a time.*

Burl knew without even testing it that Emily wouldn't welcome his premature efforts to be fatherly, and that put him in a tricky position. He couldn't discipline the child, because Lily had yet to invite him to help make any parental decision on an essential matter such as Emily's schooling. He worked to stay friendly, though this kid was often trying. She was a bookish know-it-all who spent far too much time on her computer playing a game where she made up a family and digitally ordered them about through their daily lives in cyberspace. While she didn't exactly sass Burl, she spoke to him with a veiled impatience that suggested her reserve of politeness was being worn thin by having to speak to an idiot. She was not what he would've preferred in an eleven-year-old stepdaughter, or a biological daughter, for that matter: a tree-climbing, horse-loving tomboy in t-shirt and blue jeans with a shelf of Barbies and a yen to go to church or Scout camp and dress up in mommy's clothes.

They looked up when he entered, and Lily said, "Hi, sweet," nicely, but she did sound tired. Though she had her hands full, Burl moved to the island to hug her and kiss her forehead. He was aware of Emily's large brown eyes on them.

"Hello, Emily. How was school?"

"Sucked."

"Emily," said Lily.

But Emily kept her attention on the paper napkins she was folding and positioning just so beside the plates, centered on each plate's horizontal axis. She tucked the right edge of the paper slightly under the leftward curve of the plate's outer rim so that if the rim were a cutting edge pressed downward, it would take a bite shaped like a quarter moon from the edge of the folded napkin. She did that kind of thing a lot, this visual measuring and adjusting objects on a shelf or table.

Her curt reply irritated him. It was too much like the reply he'd get from Jason.

He smiled, falsely, at her. "Wouldn't that be, 'It sucked, sir.' or, 'It sucked, Mister Sanborn. Thanks for asking'?"

She shot him a slit-eyed sideways glance but she had trouble getting rid of her involuntary grin quickly enough to keep him from spotting it. He'd almost won her over momentarily, but she was not about to concede that.

"Sorry."

He passed over his objection as to the spirit of her apology and chose to pursue his struggle with the other child.

"Where's Jason?"

"In his room, I suppose," said Lily.

"What's he been doing all day?"

"I just got home, Burl."

When he turned to Emily, she said, "*I* was in school."

"Do you know if he went to that job interview?" he asked Lily.

"I have no idea," Lily said tightly. "You'll have to ask him."

Burl sighed. "He'll probably lie," he said to no one in particular, looking for sympathy.

"No surprise *there*!" shot Lily.

Her vehemence alarmed him, and he carried its echo away to the hall as he trudged reluctantly toward Jason's room. Maybe they'd had an ugly exchange in the yard when Lily came home and he'd stormed off to his room? Almost anything set him off these days, and Burl's phone call about the trial wouldn't have improved his humor. Lily wasn't used to dealing with a teenage temperament and, as it turned out, didn't have a lot of patience with it. Whatever patience she'd been blessed with had been strained by successive revelations about Jason's scrapes with the law that he'd given—rationed out, really, you could say—in the days and weeks following the wedding. The night of Lisa's graduation party was to have been Burl's and Lily's first all-nighter. They were asleep on the sofa half-clothed when the call came from the Mesquite Police. Burl hadn't encouraged Lily to go with him to bail Jason out, and when he and Jason got home several hours later, she'd already had her sister pick her up. At the time, he told her only that Jason had been mistakenly accused of car theft, but after the wedding, his guilt had twisted his arm to reveal, gradually, more of the truth, but he had held back telling her about the charge of assault with bodily harm. For a while, she'd acted supportive and sympathetic, but since she now lived with Jason, her attitude had shifted. While once it was, *Poor kid lost his mother. We need to cut him some slack,* now it was, *We've all got our troubles, sonny boy! Get over it, straighten up, and get on with your life!*

He bent his ear to the wood but heard only a soft, regular tapping. He guessed Jason's ears were harnessed to his headset and he was either jamming with his guitar or listening to his Discman. Burl pecked at the door with a knuckle, then, without waiting for a response, he jiggled the knob.

"Jason!"

Nothing. The boy wasn't going to make this easy. Now Burl knocked hard, with his whole fist, a single wham like a judge's gavel.

"Jason!"

A muted scuffling and a rustle, a ka-bump, two thumps (feet hitting the floor maybe), then Jason opened the door maybe four inches to offer a slim rectangle of face that revealed one eye like the dot on a lower case i.

"Yeah."

Annoyed, Burl pushed the door into Jason with his fingertips, and Jason backpedaled to his desk and stood with his arms folded across his chest. The headphones yoked his neck like a horse collar. The window had been flung up hastily, knocking the blinds askew. Another flagrant violation to address. Jesus Christ! Where to start with this kid!

To buy himself a moment, he turned and quietly pushed the door back into its frame until the latch clicked.

"I've asked you not to smoke in the house, Jason."

"I had the window open."

"That's not the point. I didn't say it was okay if you opened the window."

"But I don't see—"

Burl brandished his palm to stop him. "Did you and Lily have an argument?"

"No. Why?" Jason leaned forward as if to see something in the distance more clearly, something he loathed. "Did she say something?"

"Never mind. Can you tell me why you're sitting in here diddling off instead of finishing your job out front?"

Jason smirked. "Diddling off?"

Burl let that sail past. "What've you been doing all day? How hard is it to mow the damn lawn, anyway? I ask you to do one simple thing, a thing a twelve-year-old could handle, and when I get home I see a half-assed job out there with all the tools just . . . just tossed around like you're six blasted years old and nobody taught you to put things up!"

"I tossed the mower around?"

"You left the gas can sitting on the walk!"

"Ohmagod! Call 911!"

Burl frowned. Even for Jason these provocations were over the top, as if Jason were testing whether sufficient goading might produce a major heart attack in his father or make his head pop off.

"Don't get smart, son! Did you go to that interview today?"

"What interview?"

"The one with the manager at Blockbuster. Or did you just lie to me about going down there in the first place?"

"No, I didn't lie! And I didn't go down there today because the guy isn't in on Fridays."

"The *manager* takes Fridays off?"

"Jesus, Dad! I don't know what goes on down there! Call and ask yourself if you don't believe me."

"Maybe I just will."

"Fine."

They'd worked to a pause. Burl had gotten absolutely no satisfaction on any point raised. He stood digging at his sweat-damp waistband with a thumb and watched as Jason averted his gaze and slowly folded portions of himself one by one, like a carpenter's wooden ruler, into his desk chair. Jason acted as if their next phase might involve Burl's decision to relent and remove himself, as if by this little act of taking a seat, Jason was giving Burl a preview, as it were, of what Jason's peace might be like without Burl there to disturb it. Jason astonished him these days with his shocking rudeness and utter disregard for Burl's authority. When confronted about the half-finished mowing job, he didn't even offer a reason or an excuse. Instead, he mocked Burl for objecting! Incredible!

When Jason, without even glancing Burl's way, parted the headphone collar with a speaker in each hand, stretched them like pulling taffy, lifted them up, and settled them firmly over his ears, it was more than Burl could stand.

From the kitchen, Lily and Emily heard raised voices—not shouting, no, but the blunt, abrupt maleness in the exchanges sang with anger as if their words were lightweight objects flung at one another. Emily looked up from her chore of setting out the ketchup and Burl's green jalapeño Tabasco and over to Lily as if for a cue as to how she was supposed to handle this. Understandably, the sounds made Emily uneasy; Jason's father always seemed on edge to her, and, though she'd not witnessed anything violent since she'd moved here, most of the words between this father and son were a harsh melody with an ominous underlying pedal tone, like horror movie music. Burl was bigger, older, the father, and so Emily identified with the child in this confrontation.

Lily didn't appear to have heard anything; or if she had, she wasn't going to act as if it were out of the ordinary. Emily stood at the breakfast table, head cocked so she could observe her mother through a half-averted gaze as if spying. Still, Lily continued to open and shut cabinet doors, fairly banging them as she removed a serving platter and two bowls and plopped them on the counter, then set about transferring the chicken pieces, mashed potatoes, coleslaw, and rolls from the cartons on the island. Though she had picked up the supper from the KFC drive-thru window, she would serve it as if it had come fresh from her own range and oven; she could do that at least, she felt. She was uneasy about the fight, too, but she was caught between pretending nothing was wrong, continuing to spoon out the potatoes and slaw as if the schedule somehow included this brouhaha in Jason's bedroom, that it was on the agenda for Burl and the boy like washing-up or checking the mail might be, thinking that if she were to show Emily that she was rattled it might alarm her. She was walking on eggshells these days anyway with Emily, doing her best to make her feel at home here (while making herself feel at home here), struggling to induce Emily to believe that this was best for all of them, that this life in this house was not only the best Lily could do, it was the best that could be done.

"Mom?"

Lily kept her eyes on the spoon that was slowly tracing, for the third time, the interior corners of the potato carton.

"What, hon?" Lily said cheerfully.

Waiting for Emily to speak, she kept poking the bottom of

the carton. The argument off-stage seemed to have stopped, however. When Lily did flick a glance toward her daughter, she read nothing in Emily's profile but everything in her robotic positioning and readjusting of the two mismatched condiments. She felt a twinge of guilt at having forced denial onto the floor between them, and, wanting to spare Emily from having to thrash her way through it, she turned to say, "It's nothing," with a smile. "Boys, they play rough."

But then a shout, a loud *ka-boomp*, another shout, a *clomp clomp* like something or someone tumbling down stairs, though there were no stairs in the house, a pause and in it both mother and daughter involuntarily stared wide-eyed at each other, Lily unable to hide her shock. Emily stepped back from the table suddenly as if the fight were transpiring on its surface, hugging the big plastic jug of ketchup in one hand and the tiny bottle of sauce gripped in her other fist to her chest.

As Lily stepped around the island to move to Emily, they heard Jason's bedroom door open, then movement, shuffling, voices again, not raised but urgent, Jason saying, "You okay, Dad?" and Burl saying "Yeah, yeah, it'll be all right," then both emerged from the dim hall into the kitchen. Burl was bent over with his palm pressed to his forehead, that hand outlined in red, and a rivulet coursing down his wrist and around his forearm, while Jason loomed over his back, trying to peer over Burl's shoulder as they went.

"What happened? What's the matter?" Lily asked.

"It's okay," said Burl. He straightened and stepped around Lily to the sink. "Bumped my head." He bent over the sink, lowered his palm, and inspected his hand. Blood poured from a cut over his brow.

Lily said, "Let me look at that," and moved beside him, pushing her fingers against his forehead, bending over the sink with him. "Wow, that's a gusher. That's gonna take stitches, Burl. What happened?"

"We thought you were fighting," accused Emily.

"Oh, no, hon," Burl tossed over his shoulder. "I tripped and banged my noggin on the edge of Jason's desk, that's all. It'll be okay in a minute."

"But you were *arguing*!" she insisted.

"We do it all the time," put in Jason merrily, as if it were a sport.

"We have any Band-Aids?"

"It'll take more than a Band-Aid," said Lily. She folded several attached swatches of paper towel into a compress and handed it to him. "Keep pressing on it."

Burl clapped the pad to his forehead, winced.

"What about hydrogen peroxide?" asked Emily. "Or Neosporin."

Nobody spoke or moved for a full minute; they all appeared to be waiting for someone else to take charge.

"Let me see it now," Lily said, as if she'd been waiting for the injury to heal. She moved her hands to Burl's splayed paw and gently lifted it away, looked around the edge of the sopping compress. She tsk-tsked, smoothed his hand back to his head.

"Is there a doc-in-the-box around here?"

"There's one on Town East," said Jason.

"You know where it is, Burl?"

Burl nodded.

"You're going to have to have stitches or that thing'll never heal!" She took Burl by the arm and he allowed himself to be steered away from the sink. "Emily, you come, too."

Emily said, "Do I have to?"

"Yes, now—"

"Aw, let the girl eat her supper. Jason too. No telling how long this will take. No point in having her sit down there for hours with a lot of sick folks coughing and sneezing all over her."

For this very first instance of intervening in a matter between the child and her mother, Burl was granted the blessing of oblique gratitude, though it needed to be decoded from what showed up on Emily's face as she swung her head up to meet her mother's gaze. A bit of glitter in her eye. *Don't blame me if he contradicts you—you married him. And maybe I can look forward to more of this!* Lily now faced the difficulty of losing face by conceding to good sense, but the sight of blood smeared on Burl's arm and blooming red through the paper towels, drizzling along the sink rim like raspberry sauce on a dessert plate, and glittering in a trail of ruddy dimes leading from the hall through the kitchen like evidence in a crime scene, electrified her, jangled and buzzed her decision system out of commission.

"Fine!" She pointed a mother-finger at Emily. "But no funny business, you hear?"

Emily rolled her eyes and did a very Gallic "puh!" as she turned her head.

"I mean it! Do you understand me?"

"Yes," Emily said, then added, "ma'am."

"And you are to clean up this kitchen when you finish eating, you hear?" Before Emily could even respond, Lily suddenly whirled on Jason and gave him the same finger, though it didn't point so directly at him; were it a loaded pistol, the shot probably would've gone wide right. "That goes for both of you!"

Lily's reward for her first effort to parent the two equally was Jason's deadpan poker face that, Burl knew from long experience, was like a drawn shade behind which thieves conjure up their schemes.

---

The door to Jason's room was open, so Emily treaded quietly down the hall and stood just outside. What was he was up to? A large rucksack sat like a baby Buddha on his bed while he was riffling through the drawers in his chest and tossing items onto the mattress. His earphones looped his neck, but he wasn't listening to anything, so Emily advanced two more steps and leaned against the doorframe.

"You're supposed to help me clean the kitchen."

"I didn't help you eat, did I?"

He went on, taking what appeared to be pairs of white jockey underwear from the drawer and stuffing them into the pack.

"Aren't you hungry?"

"Not now."

Since he seemed aware of her presence only in the nanoseconds required to reply, she let her inquisitive gaze take a silent inventory. She had a good idea of the room's usual contents and their placement, since she snooped while he was out and took enormous pride in covering her tracks. She knew, for instance, that he had three issues of a naked girls magazine secreted under a stack of school folders in his bottom desk drawer and a commando folding knife in the top. She had read his journal, where she learned little about his legal problems but a lot about how he pined for his true love, Lisa, and she'd read the lyrics of about three dozen unfinished songs. She had prowled his hard drive (if he knew anything about creating passwords for security, he didn't apply it) but since his PC wasn't online and he spilled his guts using a Bic and a notebook, there was little of interest on it. His games were pitiful: Solitaire, Hearts, Free Cell.

"Did you and your dad have a fight?"

Jason shrugged.

"How'd he hurt his head?"

Jason stopped midway between the chest and the bed, hands frozen with a ball of t-shirts or polo shirts between them and gave her the blessing of his full attention. "It's like we said, he tripped and hit it there—" he dipped his own forehead toward his desk. "We were scuffling a little, yeah. He was trying to take my headphones and I grabbed them back from him."

"Why'd he want your headphones?"

"I don't know. You'd have to ask him."

She really wanted to know what he was up to at this very moment, but she was afraid she'd hear what she feared was true. He was obviously worked up; his body radiated an aura of electric energy as he danced about selecting things—a handful of CDs, the aforementioned red spiral he used as a journal—and unzipping pockets in the pack to contain them. When she saw him slide the Discman in the pocket with the CDs, frown, then extract it and try it in another pocket, she couldn't contain herself.

"Are you going somewhere? Where are you going?"

He ignored her.

"Jason! Come on! Where're you going?"

"Out of this hell hole, that's for sure!"

She turned and scurried off as if, Jason thought, to sound an alarm or to call her mother, and, though it jangled his nerves a second, he neither stopped to chase her down nor speeded his packing. Now and then he cocked his ears to listen for voices, but he heard none. After a full ten minutes, she was back at the doorway. She'd changed into blue jeans and a t-shirt and a much-too-large red Rangers cap he'd given her a week ago.

"Don't you know where you're going?"

Jason lifted his shoulders, twisted his mouth as if considering a list of possibilities.

"I bet you're going to Austin to see Lisa."

He blushed. "What makes you think that?"

She thought that because she'd just spied on his Hotmail account (his password was his birthday: 080685) and she'd read the e-mail he'd written Lisa this morning and left in his Drafts folder.

"Just 'cause."

When he said nothing, she said, "Because I know you miss her a lot. I miss my daddy, too."

Jason lifted his guitar from the bed and inspected the back of it.

"I hate this place, too." Emily thumbed her glasses up her nose and, as if that habitual little gesture reminded her, she said, "A kid at school called me headlights. And my teacher said the Harry Potter books are full of Satan worship, and she asked me if I'd accepted Jesus Christ as my personal Lord and Savior, and I said in the first place my daddy was a Hindu and that I believe in the separation of church and state and it was a public school and she didn't have any right to ask."

Jason laughed. "Girl, you rock."

"So now they all act like I'm the devil and a witch! I don't like it here!" She took three steps into the room, lunged forward toward him, arms and hands flung out as if to catch a beach ball, and yelled, "I HATE IT HERE!"

Jason unzipped a side pocket on the pack and tucked a balled pair of socks into it.

"Hey, all kids hate their new school at first, you know? Give it a chance. Look at your pal Harry Potter at Hogwarts."

"You hated your school too and you didn't stay in it."

"Yikes!" Jason cringed. "Well, you're smart, though. Math's no problem for you."

Jason knelt to open his guitar case, took a polish rag from its doored compartment, sat on the bed and eased the guitar across his thighs, then worked the polish cloth across the wood. Emily vanished again, but only momentarily, and when her form loomed in his peripheral vision, he glanced up. A full book bag slung over one shoulder draped low with the weight and dragged that shoulder down.

"I wanna go back to Austin and live with Daddy. You can stay there too if you want." She suddenly thrust out her fist; in it she gripped a roll of bills. "I can pay my own way, okay? I've been saving for this. You can keep it." She stiff-armed the roll toward him.

"I can't take your money."

"I've seen you take money from Mom's purse and your dad's wallet!"

Jason's brows popped up. "You have? Wow. Well, that's different. They deserve to be ripped off. You're just a kid. I'm sorry, but you can't go with me."

"Oh, Jason! Puh-leeze! I hate it here! Especially if you're not gonna be here. They'll start yelling at me all the time! If you don't take me with you, I swear to God I'll walk out there and stick out my thumb and take the first ride that stops to pick me up! Even if it's a sex addict molester or a serial killer! You're supposed to be taking care of me, you know—"

"Who said that?"

"It's just, you know, understood because you're eighteen and I'm eleven."

Jason stopped polishing the burnished burgundy back of the guitar, lifted it, spun it neatly over between his hands so that the strings were up, nestled it gently in the red plush case.

He folded the cloth and tucked it into the drawer, brought the lid closed, latched the locks by the handle at the bottom. He heard the sniffling.

"Don't give me that."

"Do you want to see that happen? I mean it! I'm going one way or another! I'm packed. I've got money. I'll just go by myself. In fact, I bet I can get a ride before you can! Who's gonna pick up somebody like you before they pick up somebody like me? Huh? Think about that! And I think I'll just get a head start!"

She whirled to go and disappeared through the door and he heard her sneakers scuffling down the hall. He waited until he heard the front door slam, then he jumped up and ran after her. When he reached the front porch, she was walking toward the street.

"Emily! Hold up there."

She stopped and turned but didn't retreat. He bounded off the stoop and strode to where she stood at the curb. He paced about her for a moment as if she were a construction project that presented an engineering challenge, and she watched, hands to the straps on her book bag now hanging from both shoulders, one foot forward of the other.

"What about school? I thought you were like the world's biggest grade-monger."

"What about your deal with the court case?"

"I have to see Lisa and explain something to her."

"I have to see Daddy and explain something to him."

Jason said, "Look, you are not going out there on that highway by yourself and putting out your thumb, you understand me?"

"Yes I am!"

They stood frozen in stalemate for a moment, then Emily took two quick steps forward, and Jason grabbed her arm.

"Okay, okay, okay! But you have to write your mom a note. You can't just walk out like this and not—"

"I already have. Gosh, you think I'm stupid?"

# Two

At the FirstCare Med-Stop on Town East, Burl and Lily took plastic scoop chairs and waited for a doctor to examine Burl's cut. Lily was restless, agitated, and after scouring the waiting room for magazines and finding only promotional brochures from pharmaceutical firms, she retrieved her briefcase from the car and lap-desked it while she tended a file left unfinished at work.

Burl tried to keep his mind off Jason's problems and his own problems with Jason by speculating about his fellow emergency-ites. The group included at least two Hispanic families, no member of which appeared to be in distress, leaving Burl to guess that a brother or wife or child was being attended to behind closed doors. Two white girls in jogging togs, one with a knee wrapped in a yellow towel and the other with speaker buds planted in her ears, a black woman in a brown UPS uniform seated alone and reading a *Left Behind* paperback by holding it open with one hand while the other was jammed under her armpit.

Lily had put her reading glasses on, and her pink nails were clicking on a calculator. She was all business, like a female judge on TV. Hers was an unfamiliar demeanor for a female intimate to Burl, and the novelty of it, while often thrilling, could likewise intimidate. When she straightened her papers, clipped them and slipped the folder and glasses into her briefcase, he said, "I haven't had time to tell you yet. I heard from

Jason's lawyer this morning."

"Will he have to go to court Monday morning?"

"Yes."

Lily's nostrils twitched as if testing the air for an odor she couldn't identify. "I'll let them know at work I'll be taking half a day off, then. I thought the lawyer could get the charges dismissed or settle it all somehow."

Burl sighed. "Yes and no. Doctor Johnson's withdrawing that unauthorized use of vehicle business, and they'd already dropped the shoplifting charge, and he, I mean the lawyer, doesn't think they're interested in the minor in possession."

Lily looked at him with puzzlement. "So what's the hearing Monday about?"

He sighed. "Well, looks like there's going to be a charge for assault."

"Assault!?"

Several people glanced at them and quickly looked away.

"It's okay, it's okay," he murmured, laying his hand on her knee. "The lawyer is saying that if he pleads guilty, he'll likely get a probated sentence."

"Why assault, Burl? What happened?"

Burl talked down into her lap to encourage her to bend her head so that they wouldn't be overheard. "When Jason was running, this clerk from the store tried to stop him, and Jason ran into him. He didn't mean to. It was like trying to avoid being tackled while you're on your way to the goal line, you know, nothing more than that." He waited a moment. "The clerk got a few scrapes and bruises when he fell."

"Shit! Why am I just now hearing about this, Burl?"

"I told you he was in trouble, Lily! You knew he was having to go to court and that I'd had to hire a lawyer. And I told you that you wouldn't have to pay a dime for any of this, either." He knew then that he had to keep his mouth shut about the probable civil suit.

"It's a not a matter of money, Burl. It's a matter of trust, you know. Assault! That's got to be a felony! It's a crime of violence! You say 'scrapes and bruises,' but there's bound to be more to it than that!"

"*He* says he . . . maybe fractured his collarbone."

"Oh, my God! I don't know what I'm into any more, Burl. I mean, look at your head, for God's sake!"

"What's my head got to do with anything?"

People were aware they were arguing urgently through clenched teeth, and so he blew out a huge breath, leaned back with his head against the wall, closed his eyes.

"Let's talk about it later."

"Fine. And I do want to!"

Lily didn't accompany him to be examined, for which he was grateful—they'd both recognized a need to repair to separate corners between rounds. A rotund nurse in stretch pants and a voluminous scrub top sporting big yellow smiley faces shunted him into an examining room hardly bigger than a closet. Unlike such rooms in specialists' offices, it was stripped down with no prescription pads visible, nothing left lying on the counters. Not even a box of tissue. Were the patients here prone to making off with anything not nailed down?

He couldn't blame Lily for being upset. He'd withheld important information out of fear and a lack of trust, and that wasn't good for them as a couple. He wouldn't have lied to Sue, though, not about that, anyway. He'd tried to hide his drinking from her in their early years, though he knew, or found out, that she'd known anyway. But in Jason's situation, she would've been there all along: she'd have been waiting at home when he brought Jason back from the jail that night, and she would've gone with him to meet the lawyer. It was hard to judge whether he and Lily could eventually click like that. Was it just that he and Sue had spent twenty years together, grown up with each other? Or was it a matter of personalities? If so, he and Lily might never have that ease. In so many aspects of his new marriage, a lack of precedents put him at sea in making judgments.

The "doctor" who weaved twelve stitches into his forehead looked like a college boy who'd just clawed his way up out of a four-day bender. His smock was filthy, and his hands trembled minutely so that the kid had to plant the heels of both hands on Burl's forehead to steady himself while he sewed the cut. He hadn't shaved in days, though it was hard to know if this was a fashion statement or a result of dereliction. The boy's breath had a thin high strata of peppermint riding over a miasma of soured alcoholic roué, and Burl wanted to mention the Bruton Terrace AA group but didn't.

In the passenger seat of Lily's Civic, he cocked the visor down to peer at his head in the vanity mirror. A bandage the size of a playing card had been taped over the injury, the whiteness of it stark and almost glowing in the dim interior.

They drove toward home in silence, though Lily did ask, "Do you have to go back in?" and Burl said, "No, the nurse said just to keep it clean and the stitches would dissolve." He'd learned something from their relationship so far: the dynamics of working your way back to normalcy or even to a truce from a dust-up required a protocol as intricately formal as a bid on a government project. Her question had been a single complete sentence, and he'd given her precisely that as his answer. But she'd broken the ice—that added points—so unless he wanted to make her feel she was hanging out on a limb alone, he'd have to add something to equal that effort.

"The kid who sewed me up must've been moonlighting from his regular job at a mattress factory."

Lily chuckled.

It seemed like a tiny breakthrough. He'd take a bigger step.

"No kidding. He looked like he'd just crawled out of bed and he'd been sleeping in his car. Stunk to high heaven."

"I suppose they're medical students and they pick up extra cash this way."

"That makes me feel like a guinea pig. Shouldn't they be paying me?"

Lily had no comment. All this chatter was but an overture, he knew, to the rest of the music: resuming their argument about Jason and his legal problems. Still, though, he wanted to feel more at ease and wanted the same for Lily, so he said, "I think the kid might be a drinker. I was tempted to mention our group to him."

"Well, I'm sure glad you didn't!" declared Lily, as if the very idea made her angry. He was afraid to ask why for fear of stepping on another heretofore hidden mine, so he had to mull it over in silence. Would mentioning the group strip away her privacy? The longer he stewed, feeling constrained and, above all, unfairly blasted for what he believed was a generous impulse, the more pissed off he got, so the last five minutes of their ride home were spent in silence, though now the momentum had shifted his way: he had the grievance, she the need to apologize.

Inside, he paused to pick up the mail Jason had left on the coffee table while Lily put away her purse. As he was inspecting it, she appeared suddenly in the living room.

"They're not here, Burl!"

He didn't understand her panic. He strolled toward the bathroom, intending to inspect the sutured cut. "Well, maybe they went to get frozen yogurt or something."

"It's after ten o'clock. Aren't they closed? And how would they get there?"

"Maybe one of Jason's friends. Or maybe they hoofed it. Don't worry."

He said this while standing in the bathroom threshold, holding the door open by the knob and clearly signaling he meant to close it.

"You're telling me not to worry that my daughter might be out running around in a car driven by a friend of Jason's this late and neither of us knows who that might be?"

Burl sighed. "Take it easy, Lily. Maybe one of them left a note."

That was tantamount to assigning her to look for one, and she rolled her eyes and moved off toward the kitchen. He shut the door, took a long piss, gently dabbing the bandage with the fingers of his free hand, then stood at the mirror and drew back one side of the taped bandage like a door to his brain and held it open. The cut had a raw, red crusted line, the edges butted neatly and bound with black stitches, like a tiny football.

In the kitchen, Lily was moving condiments about on the table as if something had been secreted under the bottles and said, "I didn't see anything in the living room or dining room."

"I wouldn't worry, hon. Really. Jason's not very good at that kind of thing."

"What kind of thing?"

"Notification."

"Yes. And that's precisely what makes me worry."

"Look, I'm telling you they probably just went out because they got bored. It's Friday night. There's no school tomorrow. He'll take good care of her."

He spoke the last of this to her departing back. She was still wearing the clothes she'd worked in, and the heels of her black pumps clomped like Dutch wooden shoes in the hall as she went.

"I'm going to look in her room. Would you please look in Jason's?"

Burl couldn't imagine why either would've left a note in an inconspicuous place, in the unlikely case that they had left one at all. Jason probably needed to blow off steam after fighting with Burl, and he knew not to leave Lily's child here alone. Jason had been upset and surly, but he'd also instantly turned fearful and solicitous when he saw that Burl was injured (that was gratifying!), so chances were that the mood he took out of the house with him was little more than a couple ounces of irritation and a pound of concern.

Jason's desk looked less cluttered than Burl remembered, though when he was here hours ago he'd been so worked up he was nigh to frothing at the mouth, so he couldn't rely on his memory. His gaze automatically went to the sharp corner of the desk. No blood was visible there, though like most head cuts, his injury had bled copiously. But dried blood splotched the portion of Jason's bedspread that draped nearby; in the wastebasket beside the desk, flowers of white tissue stained with red blotches topped the other trash. These signs wriggled down into Burl's consciousness where they vibrated minutely and emitted tendrils of fascination. Seeing your own blood spilled sort of corners your attention, he thought.

No note on the desk, the bed, the floor. He gave the room only a cursory inspection. Turning eighteen had diminished Jason's sense of such obligations as leaving notes, after starting with little. Burl hoped Lily had calmed down by now. Standing there, he drifted back to the moment Jason was easing down into his desk chair and slipping the headphones over his ears. Where were the headphones?

He looked up and about. Lily's anxiety seemed to have seeped into the atmosphere of the room from her location elsewhere in the house, and he had to breathe in shallow drafts to avoid ingesting it. The absence of a note could seem a little ominous, if you were inclined to hop yourself up with a dose of worry. The headphones were probably in the closet.

Jason's guitar was missing, as well. For an instant, a jolt of fear zipped up his spine and ruffled his nape fuzz, but then he counseled himself into relief: this was a good sign. Jason had gone out to work on his music, probably to a park nearby or to a friend's house, and he'd simply taken Emily along. He liked to be seen in semi-public places whanging away on the thing with a pen and pad beside him to scrawl down his lyrics as they came. If they didn't show up soon, he could ease Lily's mind by driving her to some of Jason's haunts.

He went to report this to Lily. She was sitting on Emily's bed holding something metallic in her hand.

"Did you find a note?" he asked.

"No." She looked up from the object. Her eyes were large with her panic, and she held out the thing in both hands the way you'd show a beloved bird to the person who'd shot it.

"It's her cell phone!"

"What—"

"She's never without it, Burl! You know where I found it?" She didn't wait for him to guess. "Under the bed. And look at it! It's been smashed!"

She thrust the holding hands out to force him to take it. He did. He wouldn't have said it looked "smashed"—the back had separated so that the battery was loose, but he'd had cell phones at work whose covers popped off if you dropped them on a floor.

"Look at her call list!" He was still puzzling over the phone's condition, but he cut short his inspection, resettled the battery and reclamped the cover. When he passed it back, she punched at a key and fairly danced in place while it booted up.

"Oh, my God! I shouldn't have listened to you! Look what number she tried to call at 8:03. When we were at the Med-Stop!" She brandished the phone face between her fingers as if waving a cross at a vampire. He couldn't read while she waggled it that way, of course, but it didn't matter because she told him. "My cell phone! She tried to call me while we were down there."

"I didn't hear your phone ring. Did you have it on?"

"Of course!"

"Well, why—"

"Don't you see? She was calling me but the call didn't go through because the phone was thrown down or was stomped on or something!"

"Oh, now, Lily. Calm down. Don't get carried away. I'm sure there's an explanation here." He was dimly aware that the part of him that supervised personnel was being called into play and also that if an employee ranted like this, he might have her fired when it was over. Possibly she was having her period, but he wasn't about to ask.

"I didn't find a note in Jason's room, but I did see that his guitar is gone, and that's as good as a note to me. I know he's probably in a park or a coffee house picking away at the thing and working on his music. It's how he handles stress. I'm sure he's upset about the fight and about Monday. His music is good therapy."

"Well, bully for him! And do you think he just left Emily here on her own?"

"No, I really don't. I'm sure she's with him. She's probably sitting right there sipping lemonade and reading."

"Then who did this?" She shook the phone at him. "And if she needed to talk to me, why didn't she try to call again!"

"Look, maybe the call was only incidental, maybe it was about something unimportant, and when she tried to call, the back came off the phone and it quit working. Okay? There's no reason to get sinister here, you know."

"She could've used the landline."

"Maybe she decided not to call. Maybe she wanted to know if it was okay if she went out then didn't want to bother you because she was going out with Jason and thought you probably would okay that anyway, you see?"

Her breath whooshed out slowly like air from a leaking balloon; she slumped back on her heels, closed her hands over the phone. When she looked at him, the wild heat lightning in her eyes had dimmed as if a storm had passed just over the horizon. She sat on the bed and wiped at the tears on her cheek with the heel of the hand holding the phone.

"I worry about her so. All the time. What I've done to her. She's very unhappy here, I know it. And I did it."

"Aw, hon," he said, with some relief. "Give her time."

"Time is her life, too. Her childhood." Lily shook her head. "You think I'm just being an alarmist, I know. But you are in such denial about Jason."

"For God's sake, Lily! He's not going to let any harm come to her!"

"You don't know what he's going to do! Do you? Really? I'm not saying he's going to shove her around like he shoved you and that she's going to wind up with a cut like yours or a broken collarbone, Burl. But I am saying he has terrible judgment, and you indulge him. And on that score he's really a danger to my child."

"Lily, listen to me. I promise you that they're just goofing off. They'll be back safe and sound."

Lily looked at her wristwatch. "It's five to eleven now. If they're not back by midnight, we're going to call the police! Okay?" Her mouth had a thin set line but her jaw was trembling.

"Why don't we get in the car and go look at the places I know they're probably at?"

"I asked you a question. Do you agree we call the police at midnight?"

"I don't believe they'll do much until somebody's been missing twenty-four hours."

She stood, gripping the phone in her fist, then swung that

bunched fist against her chest as if thumping a vow on her breastbone. "Do you *agree?*"

Well, he *had* urged that Emily be allowed to stay at home. Burl shrugged. "Yeah. Okay."

Burl stationed himself in the black leather recliner that had been part of Lily's dowry, so to speak, and turned on *The Tonight Show*. He'd missed Leno's opening stand-up, his favorite part, by a good half hour, and the show had sunk into its routine chore of pimping a new movie. Now Leno was in the midst of flirting with a gorgeous black woman who was starring in a sequel of a hit sci-fi movie Burl hadn't even heard of, let alone seen. Burl's lack of interest in the interview perfectly matched his motive for clicking on the show in the first place: to pose as someone who has absolutely no worry about what his delinquent son might be doing out in the world on a Friday night with an eleven-year-old child in tow. Leno claimed little of his consciousness, so he was free to gnaw privately on the anxiety that gloomy possibilities aroused.

Lily's hoofing about in other parts of the house rang in his ears, though he'd told her that she ought to change into something comfortable. You could call it pacing except that she too meant to signal something through her activity—that she was engaged, preparing for a siege or a mission, awaiting the word for the charge. He hadn't been settled five minutes before she appeared in the doorway to the living room to toss a question. "Do you know the names and numbers of Jason's closest friends?" Burl gave a little lurch to bump the recliner upright simply out of respect—answering such questions under these circumstances while lolling too casually would be akin to wearing sunglasses in a job interview—and said, "Well, one or two, you know. Their names, anyway. I know where one lives, like I said earlier."

She left, but scant minutes later she was back. "Do you think his girlfriend knows where he is?"

Burl gave an inward shudder at the prospect of contacting Lisa after all the trouble with her father. "No. Lisa is at school in Austin now."

"But he could've talked to her."

Lily's dark brows were gnarled with worry in a way that radiated outward over all her features like windshield damage. Burl was a little in awe of her manic purposefulness. This was an aspect of her personality he hadn't yet encountered, and it made her mysterious and strange.

"Yeah. I suppose he could've. Probably not, though. It's something to consider, you know, if it comes to that."

She went away again. That she wouldn't leave him in peace to ruminate irritated him. He wished she'd settle down and shut up. He did have some concern, of course, but her wild behavior was sucking up all the oxygen so that he wasn't free to express it. He was afraid to let her know that he did indeed find Jason utterly untrustworthy. For God's sake, the whole uproar tonight had been about just that! If he were to admit that, she might explode into hysterics and require . . . what, hospitalization? No, she'd forced him into the role of the calm and rational party who has to humor the one given to hysteria.

Of course, Sue had done just this for him all those years: he raved and stomped around the house, not just about Jason's behavior, but about his Little League coach, the property tax bill, the supervisor who wanted something done over, the AC compressor's final collapse. Each and every thing that seemed to thwart his existence called for a tantrum. Sue, at his elbow: *Burl, honey, just calm down. Not the end of the world. Just a tax bill. It's not worth such a fuss.* She'd pray, he knew. Give it all over to the Lord. Burl didn't trust the Lord to attend to minutia, didn't think it was even fair to tax Him with it, though he never told Sue so.

Her long, slow suffering and death had had one benefit: it had burned out his rage, left it in smoldering ruin. If he'd meted out his rage in accordance to what her death required, he couldn't have stayed sane. Now, anything less than her death called for anger in proportion to the grievance. Always smaller, much smaller. Jason was all that was left in his life to test the limits of this new understanding.

Lily appeared beside the recliner.

"It's ten to twelve. Are you going to call or shall I?"

"I'll do it. But you know, you shouldn't expect too much. To them it'll just be a case of an eighteen-year-old young man out past midnight with his stepsister."

"How nice of you to belittle my concern!"

He sighed, went to the kitchen to retrieve the cordless phone, raised it to dial, but stopped. 911? For this?

"What's the matter?"

"I was thinking of calling the station directly. I know a patrolman, used to work with me in the utilities department."

"Just call 911, Burl!"

He fixed his face with an expression of innocent bewilderment. "Lily, hon, what's gotten into you?"

"You're kidding me, right?"

"No. You seem a little hysterical, to tell the truth."

"I do? Why should I be hysterical? I've spent the evening watching my daughter cower in the kitchen while you and your teenage son have a fistfight right here in the house where you wind up with a gash that requires—what, twelve stitches? And while we're at it, you tell me that the sulky belligerent boy that I and my daughter have been living with for, well, almost six weeks is actually a violent criminal, and then I come home to find that he's taken her off with him?"

He was sorely tempted to argue about "violent criminal" and "taken her off," but Lily appeared poised to yank the phone from his hand if he didn't use it immediately, so he sighed, again, and dialed 911.

When the operator responded and asked, "What's the problem?" Burl said, "Well, it may not be anything, but my wife and I are worried because our children weren't here at home after we came back from having to leave for a medical emergency."

"You call 911 about the emergency?"

"No. It was a household accident and we went to a Med-Stop."

"What's your name and where you at, sir?"

Burl gave her the information, and the operator then said, "The children had a medical emergency?"

"No, ma'am. I had a minor cut from a household accident. My wife took me to get it sewed up. When we got back, the children were gone. They were supposed to be here."

"How old are they, sir?"

"My son is eighteen, and my stepdaughter is eleven."

"They in a vehicle?" The operator's voice had dropped a few decibels and slowed considerably, then suddenly became more remote as if she were reaching away from her headset for something, and then he thought he heard the smack of chewing gum. He wondered if she'd now guessed that this wasn't urgent and that she could more or less take a break while staying on the line with him.

"No, I don't think so. Not one of ours, anyway."

"Where you reckon they at?"

"Tell them about Jason's assault charge!"

He turned his back to Lily and strode out of the room, but she was dogging his heels.

"They could be about any place, really."

"You know, most times kids make it back home safe. We get a lot of calls from folks worried about their kids, you know. Sometimes even if they get it in their haids to run, they don't get far 'cause they get hungry and tired, and they just trot their little selves right back home."

"Yes," agreed Burl. He wanted to add that his wife was the one who needed to hear this, but Lily was hovering over his shoulder. "I think so."

"But if you wanna make a missing persons report, I be glad to transfer you to somebody at the station to hep you."

"Thank you. You have a good one, too."

While the phone was ringing on the transfer, Burl hung up.

He turned to Lily and handed her the dead phone as proof of his accomplishment.

"It's like I said, they need to know for sure something's wrong before they'll do anything, and they know in most cases kids show up sooner or later. She said if they're not here by the morning, I could call the police station and make a missing persons report."

"Thanks for nothing!" When he frowned at her, she said,

"Oh, I don't mean you, Burl."

She looked so miserable and forlorn that he pulled her into his chest and hugged her firmly for several long moments. "It's gonna be okay," he murmured to the top of her head. Her hair smelled faintly of cigarette smoke. "They're friendly with each other. He may be a messed-up kid in a lot of ways, I grant you that, but I've seen him be protective of her. Haven't you? You have to admit it."

Whimpering, she nodded after a moment, her head bumping his chin.

"So let's go find something on TV and wait for them, okay? The good news is we don't have to work tomorrow."

After a moment, Lily pulled away. "You go ahead. I need to wash my face and get my pjs on. I can't believe I've been wearing these same damn clothes since six o'clock this morning."

Burl gratefully sank into the recliner and surfed their cable channels. His agitation kept him from fixing on any place to deposit his quavering attention, but surfing seemed to aggravate the condition rather than soothe it. He relinquished the restless impulse in favor of an old John Wayne movie halfway through its unreeling in which Wayne was wearing a tweed cap, the setting was a very green countryside, and the characters spoke an Irish brogue. Burl followed the film until the first commercial (for Depends), then it all segued into a mishmash of flowing pictures: Burl following the bob of the top of a white hard hat—one of his guys, in the ditch, making a connection—and something flying up from the labyrinth of pipes to strike his forehead, then Meemaw was cooing to him "Poor boy, poor boy!" as he was reclining on her bed in the nursing home. People were running in and out, it was a fire drill.

He awoke when he heard voices. The movie had ended; another had slipped in behind it. The voices might've come from the TV. He leaned the recliner upright, felt the wetness of drool down his chin and into his shirt collar and chest. He blinked, looked at his watch. It was after two!

Where the Sam Hill were those little bastards!

He heard the voice again: Lily, talking, probably back in their bedroom. To her sister? Or maybe to one of the kids?

His calf cramped when he pushed up from the chair, and he hurriedly limped back to the bedroom and came through the closed door just as she was hanging up the phone on her nightstand. She turned to him with a look of triumph he instantly misread.

"Was that them? Where the hell are they?"

"No, that was the police. I told them the whole story, and they think it's a possible Amber Alert."

"An Amber Alert? You're kidding!"

She popped up from the bed as if she'd been seated on a spring and bustled past him, full of purpose.

"They're coming to do an interview."

# Three

Jason knew to stay off the interstates, so they hiked over to Pioneer, where an elderly Asian couple in an old Lincoln Town Car with duct tape on the leather seats took them all the way to C.F. Hawn Freeway. There they thumbed in unison from the shoulder because the signs up and down Highway 175 through Seagoville near the federal prison warned against picking up hitchhikers.

Emily said, "How far do you think you'd get by yourself here?" and Jason nodded. He gave her that, at least, but it was not in her nature to make such a point only once and she beat him over the head with it until he protested. "Jesus, Emily! If I was alone, I wouldn't have come this way in the first place, you know?"

Minutes later, an old Dodge Neon stopped for them. When they managed to squeeze themselves and their gear into the two-door vehicle, the first thing the middle-aged black woman driving it said was, "I wouldn't have picked you up here ordinarily 'cause you might be excaped, but in my book a man carrying a guitar won't harm anybody but a lovesick girl."

The woman wore a floral-patterned dress with half sleeves and a string of pearls and rimless glasses whose lenses flickered as they reflected the headlights streaming on the road. Jason had taken the passenger seat and left Emily to worm her way into the back. Jason figured the woman might be a teacher, or a church lady, in any case. He guessed they wouldn't get free without being prayed over.

The woman flashed Jason a grin. "But your sidekick back there—she won't be some kind of desperado, now will she?"

"No, poor thing's a retardo."

Emily kicked the back of his seat. "You're the retardo."

"I'm off to Athens. Where are you children started to?"

This quite logical question caught Jason off-guard—he realized they should've concocted a ready answer, and he sniffed a detective's interest in it. He opened his mouth to say "Houston," but Emily beat him to a response.

"We're going to Austin."

"My. Folks usually go by way of Waco."

As Jason was working on an explanation for this, Emily blew right by it. "Our daddy's a professor at the university there."

"You don't say! Lord, you children must be smart."

"And my brother writes songs. He's gonna be rich and famous, aren't you, Jason? He's gonna be on *Star Search* in December."

"My, oh my!" said the woman, surely not believing a word, and Jason twisted about in an effort to shut Emily up with a glare.

"If you don't mind my asking, does your mama know you're out here hitching rides at night?"

Jason said, "Oh, she knows."

"She doesn't like it, though," said Emily.

Jason grimaced. "But, you know, it's like the only way we can . . . uh . . ."

"Get to Granddaddy's house 'cause he's dying, and they called Mama at work today and she had to leave right then and drive down to some other town where our aunt lives— what's the name of it, Jason?"

"Uh, Whoville," blurted out Jason, then hoped the driver wouldn't recognize the name.

"Yeah, Whoville!" chirped Emily, and Jason heard her little snicker. "She had to drive down to *Whoville* right then and we were still in school so she had to go on without us. She wanted us to take the bus but we didn't want to wait. So we're gonna meet her in *Whoville*—"this time she had to squelch a giggle—"and all go to Austin together."

"My, oh my," murmured the woman. "I hope your granddaddy's ready for his reckoning. Has he suffered much?"

Emily was kicking the back of his seat to tilt him off his composure. Clearly she was having a great time fabricating nonsense and wanted him to conspire to even greater heights, but Jason's thoughts had taken their own inevitable dark turn.

"Yes, ma'am. I'm afraid so. When they first diagnosed him it surprised us all because he'd always seemed pretty healthy except that he complained about being tired a lot. It's cancer. Cancer of the . . . liver, I think. He started taking chemotherapy and of course then he really did look sick. He lost a lot of weight and had bags under his eyes and his skin was, I dunno, kind of blue and gray somehow. He'd always had a full head of hair he was pretty proud of, and he lost it all. I gave him a hat, kind of as a joke but also, you know, if he needed to feel, well, *covered*. Being that bald embarrassed him."

"A Ranger's baseball cap," put in Emily. "Like the one I have."

"No," said Jason. "You never saw it."

"Okay, what kind then?"

"You could tell he really felt terrible," Jason said to the woman. "You'd go to talk to him and you could see that he felt really sick, but he tried not to show it because he didn't want you to worry. That was . . . that was the most important thing, even in that condition, that I'd not feel bad or suffer because he was. That's the kind of person he was, that even in his horrible pain he'd think of how you were feeling. You'd say, 'Is there anything I can get you?' And he'd say, 'Yeah, I'd love a strawberry milkshake more than anything in the world,' pretending he really wanted it, I guess, or maybe wanting to really want it, because when you brought it to him, he'd grin and make a big to-do over it, but he couldn't get more than a swallow or a sip of it down."

"That'd be good right now," said Emily.

"Maybe it was the idea of the thing," said the woman.

"Yeah. Sometimes I thought maybe he was just really tired and didn't want to have to ask me to leave. Or thought it would make me feel better to think I was doing something. Then toward the end there . . ."

"He's not dead yet," protested Emily.

"All right," said Jason. "I mean these past few weeks he's been trying to get me to, you know, talk about my future without him, what I'm supposed to do, and all, and—" Jason broke off and turned to the window for a moment.

"Sounds like you two are awfully close," the woman crooned.

"Yes, ma'am. We are. I miss him already."

Feeling upstaged, Emily began to monologue about her special relationship with their dying grandfather. He took her to Disney World and to the Smithsonian in Washington, DC, and to meet Senator Hutchison there, he bought her a pony and a Dell laptop and a mini-refrigerator for her room, he dedicated one of his books to her . . .

"Oh, my, so he's an author?"

"Yes, ma'am. He's written about a kazillion historical novels and a biography of President Washington and Lincoln and a bunch of books about astronomy, too. And, oh! He bought me a telescope so big you can see stars that aren't even named yet!"

She went on in this vein, but Jason tuned her out. Though it was a little like trying to control water from a glass spilled onto a table with only your hand, he tried to push thoughts about his mother's suffering aside, partly to honor her wish that he not dwell on how she was at the end. He tried to focus on practical problems he only now recognized. The woman was right—to get to Austin, they'd have to work their way westward from their present course toward Athens. The dash clock burned the green numerals 9:45 in the dark, and Jason wondered if his dad and Lily were home yet. Whatever they might speculate about where their children had gone, they sure wouldn't guess Athens; so far as Jason knew, nobody in his family had any connections there. It might be a good while until they reached the point where the woman would have to let them out.

Then what? Should they keep hitching this late? Or would the very hour arouse too much curiosity and suspicion that they were runaways? And if they didn't keep moving, where could they sleep for the night? Emily's wad might support a cheap motel room, but bagging it was another question. When he'd been packing in his room and imagining himself on the road, he hadn't been encumbered by the responsibility of an eleven-year-old child. In truth, he hadn't really had any practical thoughts. He'd just pictured himself along the highway, backpack and guitar, thumbing, a kind of romantic and/or tragic figure, alone in the world, a sad troubadour, showing up like Holden in somebody's headlights. Then the film would leap ahead to the UT campus, though Jason had only a vague idea of it, and to Lisa walking about, wearing flip-flops and shorts and a neat cotton blouse, hair in a ponytail and pressing a stack of books to her breasts as she sashayed along. She had insisted in the letter that she did want to stay connected, hadn't she? There he'd be, a romantic surprise, appearing out of the blue before her, the song completed and polished (he would finish it on the way to Austin), ready to play to her. And it would sweep away all her thoughts about a "new" arrangement where they allow each other "to grow" without—what was her phrase?—without "feeling that the other is going to stand in the way . . ."

The song would make her want to eat those words. Maybe that could be the title: "I Don't Want to Stand In Your Way." *Baby, I don't want to stand in your way / I hear what you say / I'm here to the end / as always your friend. . . .*

While he'd been dreaming all that like a sound track to his packing, not a single tiny brainwave had wafted out to apply itself to something as mundane as where he (they) would sleep. Well, if he had managed to escape alone, then he could curl up anywhere like the homeless do: in a doorway, or maybe there'd be an unlocked door on a used car lot, or in a bus station, or he'd make his way to the nearest airport, pretend his flight was cancelled or delayed, and just crash on the floor. He'd camped out plenty with his dad on fishing trips, so it was nothing to him to find a cardboard box and dismantle it, spread it out in a field and snooze under the stars. (Luckily, the weather was balmy and dry.)

Emily was persnickety but not frail in the slightest; she could probably rough it with no harm done, though she'd whine. What she'd said earlier was true: it was understood that he was responsible for her because of their ages. He'd been considering her welfare when he agreed to let her come, and Lily would surely give him a high grade for not letting her only child stroll onto a highway shoulder alone and thumb it. She was officially a runaway, but you could say she was supervised, chaperoned.

Meanwhile, Emily kept filling their kind, grandmotherly driver with her own brand of nonsense about her (virtual) cousins, the Simses, who supposedly lived next door. The kid could really lay it on. She lied even when she didn't have to, lied even when the truth was a better story. Lily was going to absolutely freak out when she came home and found that Emily was missing, but she'd soon figure out from the note where Emily was headed and would call her ex in Austin to be on the lookout. Jason's job was just to deliver her to her dad's doorstep in good health and let them thrash it out from there. Then he could find Lisa and try to work his way back into her heart.

They went past Mabank and the turnoff to Gun Barrel City and kept driving south toward Athens, and Jason wished he'd had the foresight to bring a map. On the outskirts of Athens, before an interchange that loomed in the night sky just at the horizon of their headlights, the driver pulled over and told them that if they wanted to go to Austin, they could go west from here to Corsicana, taking the loop ahead to avoid downtown Athens. She didn't know where that Whoville they mentioned was, but if they thought it was down near Rusk or Palestine, she'd be happy to take them to the highway on the other side of town.

"Or maybe you childern would like to come to my son's

house and get yourselves some supper with me. I'm sure if you want they can find a cot for you too, if you'd like to start out fresh in the morning. It might worry your mama something fierce to know you're out on the road like this at night, and you'd sure be welcome to call and let her know you staying someplace safe with good Christian folks."

Before he could construct a polite response, Emily jumped in. "Thanks a bunch, ma'am, but no telling what might happen to Grandpappy tonight, so we'll just keep going."

Jason was imagining that supper—he'd missed eating earlier —but he knew that snares were buried in the offer.

"Yes, ma'am. Sis is right. We'd best be moving along. It's between here and, uh, Corsicana, so we'll get out here and be there in a jiffy, thanks to you."

As Jason had anticipated, before she released them, the driver took one of each of their hands in hers, prayed vigorously for the soul of their poor ill granddaddy, and asked the Lord to watch over them on their journey. Her praying voice was wonderfully mellifluous and rich, and Jason would've put a hundred dollars on a bet that she sang in her church choir. The prayer was downright professional, he thought, with repeated phrases that set up a song-like rhythm: *Oh Lord we ask that you . . . Oh Lord we ask that you . . . And we ask that you . . . And we beseech thee to . . . And we beseech thee to . . .* When a few good full minutes later she reached an *Amen!* that rang like an auctioneer's *Sold!* he had to admit it was a good send-off. It partly compensated for the loss of the cozy auto interior and the sensation of moving ahead as, a moment later, they were standing alongside an empty dark road watching her taillights diminish in the distance.

Jason wondered if they'd made the right choice.

"Come on," he said. "We got to get up to that intersection and head west to Corsicana." He slung his pack over one shoulder, gripped the guitar case by its handle, and set off trudging the few dozen yards where they'd need to turn. When they reached the interchange, they hiked up the access to the highway heading west. From this vantage point, they could see the ambient light from the town suffusing the air above it in the distance, but there was little traffic. It was beginning to look like they might be camping in the field behind them. He set his guitar down, unshouldered his pack. Emily plopped hers beside his and rooted about in it. A water bottle appeared in her hand, and she twisted off the top and took a big swig.

"Aren't you thirsty?"

Jason shrugged. His stomach growled.

"You didn't even think to bring water?"

"I'm not thirsty."

She went back to the pack and brought something out, a tiny box. She fingered back the lid, then raised it to her mouth like a glass and tipped something from it into her mouth.

"You want some raisins?"

"Yeah, sure."

She passed him the box. The aroma of the sweet dried fruit made his mouth water. He shook a huge glob into his mouth and chewed the sweet wad slowly, savoring it. The sky was moonless; the dim aura hovering over the city didn't help il-luminate their small specific location—if anything, it kept them from seeing what might be in the dark around them. They couldn't effectively hitchhike where there was no traffic, and on a spur outside a small town, they weren't likely to get many chances. Nor could they comfortably walk without knowing what lay underfoot. A billboard far in the distance was lighted, but if it contained useful information, it was no help from where they stood.

"What did you bring to eat?"

"Nothing," he said when he'd swallowed.

"Nothing?"

"Gah, Emily! Did I stutter? I was too busy thinking of other stuff."

"Okay. I guess you can always eat snakes and frogs and ants, then. Aborigines eat larvae. Maybe you'd like them, too. While you're enjoying your nice snake sushi and ant guts and beetle larvae, I'll be having my pecan sandies and graham crackers and an orange. And—oh—there's peanut butter on the crackers."

What a smart-ass! "Do you have your cell phone?"

"Why do you want to know?"

"Duh. In case we have to call somebody." He could tell Lily and his dad to come retrieve Emily, for instance.

"Why don't you have one?"

"Same reason I don't have a lot of things."

"Everybody has a cell phone."

"Of course they don't! Just because you get everything handed to you on a silver platter, you think other people all over the world get that, too?" This sounded akin to something Burl would say to Jason, and Jason was annoyed by how Emily provoked a paternal response from him. "Anyway, let me have it a minute, okay?"

"Who do you wanna call, your girrrlllllfriend?"

"You are such a pissant!"

"A what?"

"A pissant!"

"In the first place, that's cursing, and you shouldn't curse at me, because my daddy says that a person who curses has run out of ideas, and in the second place, I don't know what that is."

"Forget it. I'm sorry."

"Okay. But what is it?"

"Some kind of insect, I guess. Will you at least look at your phone to tell me what time it is? Please."

"You mean you'd call me a name without even knowing what it means?"

"Look at your . . . *dad-blasted* cell phone!" Jason demanded, resorting to his grandmother's adjective.

"I would if I'd brought it."

"You're a liar." Jason bent to grab her bag, but she whisked it out of reach.

"I'm not lying!"

"Let me look, then!"

"No! This is my private backpack! I didn't bring my phone. Think about it! Can't you imagine how many voice mails there'd be on it right now? And they'd all be from Mom! They'd all say the same thing. And as soon as I made a call, she could have them find where I am, you know. They do it all the time on *Without a Trace*."

Jason said, "Wow! You have been working on this!"

"I'd probably be in Austin already if I didn't have to have you with me. I sure wouldn't have gone out in the wrong direction."

That stung. That she'd do better without him was so preposterous he didn't know how to answer. "Just out of curiosity, where would you plan to spend the night if you couldn't get a ride and had to stop?"

"Maybe I made a reservation somewhere."

Jason laughed. "Oh, please!"

"At the Best Western on I-35 in Waco! My aunt lives there, and when Daddy and I visit her, that's where we stay. They know us. My cousin's boyfriend is a desk clerk. At night."

"Gah. You are like such a total liar, Emily."

She crossed her arms and turned her back. They stood in that silence for several minutes. Then he said, "Hey, Emily." He spoke it calmly, a little teasingly. When she didn't answer, he sang it, "Ohhh Emmiiillly . . . " A third time he sighed, "Oh, Emily, Emily, M . . . UH . . . LEE. You know what that stands for? E is for Every, M is for Mother's, I is for Idiot, L for LIAR, and Y is for You."

Still no response. When he touched her shoulder, she flinched his hand off.

He wanted to laugh at her. But then, catching himself in a childish wrangle with an eleven-year-old, he had a moment of regret that had become familiar lately. Ridiculous. It was (or should be) beneath his dignity. Not cool, that's for sure. But now he had to find something to say that would show he was willing to sit at the peace table, without actually apologizing. Or, barring that, do something to jolt her out of her snit.

He cupped the handle of his guitar case, dipped his arm through one loop of his backpack, rose and hopped a bit to settle it on his shoulder, started walking toward the distant billboard. She might've bluffed him about going it alone when they were standing in their front yard, but out here in the middle of nowhere, deep in the moonless dark, it would likely be another story.

When he'd gone several yards, she called to his back, "Where are you going?"

He ignored her and kept walking but shortened his stride. After another dozen steps, she wailed, "Jason!"

The panic he heard in her cry—he'd extracted it, of course—made him wonder what sort of person he was, to enjoy having done that. The inevitable pangs of guilt provoked him to stop and turn to watch as she scurried to catch up.

"What?" he asked when she was beside him, panting and jabbing at her glasses to resettle them.

"That wasn't fair."

He passed over the opportunity to rub it in. "Yes. I know. I'm sorry. But you did . . . *tick* me off, you know." It was annoying to have to use his grandmother's vocabulary in conversing with Emily, as it required a lot of vigilance he found tedious.

"If I had the phone, I'd let you use it, I promise."

"Okay."

"Will you promise me something?"

"What?"

"Just say you will, okay?"

"Even though I don't know what it is?"

"Well, I want you to promise you won't leave me like that again."

He couldn't resist saying, "But I thought you were ready to go it alone. I just wanted to let you be free to get to Austin sooner and not have me as a big weight dragging you down."

"Shut up!"

The poor kid's forehead furrows were underscored by her heavy dark brows, and he was flooded by pity for her. "I'm sorry for teasing you. I'm not going to walk away like that."

"But what if we go to sleep somewhere? Promise you won't get up and sneak off?"

"Yes."

She sighed. "Thank you. You can have my cookies and stuff if you like. I'm not hungry any more. I had dinner."

"Thanks. Maybe later."

They kept walking toward the lighted billboard. It hovered

motionless on the dark horizon as if levitating. From a greater distance, it might've been mistaken for a filling station or a restaurant, and the very presence of light itself seemed to offer a vague promise of comfort or sanctuary as they trudged on toward it. It was, of course, only a façade, so the promise turned out to be empty when they were close enough to see one another's forms in the pale borrowed light. As soon as they were fully illuminated, swarms of moths, gnats, mosquitoes, and beetles enveloped them in swirling galaxies.

"Oww! Yikes!" howled Emily, hopping and swatting in front of her face.

"If I had a net, I could get myself some dinner, I guess."

Emily laughed.

"It's too buggy here."

"I think we'll catch a ride better if we're visible, though."

While they waited, Jason tossed pebbles at the bulb in the nearest hooded light.

Emily said, "What exactly does 'unwanted pregnancy' mean?"

"What?"

"Up there."

Jason followed her pointing finger to the billboard. The advertisement featured a close-up of a white girl with long blonde hair, looking away from the camera with a worried expression. The text wrapped about her urged young women to call a 1-800 number to discuss their options for adoption. The girl looked a little like Lisa, and Jason automatically remembered the last time they'd made love, months ago. She had always been on birth control pills, so he'd never had to worry. But now he thought maybe that had been a mistake, giving her all the power. Maybe if he had knocked her up, she'd have sent him a very different kind of letter. She'd be needing him. Desperately.

"It means, you know, if some girl gets pregnant but doesn't want to have a baby," Jason said helplessly, aware that his explanation added nothing.

"I wish it said how far it is to Austin."

"Or how far to IHOP."

"Or Taco Bell."

"Or Taco Bueno. I like Bueno better."

"If you could have anything to eat or drink right now, what would it be?"

"Hmm. A beef enchilada platter with rice and beans and guacamole and a Corona in a bottle so cold it almost hurts your fingers to hold it and it's sweating frost. I'd take that one right off in a couple of swallows, then I'd have another while I was eating, and then I'd have a third really slow for dessert. With a cigarette."

"I thought you were trying to quit."

"This was hypothetical."

"So you'd get drunk!"

"No, I wouldn't. Three beers is nothing. Especially with food."

"You'd be an alcoholic like my mom and your dad."

"Not everybody who drinks is an alcoholic, Emily."

"My daddy doesn't drink at all. He's Hindu. It's against his religion. That's why he couldn't stay with my mom."

"Okay," Jason said, rather than arguing. "Well, what would you have for your best meal right now?"

"My grandmother lives in Boston and she makes samosas. You know what those are?"

"No."

"They're kind of like doughnuts without the hole and they don't have sugar on them and they have stuffing inside—potatoes and peas and spices. Yumm. And chicken tiki masala!"

"You're the only kid I know who'd choose a vegetable dish."

"I said chicken!"

"Okay, chill. I was just teasing. You're too sensitive, you know that?"

The result of their discussion was that Jason decided he would like one of Emily's graham crackers with peanut butter, after all. He was sitting cross-legged on the shoulder, meditatively gumming the end of one to make it last, when headlights appeared from the east.

The vehicle was moving slowly, and it kept pausing before

proceeding toward them. They waited, curious and puzzled, Jason with his thumb out as he rose to stand.

"How come it keeps stopping like that?" asked Emily.

"I don't know."

The mystery made Jason a little uneasy, and if this weren't the first vehicle to come since they'd been on the spur, he might've let it pass. But prescreening a ride simply wasn't a luxury they had now.

At last the car moved into the light from the billboard. It was an old blue Ford Econoline van, one headlight cocked slightly outward like a lazy eye, right front fender sporting a dent the size and shape of a football. An Illinois license plate was fixed canted to the front bumper like an impaled bird. A black male was behind the wheel, and his only apparent passenger was also a black male. The vehicle was moving slowly enough that when the driver braked, the van eased to a halt directly beside Jason and Emily, as if the decision to stop for them had been made long ago and their meeting were a prearranged appointment.

# Four

Lily freshened up for the interview—clean blouse, new lipstick, lobes sporting showy gold earrings with ruby stones he hadn't seen before.

"You might want to shave and put on slacks and a nice shirt."

"Why?"

"If they issue an Amber Alert, the press will want to talk to us."

"At four o'clock in the morning?"

"They won't want to lose any time."

Having obviously lost the argument when the kids hadn't come home, he was forced to concede to Lily's plan. But holding a press conference in his living room at dawn? Wouldn't happen. Amber Alerts were for when somebody sees a guy wrestle a screaming kid into a car and speed off, for when a child disappears with no explanation and foul play is suspected, for when one divorced parent kidnaps a child to circumvent unwanted custody arrangements (and even then, doesn't the kid have to be in danger?). As for that possibility, Lily's ex had more legal custody than he used—he had custody in the bank, a big custody savings account, he was filthy rich with custody—and so far as Burl could tell, Venkat "Vinnie" Patel was your typical head-in-the-clouds professor, a fellow who'd coax a wasp out a window rather than whack it with a magazine. The problem with their marriage was not that he might beat or otherwise abuse her; it was that he hardly knew she existed.

"Tell you what," said Burl. "If it comes to that, you can be our 'family spokesperson.'"

She caught the sarcasm. Fists on hips. "What would you recommend? They've been gone since early evening, Burl! It's 3:30! They haven't called in to say they had car trouble or that they're at somebody's house."

"All right, all right."

He left her in the living room pacing and massaging her cell phone in her fist as if it were a piece of CPR equipment attached wirelessly to her daughter's failing heart. Burl trudged into the kitchen and inventoried the refrigerator, thinking he might be hungry. He panned the cartons of leftovers (realizing as he did that one or both of the kids had put away the food from dinner), without arousing any appetite, so he realized his foraging was a response to that strangely paradoxical combination of boredom and anxiety. Like when a blizzard has delayed your flight and you have to spend hours standing at the terminal window watching your aircraft take successive showers of ethylene glycol.

He shut the refrigerator door, ransacked the utility drawer for a pack of cards, sat at the breakfast table and dealt Solitaire. Hands on autopilot, he was whisked by the magic carpet of worry to the challenges of the mystery. All this time he'd figured they were larking about, but Jason did have terrible judgment; Lily was dead-on about that. Burl had thought his bad judgment might've consisted of this: Jason's upset and feels he has to get out of the house, he calls a pal, pal comes by, Emily insists on going or Jason knows not to leave her here alone, they leave, go to somebody's house or a park or a subdivision under construction, meet other kids, drink some beer, smoke marijuana (yes, his judgment is terrible), and Emily hangs about like a mascot, and the party goes later and later, the pal leaves without them, Jason crashes on somebody's floor, and Emily does too. It's a tale of woe a parent with a wholly irresponsible teenager can tell the cops, all right, but not the narrative for a milk carton.

Burl hadn't spun out that story to Lily because he hated to admit that Jason would subject her daughter to such a scenario. But that explanation was crumbling apart as well. He wondered now about other possibilities.

He abandoned his game and strode to the living room.

"You think it's possible she went to Austin to be with Vinnie?"

"How would she get there?"

"Jason might find a way. It's where Lisa is, you know."

Lily frowned in concentration. Burl was puzzled that she didn't leap to this possibility and take the obvious action.

"You could call him."

Lily nodded. The thought flashed through Burl's mind that Lily was awfully keen on the idea of an Amber Alert, but he batted it down.

Lily sighed. "Yeah. I guess. I sure wouldn't want him jumping to conclusions, though."

She pressed one number. Burl noted that she still had her ex on her speed dial. A lengthy wait—Lily rolled her eyes at Burl, tapping her foot, lolling her tongue, miming exasperation. Vinnie's voice mail greeted you with something like this: *Good morning or evening! You have reached Professor Venkat Patel's home telephone number. It is 512-566-9889 in case you wish to check to see if you have dialed correctly. I am most distressed that I cannot converse with you at this moment. However, I would ask that you leave your name and your own telephone number so that when I am free to do so, I shall return your call. I wish you good day or evening as the case may be!*

"Vinnie!" shouted Lily. "It's Lily. If you're there, please pick up!" More waiting, Lily inscribing circles in the living room floor like a captive animal with one leg chained to a stake. "Call me soon as you can, okay? I don't want to alarm you, but we need to know if you've heard from Emily today. You can call my cell or the home phone. Okay?"

She punched the disconnect tab with her thumb as if it were a loathsome insect. "Fuck!"

"Do you have this girlfriend's number?"

"No. And she better hope I never get it."

"How about his cell?"

Lily snorted. "Useless. Even if he knew where it was, the battery would be dead."

"How about her name?"

"Oh, I know her name all right!"

If Burl had the leisure, he would mull over the input he was receiving about Lily's state of mind in regard to her ex and his current squeeze, but the missing kids were a more pressing issue.

"Try Austin Information."

"She officially lives with other graduate students in an old house near the campus. I don't think it even has a land line."

Burl resisted the impulse to point out that he had proposed an action in response to Lily's *What would you recommend?* The idea wasn't persuasive to him, really, but he thought he should get credit for the suggestion.

Soon enough, authorities arrived, though not the plain-clothes detectives Lily had hoped for—to her mind, they would wield more authority than the garden-variety patrol persons who reported at the Sanborns' door unheralded with no colored lights or siren and no media posse.

Checking her watch, Lily said, "They're two hours late! You'd think—" but then the doorbell chimed again, impatiently it would seem, as it followed upon the first chime by only seconds, and Burl scurried to greet them.

"Evening, sir." The lead officer, Cpl. Robert Sanchez by his nameplate, seemed to be performing two functions at once: one was hailing Burl and the other dipping his head and stretching his neck as if to see over and around him while these pleasantries were exchanged. "You reported an abduction?"

"An abduction?"

"Yes, officers, please come in!" Lily wormed past him and popped up between him and Cpl. Sanchez. "It's my daughter."

Burl's head was still rattling as Lily busily ushered in the patrolman and his partner into the living room, where she retold her story as the officers roamed the room with their gaze, inventorying? gathering evidence? assessing the situation? Though they were normal-sized humans, they seemed outsized, an effect produced by the bristling armory of the holstered matte-black weapon and bullet belt with the glinting copper cylinders, the radios, the square black leather cases of unknown gear affixed to their waists, mysterious cords looping and disappearing into the dark blue fabric of their tunics as if they themselves were techno-marvels and would plug themselves into an outlet when off-duty.

Lily stood triangulated on the officers and turned from one to the other as she spoke, like a salesperson persuading a couple to buy life insurance. The buzz in his brain created by hours of denial dimmed as her voice broke through. He knew now he should've asked what she'd meant by telling the police "the whole story" when he had found her in the bedroom hanging up the phone.

"Ordinarily, we wouldn't be worried—or I wouldn't, you know. I mean they are officially stepsiblings now, but, like I said, Jason is a troubled kid who's prone to violence. I told the officer who took my call *two hours ago* that I was afraid that he was running away because of the hearing Monday on an assault charge. I mean, isn't his being a fugitive enough to make somebody see that she's in danger?" The officers, perhaps unaccustomed to being chided for tardiness, blinked in unison and nodded for her to continue. "He and his father had a fight earlier this evening." She whirled to wave at Burl as if he were her PowerPoint screen. "His head, it got cut, we had to go to the emergency room to get it stitched up, and when we came back, they were both gone." The female officer opened her mouth as if she might ask a question, but Lily spun on her heel and strode to the dining room, where she retrieved Emily's cell phone, snatching up a piece of it in each palm. She'd taken the back off after Burl had snapped it into place.

"And there was this, her cell phone. She never goes out without it, and I found it under her bed, all smashed up like this! And when you look at her call list, she tried to call me while we were at the doctor's and somebody threw it down or stomped on it!"

She handed the parts to the patrolman, who took them, and, as had Burl, attempted to reassemble them. The attention he'd been giving Lily sank like the light level on a dimmer-controlled lamp as he bowed his head to solve the puzzle.

"Ma'am," the woman officer said, "you think this boy is running from the law, why's he got the girl with him?"

Lily crossed her arms over her breasts and looked down at her feet. Her mouth was set in a crisp line. She glanced quickly at Burl—a little hatefully, or resentfully, he realized later—then back to the officers.

"I think she's going to be a hostage!"

"Lily!" Burl howled. "Come on!"

Boy, did that word jazz them! Cpl. Sanchez's arm swung around in an arc, and his index finger just tapped the butt of his sidearm and sailed on, unconsciously it would seem, like a compulsive checker's tic, as lightly and quickly as it would if counting a stack of a hundred holstered 9mm pistols, then the hand swooped up to his radio, which he was unholstering as he said, "Do you have pictures?" to Lily, and to Burl, "Sir, are there any firearms in the house?"

"Uh, no," said Burl, thinking handguns, but Lily crowed, "Yes, there's a shotgun! Right, Burl?" and Burl said, "Uh, yes, an old twelve-gauge Remington that belonged to my grand-dad, when you said firearms, I was—" and the officer said, "Sir, would you check to see if it's still here?" nodding to his partner.

Cpl. Sanchez followed Lily to their bedroom where Lily kept a framed photo of Emily in the shelf of the headboard, and the other officer tracked Burl through the kitchen and utility room, then through the little-used door to the garage. Burl called over his shoulder, "I've got a picture of my son in my wallet you can use if you need to," feeling, in some peculiar way, that Jason had been slighted in the picture-needing aspect of these breathtakingly escalated proceedings.

The garage had an attic space accessed through a collapsible door that folded into the ceiling. As he drew it down with the cord, the female officer stood back as if expecting something to tumble from the space, perhaps wary of an ambush. Burl felt he needed to apologize for making the officer wait in the hot, stuffy garage amidst towers of dust-covered cartons and to explain why the gun was in the attic. He climbed the rickety stairs, wincing a little each time his left leg lifted and set on a step, until his head was above the flooring up there, where he looked back at her, and said, "I keep it up here, you see. I think it's safer, with kids around. Kids have a lot of accidents with guns." He half-expected to be lauded for his precaution, but she said nothing and merely waited. He went up two more steps, saw the old shotgun's canvas sleeve, reached to unzip it enough to see that the old bird killer was couched in its sack as always, called down to her, "Yep, it's up here."

In the rafters a broom's length from his head, yellow jackets had fabricated a papery nest the size of a cauliflower, and the light and air currents from the opened door had provoked their ireful interest in him. He started his clumsy backward descent, but the officer said, "I think you better bring it down here, sir." In the background, he could hear her radio crackling, and from the house, her partner's voice, the tone of it unmistakably martial, not the courteous interrogatory inflection of the earlier interview. Burl guessed Cpl. Sanchez was on the radio—calling for back up?

He cringed across the wasps' air-space to pinch the piping on the canvas carry bag and dragged it back to where he could grip it, then brought it down, backing step by step, awkward on the narrow stairs with only one free hand, feeling a sharp twinge in his knee. He needed to take some Advil. He held it out to her.

"Mind opening it for me, sir?"

He dropped the butt to the concrete and unzipped the sheath, peeled it back from the muzzle. The brush he'd left in the barrel gave off the pleasant scent of gun oil.

"Thank you, sir. You can put it back."

It wasn't until he was halfway up the stairs that he understood she hadn't trusted him when he'd claimed it was here. Between that moment and when he was back onto the garage floor, he struggled with feeling insulted by her distrust. It disheartened him, too, as he was now beginning, slowly and maybe much too belatedly, to understand that he and Lily had mutually exclusive explanations about the condition of their children, competing narratives, and this officer's distrust might figure into the outcome. But maybe he shouldn't take it personally. Maybe it was only professional skepticism or proscribed procedure.

"There!" he declared cheerfully upon letting the door slam up into the ceiling. He bent to massage his knee then kicked lightly in the air to shake it out. "Officer Melton, I think I wanna assure you that this thing—" he jabbed his thumb toward the bandage on his forehead, "it wasn't something Jason did, at all. We were just horseplaying, you know, and I fell and hit my head on his desk. Lily, my wife, she wasn't there." Even as he was taking advantage of the opportunity to tell his side of the story without Lily present to correct him, he knew she was doing the same with the senior patrolman.

"Uh-huh. Sir, would you mind if we take a look at his room?"

"No, of course not. I'll show you the desk and everything."

As they tromped back through the house, Lily's voice drifted down the hall from Emily's room. Though he couldn't distinguish the content, what with Officer Melton's radio and her heels thundering just behind him, she sounded strident, insistent, as if arguing, though no one argued back. Burl waved the female officer into Jason's bedroom and stood in the threshold as the cop sniffed and moved about, gingerly lifting this thing or that just the way they did on *Law & Order* but not opening the closet door or the desk drawers. Her eye came to rest on the poster from the 2002 New Orleans Jazz and Heritage Festival—a trumpet player, Wynton Marsalis, in a lighted room as seen through an archway from a dark street—and Burl thought he heard a scarcely audible murmur of approval from her. Thinking vaguely that he'd capitalize on this sympathy she as a person of color might bestow upon a white boy with a penchant for black music, he said, "He took his guitar with him. That's all he's armed with, an acoustic guitar. He lives for his music. Blues. He loves blues.

He writes his own songs. That's probably where they went, just out somewhere so he could sit and write his music."

He stepped to the desk. "Right here's where I hit my head when I fell. We were just wrestling, you know, grab-ass. *He* didn't do this." He pointed once again to the bandage as if the officer might've forgotten it.

The officer nodded. She then asked if Burl minded if they looked in Jason's closet and in his drawers to see what might be missing (or present, thought Burl). Within a few minutes, he and the officer had managed to concoct a rough list of clothing and toilet articles, along with Jason's journal, and Burl at last admitted to himself that Jason and Emily were on the run. As disheartening as it was, he took a small secret pleasure in how the two had bonded, how Emily was complicit in this scheme, though Lily clearly believed she had been forced.

"I swear I just thought they were out somewhere, you know, the way kids are these days, partying. I mean he has his guitar with him. I just can't believe that he's running away. My guess is maybe they're headed for Austin. It's where his girlfriend and Emily's father live. They're probably just thinking to stay the weekend. I told my wife this earlier."

He said this to Officer Melton's back as he was traipsing after her, hobbling a bit, into the hall and then back to the living room where Lily and the partner were waiting.

"Detectives are coming, Burl!" declared Lily as soon as she saw him appear. "And probably reporters, too." She didn't sound exactly defiant; it was more as if she were hailing him from a train that was starting to roll out of the station and he was still strolling along the platform. Come on, come on!

"Lily, could I talk to you a minute in private?"

"I don't think that's a good idea, sir," said Cpl. Sanchez. "It's best that we hear everything there is to know, you see?"

"Sure. I just wanted to know if she really thinks that Jason abducted Emily. I'll agree that it sure looks like they've taken off." He swung his gaze to Lily. "But this Amber Alert stuff— you know, hon, that makes everybody really tense. It brings out the SWAT teams. You don't really think she's a *hostage*, do you, really?"

"I just don't believe we have the luxury of giving him the benefit of the doubt any more. You've done it more than once too often. There's just too much at stake if you're wrong, Burl!" Her face was twisted with anguish like a wrung shirt, and her eyes were red and tear-rimmed. She was deeply miserable, he knew, and very worried about her child's safety. Obsessed with it, really. He had the feeling that she'd turn a gun on both him and his son if it came to that. Who was this woman?

While the other three waited for the detectives to arrive, Burl went to the kitchen, got an Advil from a bottle in the cabinet over the sink, and swallowed it with the dregs of melted ice and cola from a Styrofoam cup on the counter. He made a pot of coffee. He sat at the table clenching and unclenching his fists. *Jason, Jason, Jason! What the royal purple fuck were you thinking? Kid, you give me nothing to work with here!* Lily could argue the evidence: the prior arrests, the upcoming hearing for the assault charge—and she wasn't even aware that it was a charge of assault "with bodily harm," a degree more serious than what he'd actually told her. Then there was the "fight" in his room, the busted cell phone. In his defense, Burl could only argue the ineffable evidence of his instinct as the kid's father and the illogic of taking a child like Emily hostage if Jason wanted to be a fugitive.

But how many times had he heard the mother of a stone-cold killer tell a reporter, "I just know my baby couldn't do that"? Was he just being blind? If the situation were reversed and Emily were his daughter, wouldn't he scream for the loudest alarm and the best-equipped troops? She told the officers Jason was "prone to violence," and, though Burl had recoiled from that description, he knew that from her point of view, Jason's sullenness and his outburst of temper and the charge of assault added up to that for her. And she didn't even know about the two occasions he'd slammed his fist through the Sheetrock in his room.

Cpl. Sanchez appeared in the doorway and said, "Sir, we'll need a recent photo of the boy," then left.

Now, Burl was as reluctant to produce the photo as earlier he'd been eager. Some mulish resistance rose up, and he felt balky about the investigation, wasn't sure that their having a photo would serve Jason's best interests in the long run. The officers were ganging up on Jason. Who would speak for the kid? Burl stewed about it for a long moment before he recognized that his mind had taken its usual turn toward paternal protectiveness, also known as enabling. He fought that impulse ferociously, shaking his head as if to knock it from his skull, because he now suspected that Lily might be right: he'd aided and abetted Jason's bad behavior all along by being indulgent and much too soft.

The snap in his wallet was old, from Jason's freshman year. He fingered it out of the sheath, digging gently at the bind between the boy's face and the plastic coating, separating it from the Blue Cross Blue Shield ID card that backed it. Jason, long blond hair almost to his shoulders, in a green Stars t-shirt, a long loose hank dangling across his brow. His grin was open, uncomplicated, uncool. It turned up at both corners of his mouth, evenly. He looked so innocent, child-like. Looking at this photo, you imagined that the next words out of his mouth might be *I love my dog!* or *Nobody's prettier than my mom!*

The patrolman said "recent" photo. This was the portrait of a boy before disaster roared through his life, a boy who still had a living mother and a dad who'd been sober for fifteen years. Seeing this photo blown up on a TV screen, in a newspaper, or on flyers would be deeply repugnant. It would be like subjecting that skinny happy boy in the photo to those very dangers he had supposedly created; it would make this innocent kid the target of hateful stares, obscene curiosity, hurtful names, savage handling by authorities. No, the kid in this picture wouldn't be thrown to the wolves. They could find their own damn photo.

Two more functionaries appeared some time after the uniformed officers had completed their own investigation. At the door, a hefty blonde wearing slacks and a navy blazer over a rumpled open-collared blouse blinked a leather badge holder at them with cavalier disdain for the protocol, bun crumb glued to her cheek like a beauty mark, coffee breath. She kept squinting as if her contacts pinched, and Burl wondered if the Amber Alert had dragged her out of bed too early. She might've muttered "FBI." Close on her heels came a young fellow in a straw Stetson, green Dockers, and a yellow polo shirt, a badge affixed to his belt. He represented the Dallas County Sheriff's department, and Lily yammered at him the second he crossed the threshold. Departing uniforms had already told her that the Amber Alert rules required law enforcement confirmation that a child had been abducted and is in danger of serious bodily harm. Burl could see that Lily had spent the interim between pairs of authorities honing her arguments.

By now light was easing into the street from the east. Normally, when preceded by a full night's sleep, this was a time of day Burl relished. He liked to be the first up, liked to load the coffeemaker, pad barefoot down the walk in shorts and a t-shirt to pick up the *Dallas Morning News,* and sit on the stoop with his Best Dad mug of mud and idly skim headlines while inhaling moist cool air before the day's punishing heat descended. Surveying his tiny kingdom gave him a sense of well-being, illusory or not. Now, the world beyond his door was hostile, and the light rising behind houses across the street ushered in a day that wasn't welcome. Already the phone had rung twice; the jangle electrified Lily and Burl, and they sprang to answer, thinking *Jason or Emily*—but the calls came from neighbors who'd noted the patrol car and tried to disguise their nosiness as concern for the Sanborns' welfare.

Lily and the constable stood just inside the door while Lily repeated her tale of the evening's events, though the constable took no notes. Unbidden, the female FBI agent eased onto the sofa and rooted about in her large shoulder bag.

"Ma'am, you sure now that your daughter was *taken* and didn't just go along?" asked the constable. Burl tried to catch his eye to signal *yes,* though his opinion hadn't been solicited.

"Officer, my daughter has always been a very obedient child, I'm proud to say." Burl caught the implication. "If she'd just run away with that boy she would've left me a note—no, a letter! She's very verbal!—explaining why and what she meant to accomplish by it, believe me! She's not one bit shy about letting you know what she's thinking and feeling!"

"Have you—"

"Looked for a letter or a note? I've turned her room upside down and we've looked high and low all over the house." She whirled on Burl. "Right, Burl?"

"Have you any reason to think he might harm her?" the constable continued.

"Well, yes!"

"Lily!"

Lily flipped a glance at Burl then turned away. "Well, not, you know, *try* to hurt her like she's his target or anything, you see, but he's been charged with assault, so he has a history of violence, and he *is* due to go to court Monday, so we can assume that he's on the run from the law and means to stay a fugitive, and if Emily's not a hostage in the literal sense, he'll have no compunction whatsoever in keeping her by his side if the police track him down and chase him or if he decides to hole up somewhere! Who knows? He might be armed!"

"Lily!" Burl protested again.

"You don't know that he isn't!" She brandished her face at him like a hot iron. Then she added, one click down from that outrage: "Do you?" She might be reminding him of how little he knew about Jason.

"The shotgun's still in the attic."

Lily half-sneered, turned to the constable, and circled back to the top of her story, straining, Burl thought, the constable's patience. The female agent paused in her rummaging. "Ma'am, I have to ask: if this stepson of yours was such a dangerous and violent sort, why did you leave your daughter alone with him?"

Burl's triumph lasted only a nanosecond, as Lily had very ready answers. "Well, in the first place, it wasn't my idea that she stay behind, and in the second place"—here she swung about to face Burl—"I didn't even know about the assault charge until tonight, after we'd left the house for the clinic!"

"Hmm!" grunted the agent. She looked up from her purse and fixed Burl with a disapproving gaze. She now held a rosy-colored mango in her palm. Burl had no defense against Lily's charge. His face bloomed with heat; he looked off toward the street as if expecting someone and crossed his arms over his chest. He pictured a swimming pool full of good vodka.

"I'm sorry about that, Lily. Like I said earlier"—he put the slightest weight on earlier to indicate that she'd made public a very private matter—"I was afraid, you know . . ." He couldn't bring himself to add *that you wouldn't stay if you knew.*

The mango was set on the coffee table momentarily then went back into the shoulder bag, switching positions with a writing pad and pen. "I'm going to need some information."

Her questions could've been taken from a personnel form, and, after a moment of passively listening to Lily answer, he said, "I'm going to make some coffee."

In the kitchen he opened a cabinet door and plucked a filter from a stack, settled it into the basket, pulled off the lid to the canister of grounds. Enough left for only one pot. Excuse enough. He dumped the remaining grounds into the filtered basket, and filled the glass pot to eight cups.

The female agent had trailed him. She clutched a cell phone in her palm face up, her nose twisted as if it stunk.

"You got a land line I can use? Battery's kerflunct."

"Sure. On the wall there." He fought back the impulse to ask her not to tie the line up long in case the kids called. "Would you like coffee?"

"Had too much already. So, listen, Mr. Sanborn, what's your vote here?"

Burl glanced at the wall phone as if to remind her of her purported intent. "My vote?"

"Yeah. Is the girl in any danger?"

She curled her fingers around the cell phone and dropped her fist to the table to support herself. She wasn't here for the land line. She wondered what he'd say out of Lily's presence. She'd apparently left her pad in the other room. He had the feeling he was being worked. Is Emily in danger? Could he just answer that he feels terrible about insisting that Emily stay back with Jason? Could he just say that he was furious with Jason for running away? And with Emily too for going with him? And that he doesn't feel free to say "yes" with the world outside standing ready to be set in motion against his child?

But what Lily said about how Emily could come to harm—well, that sank home. If Jason stayed a runaway, he'd quickly be a fugitive come Monday morning, and then there'd be a search warrant and a possible arrest, and it was easy to imagine Jason in a big panic . . .

The agent was inspecting his face, waiting.

"I guess it depends on what's meant by harm."

"Mr. Sanborn, please, we all know what it means." She sounded annoyed and maybe bored by this lame subterfuge.

"Yeah, okay. I don't think Jason's really violent. But he's got, uh, questionable judgment and I think he's running away from his situation because he doesn't want to go to jail and that he's liable to put Emily at risk because of it, because, you know, of what he might do to keep from being caught. Have you guys called Emily's father in Austin? There's a really good chance that's where she'll wind up if she's not there already. So all this rigmarole—" he stopped when he noted that the word seemed to insult the agent. "I mean, you know, you guys are doing your jobs, and I appreciate that."

"So, yes or no?"

He thought he deserved her impatience. His indecision and passivity disgusted him, too. It was all too easy to imagine what she thought of him as a father.

"Okay, well, if the Amber Alert will at least get somebody to notice them . . . and maybe shake Jason into getting his head out of his hiney and getting Emily to safety before something happens . . ."

"Gotcha."

She turned to go back into the living room.

"Phone's right over there."

"This one's on now, guess my hand warmed it up." Walking away, she flashed the lighted face over her shoulder.

He stared at the dark brown drizzle as the pot filled, hands gripping the counter edge. Burl had crossed the line. Goddammit, it was Jason's fault for putting himself and Burl in this situation. If it took having his picture plastered on billboards and whatever to open his eyes, then so be it. Burl had been too indulgent for too long.

But it pained him that he and Lily were at such odds. He was bewildered to find himself as her adversary; shouldn't they be on the same side? And, yeah, now that Burl had "voted" for the alert, he was officially teamed up with her. He wished he could feel better about it. A whole lot better.

When the pot was full, he went back to the archway into the living room, put one foot forward across the threshold.

"I just used the last of the coffee. I'm gonna run to the store. Be right back."

Lily was now seated on the edge of the couch, smoking, her free hand gripping the holding hand as if the lighted cigarette could shake loose.

"But Burl, the press could be here any minute!"

"I'll be right back. If I'm not, you can talk to them."

"Burl?" she called to his departing back. He knew she was thinking of that swimming pool full of good vodka, too. He waved casually over his shoulder, denying her the solid reassurance that he wouldn't stumble back roaring drunk. It was a meager and petty payback, but it was all he could muster.

"I'll have my cell in case the kids call."

# Five

Jason and Emily sat on trash bags plump with crushed aluminum cans. The man behind the wheel—"My name is Jacob"—had driven from Chicago where he lived and had picked up his passenger—"I am his cousin, Emmanuel"—in Dallas. Jacob left Chicago "it would be three days now," he said in a sing-song foreign to Jason's ears. They were driving to Houston to attend a reunion. They were not in a hurry to arrive. Jacob said that when they traveled they slept in the van and stopped in roadside parks to cook their meals. "We like our own food," said Emmanuel. Jason thought the pair might be in their twenties, though it was hard to tell because the men were that rich dark hue of Africans, and the only light available rose faintly from the dash. Their odor—cooking oil, sweat, and an unidentified spice that might've come from their food or something stowed in the van—likewise marked them as exotics. A male chorale purling quietly on a CD or tape lured Jason's ear, and when he asked about it, Jacob said, "They are singing hymns in Dinka."

The cockeyed right headlamp cast its skewed flare out onto the right-of-way beyond the shoulder and twinkled back from the butt ends of soda cans and bottles. The light leapfrogged by bounds, like a tossed net, ahead of their progress, and they moved slowly enough to decide if the object glimmering back in the bar ditch was sufficiently enticing to examine.

"We are fishermen," chuckled Jacob. He'd curled the wheel

rightward to ease the van to a stop only a few hundred yards from where Jason and Emily had joined them, and had twisted about to explain why. Then he and Emmanuel left Jason and Emily in the van while they waded in knee-high vegetation along the road, beating at it with lengths of broom handle. In the light from the van, the men were very tall and thin. Jacob wore a long-sleeved white shirt and khaki trousers, and Emmanuel, black slacks and a red shirt with black patterns on it. Their heads, closely cropped, seemed almost too small for their lanky frames. The way the men moved through the grass, bending as they flailed it, seemed faintly tribal and mysterious. Each carried a trash sack and from time to time stooped to bag an item.

"Why are they using those sticks?" asked Emily.

"Snakes, I guess."

"What're they looking for?"

"You're sitting on it."

"Cans? Why?"

"I guess they sell them."

"You can sell old drink cans? How much?"

"I dunno. It varies, I guess. Ask them."

Emily crawled over Jason and groped in the dark for the latch. When the door swung open, the air was cool and sweet from the field beyond a barbed-wire fence. She climbed out and stood. She looked back at him.

"Aren't you going to ask them?"

"I need to pee."

"Now?"

"I have for a long time. I can't wait any longer."

"So go pee."

"Where?"

"Go behind. In the road."

"What if somebody comes along?"

"You'll have time to move."

"I don't want to go in the road. It might splatter on my shoes."

"So go in the ditch over there on that side."

"It's too dark. I don't know what's there."

"Probably just rats and snakes and spiders having themselves a creepy critters ball, that's all."

"Shut up!"

The men had ventured to the far border of the light and were standing close to examine something held between them.

"You want me to go with you?"

"Yes."

"What's it worth to you?"

He was only kidding—was already untangling his legs from under his hams and was seeking a grip on the back of the front seat to boost himself—but Emily said, in earnest, "Five dollars."

"Your money's no good in this establishment. I'll do it for you out of the goodness of my heart."

They walked in the shadow of the vehicle to the far shoulder of the road. Emily insisted that he tromp down a patch of grass just off the asphalt, and he chanted, "Snakes and toads, spiders and hiders! Scat and git! Be gone with thee!" as he stomped out a circle, then he stood in the road facing the van as she squatted behind him. The men slowly made their way back toward the highway. They were laughing and talking in a foreign language, not one he could say he'd ever heard. They seemed to be enjoying themselves.

Overhead, the moonless sky had cleared, and beyond the aura of the headlights a wash of stars lay strewn across the blackness of space. It was rare to see the night sky without the filter of city light whitening it and without buildings obstructing the horizon-to-horizon reach of the canopy. He could make shapes with the stars, join the dots. Was his mom "awake" now and looking down? Did people really drift up into the stars like flaming chaff from a bonfire when they die? It was pretty hard to swallow, the whole heaven/hell thing—especially the supernatural, hocus-pocus business of how their pastor put it in their few sermons. It was nice to think it might be that way. Some scrap of consolation, anyway. His mom had believed it, for sure. But God's plan? Why would God have a plan that put his mom there and not here, not right at home with his dad? If she were still around, she would be telling him with that little grin of hers that if he didn't get a haircut she was going to buy him a collar and feed him Alpo, asking him *How's Lisa, honey?* or baking chocolate chip cookies and bringing them out to the backyard on a plate for him and Lisa to eat while they were playing on the swing set . . . the old days, the good, good, good old days. . . . Not ours to reason why, only to do or die? And die.

While he was gawking with his head cocked back and his mouth open, Emily, now beside him, said, "How many constellations do you know?"

"Well, Big Dipper, for one."

"Part of Ursa Major."

"Whatever."

"Is that the only one?"

"Uh—oh, yeah—the Little Dipper."

"Part of Ursa Minor. Can you find it?"

"You mean right now?"

"Uh-huh."

"Probably not."

"They're not constellations, anyway. They're called . . . *asterisms*, I think. Because they're part of constellations. Did you know there are eighty-eight constellations?"

"No."

"You can't see them all at once—it depends on what hemisphere you're in and what time of year it is."

"How come you know so much about it?"

"Astronomy is one of my daddy's specialties."

Looking into the sky, they fell silent. The conversation had provoked a snarl of contradictory emotions in Jason. One was irritated contempt at Emily for being a show-off know-it-all. She would become that nerd in the front row in his high school who not only knew the correct answer to every question but would also nitpick the teacher's statements. Emily's prissy display of knowledge made him want to boot her little butt. A dozen influences on his sensibility—slacker and doper pals, popular culture, even his parents for whom education was first and foremost a tool for attaining a high standard of living—all lent their voices to the chorus condemning those who pursue knowledge for its own sake, who make a habit of revealing what they've learned.

But as they hung mute in their observatory mode, he realized that she'd altered the way he was seeing the sky. Yes, he could imagine his mother sort of hovering about up there in a vague way, but Emily's hard-edged mastery of the reality sort of spoiled the view, you could say. She made him dissatisfied with his ignorance and more than a little jealous. The eleven-year-old beside him had her eyes trained overhead just as his were, but she could apparently see more. That thought was unsettling. It made him wonder whether he shouldn't know more about the sky, about everything: math, science, art, literature, history, current events. He and Lisa were the same age, and he didn't believe she had a higher IQ than his. Yet she'd been the salutatorian, was now in college, and he was here on the road in the middle of the night looking up at a sky that his eleven-year-old companion could read like a road map.

Why hadn't he learned things? Where had he been? It didn't seem appropriate to blame Emily for knowing things. Lisa had said, *It's not my fault I'm going to college!*

So whose fault is it I'm not?

Jacob showed them the Honda wheel cover unearthed in the grass. "It wasn't a rare find," said Jacob. "We have them by the dozen." Jason presumed that they too were salable, and, once they were underway again, Emily held the disc and said, "Huh! I always thought they were metal!"

"They used to be," Jason told her.

"I bet metal's too expensive and it weighs a lot more. That's why. If a car is lighter, then it burns less gas."

Jason watched her turn it over to inspect both sides, frowning. He thought, *She wants to know why they're plastic now when they used to be metal.*

They made several such stops. Emily grew tired and napped, curled in the hollow of a stuffed trash bag as easily as if it were a beanbag chair. Jason got out with the men to scour the ditches for cans. It was like a scavenger hunt. Once, he stumbled upon an old water meter and had to explain its use to the others. He thought then of his father and Lily. He had no idea what time it was—surely after midnight—and by now they'd have come home, discovered Emily's note, and probably contacted Emily's father in Austin. He'd be waiting, no doubt, when they finally arrived, and Jason would be relieved of this responsibility.

They drove past a blue "Picnic Area 1 mi" sign, and Jacob said, "We have to sleep now."

The advertised amenity consisted of little more than a widened place on the shoulder like the bulge of an ingested rabbit in a snake. There, a wooden table with a bent-pipe undercarriage was bolted to a concrete pad under a huge pecan tree. Emmanuel set up a tube-framed, two-man tent. They left their thin foam ground pads for Emily and Jason and zipped themselves up in the tent within minutes of pulling the van to a halt, taking a canteen and leaving Jason and Emily two bottles of tap water poured into Ozark containers.

Jason hated to wake Emily. He spread a pad for her in the floor of the van and roused her enough to get her to lie flat. From his pack he extracted a sweater to pillow her head. When he had settled himself on his back on the second pad, he found he wasn't very sleepy, despite how late it was. He remembered that he'd worried earlier about where they might sleep, and without much trouble, really without working at it, here they were. Their hosts were considerate and generous.

Bagging this opportunity was a thing to be grateful for and proud of. The spontaneous, unpredictable outcome of it twanged his song-writing nerve, and he began to shape an "on the road" song that captured these adventures. He pictured himself playing it for Lisa. First he would play it to her alone (while they were sitting on a blanket beside Town Lake), then the scene segued to a small club on Sixth Street, an intimate space, a small square stage with a single spot over a single stool, and he comes from the wings and takes the stool with his guitar and sings both the Lisa song and this new one, and she's there, at a table just in front of the stage. She hadn't known he was in town, even, had shown up there with a roommate or a friend.

Of course, the friend might be Chase Putnam or a dude from her UT classes he'd not heard about. That thought shot him out of his heroic fantasy like a sharp stick poked in his eye. He zoomed back to the second worst night of his life.

First there'd been the whole hassle about how he was supposed to dress. Lisa had said the party wasn't your ordinary Saturday night barbeque (her mom had spent a grand on a "garden party dress" at Neiman's), so she'd nudged him to dress up, which he hadn't minded, really. He wasn't blind to her anxiety about how he'd fit in, and though she whined that her mom had gone overboard on the decorations and the catering and her mom's dress, he suspected she was letting him know what he faced. He'd wanted to say, *Lisa, Lisa, Lisa. Chill, girl! I've been to a million church potlucks and four funerals! Trust me, babe. Did I bring an air horn to your graduation or scream when you strutted across the stage? I saw your mom roll her eyes every time some dude's name got called and forty people heaved up and shouted hallelujah in the aisles.*

Though they were always polite, her parents already had reasons for disapproving of him. In January, he'd had a very bad week, couldn't sleep or eat or study, didn't know what to do, didn't want to do nothing and yet didn't want to do anything. So he quit school. Didn't talk about it, just tried to hide. Stacked up the absences, spent some days riding the buses in Dallas or the DART rail out to Plano, where he'd get off and stroll aimlessly, have coffee in Starbucks. In good weather, he'd set up on the little plaza in front of the Angelika at Mockingbird Station, strum and brainstorm new songs. If he tossed his cap on the ground or left the case open, people would sprinkle coins in it, and he'd have the fare home.

By the time everybody figured out he hadn't gone to class in three weeks, he felt it was too late to catch up, and his counselor, Mrs. Robinette, worked it out so that he could finish courses through "credit by exam." But failing the Algebra II exam brought him down so much that he couldn't face the same in English, history, and social studies. Ronnie Blevins, who worked at Athlete's Foot, said, "Don't bother with all that. Do what I did." Like Bill Cosby, he'd scored his diploma via a GED. Ronnie sold his packet of flashcards to Jason for twenty bucks, and Jason and Lisa went over them several times a week. It embarrassed him to do it in public, so they sat in her car or at a spot on the Eastfield College campus, where such a thing looked pretty natural if you didn't see it close up. He'd taken the practice tests in social studies, writing skills, and Interpreting Literature and the Arts and had now passed them handily, but math still slammed him against the wall. (Sample question: *Two cyclists start biking from a trail's start three hours apart. The second cyclist travels at ten miles per hour and starts three hours after the first cyclist who is traveling at six miles per hour. How much time will pass before the second cyclist catches up with the first from the time the second cyclist started biking?*)

Lisa kept urging him to schedule a testing appointment, but he kept saying he "wasn't ready," meaning he was too scared.

He'd dug himself a deep black hole but, swear to God, he was clawing at the walls to inch his way out. Making one mistake shouldn't condemn him as a total loser for life. His dad, for instance, had spent almost fifteen years sober, then went through a bad patch, but now he'd gone back to meetings.

The Johnsons' party would test him. At stake was not just winning their approval, but making sure that when Lisa left for Austin, she would lay her heart right in his hands for safekeeping. And she had to trust that while she was gone, he'd be working his damnedest to fly right. Down the road there could be college for him. Austin. Or maybe it would be Sixth Street, the music scene; it was the Texas Mecca for a guy who hoped to play and sing his own songs. Lisa could sit by the stage at Antone's or B.D. Riley's and listen to him perform. Maybe by next March he'd be a featured performer at South by Southwest, who knew? He'd been too broke and too deep in a funk this spring to make SXSW, but next year—watch out!

At Sym's he'd bought a navy Haggar blazer with gold metal buttons for $49, and while he was at it got a red silk tie for $7 and blew $25 on a Calvin Klein white dress shirt. He'd used money he'd been saving to take Lisa to a Pat Green concert. He didn't realize the shirt had French cuffs until he unwrapped it the day of the party, but his dad's friend Lily (they were only dating then) found two pairs of matching buttons in his mom's old sewing box and stitched them back to back for makeshift links.

Lily and his dad planned to go to a meeting of the AA group where they'd met, then to dinner, so they'd drop him off at Lisa's. On the way Lily had Burl stop at Albertsons so she could help Jason buy flowers for the hostess.

The Johnsons' long, curving driveway had been oddly empty; not even the family's usual rides were visible as Burl's pickup turned off Barnes Bridge Road, and Jason's gut jerked in a panic. Was he wrong about the date, or was he so early nobody else had arrived? Nothing would make him feel more like an absolute dumb-ass than to dick around in the back-yard alone while everybody finished getting ready.

Two guys in white shirts were standing at the apex of the driveway's arc, and when one stepped out to greet the arriving pickup, Burl said, "Valet parking! Some barbeque, son." Beyond the white board fence that bordered the adjacent horse pasture gleamed ranks of hoods and roofs, as if an impromptu luxury car lot had been set up in the newly mown grass. Dr. Johnson's yellow Hummer hummed in the sunlight, and in a far corner of the acreage Jason spotted the family's fleet, including Lisa's black Acura and her mother's Infiniti whose silver flanks stood light and bright against the backdrop of foliage along the wet-weather creek behind the pasture. Next to that profusion of automotive splendor, Burl's F-150 was a handyman's hoopty; it was four years old with a year left on the loan, and the right front fender sported a patch of gray primer where Burl had left off his body work after banging a parking meter during his off-wagon interim. Jason prayed that he could get into the house without anyone seeing how he'd arrived.

The valet who opened the truck door with a big grin and a "Welcome, sir!" was not much older than he. Jason wondered if his chortled greeting was meant as a mocking reference to the pickup or to the cone of long-stemmed flowers Jason clutched as he dismounted.

Jason let himself in through the half-opened door, and when he reached the archway into the kitchen, Lisa's mother was standing by the granite-topped island talking to a woman Jason didn't know. A white-jacketed catering crew was setting out containers on the counters.

Huge uncovered windows in the back wall faced north and allowed for an unobstructed and inviting view of the flagstone patio, the pool and attached hot tub, and the woods that lay at the bottom of a yard carpeted by a flawless mat of St. Augustine. A banner which stretched the length of the flagstone, supported by high poles, featured clip-art mortarboards and gowns along with the message *CONGRATS LISA— ONWARD AND UPWARD!!* Under the banner, clusters of adults stood drinking from glasses taken from trays carried by waiters wearing graduation gowns and mortarboards. Children were playing in the hot tub and riding on neon-colored inflatable creatures in the pool. Lisa's thirteen-year-old cousin Andrea was sitting on the lip of the pool dipping her feet in the water, her head tilted up and one hand shading her eyes while a guy—Chase Putnam!—bent over her, talking and maybe checking out her A-cups in that chartreuse bikini top while smirking like he considered himself the world's most swahvay dude since he'd become an Aggie. Why was he here? Lisa's older sister, Alison, who went to Baylor, was standing behind him, and off to her left a duo of teens he knew only casually sat at a patio table fondling drink glasses skirted with napkins.

Obviously these people had been here a while. Had he gotten the time wrong—was he now late? Or were there two shifts and he'd been invited to a second wave where they let the riff-raff in after the cool insiders have had first dibs on the fun? Aside from that unsettling surprise, there was a second minute shock—if the men had worn blazers to the party, they'd since ditched them in favor of sweating in their shirt sleeves in the muggy heat, and he was the sole male who'd donned a tie. Chase was wearing crisply laundered shorts, tassel loafers with no socks, a navy polo shirt tucked in, and a black dress belt. No blazer, that's for sure, but it wasn't what you'd clean the garage in, either.

He felt bewildered, at a loss to account for these tremors under the ground of his expectations. Lisa had coached him; didn't she even know what would go on here?

Mrs. J's head was partly eclipsed by pots hanging from a rack over the kitchen island, and Jason sucked in a breath, sidled up behind the two and waited mute as a brick to be noticed. The cone of tissue-swathed flowers was leaking onto his shoes and the tile floor as he held it upright before him like a canister of nuclear material.

"Oh, hello, Jason! How nice you look!" She listed toward him slightly as she turned, her eyes boozy slow and their normal green made murky by a film of moisture, and he wondered if she were drunk.

"Hi, Mrs. Johnson. I brought you these." He pushed them at her.

"How lovely!" she gushed. It was the word Lily had used, they spoke the same lingo, then. That was good. His mother would've said "pretty," maybe. But Mrs. Johnson immediately relay-batoned the flowers off to her conversation companion, and the other woman—hired help, he realized now—took them as if she knew exactly what to do without being told.

He spotted Lisa as she approached the kitchen carrying a tray of dirty glasses. It was so like her to work at her own party, though her parents had hired an army of help. He toed open the back door and took the tray from her.

"Hey, babe!"

"Oh, hi! Thanks! People are sure drinking."

She leaned up to kiss his cheek, then stepped back to appraise him.

"Do I look okay enough to meet your people?"

She grinned. "Of course! You always do. Where'd you get the blazer?"

"I bought it at the best men's store in Paris on my last concert tour. It's a Pierre La Pee-yew original."

"Excellent."

"So you're proud of me. Do I have it right?"

She took his arm and smiled. "You have it right. Come on."

They made it two steps onto the patio when Jason said, "Hold up a second." His aggrieved sense of betrayal that rose from the gap between his expectations and the party's reality needed a serious massaging. "Why's Chase here, anyway?"

Lisa blinked. "Alison invited him."

"But it's your party."

Lisa sighed. "No, it's my family's party."

"Okay. I'm sorry. It's not my business. It's just—"

"Just what?"

"Just that I feel a little weird with this"—he flipped his tie up disdainfully—"when old Chase looks like some GQ model at a prep school thing. And nobody else is wearing a freaking coat in this heat."

"Daddy took his off when Mom wasn't looking, and everybody else just sort of ignored her hints in the first place."

"I think I'll take mine off."

"Aw, come on. Wear it for a bit, okay? What'll it hurt?"

He took that as a compliment and as gratitude for his efforts, but her insistence implied that everybody else could come as they damn well pleased but he couldn't afford the luxury of not playing by her mother's rules. Or she couldn't. Not with him, anyway.

He was dying for a cigarette, but since no Johnson approved of smoking, he sat on the urge. Lisa steered him to the table occupied by Chase, Rebecca, and Destiny. Rebecca was a fellow officer of Lisa's in the National Honor Society and volunteered with her to read to seniors at nursing homes, including Good Shepherd, where Lisa always made a point of visiting Meemaw. Destiny wore a skirt and a tight-fitting top that Chase was admiring. She'd sat in front of Jason in sophomore World History and spoke to him if they bumped body parts while unharnessing themselves from their book bags.

"Jason, you know Destiny and Chase and Rebecca, right?" Lisa was insisting while tugging him so close to the table the rim pressed his thighs.

"Sup," Jason said to Chase, cool, non-committal, then broad-brush formatted his half-smile across the space occupied by the other faces.

Jason and Chase endured an awkward moment—Jason suspected that Lisa's introduction had interrupted a conversation about his own relationship with Lisa. Everyone watched with an inexplicable fascination as a duo of musicians returned from a break, picked up guitar and flute, sat in metal folding chairs near the pool. They struck up something that sounded Irish.

Chase said, "Hey, Sanborn, you still busking down in Deep Ellum?"

"Aw, now and then."

"I saw you outside Club Dada when I was home one weekend. Some dudes from school and I were like totally wasted."

*So?* thought Jason. *You got a good laugh?*

"What's 'busking'?" asked Destiny, with an air that suggested her ignorance was to her credit because the thing was too peculiar to be known by a normal person.

"You know what husking is, with corn on the cob?" asked Jason.

"Yeah, sure."

"It's the same, only with beavers," said Jason.

Lisa laughed. "You remove their busks," Jason went on, and before the girl could take offense, Lisa said, "It's what street musicians do when they play and pass the hat."

Lisa leaned into him. "Jason's writing a song for us."

Jason cringed. Chase said eagerly, "What's it about?" Jason could tell this was comical and Chase was yearning to text a frat brother.

"Long distance love," she said.

"Is that the title?" Chase asked.

"I like that," said Destiny.

"It doesn't have a title yet."

"Why don't you get your 'git-tar' and try it out on us. Maybe we can help you come up with one," said Chase.

Jason flicked a glance toward Lisa, but her profile was to him. She had a hold of his bicep with both hands, and the round arc of her hip was pressed to his thigh. Did she know how embarrassing this was?

"It's not finished."

"Maybe we could help with that, too. Gimme the tune."

"I think I'm going to get something to drink. What're you all having? I'll get you a refill. Lisa?"

"Diet Coke, baby."

*And thanks for that endearment,* he thought. "Okay. Rebecca? Chase?"

Rebecca passed on a refill, but Chase said, "Vodka tonic, twist of lime."

*A proud legal imbiber,* thought Jason. The Johnsons were not the kind of parents who allowed their underage children to drink anywhere, even at home, though they allowed a finger of wine at holiday meals.

"Destiny, what's yer poison, gal?"

Destiny advanced her torso toward the table to give her sizeable breasts a gander at her glass. "It was supposed to be cranberry juice and club soda. I have a urinary tract infection."

At the bar table, Jason was momentarily startled by the bartender's astonishing resemblance to Sgt. Brookes, who he seemed to bump into at gas stations and grocery stores and ball games. Rumors went around that a math teacher, Mr. Anderson, slipped the names of unpromising students to the recruiters for a bounty paid on each enlistment, and since Jason had dropped out, Sgt. Brookes had dogged his steps. But, surely not here.

The bartender tidied up his table while waiting for Jason's order.

"You wouldn't happen to have a brother in the army, would you?"

The bartender chuckled. "Got a lot a brothers in the army." He winked at Jason. "What can I get you?"

Jason ordered Chase's vodka tonic, Lisa's Diet Coke, and Destiny's club soda and cranberry juice. He waited for the bartender to object to the alcoholic beverage and considered whether he should point to the table or claim the drinks were for his parents. Apparently Jason could get served if he wished without coughing up his fake ID, though it would upset Lisa for him to drink.

He looked over to the table. Lisa had taken a chair, and Alison had come to sit with them. They were chatting merrily like roomies on a *Real Life* road trip. Chase. What a dick. *Why don't you get your git-tar?* Why don't you fuck yourself three ways. Surely Chase and Lisa . . . she *knew* he was a dick, right? Why else did she break up with Chase even before she and Jason made up? And the million-dollar question: did they or didn't they? Lisa had said, "Don't ask me that, Jason!" What a torment *not knowing* was! Was her order not to ask an admission of guilt?

Lisa in Austin, Chase in College Station, not many miles between them, out of Jason's sight, his hearing. He didn't even know anybody there who might send him a report.

He set the drinks on a tray and brought them back to the table.

"Here you go!" he declared like the world's most cheerful waiter. "Uh, forgot mine! Gotta go back," he said to Lisa.

Back at the bar table, Jason said, "Got another order for a vodka tonic," waggling his thumb toward the table. "Triple shot, just a squirt of tonic he said."

The bartender fixed the drink in a *glass* glass. If Jason had missed it before, he noticed it now: you knew this was a "nice" party because there wasn't a tumbler of plastic in sight, and when you took a plate to set your appetizers on, it wasn't made of molded foam. If Lisa asked, he'd say it was Sprite. If she insisted on sipping, he was a dead man. Lisa was engaged in an animated dialogue with Rebecca, and Chase was raining his bullshit onto Destiny and Alison. Jason could go back and sit like a dumb-ass, worry about Lisa's identifying his drink, and torture himself by reading too much into Chase's and Lisa's body language and listening way too closely to each little word.

The sun even at a six-thirty slant was a torrid orb pushing heat at them from the west like a weather front. His face was baking. He sipped his drink. Had he ordered straight vodka?

Whew. The cold pungent bite seared his gullet, then the toxic center of it eased out into his bloodstream and weighted his limbs slightly, pleasurably, sank him onto his heels, flattened his feet, and he felt the discs in his spine collapse on one another like stacking coins. A butt would be so good with this.

Keeping his back to the patio, he strolled the flagstone apron on the far side of the pool then sauntered casually as if meandering without intent down the lawn. He might disappear into the trees along the creek, where he and Lisa had a secret spot and he could sit and smoke in peace. An old playhouse stood a few yards into the foliage, and maybe he could chill out there. He needed time to tote up wins and losses. He'd suck this one drink down and maybe get back up to the bar and return to the table with a virgin Sprite.

Some kids were prowling about where he'd intended to go, so he curled back up toward Dr. Johnson's garage. He hadn't seen his magnificent car collection in a while, anyway, and maybe Dr. J had added something. And the steel-framed garage was air conditioned. Nothing was too good for Dr. J's collection of muscle machinery; it was a temple to American automotive ingenuity, a trophy case you could stand inside.

The windowless metal entry door was hidden from the house, and to his luck it was unlocked. The air inside the garage was cool already and contained the pleasurable scents of gasoline, paint, and rubber, but his entrance brought in a draft of overheated humid air, and the thermostat kicked on the AC blowers suspended like huge beehives under the I-beam rafters. He dug a pack of Marlboro Lights from his pants pocket, shook one out, and lit it. His smoke drifted away from him. A bank of fluorescent lights in shop fixtures hung from the vaulted metal ceiling, and, after a moment's hesitation, Jason hit the switches by the door and watched as rows of long bulbs coughed up their white light. Dr. J's three splendid specimens gleamed it back as if in gratitude for the exposure. Their grills beamed big metallic grins, and he had a strange impulse to break into applause.

Close by was a 1967 Shelby Cobra Mustang GT500, white

with two wide blue stripes all the way from the lip of the hood and across the top and down the rear deck. Sweet, sweet ride! Dr. J had paid $250,000 for this car, and Jason also knew from Lisa that Mrs. J didn't learn about that until a year after the purchase. Jason stood in front of the Cobra sipping his drink and dragging off the butt. Once he had asked how fast the car was, and Dr. J had said, looking about as if to make sure they weren't being observed, "I never had the guts to take it over 120, but I could feel there was a lot more to spare."

Jason took another pull from the glass and another drag of the cigarette, holding it upright to keep the long ash intact. He looked about for something to use as an ashtray, but the garage was more showroom than auto shop. A long work-bench stretched along the wall behind the cars, but the surface was clean as an airport runway. He tugged at his left outside coat pocket and discovered that it was still stitched shut, so he tapped the ash into the inside breast pocket.

The vodka massaged his nape but hit his control center like laughing gas, and all the techies there on the bridge started swaying a bit in their chairs. The thought came that the drink was way too strong, then the second thought came to toss it down quick to hide the evidence and use the empty glass as an ashtray.

He moved on to the car he yearned to own the most: the black '73 Plymouth Barracuda coupe with its 340-cubic-inch, four-barrel carb V8. It looked like a big shark with that wide chrome-rimmed mouth and black gullet, the headlights like predatory eyes posted on either side, the wide black racing tires with the lettering FIRESTONE highlighted in white, the cool air scoops in the hood that made it look like a fighter plane. Under that hood, the engine was totally chromed out—air filter, valve covers, the block painted turquoise, new red wiring. Not a speck of oil or dirt. When Dr. J cranked it up, you heard a throaty roar from a dual exhaust and he'd swear you could feel the power of the engine through that concrete floor. It was like standing next to a diesel eighteen-wheeler while it idled.

It was a freaking outrage that this car didn't get out of this garage. Some dude buys a Stradivarius violin or a Martin D12 guitar and locks it in safe deposit box. Jesus.

He smashed the butt in the bottom of the cocktail glass. He stroked the glossy raised ridge on the front fender, then he opened the driver's door, stuck his head in. Black leather buckets, a black leather bench in the back, a wood-grained console and shifter, the instrument panel with red-fingered analog gauges, tach, and speedometer. The black leather wheel turned on a burnished stainless steel bracket bolted to the post under a round black horn hub.

He could picture himself behind the wheel but knew it would likely be Lisa's goofy little brother Chris who'd get the chance to drive it. Some kids have all the luck. Jason would be lucky to borrow the old truck once Lisa leaves for school. Sure, he oughta get a job that would allow him to buy a car, but what minimum-wage slave could afford the insurance and upkeep? *There's a reason poor folks ride the bus, Dad.* Lisa had always been good about not humiliating him over this, and since she got her car at sixteen, the two of them had used it for their transportation. He bought gas now and then when it pinched too much to be such a wussy freeloader, and she let him drive it when they both knew his being a passenger in his girlfriend's car might be an embarrassment, but it didn't fool anybody. Lucky Lisa, lucky Chris, lucky Allison. They got themselves born to a doctor, not to a hoopty-driving alky who works for the city as a sewer inspector, who couldn't have made the mortgage half the time if it weren't for the extra pay his mom brought in as a secretary at their church. Screw him. If Mom hadn't died, things would be different. *If Mom hadn't died.* Jesus fucking Christ, he was so tired of that tune!

And now Lisa. Not dead, no, but so far away for a guy with no money and no wheels, she might as well be at school in Australia. He shouldn't have told her he was working on the song. *Get your git-tar.* The trouble was that every time he tried to sketch out a lyric, he got pictures of her there in Austin with other people—a whole life—and him here alone, and the whole thing was just so freaking sad that he couldn't bring himself to write another word. So far the song was like one long pathetic moan—*Leeeeesssa!! Leeeesssaaa!!*—from some loser, and he wouldn't sing it aloud in front of an audience even if somebody gave him this lovely 'Cuda.

He'd just lit a second smoke when the entry door opened, and Dr. J came in with two other men. Lisa's father looked up at the overhead lights and called out, "Anybody here?"

Jason hastily stabbed the butt into the glass and eased the car's door to. "It's me, Jason, Dr. J. Here."

He waved over the top of the car. He'd been busted, sort of. The crime wasn't well-defined yet, though the sense of guilt was potent. Lisa's father nodded and ushered his two companions to the far side of the Cobra. Jason could hear Dr. J unreel his anecdote about how he'd hidden the Cobra's cost from Brittany for a year and how she'd refused to sleep with him until he'd agreed to let her spend the equivalent on something frivolous she wanted. "What'd she get?" one guest asked. "She's still shopping," said Dr. J, and they laughed.

Jason considered detouring to the workbench and ditching his glass, but in the meantime the trio was sauntering his way, so Jason felt he had no choice but to join them. He came up as a guest was asking, "How often do these cars get driven, anyway?" The question delighted Jason, if only to hear Lisa's father confess that they were rarely driven, thereby confirming Jason's sense of injustice.

"Now and then," said Dr. J. "I take the kids out from time to time. Brittany won't go, her way of protesting."

His audience gave the obligatory chuckle of long-suffering husbands, and Dr. J, wheeling suddenly toward him, said, "Jason?" Jason thought for an instant that he was about to be introduced, so he stepped nimbly forward and shifted the glass to his left hand to use his right for shaking, looking up into Dr. J's face and seeing too late the expression on it. "It's obvious you've been smoking in here." His eyes darted to the cocktail glass. Before Jason could respond, Dr. J said, "If you had to pay the insurance on these vehicles and this building like I do, you wouldn't even *think* of doing that." His jaw muscles pulsed as if he were grinding his teeth, and his mouth was a long horizontal nail, a line drawn in the sand. His gaze lasered Jason's brain. Jason flushed.

"Sorry, Dr. J."

Lisa's father simply swung away with his back to Jason, the way you'd block somebody under the basket if you had the ball, and said to his companions, "Now, this one—I've always had a weakness for the old Stingrays," and with a hand on each of his pal's elbows, barkered them around to the rear of the car, visually tagging each of their two faces as he talked. Jason got the point: he was not to follow. Dr. J's dressing down was what he'd say to the garbage man who'd left the empty can lying in the alley.

Nothing left to do but slink away. When he was outside, he stood a moment stewing. *If you had to pay the insurance. Oh, fuck you and your paying for shit! Jesus fucking Christ, the fucking building is made of STEEL. It has a CONCETE FLOOR, a galvanized tin roof, iron rafters! Dr. J, please tell me one fucking thing that is flammable in there!*

Lisa's dad was probably just looking for a reason to bust him. If it hadn't been smoking, it would've been carrying the glass around. *It might be dropped and shatter! Some child might get a sliver in her foot! Call OSHA. I have to pay for liability and health insurance, Jason!*

Or, like as not, it was just the idea of Jason's being in the building in the first place without a security guard. *If you're so worried about that, Dr. J, then you should've locked the freaking door!*

His head was about to explode. One wrong word from Chase, one little sneer . . . *Git-tar.* Dickhead!

---

Emily grunted and stirred in her sleep. He might've cursed out loud, he thought, and disturbed her. The memory of his humiliation in Dr. Johnson's garage, coupled with Chase Putnam's presence at the party, still smarted deep in his tissue, turbo-charged his blood. He really should've called it a day right then. Things had been going south since the second he stepped inside the house. There'd been no way to salvage the possibility of all this ending well, really, after that encounter with Lisa's dad.

But instead of sneaking away from the party, he'd smoked another butt in the woods to calm himself, then trudged back to the bar and ordered a Sprite. He had stared wistfully into the fizzing surface while wishing that he hadn't succumbed to the temptations of the cocktail and the smokes. Then the blunder in the car museum wouldn't have happened. Now instead of earning points, he'd lost whatever edge his wardrobe had supposedly gained. He was worse off than before he'd come. Their patio table had been removed, and he arrived at the vacant spot with a bewildering sense of dislocation. He didn't seem to be living in the same time zone as everyone else. Lisa, Allison, and their mother were standing at a table set up on the pool apron. Mrs. J was pointing beyond the pool to a raised platform where two dudes in ponytails were fiddling with sound equipment. A band? Dancing? That at least would give him a chance to rub up close to her.

Jason glided up unobtrusively and waited. When Lisa noticed him, she stepped away from her mother. "Where've you been?" She seemed cross.

"I had a smoke in the woods."

She rolled her eyes.

"I didn't want to freak anybody out."

"Well, you just left me there."

Jason shrugged. It was weird that she should feel abandoned, considering that it was her house, her family, her party. What was she today, Gradzilla?

"Sorry. You looked pretty happy to be with Chase, to tell the truth."

"Jason."

"Okay. I didn't mean it."

They stood in silence. Jason took a long slug of the Sprite. "Wanna drink?"

Lisa shook her head. "Anyway, I was looking for you."

He smiled. "Here I am, a *sus ordenes*." He mock-bowed.

"I need to explain to you about dinner."

Dinner needed an explanation? "Okay."

"It's a sit-down, not a buffet."

Jason said, only half-joking, "So I won't pick up a utensil until after you've picked up one, right?"

She smiled, pained. "Thing is, I'm sitting with my parents and Alison and Chris and Uncle Gerald and Aunt Barbara. It's a family table."

He shrugged. "That's cool. Where do you want me? Just tell me who's the lead eater and I'll take my cues from them."

Posted at his assigned table were Lisa's two cousins, Andrea and her ten-year-old brother Matthew; Mrs. Dowling, the piano teacher who had been giving them and the two Johnson sisters lessons for many years; and Destiny and Rebecca. Chase was posted at a table that, so far as Jason could tell, wasn't socially advantageous to his own: two grade-schoolers and Dr. J's two partners and their wives. Jason had chosen a chair that allowed him to observe Lisa, though her back was to him. The delicious half-moon of flesh exposed below her nape by the dipping curve of her dress, the soft tanned knuckles of her spine, her newly styled hair sweeping back and forth across her shoulders as she turned this way and that. It killed him to watch her from afar. He kept expecting her to twist about to find him, smile, blow a kiss—anything to show he was in her mind!—but he waited in vain as everyone dealt in various ways with the salad, a tumble of green and red vegetation the likes of which he'd never seen, with strangely wrinkled olives and sundry, unpalatable-looking chunks that might be artichoke or other foreign plant life. He toyed with it, as did the boys; Mrs. Dowling marveled at what she called the "presentation" but only picked at it; Rebecca chowed down heartily on it while Destiny ate the olives in her salad and in Jason's. He'd carried his Sprite to the table and declined the iced tea and wasn't offered wine, so during a lull in the salad trials (this was like an immunity challenge from *Survivor: Africa* to him) he took his empty glass to the bar table, asked for another Sprite, and when the bartender had turned to take another order, sloshed vodka atop the bubbling soda.

He gave up on the food. He sat and watched Lisa lean over and hug Alison's neck, laugh, swing back. She was having a fine, good time. Now that he thought of it, each time he saw her with other people she was in a much better mood than when talking to him.

During dessert, Lisa's father stepped onto the platform and tapped the mic three times. Gifts from guests were stacked on a nearby table. Jason checked to make certain the heart-shaped gold locket was still in his jacket pocket. It was a poor substitute for the song that he'd planned to surprise her with, but it was all he could manage when it became clear the song was stuck under the mud of his mind.

Dr. Johnson said he hoped everyone was enjoying themselves and he thanked them all for helping celebrate "this important passage in a young person's life." He said that Lisa had always been their most studious child—"no disrespect to you, Ali, because we're proud of you, too, you know"—and that nothing pleased him and Brittany more than to be in the audience as she gave her salutatorian's address. He thanked those who had helped Lisa attain such success: her mother got a rousing round of applause, then her sister, her brother, and "Lisa's good friends, Rebecca and Destiny," who provided loving support, etc., and then of course Uncle Gerald and Aunt Barbara were singled out for recognition. Then, as an afterthought, old Mrs. Dowling was hailed from the podium, and Andrea had to help her up from the table to take her bow.

Jason tongued out the last sliver of ice in the bottom of his glass and wondered if now would be a bad time to get a refill. Dr. Johnson said that he and Lisa's mother had thought long and hard about a gift for her. He called Lisa up to stand beside him on the platform. He stepped over to the gift table, selected a foil-wrapped package, and brought it to her. She awkwardly undid it, then she lifted an object from a box. A smile crept over her face. She held it up. So far as Jason could see, it was a large book.

"I guess you guys probably can't tell what this is." Lisa turned it toward her face. "But I've known this book since I was old enough to read titles." Her chin trembled and she ducked her face. Dr. Johnson leaned into the mic.

"This is the *Gray's Anatomy* I used in medical school. I know she's going to need it eventually when she starts that long walk in the old man's footprints. Lisa, honey, I am so proud of you, and I know you've got a wonderful future ahead of you, though I have to warn you that scrubs have got a long, long way to go before they'll ever make a fancy fashion statement."

They hugged, and before they separated, Lisa strained up on her toes and kissed her father's neck, and Jason could feel the kiss burn there. Lisa then treated everybody to a tearful, abbreviated version of her salutatorian's speech, musing that no one gets anywhere without climbing on the shoulders of those who'd gone before and not without being boosted by friends and family. This speech had drawn much interest in Jason when he'd heard it a month or so ago at graduation, as he'd waited for mention of his name, or, at the least, his role as "special friend." But he'd been disappointed then, as he was now, when she made a point of thanking her parents and her siblings but said not word one about Jason, who believed that he should be the most important figure in her life.

Her father's words about Lisa's future sank in as Jason nursed the wound of being overlooked. Her father wanted her to be a doctor; he knew Alison wouldn't go on to med school, and Chris was way too ADHD to score the kind of grades he'd need to live up to Lisa's record. College would take four years, then there'd be, what, four years or more of medical school, and then she'd be an intern or resident or whatever they were on *ER*, working 24/7, hooking up in the locker room with other doctors, everybody who isn't one shut completely out of her life. It's like he was seeing Lisa for the last time, really. Not literally, of course, but this was the beginning of the end unless he could find a way to stop this train before it left the station.

Maybe she really didn't even want to be a doctor! Did her dad ever ask her that?

As Lisa wound up and nodded to the claps and whistles, Jason got up from his chair and sidled to the bar and while the bartender was occupied, he helped himself to more ice and Sprite and vodka. Onstage, Lisa had started to return to their table, but her father tugged her back to the mic.

"Now, honey, you didn't really expect that a dusty old text-book was all you were going to get for graduation, did you?"

Lisa grinned. Dr. J whistled to someone beyond the patio, and while everyone turned to watch, down at the bottom of the yard beyond the garage a red Miata turned off the drive-way and glided quietly over the lawn toward the pool. The top was down. Dude with sunglasses behind the wheel.

"Oh, Daddy!" sang Lisa. "It is so cute!"

Dr. J beamed. Lisa hugged him and kissed his neck once more.

What would happen to the old Acura? Losing it put Jason in a panic. It was their car, the scene of many hundreds of hours of conversation, of making love—they'd burned up their virginity in a mighty blaze in the backseat of it! They had studied in it, driven to Austin in it for SXSW and to Padre during last year's spring break and slept two nights in it. He'd rotated the tires and checked the fluids and changed out the wipers and a headlight bulb and knew that when you had it in Park and wanted to go to Reverse, you had to jiggle the shifter just a tad to make the gears click into place. He knew when he saw it pull up in front of his house that she was there. To him, it was a kind of metallic garment for her, as comfortable and familiar a signal of her personality as her ponytail and scrunchie, the way she could never kept track of her glasses, or the cute way she said "ab-so-LUTE-ly." When you got into that car, you could smell Lisa: lip balm and shampoo, her thyme-scented soap she bought at Bath & Body Works.

He sat momentarily stupefied as she trotted eagerly down the hill to where the car was now parked, trailed by Alison and others. The driver, apparently someone from the dealer-ship, got out, kept the door open, smiled as she bounced into the seat. Jason knew Miatas. They were high-dollar toy cars to him, even if you could supercharge an MX-5, and they were hot on the road-racing circuit. It was tiny. No backseat. Mostly you pictured a girl with her hair streaming out behind her or tucked under a baseball cap as she cruised along alone. Now Lisa had two automobiles. This new one would obviously go to Austin with her, and the other she'd leave here to rust in the driveway, let the battery run down, the tires go flat and crack, until eventually Daddy would have it hauled it off or sold to a wholesaler.

"Jason! Jason!" she was half-standing behind the wheel and waving at him. He waved back, and she beckoned.

He set his glass on the grass and, realizing that he was unsteady, coached himself to step with care. He went slowly down the incline of the backyard, feeling as if his head were bobbling on a spring.

"Oh, Jace—isn't this so cool?"

The car had become a rallying point for the guests, but while he was making his way to it, a good many had drifted off after paying their respects. Only "the young folks"— Chase, Rebecca, Destiny, and Alison—were hovering over the tiny vehicle, the girls oohing and ahhing as if it were an awesome fashion accessory.

Lisa ran her hand over the dash and touched the controls as she rhapsodized to the others who stood on the passenger side. Chase had a thigh pressed to the door and his forearm draped over the windshield's frame as he leaned into the compartment. He looked up and caught Jason's eye.

"Hey, babe, let's go for a ride!" Jason said, gently cupping Lisa's nape but looking at Chase.

"Now?" She laughed. Her head swung back and forth from him to the others. "Well, . . ." she was tempted but shot a glance over her shoulder as if to see whether a backseat had magically appeared.

"Yeah!" Before she could hesitate further, Jason clambered over the rear deck, startling Chase backwards, and fell feet first into the passenger side. On his way down, he kicked the dash and left a small black streak on the beige leather. He grinned at Chase.

"Crank her up!"

He pointed to the key protruding from the ignition. Lisa

grinned, turned it; the engine quietly and instantly struck up its happy little hum, and, after a moment spent studying the shifter markers, she palmed the knob, stepped on the brake, and eased it into Drive.

"Bye, bye!" yelled Jason as she trundled the little car slowly over the grass toward the driveway that led to the garage. Lisa checked the rearview and waved over her shoulder. She stopped at the driveway and pulled the seat belt across her breasts, and he followed suit.

"Isn't this the neatest car?" Lisa pulled onto Barnes Bridge Road carefully, feeling her way, finding her fit with the tilt wheel, wriggling her hips into the leather bucket. "Here, hold the wheel." He held it with his left hand while she slid the seat up a notch, then she took it from him with a decisive, proprietary gesture that left him feeling as though his hand had been slapped down.

"I was hoping your dad would give you the 'Cuda."

"Oh, that ugly old thing?"

The road here was curvy and busy on a Saturday evening; it was hard to talk with the top down and the wind rushing by, whipping her hair, and she was preoccupied with her driving. He leaned down into the dash, located the AC control and clicked it on H so that the vents gushed cool air.

"How's that?"

"Good!"

"I like your friend Destiny."

"What?"

He leaned toward her. "I like Destiny!" he shouted.

"Oh! Good! She's great!" Lisa shouted back.

Lisa never let him smoke in the old Acura, but this car was presently topless, so he dug out his Marlboros and stuck one in his mouth. When she looked over at him, he could see her processing the image and working on a response but apparently deciding not to object. He scanned the dash for a lighter and couldn't find one, wound up hunkered in the floorboard with his head tucked between his knees almost under the dash until he got it burning with his Bic. Now that he'd managed to get her to himself, he could give her the locket and try to find out where they stood about the future, get some kind of pledge from her, let her know that he would wait, and wait, and wait—wait for freaking ever, if that's what it took to keep her.

They went east just past the power station until the road ran out and spilled onto a large graveled lot overlooking Lake Ray Hubbard. This early in the evening, the small park was busy with Hispanic families at picnics, the children wading along the beach and swimming. Lisa pulled into the lot and made a wide circle, and, when it appeared she might simply U-turn and head back home, Jason said, "Pull in here a minute, okay?"

"We oughta get back."

"Oh, come on, for God's sake!" He sounded angrier than he meant to and tried to undercut it. "I haven't had a second with you all day. Okay?"

She eased the Miata to a stop with the front bumper inches from the metal guardrail. Through the windshield, the lake glittered metallic orange in the last rays of the sun going down at their backs. The digital dash clock showed 8:45.

She turned off the engine. "Sorry," she said. "All day long I've just felt like everybody's pulling at me every second." She turned in the seat, smiled, reached her hand out to caress his cheek, bent forward with lips puckered for a peck; when he kissed her he greedily tried for something more passionate, but she gently pulled away.

"Silly," she murmured.

"Chase is such an asshole!" he burst out.

"How much have you had to drink?"

He looked away. Started to deny it, then said, "I had one. When he did. I had to get the damn thing for him, you know."

"Okay. Just don't have any more. Okay?"

"Did your mom or dad say anything?"

"No."

"Did he tell you he caught me smoking in his garage?"

"No. Jason! God!" She swung back forward and laced her arms over her breasts.

"I know it was stupid. I apologized to him."

He could hear her left foot softly tapping against the floorboard. She was looking off toward the power station. He watched her breasts rise and fall with her breathing. He recognized that raggedy kind of breathing that preceded tears.

He unlatched his seat belt. "Hey, let's stroll." He searched briefly for the door latch, located it, opened the door, and pulled himself up out of the car as if from a deep hole. He braced himself by clamping his hands over the window ledge.

"Come on, babe." She hadn't moved yet. "I got something to show you."

He walked around the rear of the car and opened her door, extended his hand for her. She took it; he pulled her up, but kept her hand in his and led her down through the grass toward the far edge of the park, where the woods formed the southern boundary. He took her to the water's edge and slipped his arm about her waist. After a moment, she surrendered, sank into him, and her arm looped about his back. She breathed deeply and deliberately three times, then exhaled with a sigh. Not a good sign. She'd recently started yoga and told him she was learning how to defuse stressful situations using her breath. But maybe it was the party, her parents' unreasonable demands and expectations.

He dug in his right coat pocket for the little box and drew it out. He held it up before them. "I got you something."

She turned; her eyes were tear-rimmed, but she smiled weakly as he handed her the little jeweler's box wrapped in gold foil festooned with curliques of ribbon.

"It's just something to have, you know, to think of us. I'd hoped to finish the song. That was going to be your real present. Well, I mean it will be a present when I do finish it. I will. I promise I will."

They parted while she undid the ribbon, unpeeled the paper, eased off the lid, and looked at the locket lying in its bed of cotton. She lifted it out on her fingers and dangled it for inspection.

"It's very pretty, Jason."

"Look inside!"

She parted the halves with her fingernail and swung them apart on their tiny hinge. Two heart-shaped photos were tucked into the halves. He'd bought it online for $139, chosen it among a bewildering array of lockets because it had an image of a guardian angel on the face and on the back an inscription in ornate script, "May Your Guardian Angel Always Love and Watch Over You." The sentiment matched Jason's deep fear that he couldn't help her or watch over her himself after she'd gone. And he chose it because when the two halves were opened on their tiny hinge, inside were couched small snaps he'd carefully and tearfully scissored to fit, one of them both in their prom finery junior year that his mom had taken, and the other of them both with their heads together, in a photo booth.

"Aw, that's so sweet!"

Lisa leaned forward for another kiss, and this time she held still for his efforts at sparking her fire. She responded with earnest intent, he felt, as if she meant to honor his feelings. That made his spirits plummet almost as far and fast as they would've if she'd simply pulled away again.

He broke off and clutched her with their heads together. She had the locket in her free hand, and he put his free hand down to it so they could hold it open like a shared hymnal.

"Thing is," he said, his voice trembling, "when I was making those pictures I was thinking of all the happiness I've had with you. I thought that if you had these with you and could look at them anytime of the day or night, even if you're in class or something, then you'd remember, too."

"I won't forget."

"Do you still love me?" He absolutely hated to hear himself ask that, and he held his breath to keep from breaking into sobs.

He felt her head bob against his chin. She drew him closer with the arm that was around his back.

"I still love you," he said. "More than ever, Scout's honor."

She squeezed him again, and, feeling his throat tighten and his eyes start to burn, he laughed, shrugged upright, then kissed her cheek and ear, releasing her.

"Can we hook up later on after the party?"

"Aw, Jace."

"What?"

"Everybody's gonna want to stay."

"All night?"

"We'll see. Okay?"

She was humoring him. He felt that she'd been "handling" him for days about this party, cajoling, coaxing, hinting, outright manipulating, faking—lying, really, when you came right down to it. She had no real intention or willingness to let him make love to her.

"You know what I think? I think the truth is you really don't want me to be at this goddamn party, and you don't want to be with me somewhere else, either."

"No, the truth is I don't want to be at this goddamn party." She clenched her jaw the way her father did, then apparently allowed herself to go on. "And I do want to be somewhere else with you. Like last year, that's where I want to be with you."

"Before I became such a fuck-up and had my mother die on me, right?"

"I wasn't talking about your mom at all, Jason, and you know it. I was talking about all the bad choices you keep making. Those aren't my fault, you know. It's not my fault I'm going to college!"

They stood with the silence ringing like an alarm bell between them.

At last, she sighed. "We need to get back."

"No, you do."

"Whatever."

She bent to pluck the wrapping paper from the ground. The raw orb of bruised feelings between them kept him from reaching over to take her hand, but he still felt a need to accompany her back to the Miata so he wouldn't appear to be shunning her. They moved in tandem at about an arm's length apart toward the lot, but she suddenly detoured to the trash barrel to toss the wrapping paper. He halted, waiting for her, while she stooped again at the barrel to pick up someone's beer can and deposit it as well. He was aware that she was carrying the locket in its box, not around her neck. He stood in her path and when she caught up, he turned to walk with her.

"Okay if I drive your car?" Jason tried for a tone of utter neutrality, as if this question were wholly apart from whatever other issue they had between them.

"Aw, Jace . . ."

He fumed. "I'm not gonna hurt it, you know."

"You've been drinking."

"I had one drink!"

She shot him a quick look that he could read all too well; she was embarrassed for him, for his pathetic lie.

"I'll let you drive it sometime soon, I promise."

"I guess you have to check with Daddy first."

She stopped dead. "No. I don't have to ask my father, Jason! For God's sake, can't I even enjoy my own frigging present?!"

On the way back to the house, the tension got to her; she dipped her face briefly into the dash and touch-padded keys to click on the radio. Linkin Park's "Crawling" burst out of the speakers, and she didn't bother to fiddle with the volume. He snickered. She was more the Faith Hill type. Jason could dig these lyrics: "*Crawling in my skin / these wounds they will not heal / fear is how I fall / confusing what is real.*" He wondered if she were paying attention to the music. He slouched in the seat, arms crossed, head swinging to watch the treetops pass as they went back on Barnes Bridge.

He replayed her whining complaint about enjoying her present, amplifying the undertones. *For once, Jason, let me have my own stuff without having to share it with you. For once, Jason, don't be a frigging beggar. Jason, I am frigging tired of your frigging freeloading!*

She wheeled the little car to the walkway leading to the Johnsons' front door. The valet on duty stepped out to greet them, and when he opened her door, she said, "Put it out there," nodding to the pasture. Without speaking to Jason, she strode down the walk toward the house.

The valet walked around the hood to open Jason's door, and something about the set of his mouth pissed Jason off. The kid opened the door in a grandiose, mocking way, but Jason had already scrambled over the shifter and into the driver's seat.

He grinned.

"S'allright, dude. I got it."

---

Light from a passing truck momentarily whitened the old van's inside walls with a strobe-like flicker, like an intangible but nonetheless perceptible lash to his shame. He could remember too clearly how he'd felt at that moment he'd landed in the Miata's bucket seat behind the wheel. He'd been such a smart-ass, cocky dude, like he'd really put one over on the jerk of a valet and Lisa as well. But the picture of the valet's smirk was etched in the air before Jason's eyes as well, and Jason could see now he'd let himself be baited. Lisa said he'd made bad choices. Here was another, worse than the ones before it: he could've and should've actually parked the car.

# Six

Burl had actually parked in the Albertsons lot before recalling that the trip to the store for coffee was only an excuse to get away from the house, and he couldn't summon the energy to troll the aisles. He couldn't recall feeling so tired, so jangled, jittery, woozy-headed. It must have been years since he'd had an all-nighter like that. Sober, anyway.

He drove to the Long Creek Cemetery, parked in the lot of the Baptist Church adjacent to it, got out. Though it was still before eight, already he saw a few other visitors in the cemetery's east end. Weekends he usually ran into people he knew by sight, though more often he dropped by during the week when his work brought him this way. Being here this morning carried its usual freight of emotional discomfort: aside from the sorrow of grief, there was the guilt of not telling Lily that he'd visited Sue's grave. Not that it was forbidden, exactly; at the outset of their courtship, Lily knew he was suffering and seemed to encourage him to come. Soon, she wanted to come too. To support him, she said. But it made him feel *watched*, chaperoned, as if Sue were a living ex-wife who might make an underhanded play if she could catch him alone. Lily always took his arm and hovered so close to his side it was hard to bring himself to step up near Sue's headstone, and Lily's presence certainly made uttering endearments out of the question. So he started sneaking away during work to spend a few contemplative moments, often stopping by Albertsons for flowers.

Sue was no threat to Lily. How could she be? But this subterranean conflict over the two women always made him antsy and unhappy. Lily never said she wanted him to forget Sue, but it would be human and natural for her to feel that when he was recalling Sue and their life together with a sad and poignant fondness, Lily was crowded out.

As for Jason, so far as Burl could tell, after the burial, he'd never once visited his mother's grave. He could guess that Jason hadn't wanted to relive the funeral service, and then, once he started going wrong, it would be hard to face his mother and not feel that he had failed her miserably in her absence. Burl felt that way, for sure, and it was like a massage for his masochism to stand in front of that granite marker with his head bowed a little as if receiving a sentence from a judge, as he imagined what she might think.

Sue's pink granite marker had a smooth tablet inset adorned with carved roses and a cross. He walked alongside her imagined buried form and patted the stone's shoulder. The brass flower cup affixed to the stone's base was empty. He'd last placed a spray here a couple weeks ago; coming empty-handed now and seeing the cone hollow like that gave him a pang.

"Hey, girl." He looked about to see if anyone stood within earshot. It wasn't that he minded someone knowing that he talked to the dead—a common practice out here—but he didn't want to air the family's dirty laundry in public.

"I've done it this time. I guess I could blame this on Jason, but maybe it's true that if I'd been harder on him all along since you've been gone, maybe he'd be in better shape. Thing is, you know, I can see how he's really hurting but I just don't know how to say or do the right thing. That was always your department, and try as I might to think of how you'd handle this, try as I might to do as you'd do, things are just too different now for it to fit. He went off the deep end last night, I mean worse than the night he stole Lisa's car and wound up arrested, and I had to okay the plan to just . . . well, to just sort of call down a whole damn thunderstorm of authority on the kid. I guess I need to know if you'd think that was the best thing to do."

As usual, Sue had no reply. Normally he counted on the presence of the stone and her imagined buried form to inspire a memory he could glean for tips on how to proceed. Of course, most of what he'd had to cope with since her death was utterly unprecedented in their family life, so conjuring up any slice of their history that might be meaningfully comparable wasn't possible. Jason and that pal from Cub Scouts, tossing water balloons at that old woman's car, or the time he called his soccer coach a "dumb butt," or when he and Matthew Jenkins smoked a cigar apiece and got sick, or when Eva Sanchez's mother complained that Jason was sending unwanted mash notes to Eva during class.

The good old days.

But here was a thought—maybe Sue wouldn't fare any better than Burl had with the wide range of more egregious infractions, actual misdemeanors, and a could-be felony. She might feel just as helpless and bewildered. Though, on second thought, at least they could thrash out the possible solutions together.

That brought him to this new peculiar state that he and Lily had slid into over the past twelve hours. Sure, he and Sue had had disagreements, but he'd never felt that she was an enemy. He knew that she knew that at the other end of their disagreement, they'd be there together with a compromise or a concession that restored their harmony. Lily's bristly coldness kept him far beyond arm's length. It was as if she believed that he would do anything to undermine her best plan for her daughter's safety, as if he would willingly and readily sacrifice Emily for Jason, and that if she didn't stay on her toes he'd do it behind her back. She didn't trust him.

Well, she knew he was a drunk, and, being one herself, she knew that weakness was like, well, like a swimming pool full of good vodka that you're standing in up to your chin.

He wanted to discuss his marriage to Lily with Sue but didn't feel it was appropriate. It would violate whatever implicit trust, however meager, Lily might still have. And there was Sue's inexperience, too. Sue seemed too innocent now, too naïve, too trusting to have good advice on the subject of his and Lily's relationship, and, unexpectedly, he felt oddly superior, as if having the experience of a second spouse had made him wiser, even in his befuddled state, than Sue had ever been.

He sighed. A mockingbird alighted briefly on the shoulder of her stone, danced on its tiny claws, its long tail cocked saucily upright like a visual Bronx cheer. Then it blurted berserk gibberish from blendered bits of plagiarized calls.

"That's your answer?"

The visit left him in a more directed, stronger state of mind, and he picked up on strands of possibility left dangling last night. Jason had a pal he'd been hanging out with during these past errant months, a pal who, like Jason, was a dropout. When they were together, they fairly oozed an up-to-no-damn-good air of belligerence, arrogance, and snide superiority.

The pal, Scott something (Jesus, shouldn't Burl have at least learned the kid's full name?), lived with an uncle and aunt (so Jason said) at the house Burl pulled in front of moments later. He'd once delivered Jason here and once picked him up after Jason had spent the night. It was in an older neighborhood with houses much like Burl's own, with brick veneer and siding combo, one-story, an attached garage accessed from the front. This one stood unlandscaped but for a low row of half-dead boxwood hedging along the sides of the concrete stoop. Windows facing the street were backed with aluminum foil.

Neither time that Burl had driven here had he seen parental figures, so he had no idea what to expect after he knocked. He checked his watch—it was 8:45 now. Saturday morning, folks might be up, might not. He heard no sounds from the other side of the door. After a moment or two, he knocked again.

A ZZ-Top sort answered—long gray hair, long gray beard, bare to the waist, tattooed forearms. Said nothing. Waited.

"Yeah, sorry to bother you so early, but I'm Jason Sanborn's dad. Is Scott here?"

"Scott? We kicked his sorry ass out way back last month."

"Uh. Thing is, my boy is missing, and I thought Scott might know something. Would you have any idea where I could get a hold of him?"

The fellow's demeanor morphed a tad soft as Burl's parental woes made him an ally and not a bill-collector or detective.

"Naw, hell. I'm sorry. He don't 'sackly write home. Jason's missing?"

"Well, we think he's probably gone down to Austin to see his girlfriend, but he left a *lot* of loose ends dangling."

"Them boys." He shook his head. "I wouldn't worry too much. That kid looks to have a pretty good head on his shoulders, really. He'll turn up I reckon."

Burl wanted to kiss this fellow's cheek. A character witness?

"Thanks. I hope so. Sorry to have bothered you."

"Good luck."

Then, on the chance that Jason, disturbed and intent on bolting, might've gone to see Meemaw before leaving, Burl drove to Good Shepherd. In the communal parlor several patients were already parked before the big-screen television, on which a children's cartoon show was in progress, though someone had muted it. At the staff hub, he got the day's code for the Alzheimer's wing, and, once on the ward, found the orderly he knew as "L.J." wiping off a table in the dining area.

"Hey, L.J."

"Hey, Mr. Sanborn, What's shakin', bacon?"

"Not much. Are you doing a day shift?"

"Pulling a double."

"So you were here last night?"

"Yeah."

"How's my gal doing?"

"She ate good this morning. I gave her a shampoo last night!"

"I bet she liked that."

L.J. looked worried. "Well, sometimes it's hard for her to understand why we're putting water and soap all over her head, and it kinda freaks her out at first." He grinned. "Then I put some on my own head and she laughs at me."

"Fine. I know you're doing a good job, son. And I appreciate it. I was wondering if you'd seen Jason. Maybe he stopped by last night?"

L.J. stopped wiping the table and leaned on the bunched-up cloth, frowning.

"No. Not last night."

"This morning? Any time yesterday?"

"Aw, no. Maybe last week sometime."

He clapped the boy on the shoulder. "Thanks, anyway. I'll just pop in to say howdy to Mrs. Larkins, then."

But he left the ward without going deeper into the hallway to Meemaw's room. In the parlor, the television was still muted, but the image on it stopped Burl dead. Jason's face, from last year's high school annual. Sneering, hair dangling across his brow, dingy curls draping over his collar. Lily had no doubt dug it up from Jason's room.

"Shit."

Then Lily was talking into a microphone held by a reporter, looking fresh with lipstick and brushed hair, fresh everywhere except in her eyes, and Burl blurted out, "Uh! Hey!" waving to the room at large as if to alert whoever might be sitting on the remote to click on the sound. Heartsick, he blew out a big breath and merely stood without speaking as Lily stood speaking without sound. Behind her, the horizon of their sofa, the living room's north window. He watched her lips move, disclosing glints of her white-capped lower teeth, ripples of emotion fleeting across her forehead and cheeks and chin like minute tremors of anxiety. She wore the properly anxious, tearful expression of a mother whose child was missing. The world would see her this way—authentic, credible, a victim herself.

Now a uniformed deputy appeared on-screen, talking while being garroted by a scroll glittery with a phone number, then that image gave way to a large poster or card with inset photos of Jason and Emily and their ages and vital statistics.

He wondered what Lily might have said about Jason to the public. He shook suddenly with a deep groan as he recognized that during all this uproar, they'd all been focused on the danger to the *child*, and now he could picture the danger to Jason as well. A car chase, a foot chase, perhaps shooting, if the pursuing officers were worked up enough and felt threatened. Rodney King footage. Jason lying on the pavement, kicked and whacked by batons.

As Burl strode out of the building, he cursed himself for abdicating his part in the public presentation, leaving it to Lily to characterize his son in a way that best suited her purpose, though she wasn't being conniving so much as desperate to provoke the world to help her get Emily back. If nobody was present in Burl's own home to speak up for his son, that was nobody's fault but his.

How many fucking things can you do wrong in one twenty-four-hour stretch?

While he drove down toward home, he one-handed his cell.

"Hello," someone answered.

"Who's this?" Now they'd commandeered his telephone! At the least they could let Lily answer.

"Who are you calling?"

What, did this fellow think Burl was the "kidnapper" making his ransom call? "This is Burl Sanborn. Put my wife on, please."

"Oh. I believe she's lying down right now, resting."

Burl swallowed back the impulse to scream, *Put her on the fucking phone, asshole!* and said, "Well, I just wanted her to know I'm on my way home. I wanted to check at a friend of Jason's house first. Did the kids call?"

"What's that friend's name now?" He spoke as if Burl had asked him to take dictation. "You got the address?"

"So they haven't called?"

"We'll let you know."

Burl ground his thumb into the disconnect button until not only was the call broken, but the phone cycled off and the screen went black. He tossed it onto the seat beside him.

A van with a billboard-sized logo on its flank was parked in front of Burl's house. The local Fox News affiliate. Protruding from its roof stood an aluminum mast topped by a huge concave disc festooned with antennae and bewildering electronic gee-gaws. The sight alarmed him, not only because it signaled to the neighborhood that someone at this address had done something newsworthy, but because the very nature of the electronic array, bristling with steel, copper, and titanium and interlaced with optical fiber, seemed faintly martial and invasive.

Parked behind Lily's Civic in his driveway was a beige Crown Vic sedan, leaving no room for his truck. He parked up the street and sat a moment appreciating his non-proximity to all that was transpiring at his address, but then he sighed, eased out, locked with his remote, trudged down the walk. In the cab of the news van, a driver chomped off the end of what appeared to be a breakfast burrito. The van windows were up, the AC running no doubt, and either the engine was idling or a generator inside the cargo compartment was churning juice to run the machinery that transmitted Burl's woes to a planetary audience.

The female agent was still in his living room, her blazer draped over the back of their easy chair. She'd commandeered the crossword puzzle page out of his morning paper and was slouched on the sofa, frowning as he entered. When she recognized him, she tossed the paper onto the cushion beside her as if she'd had no interest in it.

"I see the press is here," said Burl. "Where's the reporter?"

"In the van, I guess."

"So the kids didn't call?"

"Oh, no."

Her apparent opinion of him—moron, dipshit, lame-ass dad—stung. "I checked at the nursing home where his grandmother is, you know, to see if maybe he'd come by on his way out of town. And I also dropped by the house of one of his pals to see if anybody knew anything."

"Any luck?"

"No. Has anybody gotten a hold of Vinnie yet? If not, I'm gonna try that myself."

"You talking about the biological father, right? She's left a buncha messages already."

"Where's Lily?"

"Lyin' down I think."

Or hiding out in their bedroom, where maybe in her closet, hidden in a boot, there's a pint of schnapps or gin.

"Okay. Well, listen, I'm gonna check on her. Give us a call if—"

"A'course. You'll be the first."

He tapped with a knuckle on their bedroom door, said, "Lily?" waited a moment, then eased it open and entered. She was lying supine and fully dressed on their bed. Since they'd not slept in it last night, it was still made. Her feet were bare. An arm was flung across her eyes.

"You awake?"

She nodded.

"Sorry I've been gone so long. I went to see if Jason had spoken to Meemaw, and I went to his pal Scott's house. I couldn't stand just sitting here doing nothing."

She sighed, sat up on the edge of the bed, pawed the items on the nightstand, found a pack of cigarettes, took one, stuck it between her lips, then grimaced, snatched it out and tossed it back onto the table.

"I saw the interview while I was at Good Shepherd."

"Oh yeah?" She looked pleased and hopeful, then rubbed her face with her hands.

"The sound was off, though."

"I hated having to broadcast our troubles to the world. It was really humiliating."

"I'm sorry I wasn't here. I know you did the right thing, though. And maybe somebody will spot them, or maybe they'll see it and come to their senses."

"Jason, you mean."

"I don't see any reporters in this room."

"Burl, I just can't believe that Emily would run away and not at least leave a note. I just can't."

"Maybe she was mad enough at both of us to want to punish you that way. Maybe she was really upset about the fight Jason and I had, and she was on his side and blames you for bringing her here. Or maybe she knows the worst punishment she could inflict on you isn't just leaving—it's also not letting you know what's on her mind, making you worry."

This was perhaps the fanciest assessment of a human act that Lily had ever heard Burl utter, and it was the kind of analysis she was most inclined to credit.

"You could be right."

"So let's call off the dogs."

"But if you're wrong, I'd never forgive myself if something happens to her. Oh, Burl, I feel so bad about all this! I hate what it's done to us."

Elbows on her knees, she couched her face in her palms as her shoulders shook. He eased down onto the bed beside her and slid his arm across her back, massaged the nape of her neck, then cupped her far shoulder and drew her toward him.

"It's enough to drive a person to drink, all right."

She nodded. After a minute, she rose up, took his free hand and clutched it.

"We need to be together on this," said Burl.

"Yes! God, I've felt so completely alone and I know that's not fair. I've just been so down on myself seeing how unhappy Emily is living here, and I know it's all my fault. It's hard to admit that, you know. It's a hell of a lot easier to blame you and Jason."

From the first group meeting that he'd seen Lily, he'd always admired her openness, her willingness to dig down and give a full accounting of her behavior.

"And I feel down on myself for making you both so unhappy and for just plain failing to be the right kind of father to Jason. I feel lost at sea all alone without Sue being his mother."

"I know that. I'm just sorry I can't help you more with him."

They rocked side to side in unison for a moment.

"Burl, if you want to call off the alert, then do it. Okay? I'll leave it up to you."

It surprised him how much her concession filled him not with relief but with dread. It was far more comfortable to have her pushing him to take a step than to make the decision alone.

# Seven

Smoke woke him. Emmanuel had built a fire in a stone circle and had set a blackened grill across it. He stood over the fire, squinting with his head craned to the side to avoid the smoke while he positioned a skillet over the coals. From a small blue cooler he plucked plastic bags and set them on the picnic table. Jacob was apparently still asleep, as was Emily.

Jason crept out of the van and stretched. It was near dawn, and a layer of blue-gray haze hung over the field across the barbed-wire fence. Beyond the field, the woods were still a dark, undifferentiated mass. Three red-winged blackbirds alighted briefly on the top strand, yelled at one another, flew off. The fragrance of honeysuckle drifted into his attention.

"Good morning," said Emmanuel.

"You're the cook, huh?" Jason slid onto the bench at the table.

"Yes, until someone says 'This is not good,' then that one is the cook!"

"My stepmother's that way."

Jason wished for coffee but none was being perked. He watched while Emmanuel lifted eggs from the cooler, broke them on the rim of an empty thirty-two-ounce can from which the label had been stripped, dropped them into it. The walls of Jason's empty stomach lurched and rubbed against one another like cold hands seeking warmth. He should've had the foresight to eat dinner before they took off last night, though it would've meant a loss of face: not eating showed you didn't need anything from the people who brought food into the house. Poor planning. He wondered what Emily had in her backpack. He didn't expect to take food from these fellows as they were obviously dirt poor, but he knew if it were offered, he'd surrender. Eating showed you did need something and were willing to accept the help.

Emmanuel chopped onion, a small green chili pepper, and a tomato on a cutting board and added it to the eggs. He sprinkled oil from a can in the skillet. He plucked a plastic package of round bread-like thick flour tortillas and placed two on the grill. He stirred the contents of the can vigorously and added salt and pepper to it. Then he poured the eggs into the skillet.

"You would please join me, Jason?"

"You don't have to ask me twice."

They ate from plastic plates taken from a grocery bag. The bag had the name of an upscale grocery chain in Dallas, Jason noted. The grilled bread, like a thick, unsweetened pancake, was chewy and delicious.

"What's this bread? It's great! Is this something from where you come from?" Jason was aware that he'd made a reference, and none too slyly, to the young men's obvious foreign extraction and hoped the underlying intent of the question would be addressed.

Emmanuel chuckled. "No, no. It is *roti*. From India. But made here in America." He winked at Jason. "It comes from the grocery where I work." While Jason was silently considering alternative probes, Emmanuel said, "We are from Africa."

Emmanuel said that he and his cousin and their friends in Houston were meeting to celebrate their arrival in the United States five years ago. Church groups brought them over from refugee camps where they'd been for many years. Some went to Minnesota, some to North Dakota, some to Chicago, Dallas, Houston. They were just boys, then. They knew nothing. The church organizations put the boys in apartments together, and one church even appointed a member of the congregation to deliver groceries and teach them how to use the gas stove and the refrigerator.

"The refrigerator?" asked Jason.

Emmanuel nodded, smiling. "Yes, if you have a box in the window that makes cold air and a bigger box standing up in the room that does the same, how do you know to keep the door to *that one* closed?" The camps had generators, but no refugee had control of a machine run by electricity. In America, the new world around them was strange and frightening. Jason considered all the things in his home that he operated without any thought of how he learned their secrets: can openers, lamps, flush toilets, telephones, doorbells, garbage grinders, hot and cold water faucets, furnace thermostats, toaster ovens. Outside the door lurked even larger unknowns, some dangerous, all bewildering: traffic lights, vending machines, elevators and escalators, automatic doors, bus and train routes, the English language!

"And oh, my friend—" Emmanuel shook his head. "You must see through the eyes of a boy who has never been inside the American supermarket to understand how such a thing can make you tremble. It is like an ocean when you are dying of thirst. All around, food, food, food! You do not know how to choose one thing or the other. It takes many years to learn."

Emmanuel and his fellow refugees were born in villages of thatched huts to a people who raised crops and cattle. He told Jason how the *Janjaweed* rode through the village killing men and raping the women and setting fire to the crops and houses. Everyone who could fled into the countryside. He was only five. The Arab raiders killed his father and two of his older brothers and took a sister away with them. They took many young girls. He and his mother and others walked for many miles for many weeks. Once they had to cross a river filled with crocodiles, and one child was snatched from its mother's arms and eaten.

Jason controlled an impulse to blurt "Fucking crocodiles? No shit!" He sat very still, listening. He'd never heard anything like this firsthand, and it made him wonder how much of this kind of thing had gone on, was going on now, out there in the world beyond the near border of his ignorance. Who were these raiders? Why did they do this? This African fellow, his host who had generously shared his breakfast, had lived in some part of the planet Earth that operated under entirely different rules and subjected its inhabitants to horrific circumstances. Maybe more of the planet was like that than he'd ever dreamed.

Emmanuel told Jason that he and the survivors had walked without food and very little water for weeks until they reached a refugee camp in the desert. It was filled with thousands like them from many other villages. They had to walk out of camp every day to find firewood. Groups from Europe and the United States delivered parcels of food, but many in the camps died of disease and starvation. Emmanuel's mother died there.

Jason was on the verge of telling Emmanuel that his mother had died, too, but Jacob had emerged from the tent and was standing beside them with a hand towel and toothbrush clutched in a fist.

"Brother," he said, "You shouldn't tell about these sorrows to our guest. It's not for children's ears." Jacob waved to Jason as if in apology to him.

"I'm eighteen!" Jason protested.

"I was a child when it happened," said Emmanuel.

"But it shouldn't have!" Jason said.

Emmanuel shrugged. Jacob smiled at Jason and said, "Why has the cook stopped cooking?" and with that Emmanuel rose to start a new round of scrambled eggs and *roti*. Jacob started breaking down the tent and tidying up. Jason watched from the table as Jacob strode to the perimeter of the mowed picnic area, turned his back to them, dunked his head with water from the canteen, brushed his teeth, then walked down into the bar ditch along the highway until only his head was visible. Jacob's head held steady and bent slightly down for about the duration of a young man's morning stream, and his modesty impressed Jason.

Everything about these men impressed him. He felt as if he and they belonged to a tribe of wanderers, and in the dawn light suffused with the pleasant dampness of morning air, this impromptu encampment seemed blessed with an aura of superiority. His nape hair tingled with a frisson of pleasure at the experience of meeting these Africans, sleeping in the van, eating that breakfast with the Indian bread, hearing that story. These guys were so fucking cool! Definitely song-worthy! Their lives were so much richer and full of tragedy and purpose than those of the dweebs and slackers he knew in Mesquite! He wished Lisa could meet them.

His eyes stung as he blinked back tears. This was fucking real life! It seemed that until this moment he'd moved about blindly with his head up his ass, making stupid mistakes. But now that he'd been befriended by these Africans, his intrinsic value as a person of merit and potential had soared. Jacob and Emmanuel had initiated him into the underdog pack. Now Jason knew what was truly valuable, what was not.

From here on out, he would be a more serious, mature person. Lisa would be the first to hear about it.

While he was ruminating with considerable relish about his recreated identity as a person of superior moral weight and his rosy future in that persona, Emily slung her backpack onto the table, legged herself over to sit across from him. She rummaged about in the pack. She looked grumpy, her hair a thrasher punk's spiky 'do.

"Emmanuel will make you some eggs." Saying it, he felt as if he were one of the Africans' party, a kind of host, and she the guest.

"I hate eggs."

She stuck her face in the mouth of the pack, squinted, then her little hand darted like the head of a striking snake into the cavity and out again. She'd found a Nutri-Grain® granola bar. She started worrying the wrapper. The thing was like an insult to Jason, somehow. Or her having it was. Like her computer and cell phone and the TV in her room. And now, this: her unexamined presumption that food would be available to her as a matter of entitlement, to accept or reject even with contempt. Well, that needed correcting. Since he now belonged to the club of outsider underdogs, he was qualified to give moral instruction.

"You should offer to share that with them."

She stopped chewing and frowned in mock disgust. "Why? I'm not eating any of their eggs."

"You should share with people who are less fortunate than you are. They've been through all kinds of terrible stuff."

"Like what?"

"It's not something a child should hear."

"I bet they're from the Sudan . . . Darfur, right? We saw a documentary about some of them in my school in Austin. It was called *The Lost Boys*. I bet that Jacob and Emmanuel even know some of them. Maybe they were even in the movie. It's still all going on over there. It's genocide now. Even President Bush said so. You can go online and read all about it."

She licked a honeyed fleck of grain off her fingertip and shot him a wicked little smirk. "Anyway, you're so worried about it, give them your granola bar."

---

Their hosts were in no hurry to get on the road. With their few utensils cleaned and the tent stowed in the van, the two Africans set to harvesting the fallen pecans. Their green husk quarters were strewn on the picnic table and underfoot about the tree, and Jason pitched in to collect the pale brown striated nuts. They ate a few as they went along; the shells were easy to crack with your teeth, and you could pick the rich, sweet meat so that the naked halves were intact. They filled a grocery sack, but when Jason suggested bumping the tree with the van, Jacob said, "No, no. We will leave some for the next person."

Emily sat swinging her heels at the table, listening to a CD from her own collection on Jason's Discman. It annoyed him that she didn't volunteer to help. He felt it gave their hosts a bad impression. Wearing earphones shut everybody out. While Jacob and Emmanuel scoured the perimeter of the campsite, Jason slipped up behind her and pried off the headset.

"Hey!" She whirled to grab it, but he held it out of reach.

"Why don't you help us?"

"I don't want to! Let's go! I wanna get to Austin."

"Don't be a brat. Be patient, okay?"

But when the pecan harvest was finished, Jacob and his cousin wanted to explore the near bank of the Trinity River. They'd crossed the bridge last night just before reaching the picnic site. By this time, Saturday morning traffic on the primary link between Athens and Corsicana constituted a rural rush hour largely composed of Chevy and Ford pickups, freighters full of Chinese-made goods rumbling along on eighteen wheels, and the expected assortment of family Camrys and SUVs—a rich pool of hitching possibilities.

Jason was tempted to surrender to Emily's whining, but he resisted because there was something so cool and interesting about Jacob and Emmanuel that he couldn't bring himself to leave them if he didn't have to. They spelled adventure, and his curiosity was far stronger at the moment than his need to get to Lisa, though the two were related. He needed something to deliver to her, an account of an experience so compelling that hearing it would be necessary for her continuing existence, her happiness and satisfaction, and it would make her admire him. She'd feel that though she was surrounded by college boys, they were all bland clones with stale middle-class tastes and ideas, and none could possibly compete with Jason when it came to knowing real life and living it, too. Yes, he and Emily could abandon their captured Africans and they'd probably get a ride within a few minutes, but while a preacher in a beige Buick could zip them west along their route, it was likely he'd have little to offer except unwanted advice or a cautionary tale about the perilous future of their souls. Jason had decided that he wanted to be the kind of person that this kind of thing (meeting African wanderers) happened to, the kind of person who then translates such an experience into song. A rambling troubadour.

"I'm going on alone, then," said Emily. Jacob and Emmanuel were easing their way through the barbed wire fence that bordered the picnic area by lifting the topmost wire and standing on the next one down, wadded trash bags stuffed in their rear pockets.

"Go ahead. Be sure and lock up before you do."

"Shut up."

He held the side door open, ready to shut it. "So, you going or not?"

She reached into her pack and drew out a book. She would wait, then.

"You should come with us down to the river."

"Why?"

"You need to get outside more. You don't play outside enough. You've always got your nose in a book or you mess with the Sims on your computer. Being with these guys is a once-in-a-lifetime opportunity."

"How do you know I won't meet a whole tribe next year or something? Besides, you're not my mother, so you can quit acting like you are."

"Suit yourself."

On the other side of the fence, a beaten path, apparently made by fishermen, swimmers, or kegging kids on their way down to the water, led alongside the pasture and cut down into the woods. The path was laced with litter: cigarette boxes, beer bottles, fast-food wrappers, disposable diapers. Jason crossed in and out of olfactory strata that reeked of piss and shit where picnickers, obviously lacking a porta-potty, had made use of the nearest obscuring shrub.

Jacob and Emmanuel went ahead, harvesting aluminum, stepping off the dirt path to stoop and pluck or meander farther afield. Jason soon caught up with them as they stood on a trodden lip above the turbid, stinking water, an anglers' stand no doubt, as it was littered with bait wrap and cigarette butts and bottle caps, a discarded Garth Brooks CD *(Ropin' the Wind),* and signs of quick-shop snacks: Slim Jim wrappers, Vienna sausage cans, Dorito husks. They were passing an object between them that turned out to be a mud-clotted Revco reel with several maddening hours' worth of tangled line.

"It's for fishing." Jason was enjoying the role of guide to Americana. Feeling knowledgeable was an unaccustomed pleasure.

"Yes," said Jacob. "I see now."

"Somebody tossed it because the line's all knotted up, probably got frustrated."

Emmanuel beamed. "One man has the trash, and the other has the treasure."

Jacob was looking down into the water. This time of year, at the far end of a long summer drought, the river had shrunk into its bed like a terminal octogenarian resigned to dying, leaving scum-coated flotsam embedded in the mud: a yellow plastic Pennzoil bottle, a six-pack ring, a child's off-brand running shoe, a green Skoal tin. The opaque water was a dark gray-green and seemed to be hardly moving. A turtle poked its snout up like a knuckle, sniffed, dived.

"We fish here?" asked Jacob.

"Aw, I wouldn't."

"No?"

"No. Too much pollution upstream—fertilizer runoff, factory stuff from Dallas, you know. PCBs."

Jacob pointed to the reel. "Someone fishes."

Black dudes. Jason opened his mouth, shut it. "Poor people," he said finally.

"Ah," said Emmanuel. "We have eaten many bad things when we had to—snakes, lizards, grass soup, sticks, bugs."

"I once ate a leather strap," said Jacob.

"No shit?"

"No, not shit," grinned Jacob. "But I have drunk my pee."

Emmanuel made a noise with his mouth and tongue, a kind of cluck, and went "tsss" softly, as if to quiet his cousin.

The three followed the path beside the river. The Africans continued to feed their trash sacks with cans, and Jason looked for other items he thought they might find useful or interesting. The yield thinned as they worked farther from the highway, but Jason's finds included a t-shirt with the slogan "I'm with Stupid" enclosed within an arrow. The Africans were highly puzzled by the message and couldn't shake the idea that "with" in this context meant "having," as in "I'm with (having the characteristic of, or being) Stupid," and Jason, finally, got across the idea that "with" meant "accompanying," and "stupid" referred to another person not wearing the shirt. Though they understood at last, Jacob still seemed mystified as to why someone would wear a shirt that insulted a companion so gratuitously.

"It is for punishment, maybe?"

Emmanuel laughed. "No, no! It is a joke."

"Yeah," said Jason. "That's it."

The shirt was a keeper. The catch eventually included three unmatched socks, a round Danish shortbread cookie tin containing one red Lego, several plastic writing pens of various styles, half a dozen bobbers, nylon basketball shorts, a mud-caked bra with broken hooks, a place setting for three of plastic forks, knives, and spoons, a large-print *Reader's Digest* whose water-soaked pages had been sun-baked to a texture akin to stiff crepe paper and whose swollen contents fanned open like a ravaged carcass.

Some items were left where they were found, others tucked into the bags, though Jason couldn't have said why some made the cut but not others. (Yes to all clothing regardless of condition, no to plastic utensils.)

Returning to the van, Emmanuel told Jason that he and his roommates in Dallas, four other Sudanese refugees, had furnished their apartment almost entirely from Dallas curbs in the monthly round-up the city held for bulky trash: two easy chairs, a sofa, several small tables, bookshelves, rugs, dishware. He never ceased to be amazed at the bountiful harvest of free goods available to anyone in America who wished to collect them. Jason's own scavenger gene was recessive, and he'd always been faintly in contempt of trash-pickers who went through your cast-offs and tossed items into their old pickups (and Burl was always annoyed when they failed to restack the remaining heap). However, seeing this cornucopia through the eyes of the two Africans, he was coming to view this gleaning as a sign of resourcefulness and thrift, old-fashioned values his Meemaw would appreciate.

The van was locked. Emily was gone. She'd called his bluff? "Emily!" he yelled, circling in the shoulder and scanning the woods on the other side of the highway. Heart thundering in his throat, he danced antsily in place while Jacob unlocked the van, hoping that she'd merely wandered away looking for them, but a glance inside showed him Emily's pack was gone.

"Damn her!"

Jacob and Emmanuel watched in silence as he stomped about the van, his anger radiating a force field keeping them at a respectful distance. Jason trotted along the fence line, peering into the woods. He kept screaming for her. Then he crossed over to the other side of the highway, marking time momentarily as he was buffeted by the backwash of a tanker, hollered her name into the stand of trees.

"How long have we been gone?" he asked when he came back to the van. Jacob shrugged. Emmanuel said, "Thirty minutes, perhaps. Maybe more."

Jason was on the verge of ordering the two to jump in the vehicle and haul ass down the road after her, but he checked himself. He was heartsick. His only responsibility had been to see that she arrived at her father's house safe and sound, and he'd flunked this test royally. God only knew what could happen to a little girl alone on the road with her thumb out. And he'd be blamed. Rightly so, too. He should've made her come with them, shouldn't have trusted her in the first place—he knew she was a devious little shit. Images unreeled like a fast-forward montage: Emily's thumb, the leering smirk of a meth-addled trucker, the kid trapped in the cab, Lily sobbing over the crumpled form of her only child lying nude in a shallow grave covered by leaves. . . . He could explain, couldn't he, why she had run away from home with him? That he'd had no choice? That she was going to do it alone or with him? Now, though, he saw he'd had the option to stay home himself and keep her there by force until his dad and Lily came back. Then he could've slipped off later in the night, out his window. But no, he'd been in such a fucking hurry! His head was ten feet up his ass!

Jacob said, "You think the child is doing the thumb?" He mimed hitching.

"I guess. But I hope to hell not!"

Emmanuel said, "Maybe she has walked ahead. We can go look."

"Would you mind? I could stay here, you know, if you wouldn't mind doubling back. We could buy you some gas, you know . . ."

Jacob waved away the offer. He opened the driver's door and took the seat behind the wheel while Emmanuel loaded their sacks and items gathered on the hunt, then he stepped up into the passenger's seat. Jacob started the engine while Jason was standing beside the open rear door, and it occurred to him that if they didn't find Emily, they might decide to drive on.

"Hold it a sec. Let me get my gear."

He stepped into the van to retrieve his pack and the guitar, then heard Emily screaming, "Wait! Wait!"

She was running out of the woods on the near side, carrying her pack in her arms like a grocery sack, waving frantically at them.

"There she is!"

Jason tumbled out and paced beside the van, legs trembling. His cigarette-holding hand popped up to his mouth, whisked his cheek, fell to the side. At the fence, Emily tried to hurry between the strands, lifted the pack through and set it on the ground, squirmed through the barbs, hopping on one foot as she cleared the wire, snatched up the pack, came at a dead run, hair flying from the wind.

"You were gonna leave, weren't you!" She danced about him, furious, chin quivering.

"Where the hell have you been? I looked for you! How could you go off like that? I thought you were out there." He waved wildly to the highway as if the ribbon of asphalt led straight to the dark mouth of the underworld. "We were going to go looking for you! You have any idea how that scared me?! Where were you?"

"I went looking for you guys."

Jason was aware that Jacob and Emmanuel were sitting quietly almost within arm's reach, their dark, round, close-cropped heads steadfastly turned forward as if to give the illusion they weren't witnesses. Jason said, "We'll be back in a second if you don't mind? Or you could go on without us. We can catch a ride."

They both turned. Jacob frowned. "Oh no! Please!"

Jason led Emily to the table under the tree by cupping her elbow. His hand was shaking.

"Emily, you scared the crap out of me, you know that?"

"You said I should go on alone if I wanted to."

"You knew I didn't mean it."

"And you should know I wouldn't have, either!"

"Why'd you take your pack with you then?"

She sat on the end of the bench and turned away, shoulders sunk inward like folded stubby wings. He couldn't read her silence, but usually when she got this way she was sulking, resisting interrogation. It irritated him to no end. He'd rather argue outright than deal with someone's stony pouting.

"Why'd you take your pack if you weren't going to go off alone?" He put a detective's hard edge to the question.

"I needed it."

He thought maybe she meant that she needed it to hold things she might find, but she added, "In case I came back and you were gone. I wouldn't have my stuff with me."

He sat on the bench. It was gradually sinking in on him how little she trusted anyone.

"You actually thought I would really leave you here?"

She nodded.

"What makes you think that?"

She shrugged, a quick violent spasm rippling her back.

He sighed as he recalled the trick he'd played last night walking away and leaving her standing alone in the dark. "Emily, look at me."

She raised her sorrowful face; her lashes were plastered together with tears. He raised his right hand in the pledge position.

"I swear to you right here and now that I won't let you out of my sight between now and when we get to your dad's and he says everything's okay. All right?"

Something glittery and sharp flicked through her eyes for an instant, as if she'd heard all this before and the temptation to believe it was hurtful in itself.

"I promise. I swear on Meemaw's grave."

This only seemed to puzzle her.

"What can I do to make you believe me?"

This did interest her, maybe as a challenge. Her lips pursed and she bit her upper lip, frowning.

She pointed to the fence. "Smash your guitar over the top of that post."

"Emily! Come on!"

"Well, so you don't really mean it, then."

"Of course I do! Look, if somebody took you, you know, kidnapped you, and the ransom was my guitar, I guarantee you I'd give it to them to get you back. But if I bust it up like you're asking, well then, I wouldn't be able to play the Emily song for you."

"The Emily song?"

Jason nodded, grinning.

"How's it go?" Suspicious, now.

"Right time and place, kiddo. Not here and not now."

"Really? You wrote a song for me?"

"Uh-huh." He grinned, winked.

"You better have."

She eased off the bench, gingerly lifted her pack from the table between her arms. The paw of an animal suddenly waggled through the partly unzipped top.

"What the . . . heck is that?"'

She opened the pack and dipped her hands into it, then drew out a cat and cradled it like a baby.

"It's a kitty. He's just like Marvel, the one I used to have."

The tabby might've been a kitten last year. "Emily, where'd that cat come from?"

"I found him in the woods."

"He's a wild cat, then. You should let him stay there."

She turned a defiant face at him. "He has a flea collar."

Sure enough, the cat sported a faded plastic band around its neck. "Well, then, he's somebody's pet, and they might be looking for him. You better just leave him right here."

"I'm not going to leave him! He's starving!"

Jason could feel the minutes ticking away and worried that his hosts might run out of patience. He clearly wasn't going to argue Emily out of dumping this beast on the side of the road here, but he could hope they'd find a "suitable home" for it later, such as a truck stop dumpster or with another feline family. Or maybe Jacob and Emmanuel needed a pet.

"Just don't give it a name," said Jason.

"His name is Trippy. I named him that because I found him on this trip."

Cradled in Emily's arms, the yellow-eyed cat stared at Jason evenly.

# Eight

In Corsicana, at the interchange with I-45, Jason insisted on buying ten dollars worth of gas, and while he was inside the Shell Mini Mart he perused a map and decided that they could go south with the Africans toward Houston on I-45 to Buffalo, then hitch west to Round Rock. Coming out of the station, he spotted the golden arch hovering brightly over the interstate and talked Jacob into scooting on down the block to Mickey D's for coffee. They all went inside to wash up, then at the counter Jason noted they'd just slipped under the 10:30 breakfast wire. Not knowing from where or when their next meal might come (he was thinking like a disaster victim), he took an order from Emily for hotcakes, sausage, and orange juice and doubled it for himself. She sent him back for milk (not for herself, it turned out). When he asked Jacob and Emmanuel what they might like, they declined, patting their tummies as if the scrambled egg and *roti* they'd had three hours earlier had stuffed them to the gills. They weren't coffee or tea drinkers, either. They each spent quite a while in the restroom, as if they might be sponge-bathing.

Aside from his and Emily's breakfast, Jason brought back to their table a to-go sack containing two egg McMuffins and two large orange juices, which he planned to leave in the van without mentioning when they dismounted down the road and said good-bye.

On I-45 they made good time heading south, as the volume and speed of traffic made dropping out of the flow and reentering it too harrowing for Jacob, and the road crews regularly picked up litter and mowed the expansive right-of-way. Jacob nudged the van along the slow lane at a staunch and steady fifty-five, windows down (the AC had long since quit working), and since on a Texas interstate, "slow lane" means anybody going seventy-five or under, the boxy heap was an obstacle for other drivers. They tailgated, honked, and blinked headlights as they zoomed by in a furious rush with their heads rolling sideways to flick glances of irritation at this pokey, coal-black driver or lifted chins in contempt as they sailed past. Being on the slow boat instead of the showboat was uncomfortable for Jason. It embarrassed him the way a child is embarrassed by his parent's fondness for an article of very unstylish clothing. He wanted to hide.

Before long, though, Jason flip-flopped because he couldn't take standing in the corner with laggards and losers, slowpoke old farts, those like his dad who obeyed the rules or inched beyond the limit only when absolute safety allowed it. He traded his embarrassment for contempt of the speeders and mild indignation. He was proud to be out of step, like he imagined his hosts were. Let the bastards burn their gas like spoiled brats. The dude in the black Navigator road-hog with the Ducks Unlimited sticker's gonna get to Houston five, ten, maybe fifteen minutes before this van does, and for what? What's he gonna do with those minutes gained at the expense of the planet? Sit in a bar yakking on a cell phone? Piddle it away watching the tail end of a football game he has no stake in and won't recall tomorrow? Jason and company, on the other hand, were *traveling,* drinking in, recording, noting, absorbing the passing scenery (flat bland countryside with occasional stands of pine, cows, and a pumping jack or two), making the journey more important than the destination.

Bubba vs. Buddha, the smackdown!

If Jacob and Emmanuel were aware that driving at this speed had any such moral component attached, they made no show of it. They seemed content, indifferent to the passing parade of newer, speedier vehicles and huge, gleaming trucks whose tires were thrashing the asphalt under them as they ground past enveloped in a whining aura of clatter and moans. They respectfully allowed Emily to interview them, and Jason took notes on their answers. *Where are your families? Do you have sisters? How old were you when you had to run away from the Arabs who raided your village? How long was it between then and when you arrived in America? How many refugee camps did you stay in? Which was the best? Which the worst? What do you do now? Will you ever go back? Do you have girlfriends? Are there any Lost Girls?*

Even though he relished hearing their stories, Jason poked her in the ribs and frowned when she turned to face him, trying to suggest he thought it was rude to ask so many personal questions, but she merely glared back and sneered, perhaps suggesting that his lack of intellectual curiosity was a problem, not an asset. Though Jacob didn't mention crocodiles to her, the bald facts of their decade-long exodus fell over her like a mantle of authority that evoked in Emily a rare, child-like softness that Jason rarely witnessed. Jacob's mother was one of his father's three wives, and she was killed in the first attack. He had two older sisters who were taken away by the raiders, and he never saw them again, though he always looked for them when he came into a new camp. Two brothers were killed as well. The children on the run hiked from village to village trying to stay ahead of the war, only to find themselves swallowed and surrounded by it again and again. They walked with thousands of other refugees through swamps and desert, and everywhere they went they were like locusts devouring anything edible in the countryside. There was never enough fresh water. They were always thirsty. They walked for months without shoes. The crossed the Upper Nile several times, once chased by soldiers firing on them, and many drowned or were shot in the water. No one in a village or town wanted to see them coming, and sometimes robbers stripped them of what little food or clothing they had. Boys without families were seen as prey.

"But we are here, cousin!" interrupted Emmanuel. He twisted to smile at Emily, though if you'd only seen his eyes you'd never have known it.

"Yes, yes," Jacob said. He was agreeing to restrain himself. "You ask me what has been the very best refugee camp? I tell you—it's America."

They all chuckled, as it was apparent he'd intended to make a joke, but in the silence that lapsed afterward, Jason mulled over the darker implications. The notion of a permanent rootlessness, a yearning for a home that could never be fulfilled, lay at the heart of their story. They'd never be Americans the way he and Emily were, yet they'd never be fully Sudanese again in the village of their childhood, either. The thought was frightening and sad. He wished he could help but felt helpless. But he warmed to the idea of telling their story, being their champion that way. Some dudes like U2 were into music as public service. Maybe this was Jason's calling!

At the Buffalo interchange, Jacob took the access to the frontage road and delivered them to the shoulder of 79 going west. Jason borrowed a pen and paper from Emily and asked the two Africans to write their names and addresses for him. They complied, inscribing the information in a deliberate and very legible cursive that evoked pictures of something old-fashioned for Jason, like a white frame schoolhouse in the old West. He couldn't have said precisely why he wanted this record—maybe just as that, a record, a souvenir, tangible proof—but he had vague intentions of a future connection.

He and Emily stood watching as the van U-turned and the fellows, waving, headed back to the access to I-45. Jason felt suddenly bereft, weighted with responsibility again, alone, and his nerve endings waggled, jagged and loose from too little sleep. He longed to just be beamed over to Lisa's dorm, and for the umpteenth time, he cursed his decision to bring this kid along. But she was undeniably present. At the moment, she was discreetly picking her nose, the red Rangers cap askew, her white sneakers soled with a rime of mud. She held the cat by one arm, and the tension in its shoulders suggested it was about to leap away.

Jason considered their surroundings. This was a busy interchange, one of those ubiquitous crossroads in the interstate system where tributary highways join the four-lane divided stream, and franchise operations huddle to concoct faux towns which are larger in some cases than the real communities dying two or three miles away from the highway.

He inventoried the restaurant options: Shell Mini Mart, Tiger Travel Plaza, Pizza Inn, Dickey's Barbeque, Pitt Grill, Sonic Drive-In, Dairy Queen. It was comforting that food was readily available. He guessed it was around noon, as the lots of these food emporia corralled small automotive herds.

"You hungry?"

Emily shook her head. "We had two breakfasts already."

"Do you think we should eat anyway?"

She seemed surprised to be asked for an opinion. "Uh, no. Why, do you think we should?"

"I was just thinking, you know, that if we did get hungry later we might not be anywhere near food."

Emily shrugged. Jason recognized his own ulterior motive: sitting in Dairy Queen with a burger and fries and a chocolate shake meant not standing out here on the road in the sun trying to thumb a ride. Eating lunch was a form of procrastination. It was probably a hundred twenty miles to Round Rock, twenty beyond that to downtown Austin. The ride might take several hours, depending.

They could take a break. He could think about the songs burning in his imagination. He wasn't a multitasker, and he couldn't hold many things in his attention at once. His awareness was a spotlight, not a floodlight, and at the moment, the life of the two Sudanese refugees still glowed in his mind just to the forefront, though barely, of all his thoughts of Lisa.

Whatever might be transpiring back home in Mesquite was of no interest or consequence to him, including not only his need to appear in court in hardly forty-eight hours, but also whatever measures Lily and his dad might be taking to track them down. He was jolted back home momentarily, though, when he spotted a DPS trooper's car gliding down off the frontage road in the distance.

"Come on," he urged Emily, picking up his guitar and pinching her elbow. "Let's walk, and hurry, okay?"

He turned his back to the cruiser in the distance, and they scurried for shelter in the travel plaza a few dozen yards away, where a huge caliche lot held slumbering semis parked like a freight train broken into segments, and the drivers at the pumps under the awning were gripping the big-bore nozzles like hefty handguns.

At the Dairy Queen, Jason hoped the lunch mob would blanket them, turn them invisible. Every seat was taken, though a short wait yielded a booth in a corner. Jason ordered coffee for himself and a Dr Pepper for Emily, and while they sat drinking, Trippy wriggled free from Emily's pack between her feet and shot through the forest of shins and shoes. Emily scrambled after him, yelling his name; the uproar produced a humorous hubbub, with several other children merrily joining the chase, but Trippy darted into the hall that led to the restrooms and, just as the Women's door swung open, dashed inside. While Jason sat silently cursing, Emily slipped through the restroom door and found Trippy happily cradled in the arms of a young woman wearing a Texas Women's University sweatshirt. She readily gave him over to Emily.

A brief conversation followed—the girl was with her boyfriend, who was waiting in his car (she'd only come in to use the restroom), and they were on their way to Austin to visit friends. Emily said she and her brother were trying to get to Austin before their grandfather died, and because their mother had had to leave last night, an uncle was supposed to come take them this morning but he hadn't shown up. So they were hitching.

As Emily returned to the booth with the cat, the older girl's hand was draped maternally on her shoulder and she beamed at Jason, clearly pleased to offer aid to grieving travelers. Emily said, "Jason, this is Angela. She and her boyfriend are gonna give us a ride to poor granddaddy's house in Austin! So we can get there before he *expires*."

Angela's boyfriend was at the wheel of a yellow 2001 Mustang with a yellow First Cavalry sticker on the back window. The passenger compartment was approximately the size of a fighter-plane cockpit, and the two-door configuration required Jason and Emily to squeeze past the front seat backs and into small buckets and hike their feet up on watermelons resting in the floor well. Despite being cramped, Jason was pleased not only to have a ride all the way to Austin, but also, the car aroused his envy, giving him the twisted pleasure of vicarious ownership.

Though the boyfriend, Alex Vargas, was clad in cargo shorts and a plain black logo-less t-shirt, he had a grunt's tan rim across his forehead, a close-shaved noggin, and a scab-encrusted tattoo on his right forearm that appeared to be an eagle's head swathed by red, white, and blue bunting. He was quick to let his passengers know that his outfit at Hood would be shipping out soon for the Middle East. He was a Private First Class, he said, a Bradley driver. Jason guessed his age at maybe twenty or twenty-one, though the sunglasses with mirrored lenses made it hard to say.

*Wow!* thought Jason. The world was brimming with opportunities! First there were the Africans, and now here was his chance to get unfiltered info about military life without provoking the aggressive colonizing instincts of a recruiter. Despite his efforts to avoid Sgt. Brookes and his partner, since Lisa had gone to Austin and his old pals seemed to have drifted off, it had gradually sunk in that Jason needed to figure out a way of paying a monthly nut. He couldn't just keep on living in his old bedroom with his dad and Lily down the hall as if he were a child. For one thing, he didn't want to have to argue about rules or listen to his dad nag him about chores or getting a job or how he was dressed or what he was doing in his room. He needed to be self-supporting for many reasons, and chief among them was this dude's yellow Mustang.

"So how you like the army?"

"It's cool. Three squares, good buds. Feels right, you know?" He flung a grin over his shoulder. "I'm working on Angie to join up."

"Not in a million-trillion years."

"Aren't you scared about going to Iraq?" asked Emily.

"Hell no! We're gonna kick some raghead butt. Saddam's history. We got to Baghdad in like three minutes. I'm just scared it'll all be over by the time my unit gets there."

"He's gung-ho," said Angela. "And I'm hum-ho." She'd put Emily's backpack in the floorboard between her feet, then she pulled Trippy free to hold him. Jason thought Angela might be a good prospective owner.

Jason told Alex about Sgt. Brookes's efforts to sign him up, and he had Alex laughing and pounding the wheel.

"Thing is, I'm thinking that down the road I wanna be a singer and songwriter, and they're telling me that I could probably go into the army band or something if I want. Or get stationed in like maybe New Orleans, where in my time off I could play in clubs."

Alex laughed. "The band? Whatta you play?"

"Guitar, some keyboard. Well, a little."

"You ever see a guitar in a marching band?"

"No, but, you know, there's all kinds of percussion, drums, stuff like that I could do."

Alex shook his head sadly. "They ain't sending you to the music department, amigo."

"Well, I figured they lie to people all the time. But they seemed desperate enough to make the offer, you know."

"Hey, you don't wanna be in the band, anyway, dude. Too many fags and shit. You go army, you go *army,* dig?"

For the next hour or so, Alex told boot camp tales, a good many of which Jason felt weren't fit to be heard by an eleven-year-old girl. But he was an avid listener. Forced marches in desert heat, punishment by push-ups, absurdly pointless tasks, rotten chow, sadistic noncoms, annoying idiots in the ranks, sleeplessness, exhaustion—Alex relished every second of it. He'd endured an initiation and passed into a state of grace. Now he belonged, and, gripe as he might about his present CO or the dumb-ass gunner on his Bradley, Jason could hear the pleasure, could sense how the soldier treasured the bond with his mates. If Jason didn't already envy Alex for owning a yellow 2001 Mustang with a First Cav sticker on the back window, there was also his condition as a young man with a sense of purpose. Alex felt fat with the satisfactions of fellowship. Jason could imagine himself in a barracks, sitting on a footlocker maybe, in fatigues and t-shirt with dog tags dangling, strumming on his guitar while his good buds sat around sucking brews and listening to his boot camp ballads. Iraq—that'd be something to sing about, all right.

As they passed Loop 620 north of Austin, Angela said, "Where's your grandpa live, anyway?"

"It's pretty close to the UT campus," said Emily. "Our granddad's a professor there."

"No kidding!" said Angela. "What's he teach?"

"Retired now," put in Jason. "'Cause of his bad health, you know." He elbowed Emily.

"He taught physics and astronomy."

"Wow," said Angela. "He must be really smart."

"He's certified as a genius," said Emily.

"Wow. Hope he pulls through okay. What's he got?"

"The doctors don't really know. It's something really rare," put in Emily.

She might have been trying to give the mythical grandparent a condition befitting a genius, but vagueness could inspire further questions, so Jason added, "Something in his heart. Like regular heart disease, kinda."

Once they cruised I-35 south below the Fifty-first Street exit, Emily seemed to know exactly how to get to her father's place, and within a few minutes Alex had tooled the cool Mustang across on Thirty-eighth and into a residential neighborhood north of the campus. Emily directed him down a quiet, tree-shaded street and along a row of townhouses and stopped him before one that looked indistinguishable to Jason from all the others on the block.

"This it?"

They crawled out of the backseat with Jason's gear and his guitar. While Emily was slipping on her backpack, Jason noticed Trippy still in Angela's lap and said, "You like that kitty? We found him on the road, he's a stray, needs a good ho —"

"No!" yelled Emily. She plunged into the passenger compartment to scoop up the cat, and Angela, readily relinquishing him, said, "I would if I could, but I live in a dorm."

They waved good-bye and watched the Mustang cruise to the end of the block.

"So, hey," Jason said. "We're here! We made it in one piece! You think he's home?"

"Hope so."

Now that he was seconds away from being free of surrogate-parental responsibilities, Jason rode on a wave of good fellowship. Feeling charitable and kind toward his temporary ward, he eased his arm across her thin back and cupped her nape as they strolled to the door. It had been an adventure, after all, and looking back on it, he was glad she'd come along. She'd been good company, really, and for the first time in his brief experience living alongside her, if not *with* her, he was pleased to have this sort-of sibling. A stepling. Down the road, next few years if he was still hanging in Mesquite, the thought that she'd be there too made for a rosy prospect.

They'd sure pulled one on the old 'rents! He chuckled.

"What's so funny?"

"I was just thinking about the looks on your mom's and my dad's faces when they got home last night and we weren't there. I bet they about crapped their pants, man. You think she already called your dad?"

"Prob'ly only three hundred times."

Six concrete steps and a paneled oak door with a brass knocker were all that separated him from the end of phase one and the beginning of his quest to reclaim Lisa. They went up the steps and stood in the shade of the overhang. A black upright metal mailbox, fixed to the brick by the door spouted letter-ends out its top like hankies stuffed in a lapel pocket. The sight of it jolted Jason.

Emily leaned up on her toes to whack the brass knocker in a distinct rhythm that sounded like a signal: *bap-bap-bap-bap-bap-BAP!* She waited, frozen for a few seconds, then knelt to rummage about in her book bag, clutching Trippy under her free arm like a football.

"Your dad doesn't pick up his mail?"

"Not when he's not here."

"He's not here?!"

"I dunno. He goes to lot of conferences all over the world."

Shit. Helplessly he looked up and down the street as if a neighbor might magically appear to assist them.

But then Emily said, "I've got a key."

Which she produced, then stepped to the door and inserted it into the lock. She grimaced and grunted as she jiggled the key, jerked it out, peered at it closely, almost pressing it against the lens of her glasses, then tried it again.

"You sure this is the right house?"

Emily just sneered and shoved the key back into the lock. Jason furtively eased a protruding letter upward until the address label was visible.

"Who's Melody Kincaid?"

"One of Daddy-ji's graduate assistants."

"Who?"

"My daddy—his assistant."

After a few moments of watching her worry the lock, Jason said, "Let me try it." But he couldn't ease the fingers through the tumblers inside the lock, either.

"Maybe he changed the lock."

"He wouldn't do that!"

"Why not? People do it all the time."

"'Cause he'd know I couldn't get in! He wouldn't do that unless he sent me a new key, too."

"Maybe he sent it to your mom."

Well, that was a dark possibility for Emily. Lily might have deliberately kept that knowledge secret, though if her father was such a terrifically wonderful certified genius, you'd think he'd have told his daughter about this on one of the many non-occasions that he didn't take advantage of his custody arrangements to not see her.

She sat on the top step of the stoop, cat in her lap.

"You know a neighbor who might have a key?"

She shook her head violently. "I hate her! She's a dumb cow!" Her eyes pooled with tears. Her mother, not the neighbor. Her disappointment was aggravated by exhaustion. And their last meal had been that breakfast at the McDonald's off I-45 with the African dudes.

He was disappointed, too. He eased down beside her on the stoop, plucked Trippy from her lap so that she could blow her nose, and noted absently in a way that was faintly distressing that the cat settled into being held and petted quite readily and purred much too loudly.

"What do you want to do?" he asked finally.

She shrugged.

"You think he's out of town?"

Shrugged.

"When does he have to go to work? Monday?"

"Prob'ly Tuesday."

Jason sighed. "Well, we can't just sit here, that's for sure."

"I can."

"Emily! There's no telling when he might be back!"

"You don't have to wait with me. I'll be okay. This is my home."

It was on his tongue to ask when was she last here, but he held back the impulse. "Do you have any friends in the neighborhood?"

"I know three other kids in the next block but they don't like me and I don't like them and their mothers don't like me, either, so you can forget about trying to dump me on them."

"I wasn't thinking that."

"Oh, yeah, I bet."

"No, really—I was, was thinking that maybe a friend could cat-sit for a while and you and I could go down to Sixth Street and do some busking, get a few bucks, you know, and eat a burger. Then we could call your dad from there, and even if he's not here right now, you could leave a message letting him know that you're here, and you'll be checking in to find out when you can come home."

"I'm not leaving Trippy with any of them!"

"Not even for a couple hours?"

"No. I said they don't like me. They'd take it out on him."

Sometimes her bitter distrust astonished him. "He was a stray cat when you found him. How do you know he's not happier that way? Maybe we should take him to a park or some woods and let him be free."

"Free to starve to death!"

"Whatever happened to catching mice and birds?"

"He's got a flea collar. He's used to getting his food from humans. I think he's probably hungry right now."

Jason got up. "Come on. I'm not letting you stay here by yourself. Bring your damn cat along, then. But let's find something to use as a leash, or he'll get loose and run into the street and you'll go after him and you'll both get squashed."

"Okay, but I need to leave a note."

Jason ripped a blank page from his journal and gave her a pen. While he held Trippy, she pressed the paper against the porch pillar and scrawled something, folded the paper, wedged it between the door and the frame.

Since it was a September Saturday and the Longhorns apparently had an away game, the traffic along Guadalupe was light, though the sidewalk along the store side opposite the campus was filled with students shopping, drinking, and hanging out. Emily had found a piece of brown packing twine and had fixed one end to Trippy's flea collar, but the cat wasn't of a mind to be either led or walked like a dog, so she quickly scooped him up again but left the twine attached.

At the intersection with Twenty-first, he did a quick calculation, subtracting six from twenty-one to conclude they still had fifteen blocks to cover going south to get to Sixth Street. According to Burl, there were about twelve blocks to a mile. He wondered if Emily were up to walking that distance carrying her bag and the cat.

Then he looked left and saw the Dobie tower complex—Lisa's dormitory! Right on this street! He remembered that she'd said that there was a kind of shopping mall on the ground floor with a movie theatre, fast food, clothing boutiques, and the like.

He stood at the corner looking at the dorm—fifteen

stories? Twenty?—glass and steel, like an office building in downtown Dallas, maybe. His gaze swept up the multiple towers, down each vertical block, scanning the windows, vaguely thinking that he'd catch a sign of Lisa. Maybe she was up there in her room right now, reading, eyeballing TV, catching tunes, washing her hair . . . well, Saturday afternoon as it was, she was most likely out some place. Out some place with friends, new friends, or a *new friend?* She might be down in College Station with Chase, for all he knew. Or maybe he's come up here and picked her up and they're out. . . .

"What're you looking at? Are we going someplace or not?"

"Uh, yeah. We're gonna go set up over there, by that building. Come on." He gripped her bicep loosely and steered her across the boulevard on a Walk light. A small plaza opened up around the building across Twenty-first from the dorm and the ground-floor mall, and he led Emily to a low wall, where he stopped, set his pack and guitar on the ledge, and told her to sit there.

"What're you gonna do?"

"I need to check on something, okay? Five minutes. Just watch my stuff and stay right here, all right?"

"Does she know you're coming to see her?"

Startled, he blurted, "Who? Lisa? What makes you think—"

"'Cause a lot of first years live here."

"I just want to check to see if she's at home."

"Then what?"

"I'll call and make plans to hook up later. You know, after you're safe at home with your dad."

"There's a Subway in there. Will you bring me back a Diet Dr Pepper and some milk for Trippy, please?"

He passed through one of the many openings in the bank of glass doors under the protected overhang. His hands broke out in sweat. People were thronging in and out of the main mall inside, and it was intimidating to imagine living in a mall (or above one); it seemed like living in an ant farm to Jason. He had to walk about for several minutes, too timid and proud to stop someone and ask for directions to the entrance of the living quarters proper.

Students were waiting about the doors of a bank of elevators, waiting, so he guessed they were ascending to the residential floors. He could join them, but he had no idea where Lisa lived; he couldn't recall now if she had ever mentioned a room number or a floor, though searching his memory, it did seem that she mentioned a "nice view of downtown." That meant nothing.

On the far side of the elevators, he found a counter running diagonally across a room. Behind it, three college-age youths, two male and one female, all three wearing dark blue polo shirts with white insignia, were chatting and tossing a hacky-sack between them. The scene shared a vague similarity to a hotel's front desk, so he stepped up to the counter.

The girl gave him her attention.

"Hi! Can I help you?"

"Are you guys the people in charge? My sister lives here in this dorm? And I'm coming in from out of town, you know, kinda on the spur of the moment, and I thought maybe I could get her room number and surprise her?"

The two dudes shot him an "aw-huh" look, and the girl cocked her head. "I'm sorry, I can't do that," she said quite sweetly. He must've looked terribly woebegone upon hearing this, because she added, "I could look her up and call her room for you, though." The two dudes then gave each other another "aw-huh" look, and Jason knew that if the girl hadn't been present, he'd still be standing at this counter waiting to be noticed.

He gave Lisa's full name, and the girl slid into a desk chair, mouse-clicked, picked up a phone, dialed, waited but looked at him while it rang on the other end, smiling prettily, her teeth white against her burnished olive skin—she was cute, all right!—giving him the impression she was so very earnestly in his service trying to unite members of his family, smiling as she listened. Then squiggled her brows in disappointment. She covered the mouthpiece.

"Voice mail. Should I let her know you're here?"

"Uh, no. Thanks. I'll call her cell."

Which might be true if he hadn't already considered it a

hundred times in the last twelve hours and gone lame-ass limp before working up to it. If he called from a pay phone and her caller ID posted that puzzle in the window, pure curiosity might drive her to answer. He could leave a message on her voice mail, but that would tip his hand about being here and give her too much space to locate an excuse: *"Sorry, didn't check. Sorry, wasn't here."* *Sorry, you're so fucking sorry.*

But sooner or later, he'd have to dial it and ask her to meet him.

Were he a free man, he'd glide up to that third floor and walk the hall, then try the fourth, the fifth, all the way up twenty-some floors. He'd be in no hurry; he'd have nothing else to do. He could stroll casually along, passing each open door—*Hey, you guys happen to know Lisa Johnson?* Or read the ID cards on the door, if they had them. Or just get a good gander at what kids who are here look-sound-smell like. How they talk, hints on how to walk and talk and behave, so she'd at least like him again.

But he wasn't a free man. And he'd already been gone fifteen minutes. Emily was so unpredictable, she might've sold his stuff or walked off and left it.

He emerged from the building carrying one Styrofoam cup of milk with a lid and another of a Diet Dr Pepper, along with a plastic bag containing two tuna subs, one with everything but onions (his), the other plain but cut in half. He'd also bought a package of Sun Chips Original because Emily liked them.

Trippy, perched on his haunches on top of the retaining wall, had his face buried in a paper cup with a TCBY logo while Emily stroked his spine and grinned up into the gooey-eyed faces of two very hot girls, both blondes with tanned, sleek, long legs and their hair in ponytails, both wearing flip-flops and shorts, snug sleeveless t-shirts, sunglasses. One was still working on her cup of yogurt. Emily had obviously way-laid them on Trippy's behalf.

"Here's my brother now!" she yelped. "Did you find Lisa?" He shrugged no. The two hotties pivoted and eyed him with avid interest. "I told them all about how you guys were sweethearts all through school and were never ever apart but then her parents moved her away but you didn't know where exactly and how you've been searching all over the country for her for months now 'cause you can't forget her and everything. And about all your songs and stuff."

His face tingled with heat.

"Hey, he's blushing," one girl told the other. They exchanged an "awww!" expression.

"Sunburn," growled Jason. He handed the bag to Emily and set the drinks on the wall. "There's a tuna sub and chips. I had them cut yours in half in case you wanted to give some to your pitiful-ass alley cat."

"Thanks! Jennifer gave him some of her yogurt!" Emily pointed at one of the blondes. Her snug top was a watermelon color. The other's was the hue of the inside of a kiwi. Her arms were long and tan and tight, too. These girls were obviously pool and gym rats. "They live here in Dobie."

"We don't know your girlfriend, though," said the one-not-Jennifer. "But we could help you look for her!" She shoved her sunglasses up onto her head. Her eyes were bright with interest in the drama. "Like if you've got a picture or something."

Emily had neglected one crucial piece of exposition in her fictitious narrative: Lisa probably didn't want Jason to find her. She was lost on purpose you could say. Not exactly hiding from him, he knew, but probably not eager for him to show up unannounced, plant himself on her doorstep, and elbow his way into her plans for the afternoon. Or night. Or the rest of her weekend. Her life. He sure didn't want an audience of strangers witnessing whatever humiliating reception he might get.

"Thanks, that's really nice of you to offer. But . . . well, I think she probably hates my guts. I hooked up twice with her best friend."

That cleared the air of the sentimental miasma of unfulfilled romance, all right. Not-Jennifer swung on her heel and tossed her empty yogurt cup into the penis-headed trash receptacle nearby, but Jennifer hung back long enough to say pointedly and sweetly to Emily, "It was really nice to meet *you*, Emily, and your kitty Trippy. I hope you find your real father someday soon."

"Was that true about Lisa's friend?" Emily asked after they'd settled on the wall and had unwrapped their tuna subs.

"No. No way. I'm stupid but not that stupid."

"Why'd you say it, then?"

"I didn't want those bee-ot-chiz messing in my business."

"They were nice."

"You shoulda asked them if you could stay in their room, then." He'd meant to be sarcastic but now it occurred to him too late that this had been a missed opportunity. "They'd probably love to smuggle your pal into the dorm with them. You guys could be up there right now, napping on a nice soft comforter and taking a nice hot shower. Damn!" He slapped his thigh. He laughed. "Come to think of it, if I hadn't been such a dick, maybe I'd be up there, too. They really ate up that story about the lost lovers and all."

"It's kinda true, isn't it?"

He shrugged. "I think you're maybe the biggest liar I've ever met."

"I don't lie!"

"Liar."

She took a sullen, meditative munch from the half of the tuna sub she'd saved for herself. He'd hurt her feelings. "Like what was all that about searching for your real father?"

"I am!"

"Well, yeah. Technically, I guess."

"So?"

"So you'll make a good lawyer some day."

"I'm going to be an astrophysicist."

"And I'm going to be on *American Idol*."

"When is the audition?"

She believed he was serious? "I was kidding. That's all sell-out pop crap, Emily. Nobody on it does their own stuff."

"I think you're good enough, though!"

Now and then a little unexpected ray of sincerity broke through her perpetually overcast skies, though when it did, it always seemed to convey a hint of ludicrous condescension.

"Well, I appreciate that."

He balled up his empty wrapper and stuffed it into the plastic bag. Speaking of music—time for some tunes. Although his original plans had been to go to the musical Mecca of Sixth Street and play, setting up here would allow them to watch the door in case Lisa happened to come out or go in. Later, when Saturday night was in full swing and Emily was safe at home, he could amble down to Sixth.

Either way, he was here in Austin! But where was Lisa?

# nine

Lisa waited in the water, bobbing on swells, the slalom ski floating and held lightly by her side between her thumb and fingers. In the distance above the glittering, sun-struck surface of Lake Travis, Chris brought the boat back around to pick her up. Water glistened on her eyelashes as her feet dangled in a stratum of cooler water; the temperature on this Saturday afternoon was a perfect eighty-six degrees. She blew bubbles on the water and shook her head to free her hair from her face while the boat surged toward her. She thought she'd skied well, considering it had been a couple of months. It had been a nice stroke of luck to meet Ashley and Chris at orientation: Ashley's family lived in Breckenridge, but her dad kept a house and boat on the lake here. This was really the first "vacation" weekend Lisa had allowed herself to take since classes had started, though she'd spent an hour in the library this morning before Paige picked her up there.

Had Nicholas seen her ski? She knew he'd noticed the new turquoise bandini; or, at least, the parts tucked beneath it seemed alluring to his gaze, though he wasn't sleazy about looking. Not that she was trying to get anybody, but it was fun to be free, at least. Fun to just hang out with no obligations or responsibilities. Fun to relax for the first time since classes started.

Chris cut the throttle, and the boat pushed rollers at her that gently dandled her in the water. Paige leaned over to help her up the little ladder on the back. Lisa expected someone else to take a turn, and she was a little surprised when Chris reached to lift the ski into the boat.

"Are we through?"

She came up the ladder into the boat, aware that her breasts bounced a little with her steps and glad that she hadn't chosen anything more revealing. Nicholas, Ray-Banned, tan-abbed, grinned. "Looking good out there, Lis."

Paige was now holding a cell phone and pointing it at her. "Ashley called from the house. There's some cops there wanna talk to you."

"Really? Cops?" Her wet soles slipped on the varnished wood, and she shot a hand out to steady herself on the rail. She reached for the phone, but Paige said, "She already hung up."

"Cops? What for? Did they say?"

Nicholas said, "Probably found all those pills in your purse."

"That's not funny. I don't have pills in my purse."

"Just messin' with you."

"She said they didn't say," said Paige.

Chris curled the prow back toward the Carpenters' dock on the northern shore a couple nautical miles away. A thought about Nicholas flicked by *(He's a jerk! Didn't know that!)* as Lisa turned her back on the others to towel off her head, feeling self-conscious. She was suddenly an outsider about whom there was a mystery, maybe a tragic or sordid one. She fell instantly into a black hole of anxious speculations. Her mom felled by a stroke? Her dad have a heart attack? Her little brother hurt or killed in a wreck? The day had gone too well, she'd been enjoying herself too much; she just knew that some payment was being arranged Up There in exchange for getting what she thought she'd wanted. Just when she was feeling on top of the world, sure to get a Tri Delt bid (and not just because she was a legacy), sure that this school was the right choice, sure that college itself was a grand and glorious enterprise where she would make her mark, sure that her new friends, all Plan II honor students, would be lifelong attachments—well, that's when pride sets in and the gods plot your fall, isn't it?

No, that's crazy. Maybe it's nothing. Had she left her Visa card at Saba Blue last night? Too many mojitos? That's nuts, too—they wouldn't come out here for that, would they? And how'd the cops know she was here? Tera must've told them—which would mean they'd gone to her dorm looking for her!

By the time the boat was back-churning to ease alongside the Carpenters' dock, she was almost sick. Worried, jittery, standing on the dockside of the boat and waiting to leap over the gunnel, she half-expected to see policemen there, but it was only Ashley, though behind her Jorge was walking up the slope to the house, as if to report that the boat was coming in.

"What's going on?" she asked as she scrambled out of the boat. "Are the police still here?"

"Uh-huh." Ashley's brow was knotted in earnest and her mouth was set in a thin, prim line, giving Lisa the impression that she didn't care for how this visit had upset plans for partying. "And they like searched the house!"

"Searched it?" said Nicholas. "Did they show you a warrant?"

"No," said Ashley. "And they said they weren't *searching,* they were just *looking,* and they always had a 'warrant'"—here she sneered to imitate the way the police had supposedly said it—"to look. *A looking warrant.*"

"What were they looking for?" Lisa was vastly relieved now that it didn't seem that a Johnson family emergency had provoked this visit, but she was growing bewildered. If not an emergency, what? A mistake? Mistaken identity?

"They said nothing in particular."

"I bet!" said Nicholas. "Tell 'em they—"

"I've already called my dad," interrupted Ashley. "He talked to them. It's nothing to do with us," she said, not looking at Lisa. Lisa blushed and set off up the grassy slope toward the house. She was embarrassed to be the source of this disruption, but now she did feel calmer. It wasn't her family, and it was probably either a complete mistake, or maybe a theft she didn't yet know about.

Jorge greeted her at the patio door, sliding it open, and saying, very earnestly, as if he were the host in a funeral home,

"They're out front in their car."

"Did they say anything about what they want?"

"Nope. They did look around, though."

"I heard."

"But they, you know, didn't open drawers, just walked the rooms."

"Okay. Thanks." She smiled weakly and falsely at him as if to suggest that this was all nothing to her, really. As she passed into the living room, feeling chilled by the frigid AC blowing on her damp swimsuit and hair, she had a moment's hesitation, almost turning right into the guest bedroom where she and Paige were to stay tonight to dig out a t-shirt and shorts, at least, from her duffle. But she nixed that idea out of fear that the officers would think she was dawdling or balking, or simply unconcerned. Truth was, she was scared spitless and still had no earthly idea what they might want. She didn't do drugs. Yes, her driver's license had been altered a tad to bump up her age (okay, but do they track you down for that? Don't think so!), but she'd never written a hot check or shoplifted (here in Austin, anyway, and not in the past four years!)....

She went out the front door, grateful for the heat. At the curb sat an off-white four-door sedan with black tires, a Ford maybe, two figures inside it. As she came down the walk, the driver's window slid down. The cop behind the wheel wore wire-rimmed sunglasses and a green polo, and his fair hair was sort of spiked in a modish way. He looked young and harmless except that when he hiked up his glasses his gaze was, well, *impertinent,* she thought. Offensive. Sexual but also somehow derisive.

"Hi!" she said brightly, in her best head-cheerleader mode, "I'm Lisa Johnson, and they said you needed to talk to me?"

"Yeah," said the driver. He turned off the Ford's engine. "You know a Jason Sanborn?"

"Jason? Yes! Is he okay? Did something—"

"You seen him in the past twenty-four hours?"

"No! What's this about, anyway?"

"Mind telling me what your connection is to him?"

"My connection? I, uh, guess you could say we're friends.

We used to date."

"When's the last time you saw him?"

Lisa was reeling. She scanned her memory, but images from her life in Mesquite were jumbled, hazy. She felt she'd all but forgotten the place existed, aside from her family and their home. Everything that had to do with Mesquite seemed to have occurred eons ago. "I guess right before school started here, you know. A month ago, at least. What's going on? What's happened?"

"You got no idea, right?"

"No," she said, though she was thinking, *With Jason, you never know what it's going to be. Almost nothing would surprise me.* "No idea."

The cop's face softened, his gaze met hers with something approaching kindness—or, at least, hostility had momentarily evaporated. Now he was going to be the bearer of bad news.

"There's an Amber Alert out for his stepsister. He took her from the family home and ran off."

"You're serious?"

He nodded.

"Look," said Lisa. "I know Jason's done some really freaky things in the past, but believe me when I say he did not kidnap that kid! When I saw them together, he was treating her like a little sister and she was eating it up."

"When was that?"

"This summer. I don't remember what day. At the mall, at the shop where I worked. Amy's Hallmark," she said, then added, inexplicably, "The day his dad married the girl's mom."

"Uh-huh," said the cop. The radio crackled as a voice spoke over the air; the passenger-side officer responded with something unintelligible to her. The driver reached to turn the ignition key with his right hand and held out his card between the fingers of his left. "Whatever. Any way you look at it, we need to talk to him. I'm thinking you're gonna want to do the right thing if you hear from him. Just call us. It'll just be between us, you know. He doesn't have to know."

"Okay," she said, taking the card.

"It's my cell," he said, pointing to the card. "Any time, you know. Even if he rings you up at two A.M."

"Okay."

"Like I said, he doesn't have to know."

This second mention offended her. "If he calls and I call you, he'll know it because I'll tell him."

"Whatever."

His window slid up; the Ford eased away from the curb, and she stood at the end of the walk trying to compose herself. She felt eyes on her back: her friends were probably watching at the living room windows. They'd expect a report. Lisa was involved in some kind of drama; it had abruptly chopped right into their afternoon and evening's fun but also offered the excitement of something extraordinary.

She didn't want to be the center of this attention. She'd only just begun to feel that she fit into the group, wriggling into a comfortable spot under the protective coloration of likeness: mutual interests, age, background (well, Nausheen was Pakistani). Now she felt that this cloak of invisibility had been stripped away. She was that person you thought you knew but who turned out to know people that the police were searching for.

*Jason! Might've known!* She'd certainly fooled herself into thinking that the letter she'd sent scarcely a week ago or so would ease him out of her life. Well, give her some space, the boys were always saying. That a girl might need space too was never more apparent than at this moment, when she would have to go back to the house and try to minimize everything, to reduce the glare of the spotlight, to ease her new relationships back to where they were before the cops arrived. To erase, somehow, the idea that something had happened to Lisa.

She had no pockets, so she curled the card into her left palm. When she went inside, Jorge was at the front door, but the others had scattered. She felt as if she'd suddenly contracted an infectious disease.

"Everything okay? Anything I can do?" His gold wire-rims pressed the rosy pudge of his cheeks. He was such a sweetheart.

She smiled. "No. Thanks. They're just looking for some information."

Before he could ask what information, she said, "I need to check my cell." She went into the guest bedroom, stripped out of the swimsuit and hung the pieces from a closet doorknob, grabbed underwear, a t-shirt, and shorts from her duffle, and quickly changed. Her cell was sitting on the nightstand of the bed she was supposed to sleep in, and she picked it up and turned it on. While it booted up, she walked toward the kitchen, feeling a need to be present to prevent them from talking, or at least to explain away the interview.

They were all huddled around the kitchen island eating chips out of bags and bottled salsa and guacamole Ashley had made earlier. They all turned to her.

Paige said, "We started without you. Wanna beer?"

Lisa said, "Uh, yeah, okay. Sorry about all the drama."

"Oh, hey, it's okay," said Nicholas. "What's it all about, anyway?"

Before Lisa could answer, Ashley said, "My dad said it was something to do with your boyfriend." A slight interrogatory curl lapped at the end of her sentence.

Lisa burned. "No. He's not my boyfriend. Just a guy I knew back home." She moved to the refrigerator to get herself a beer hoping that she could choreograph herself off the stage, so to speak, but Chris asked, "So what'd he do?"

"They said he—" She stuck her head as far into the box as she could get it. "They said he like took off with his little stepsister or something."

"Took off with her? Like a pedophile?" This might've been Chris asking. They were too quiet, each one listening far too intently.

"No, no! Just—" She took a bottle of Shiner Bock off a shelf and turned to shut the door. "Just ran away together. At least that's what I think."

"My dad says there's an Amber Alert."

*Jesus*, thought Lisa. *If you know so frigging much, why is everybody giving me the third degree?*

"Wow!" said Chris. "Hey, turn on the TV." He pointed at the TV set on the counter, and Ashley picked up a remote to flick the set on. Lisa had an almost irresistible urge to flee the room but reasoned that running away would be worse in their eyes than just staying there. She could pretend, at least, that none of this really had anything to do with her. Ashley surfed through a couple dozen channels without finding any mention of the supposed Amber Alert.

The voice mail alert rang on her phone. She glanced at the screen.

"Wow. Fourteen missed messages!" she blurted out.

"You're so popular," said Ashley. She opened the refrigerator, took out two tomatoes and a cucumber, and set them on the counter. Nausheen reached into a cabinet, fished about for a moment, and pulled down a big wooden salad bowl. The guys were supposed to grill, but they were too engrossed in the *Cops* episode in their own lives to function, Lisa guessed.

She scrolled through the list of messages quickly: her dad (more than once), her mom, her sister, her roommate Tera, the rest from unknown numbers. She was about to excuse herself to call her dad or mom, when Chris said, "Hey! Here it is!"

They all turned to the TV. Nicholas said, "Hey, turn up the sound!" but the alert was apparently almost over, and by the time Paige had located the Mute, the anchor had already gone on to a story about a nineteen-year-old Marine, a recent graduate of Westlake High, who was just killed in Baghdad.

But they'd seen the ID photos of Emily and Jason. The one of Jason was a yearbook picture, eleventh grade. She knew it well. Metallica t-shirt, needing a haircut, a badass snarl worming across his mouth.

"Is that the guy?" asked Nicholas.

"Uh-huh."

"Girl, what were you thinking?"

They all laughed.

"Beer goggles," said Chris.

"Been there!" chuckled Nicholas.

"He's okay," Lisa said weakly. "You know—" she sneered. "High school."

"So did you know anything to tell the cops?" asked Jorge.

"No, not really. I haven't seen him since school started."

"Where's he go?" asked Jorge.

"He hasn't graduated yet."

Paige laughed. "Ooo, she likes the young stuff."

Lisa thought she might just wither and die on the spot if they didn't shut up.

"Boy toy!" said Nicholas.

"He's a dropout!" Lisa declared. She felt tears coming and clenched her jaw. "He's a dropout and a loser, but we've been hooked up since we were in like the sixth grade, and . . ."

They were looking at her, frozen, waiting for her to break down and bawl, but she wasn't about to cry in front of them.

"And I wrote him a letter over a week ago to tell him it was over! Okay? Is there anything else you need to know?" Dead silence. "Excuse me," she murmured and strode from the kitchen.

In the guest room, she sat on the bed, buried her face in her hands and sobbed silently into her palms, rocking herself. *God, whatever he's done, it's my fault for sending that letter!* She had known he wouldn't take it well, no matter how she said what she had to say, but she didn't want to face the truth that it would tear him up. She'd kept thinking, *Well, this is civilized, grown-up, the way people who are adults talk to one another about important things,* as if to forestall or disarm him from having some kind of . . . some kind of Jason reaction!

She sucked in a few ragged breaths to bring herself under control, swiped her eyes on the hem of the spread, then scrolled her "Missed Messages" queue, wondering who to call back first. She wished she'd driven her own car here. She knew she'd lost it in front of her friends, even made it sound as if she didn't believe they had any right to know what was happening. But that was what Jason had done to her. Toxic baggage she'd brought along. Damn him.

Paige knocked, then cracked open the door.

"Can I come in?"

Lisa nodded. She turned the face of her phone against her

thigh. "I'm sorry I was so rude in there."

"Oh, hey," said Paige.

"I guess I'm pretty upset."

Paige sat on the bed beside her. Lisa's next thought came unbidden: *You need a bigger halter top.*

"Don't sweat Ashley. She's always a tight-ass."

"Oh. Okay. Thanks." So it wasn't just her imagination. She was spoiling Ashley's party.

"Do you need to go someplace?"

"I don't know yet." She wondered if they'd sent Paige in to ask because they were uncomfortable. "Thanks, though. Maybe."

After a beat, Paige said, "Do you think that he like, you know, abducted her or anything?"

"No."

"But why would they have an Amber Alert if the kid wasn't in danger?"

Lisa thought now that Paige had come alone to get the inside scoop for herself under the guise of being considerate.

"I don't know why. I think it's going to turn out to be a big mistake." Her gaze flicked reflexively to the detective's card on the nightstand.

"Do you think he'll call you? *Did* he call you?"

"I don't know for sure. He doesn't have a cell phone that I know of. Could be some of those numbers are from him calling from a pay phone or somebody else's cell."

"He doesn't have a cell phone?"

"No." Had she stuttered? Why was everything about Jason such a frigging wonder to these people?

"Are you gonna call him back?"

Lisa struggled to keep her patience. "I haven't called anybody back yet. I hardly know what's going on."

"I guess I ought leave you to it, then," Paige rose from the bed. The backs of her thighs were stamped with the bedspread's weave, and wrinkles criss-crossed her cellulite. "Just let me know if you need to go somewhere."

"'Kay. Thanks, Paige."

"No problema."

The phone in her hand was weighty as lead. To consider speaking to one of these callers made her gut ache. She wished she hadn't told Tera where she was going today; then the only way she might've been reached was through her cell, and maybe she'd have been lucky enough to have kept it off all evening and night, though that wasn't her habit. Her dad, who paid the bill, expected her to keep it on; it was one of the many little struggles between them. Sometimes the phone felt like an ankle monitor. Dad could get really freaked out over nothing— not that *this* was nothing. Mom was more level-headed and calm, relatively speaking.

She pressed number three on her speed dial.

"Lisa, honey, where are you? We've been trying to get hold of you all afternoon! Your roommate said you were out at Lake Travis. Are you all right?"

Lisa reassured her mother, explained the cellular blackout, saying, "I've been out on a boat all afternoon," and told her about the police interview. No, Jason had not called, she said (not mentioning the other "missed messages" she had yet to identify and return), and she was safe. She'd told the police that she would let them know if Jason did contact her.

"They say he was headed for Austin," her mom said. "I think that boy has always had a screw loose or something."

Austin? Lisa's heart sank. For certain, then, she would hear from him. He was coming because of that letter.

"Emily's dad lives here," said Lisa. "Maybe he's just bringing her here to see him."

Brittany sighed. "Oh, honey, I just wish you'd stop feeling like you have to defend him all the time! You're better off without him and you know it."

The part of herself that was a daughter arguing with a mother about her boyfriend flared up suddenly inside and she opened her mouth almost as a reflex to object, but that old muscle had grown a little lax in the past couple of months. She found herself saying, "I know, Mom. You are right. But I wasn't defending him as much as I was just trying to find the simplest, most logical reason why they ran off together. Innocent before proven guilty, okay?"

"Hon, here's your dad—he wants to talk to you."

"Mom! Just tell him I can't talk now. I'm driving back into town. I'll call him later. Love you!"

"Love you," Brittany said quickly and instantly disconnected, eager to do the proper parental duty by not keeping her daughter on the phone while driving.

Not surprisingly, while Lisa mulled her options, her phone rang; the screen ID'ed her dad, of course. She let the call shunt to voice mail and tossed the phone onto the bed. The phone was like a portal to a spooky room of old bad feelings, and they were creeping over her. Jason was haunting her. Example? Feeling she had to stick up for Jason when her mom criticized him.

Being hooked up with Jason was like having a debilitating affliction that came and went, one that sometimes kept you from doing things other kids did. He didn't have the money to go here or there, he didn't like the people that were going to be here or there, he didn't like to hang with "posers" and "dorks" or people Lisa might otherwise choose to be around when away from him. Being on this campus had been a tremendously liberating experience: she didn't have to worry about whether he felt he was fitting in, or whether he was being snubbed, or if he was having a good time. Her therapist had talked about being codependent, but getting yourself unhitched from that symbiotic attachment was hard. For instance, you might think that if you wrote a "let's just be friends" letter, then that would effectively snip the last thread and you could float free. Instead, the letter had landed like a bomb in his life, and next thing Lisa knew, Jason was all over the TV as the object of a manhunt. Worse, he was obviously on his way to see her.

Jason couldn't just drive to Austin like any normal person! *Yes, Mom. You are right. You are right. You are right. Only trouble is . . . if I'm not on his side, who is?*

"Goddamn you, Jason! Get out of my life!"

# Ten

He did Robert Earl Keen covers to warm up, then strummed a rough-hewn version of the Lisa song, working out the harmonic kinks, the lyrics, the rhymes, the rhythms, free to do anything since no one stopped to listen and the only audience he held for more than a few bars was Emily. She went into the mall to call her father and reported back that his answering machine must be full of messages because it left no cue for her to speak.

"It's this old tape kind. I bet Mom's left him a thousand and he probably just doesn't want to listen to them."

She repeated this trek every fifteen minutes or so, each time knotting the end of Trippy's tether to a bike stand. People here were less enthusiastic about listening to a busker than they were at, say, the plaza outside the Angelika in Dallas. Maybe street music was too common. He ran through his repertoire of originals within a half hour and started back at the top, finally catching a few passing listeners, all students so far as he could tell, who favored him with appreciative expressions that applauded his enterprise if not a snatch of music their ears had plucked from the air. Most tossed change into his open case. That no one sat out a tune from opening to ending was disheartening but not utterly discouraging. It relieved him of performance jitters, allowed for experimentation or some correction of mistakes, like making different takes of a track during a recording session. He kept telling himself, *You have to start somewhere.* This was a good warm-up for a session on Sixth Street later.

As evening eased into the plaza like a fog, duos, trios, and quartets of young people emerged from the dorm wearing the bright and eager look of a Saturday night's fun lying before them like a banquet buffet. Girls had shed shorts for hip-hugging, belly-button-boasting two-hundred-dollar jeans and designer tops, ears, and necks aglint with bling. They cast perfumed wavelets of aromatic confetti as they passed like parade float fixtures on their way to somewhere better. The shadows of twilight brought a softer air to the little plaza, diffused the sounds, and shifted the eye to the lights inside the building, making Jason feel less visible but more audible, more fitting to the setting: he was part of the Austin nightlife now.

While Emily was inside, two girls stopped to complain about his cat being tied up. Later, a dude who was a dead ringer for the youth pastor of their church back home asked if Jason knew if his spot was authorized for busking. He said, "Uh, yeah. Got a permit and all."

Emily worked her own deal on passers-by. She concentrated on young women alone or with one or two friends. She stepped into their paths while holding Trippy in her arms, then announced, "My cat is a magical cat! He has special powers!"

Invariably, this stopped them. "Special powers? What kind?" they would ask, smiling sweetheart smiles. Most of them were big sisters or little sisters, former or present babysitters, lovers still of stuffed animals and flower-adorned stationery.

"I can show you, but only if you promise to donate to his cat-food fund!"

"How much?"

"Oh, anything!"

Then she'd tell one girl to cradle him in her arms like a baby. When Trippy was comfortably abed in her arms, pillowed against fragrant breasts, he had a very visceral purr that vibrated through the holder. His eyelids drooped and he'd smack his feline lips as if dreaming of his mother's milk.

*Awww. Awwww. Awwww. Such a cute kitty!*

"So how is he magical?" the holder might ask, eyes glazed, almost drunk with kitty-ecstasy.

"He makes you feel all better—all goose-bumpy!"

True enough, they'd laugh. Each would take a turn, smiling in self-mockery. Knowing they'd been taken but not taking offense, digging into little leather club-going purses the size of cigarette packs dangling on the ends of long spaghetti straps, giving her quarters and now and then a buck or two.

Emily grew bored with this game, but Jason saw that between them they had scored enough for dinner. He already had money enough to eat without his take this evening, but using cash earned by performing appealed to him.

By now it was full dark. They toted their bags and his guitar into the mall, where Emily tried once again to contact her father and Jason ordered a chicken sandwich and fries for her at Annie's Burgers and a cheeseburger and fries for himself. He watched the counter girl make chocolate milkshakes from scratch and ordered two.

They both buzz-sawed their food, and Jason unexpectedly found that on the other end of his appetite lay not satisfaction but rather a heavy sadness and agitation that made him yearn to fall into a twelve-hour coma or get stupid drunk and stupor stoned. Somewhere, at that moment, Lisa was doing something, maybe even nearby. A stone toss, a big loud shout away. Or not. Emily pulled a book from her pack and stretched out on the booth bench across from him with her back propped against her pack and her feet dangling off the end. Trippy lay leashed underfoot.

"What's that book?"

Emily angled the cover: *A Single Shard*. Went back to reading.

"Any good?"

She sighed with impatience. "Really good." Went back to reading once again.

"What's it about?"

"Jayyy-son!"

"Come on. I might want to read it."

"Okay. It's about this orphan in Korea in the 1300s, and

he's poor and doesn't have any parents or anything and lives under this bridge with a friend, and he starts learning to make pottery and everything from this master pottery maker." She paused to see if she'd said enough.

"The 1300s?"

"Yes." When he kept silent, she turned back to the book.

He gave her a minute or so. Speaking of orphans, "What do you think we should do if your dad's not back tonight?"

"We'll go to the library."

"What for? To get more books? Do you have a card or something?"

She snickered. "You'll see."

They killed an hour sitting in the booth, Emily reading, Jason writing in his journal about their adventures, toying with lines for lyrics (*carryin' home inside their heads / no one to trust / lookin for bread . . .*), humming tidbits, poking at the membrane of diatonic melodies hoping to find a hole. He'd pause, look up, feel his hand grope for the wedge of bad news between the back cover and last blank page, resist, dig back in. It was far past time to call her cell; he should've done it before even leaving Mesquite. But never too late. (*Far past time / never too late . . .*) A 99 percent chance he'd get her voice mail. What to say? (*Tryin' to say / what can't be said / tongue like a rock / heavy words from yesterday . . .*) *Hi. I'm in town just off the cuff and on the spot and spur of the moment. Didn't get a letter. What letter? You sent a letter? We need to talk. Say anything but that. Please let me see you. Please can I see you? Promise I won't. Promise I won't fucking cry?*

Some time past eight, Emily went to call again and came back jubilant.

"He's there now!"

"Hey, great! Did you tell him where you were? Is he gonna pick you up?"

"Well, I didn't actually get to talk to him."

"Who'd you talk to?"

"Nobody, but, see, I let it ring about thirty times and the machine never came on at all. That means he must've come home and milked all the messages."

Jason sighed. "So why didn't he answer the dad-blasted phone?"

"I dunno. Maybe he's in the shower or went to the store or he's out in the yard or in the garage or something. Now I know he's home, though, and you can take me back there, okay?"

"Doesn't he have a cell phone?"

"He owns one, but he never knows where it is or remembers to turn it on."

"He must be your absentminded professor."

"He's not absentminded. There's lots on his mind—just not boring trivial stuff."

"I forgot—he's *certified* as a genius. Do they give you a wall plaque or a lapel button for that?"

"Shut up."

By Jason's reckoning, the hike was a good mile and a half back to the townhouse, but a renewed energy lightened his step. The night was now his to devote to finding Lisa, making his case, begging for a chance. Emily flagged, though, fagged from the long day and last night's fitful sleep in the Africans' van. He hoisted her backpack onto his shoulder and left her free to carry Trippy, but she trudged along despite her presumed eagerness to get home.

The porch light was on but the mailbox was still full. Emily grinned as she stood at the door and rapped the brass knocker with her personal signal.

While they waited, Emily jostled the cat in her arms. "I know he's gonna love Trippy. Trippy? We're home, kitty! Aren't you glad?"

Another brassy rap. Someone called out, "Hang on!" They heard lock-scratching on the other side, then the door cracked open. In the crack, a young, sleepy-eyed female face appeared.

"Who are you?" Emily demanded before the girl could speak.

"Jenny. Who—"

"Where's Daddy-ji?!"

"Uh, oh! You're Emily?" Now she was all smiles, tugging the door back. She was braless in a large t-shirt with a Princeton logo, sweatpants, her red hair all tousled. "Gosh, come in. Did he know you were coming? We just got back from Brussels and we're like totally lagged."

The living room was dark, the blinds drawn; Jason could make out the shapes of a couch, a love seat, an easy chair, the cold, dark face of a TV. On the couch lay an uncoiled sleeping bag, halves spread open, the body rumpled like a huge depleted python, head a pillow in a white case. Sweat on Jason's arms and face crystallized in the AC's chilly air. An overhead fixture in the hall backlit the girl as he and Emily stood with their gear.

"I'll, uh, get Vinnie. He's zonked."

"Professor Patel! Who are you?"

"Jennifer Bolens. His TA—graduate assistant."

"I know what a TA is! Where's Melody?"

"She graduated. Your dad didn't say anything about me?"

Emily dropped her bag and released Trippy to the floor. "Daddy-ji!!" she yelled. She started for the hallway, but the girl walked in front of her, backwards.

"We got in just a while ago and we were up way late last night with some people from the conference and the plane from New York had some trouble so we had a stop in Detroit, so he's like really exhausted—"

Emily pushed past her and banged on her father's bedroom door.

"Daddy-ji! It's Emily!"

While they waited, the girl noticed Jason as if for the first time. She converted both hands into spread-finger combs and raked her hair back from her face and over her shoulder.

"I've been hoping to meet you," the girl said to Emily. When Emily pointedly ignored her, Jennifer swung toward Jason as if she'd meant him all along. "Hi, I'm Jenny."

"Jason."

The Certified Genius eased his bedroom door open only enough to wedge his moon-shaped face into the crack, four fingers curled around the edge. Cuff of a pj sleeve. He had Emily's dark brows and large glassy brown eyes that looked very nearsighted and weak without the correction spectacles offered. He blinked at her.

"Punkin? What are you doing here? Where is your mother?"

"Oh Daddy!" she wailed. She launched vigorously into a tale of woe at a breakneck pace, rat-tat-tatting and spraying him with her blast of non-stop complaints as he stood squinting as if struggling to wrench himself into full consciousness. She *hated* the house, the town, her stupid school especially, it was full of redneck ignoramuses, and Jason's dad was always mad at her and her mother always took his side—

"Wait, wait, wait!" protested the CG. He held a palm up. Jason caught a glimpse of a buttoned pj top, bottoms, opera slippers. Jason had never known any man who slept in matching buttoned pj top and bottoms or who wore those leather slippers. "How did you . . . ?" The professor shook his head as if clearing his ears of water. "Wait, just wait. Go into your room, I will be out in a minute."

He shut the door. Emily whirled and strode off down the hallway and Jason followed. She led him into another bedroom, or what had once been a bedroom. There was no bed, only desks and tables full of unfamiliar computer-like equipment, a huge telescope on a tripod, a beat-up sofa, a large white marker-board on the wall which showed scrawled mathematic formulae or the like.

Emily, obviously stunned, stood frozen, her eyes magnified to huge bold orbs behind her lenses.

Jennifer appeared in the threshold.

"What did you do to my room!?"

"Was this your room?" Jennifer waved to the tables choked with equipment. "It's a project a bunch of us are working on. It's about—"

"My stuff!" Emily yelled. "Where's my stuff?"

Jennifer looked panicky and helpless. "Uh, there's a box in the closet with some, you know, Barbies and things like that. Is that it? Uh, I'll be right back." She fled.

Emily leapt to the closet and breaststroked back the accordion doors. She dropped to her knees, tore open the flaps on a carton, pawed through the contents, raking out stuffed animals and books and clothing, CDs, Legos, pencils and pens, costume jewelry, loose sheets of notebook paper with crayoned still lifes.

"What're you looking for?"

"Stuff I had on my special shelf," she sniffled. She was mewling, her jaw muscles working as she clenched to keep silent. "Special things I left."

She jumped up and stormed back down the hall. Jason trotted to catch up with her; she burst through the CG's bedroom door without knocking, screaming, "Daddy! Where are my glass sea horsies!? Where's my scrapbooks? What happened to my room?"

The CG artfully rotated so that Emily and Jason were allowed only a dorsal view of his nude backside with its long, dark cleft—he'd gotten one foot into a pair of voluminous boxer shorts before she'd barged in—and he was hopping awkwardly to step into the remaining leg hole while waving at them to go away or look away. Meanwhile, the TA (pert-breasted, Jason noted) had stripped off the t-shirt, perhaps in preparation for donning a brassiere and dressing, and was seated on the bed up to her elbows in the inside-out shirt.

"You get OFF my daddy's bed!" Emily screamed. She bounded onto the mattress and tackled the girl around the neck, and they both bowled onto the floor. She got the girl in a half nelson from behind, wrapped her legs around the girl's waist, and clamped an earlobe in her teeth.

"Emily!" shouted the CG.

"Ouch! God*damn*! Vinnie! For shit's sake, help!" the girl gargled. She swatted uselessly at Emily over her shoulder. The professor clutched Emily's bony shoulder with one hand while yanking up his boxers with the other.

"Emily! You must stop this!"

Emily released her hug-hold and kicked at Jennifer's back, and the girl scrambled up from all fours, fled into the adjoining bathroom, and slammed the door. "Holy shit! I'm bleeding!" she screamed.

Sobbing, Emily dashed from the room.

"Emily!" her father called out. "What's the matter with you?"

"You mean you really don't know?" said Jason.

Jason heard the front door slam. He was still shouldering his own pack, and as he passed through the living room, he scooped up his guitar case by the handle, thrust an arm through the loop in Emily's bag, and chased after her. She only had a few seconds head start and was unencumbered, but when he reached the front walk he spotted her maybe a hundred yards down the street, running full speed back toward the campus. He jogged along behind her as fast as he could travel carrying both packs and his guitar. With longer strides and the physical reserves of an eighteen-year-old youth, he began closing the gap some three to four blocks from the professor's house.

Then Emily simply stopped, plopped down into a hunker on the curb with her feet in the street, put her head on her knees, and wrapped her arms around her shins. He could hear her bawling a half block before he caught up with her. She sob-gasped in huge noisy drafts that alarmed him; it sounded like a medical condition. Jason sat beside her, draped his arm across her shoulder and simply waited out the storm.

When she had worked herself down off the ladder as it were and was two or three shaky steps from toeing earth, he wondered, *What now?* He had no handkerchief but knew she had tissues in her pack and he dug one out and handed it to her. She blew her nose with a snot-rattling honk and balled the tissue into her fist.

"Maybe you shouldn't jump to conclusions." She had no answer, so he went on. "I mean, she did say she'd been looking forward to meeting you, right? If she was, uh, doing something bad with your dad, you know, I mean she wouldn't say that, right? To be fair to him, we didn't give him any warning. We just showed up, and—"

"I tried to call a hundred times!"

"I know. But they were, he was probably totally wiped from the trip and everything. Did you see where she was sleeping on the couch, the sleeping bag and everything?"

"She was NAKED in my daddy's bedroom!"

After a minute, he said, "He seemed really happy to see you.

I know he'd love for you to come back and stay."

She rocked on her heels a long moment. "Jason, did you really break that man's collarbone?"

"God! It was an accident! I didn't even know him. Why in the world would you ask me that now?"

She shrugged. She buried her head again, and though she didn't start crying, she gave off a dark air of utter misery.

"He seems like a really great dude, Emily! I can see why you'd want to, you know, stay with him instead of living in the butthole of the world—Mesquite, Texas. He seems like *really* smart. And that girl Jennifer is helping him do research on that project. You could stay here and help too, I bet. Maybe you and your mom could work it out so that you could stay here instead of in Mesquite with us, you know."

"Mom won't let him have equal custody."

"But maybe now that you've come here on your own, she'll know just how serious you were and will listen when you say you want to live here with your dad."

She was silent and unmoving for a good five minutes while Jason waited. They were a block off Guadalupe, and now the street seemed busier, the nightlife calling from the near distance. Oh, why oh why was he cursed, chained to the obligations of a babysitter in the most important hours of his life, when he so desperately needed to be free? Whoever heard of an eighteen-year-old dude having to babysit on Saturday night in Austin? Whoever heard of having to babysit when you needed to prove to the only girl you'd ever loved that she should come back to you?

He could simply grab her arm and drag her back to her father's place, put the Genius in charge of her.

"Jason, would you be mad if I told you something?"

"Gah! How can I know that unless I know what it is?"

"Okay. Never mind."

"All right, all right! Emily, I'm getting really tired. I need to rest, you know, catch some zzzz's, get my breath. All this crap hanging around here waiting for your dad and then walking to the dorm and the mall and then back again and then all that crap back at his house has got me really wore to the bone." This was an expression his mother was fond of, he remembered. Wore to the bone. "What the fu . . . fuhddledy-diddle is it you wanna tell me?"

"I think I want to go home. To my mom."

"Great! Well, go tell your genius dad to take you or call her to come get you or get him to put you on the bus or buy you a plane ticket."

"See. I knew you'd get mad."

"I was making suggestions."

"I can get there without your help. I don't need you to tell me how to do it."

"Fine. Go, then. Get up right now and stick out your thumb."

"I would, but I have to get Trippy from Daddy-ji's."

That blasted cat! He'd totally forgotten about it. "So do it. Go get your cat and hit the road."

"I can't go back there. *Ever!*"

"Well, Jennifer looks like the kind of girl who'd take good care of a cat."

"Would you go get him for me?"

"No. Absolutely not."

"Okay, then I'm staying with you until you go home."

"Suit yourself. Maybe I won't ever go." For the first time since leaving Mesquite, he remembered that he was due in court on Monday morning.

"Then I won't, either."

Enough of this. Lisa, Lisa, Lisa. "I need to get to a pay phone."

"There's one in the library."

"What's this about the library with you?"

"There's a secret place in it I go sometimes when I want to hide from people. I bet we could sleep there."

He considered this a moment. "So you'd be okay there if I had to go see somebody for a little while?"

"Yes, but only if we can come back tomorrow and you get Trippy."

"It's a deal."

# Eleven

Burl was careful to arrive five minutes early for his 5:30 meeting with Lisa's father. Since the doctor's clinic was closed Saturdays, the parking lot was empty but for a white Astro van with a magnetic sign reading *Martinez Cleaning Service* on its passenger door. He pulled his pickup into the first slot left of the handicapped spaces in front, shoved the shift into Park, cut the AC to low and left the engine idling. The clinic was housed in a brick one-story stand-alone between a Taco Bell and a vacant lot owned by the clinic, where presently, amidst the crabgrass and knee-high thistles adorned with windblown plastic sacks, two boys, hatless in the blazing sun, were tooling their bikes up a makeshift plywood ramp propped by paint buckets. Though he couldn't hear them, their wrist-twists and cheek-bellows signified motocross imitations. *Rudden, rudden, rudden.* They flew up and off the shaky ramp, and he reflexively registered the danger, parental warnings scrawling across the scarred surface of his exhausted brain. But his spirit was balmed by memories of being that young, of having fun! Jesus, it's great to see this, really. They're not parked in front of a TV or PC, how rare. Good old-fashioned American boyhood, *Saturday Evening Post* style. Mayberry. Beaver. Those shows weren't that far off the mark, were they?

So what the hell happened to all that, anyway? One minute your kid is on skates or at the top of the monkey bars hollering *Hey Daddy! Look!* and the next he's wrestling you to a fall requiring stitches and you're sitting in a parking lot waiting for his girlfriend's father to come rub your nose in your own crap.

Taco Bell's smell provoked a boil-up of hunger and nausea in his blood. He needed to eat, but nothing would satisfy. Aside from the peanut butter sandwich and glass of milk he'd wolfed hours ago, he hadn't eaten since yesterday's lunch, and with only an hour's nap around noon today he was limp as a rag. Too anxious to eat, really, yet anxiety led him toward filling himself with something. In the old days, or not so old days, several slugs of ice-cold vodka could knock the edge off in seconds flat. Just the thought of it. . . .

Moments later, a navy-blue Tahoe wheeled into a handicap slot, leaving one empty space between the two vehicles, like men choosing urinals in a public restroom. Burl scurried to be first on the ground, thinking this would show deference, but he found himself having to stand alone while the doctor took his sweet time shutting off his engine. The Tahoe's windows were an opaque smoky tint, and when the doctor finally exited, he was slipping a cell phone into the pocket of his white golf shorts. He was wearing pristine running shoes and a blue-striped polo, Ray-Bans. Not offering his hand, he nodded and said, "Mr. Sanborn."

Burl pulled back his hand, which had been at the ready, and said, "Doc Johnson, thanks for meeting with me," even though the meeting had been compulsory for Burl and at the doctor's behest.

The doc stepped under the awning to the clinic's front door, bent over a silver hoop, and peeled away several keys as if turning pages. Burl studied the man's haircut. He had thick sandy hair that appeared to have just been—not barbered—*styled,* the strands so coarse and sturdy that his 'do probably stayed in place even on the links in a stiff breeze. Jason said Dr. J paid a hundred bucks a pop, or so Lisa claimed. Burl's haircuts ran twenty, including tip.

They went through the clinic door into a lighted reception area. From somewhere in the building came the whine of a buffer or vacuum. Without checking if Burl were behind him, the doctor struck off down a corridor whose floors had been freshly waxed. There was not a soul in sight, and the setting spooked Burl. He'd presumed the doctor had chosen to meet here because he had other business to attend to, that the choice of venue was incidental, not deliberate, but when the doctor stepped into his office and hit a light switch, and as the fluorescent fixtures blinked on, Burl suspected that the doctor didn't want him anywhere near his home. This was the way you'd meet a hitman, a blackmailer, a family black sheep who shows up looking for a handout.

"Go ahead and sit there. I'll be right back."

Burl took the patient's seat—a wing chair with a green and gold brocade fabric—in front of the large cherry desk. In Lisa's father's absence, Burl unleashed his gaze. A triptych of photos in a hinged gold frame was propped on the glossy surface within arm's reach, and Burl dared to lean and tilt it slightly. In the center panel the Johnsons stood in beachwear, Dad and Mom with the three youngsters arrayed before them, Dad with his hand on the older girl's shoulder, Mom with a hand on the son's. Lisa in the middle, looking about twelve, still a kid. This would be about the time, then, that she and Jason became pals at Sunday school.

He delicately shoved the frame back into its original position. On the wall the usual panoply of framed certificates, diplomas, Burl guessed. Every doc displayed them. Was it a legal requirement or just custom? Who among the patients would know if they're phony? Framed prints of ducks. Oh, yeah, the doc owned expensive shotguns, shot skeet and quail and ducks and dove, he recalled. Golf. Skiing. Did doctors take courses in med school about occupationally appropriate recreation? If it costs a wad the size of a grapefruit to do it, a doc's bellying up at the counter to sign on. Even the ones Burl had known in AA had no idea how the other half lives, and they always had the hardest time breaking down. Perhaps they imagined it'd be easier to admit your mistakes to your lessers than to your peers, but in the end they found that it's really harder.

The other man returned carrying a canned Diet Coke, stood behind the desk, and slipped a tattered *Golf Digest* from a nearby shelf to use as a coaster.

"Sorry. It was the last one."

"It's okay. I don't drink them."

"Oh." Then: "Oh, yeah."

Burl unpacked that to hear, *Oh yeah, I just remembered what it is you drink.*

"I could get you some water. There's not even coffee on the weekends."

"I'm all right."

The doctor leaned back in the leather armchair and crossed his legs so that one big white Nike was jammed against the drawer facing Burl and its toe stuck over the desktop like the nose of a turtle. He rocked a little.

"Thanks again for agreeing to meet with me," Burl offered, hoping to move things along so he could bolt. He felt as if he might explode. Dr. Johnson's studied coolness—he was still wearing those fucking Ray-Bans, for Christ's sake! Like a Mafiosa!—was eating at his patience and tolerance. Burl felt the doctor was toying with him.

"It's like I told the detective," Dr. J said. "I could just give out her cell and her address on the phone to him or to you, but like any good parent, I want to protect her."

*From??* "I understand. The Austin police, they're the ones asking. They're looking after her interests, too."

The doctor stopped rocking and gave Burl a half-smile. He suddenly uncoiled his crossed leg, dropped that foot to the mat, and swung forward. He used both hands to remove his sunglasses, pinching the corners between thumbs and index fingers. He set them upside down on the desk, ear-piece ends pronged at Burl, miniature horns, and he blinked as if unaccustomed to the light. His irises were blue-green like Lisa's.

"I'll give them to you, but I want something in return."

"All right," Burl replied instantly.

"I want your pledge that your boy will never contact my daughter again. In any way. Snail mail, e-mail, text message, phone, all that, any of that. And I'm gonna obtain a restraining order so he can't get his sorry self within five hundred feet of her. You know I gave in when your lawyer wanted that auto theft charge dismissed, but it looks to me as if it doesn't do one damn bit of good to cut that kid a break. I've got half a mind to have it reinstated."

The doctor aimed his gaze at Burl's eyes but quickly flicked his own uncovered eyes away when Burl didn't flinch. Burl hardly knew which phrase in that little speech to handle; the whole thing made him seethe. He clenched his jaw then ground his teeth, chewing on nothing for a moment. The pledge of non-contact? That was laughable. Clearly Burl no longer had the slightest control over Jason. Restraining order? Jason had done nothing to Lisa, so there were no legal grounds. *You're a poor excuse for a parent, Mr. Sanborn?* Yeah, that one might stick.

But Jason's "sorry self"? *Those are fighting words, Dr. Johnson.*

Burl cleared his throat. "I can promise that Jason will steer clear of Lisa. But I want you to know that all this business about an abduction is a big misunderstanding. He and his stepsister decided to go to Austin so that she could be with her father there. My wife, Lily, she panicked about it all, and just between you and me, she overreacted. She doesn't want anybody's kid to get hurt, and that's why it's important that the police down there talk to Lisa in case Jason should happen to call her."

"They want to use her for bait?"

Everything the doctor said seemed calculated to provoke Burl. He counted to ten. "Well, I'm sure they want to know if he calls her, of course, so they can talk to him. I know they wouldn't put her in harm's way." Burl leaned forward, pushing his heated face over the doctor's desk. He'd taken about all the ass-kicking he could stand here. When you got right down to it, the Austin police could probably get Lisa's information from UT security and the phone company, but that wouldn't mean that Burl would have her number. "Look, I don't know what else to say to you, sir. I sincerely apologize on behalf of my family for whatever trouble my boy has caused you and your daughter. And, believe me, I wouldn't have dragged you into it today if I could've helped it." He wanted to add that if the good doctor had just given the fucking number over the phone, neither one of them would have to be here now. A ten-second phone call instead of two hours out of their lives, two hours the doctor could spend bass fishing or on the links or shopping for another quarter-million-dollar toy.

The other father sat mulling it over. It was apparent he wanted to make Burl grovel.

"So you promise to keep that boy away. Do we understand each other?"

*Am I a fucking idiot?* "Yes, like I said, he won't be coming around or getting in touch some other way."

Dr. Johnson slid open the top right-hand desk drawer, plucked out a prescription pad, and tossed it onto the desk. He dug around in the same drawer and produced a blue-capped Bic. He held it expertly, knuckles dusted with reddish-blond fur, a big gold class ring with a ruby, like an extra knuckle, prominent on his finger. *The doc prescribes. Burl takes his medicine.*

He ripped the page from the pad, crabbed it with one hand across the table toward Burl, spinning it to put the print toward him. "That's her dorm room number, and the one below is her cell."

Burl folded the paper and slipped it into his shirt pocket. "Thanks very much, Dr. Johnson. I—my whole family—we all appreciate this very much."

"Don't thank me; thank my wife. She's the soft touch."

---

Soon as Burl had closed his pickup door, he clapped his dead cell phone to his right ear while the doc got into his Tahoe, flicked on his headlights, and pulled away from his handicap slot. *Let him think Lisa's getting the call right this minute.* Truth is, if he turned on the phone there'd be at least one message from Lily, and, while it could be news about the kids, most likely she'd found out that he'd talked to that reporter behind her back and played down the danger. Burl couldn't help himself.

He was miming a call partly because his hands were trembling too much and he didn't feel nearly calm enough to drive. *Asshole!* What he wanted to do was back the pickup to the edge of the lot, then cram the pedal to the floor and slam right through the front of the building. See if he could put the bumper of the F-150 right up against that cherry desk. Like as not, though, Burl would be the one to take the hit for the damage. Nobody else. Typical, really.

"Goddamn you, asshole!"

He slammed his open hands against the steering wheel. *You really are a piece of shit, amigo, you know? What with making me drive down here and kiss your ass just to get a phone number, showing me your kingdom, your power and glory. Talking about my boy like he's John fucking Dillinger or Charles Manson, for Christ's sake. Don't you have any idea at all of what Jason feels for your daughter? Doesn't that count for anything?*

Burl counted to ten, slowly, this time aloud. He said the Serenity Prayer, but it didn't make him feel serene, only weary.

He drew the slip of paper from his pocket, turned on his phone, closed his eyes and lay his head back while it booted up. The ring tone alerting him to two missed messages from Lily brought him back to consciousness.

He dialed the number on the prescription pad. It rang three times and slid into voice mail with a simple "Hi, it's Lisa. Leave me something!"

Burl said, "Lisa, hon, this is Jason's dad. I'm sorry to be bothering you, but Jason's gotten himself into a pickle, and we think he's down there in Austin and there's a pretty good chance he'll try to contact you. Would you please tell him to call us? It's really urgent. And would you please call my cell if you hear anything from him at all? He's with his stepsister, and her mother is pretty frantic to know if they're all right. That's all we want to know—are they okay. Thanks, hon."

He sat looking at the face of his Nokia, the phone cradled in his palm, his hand lifting and sinking as if weighing it.

Maybe he should've mentioned the police, but, really, the Austin cops probably had already found out where Lisa lived and maybe her number as well.

He sighed, hit number two on his keyboard.

Lily picked up on the first ring. "Burl, did you get it?"

"Did you hear anything from Jason and Emily?"

"No. Nothing! The alert's been on all the radio stations, I heard it on KRLD, and the detective here told me that it's on those electronic billboards, too, on the interstates. It'll be on the six o'clock news again on all the stations, so we're hoping that will help." She spoke as if Burl were a well-meaning neighbor. "Did you get it, Lisa's number?"

Burl sighed. If he said yes, she'd insist on having it. "No, dammit all. He backed out. He said he didn't want to get her dragged into our sorry business."

"Well, that's nice!"

"He's a piece of work, all right."

"Are you coming home now?"

"I think, I'm thinking of other leads. I'll be there in a bit."

"The police don't need his permission to check with Lisa!"

"I know that, and I guess he does, too, and he just figured the least he could do is send me on a goose chase, make me jump though some of his frigging hoops."

The silence hummed and crackled, and Burl wondered if she'd covered the phone and was talking to someone else, but then she said, "Good God, I am so tired!"

"Me, too."

"Just try to be here when the Channel 39 news comes on, okay?"

"Wouldn't miss it for all the world," Burl said wearily and punched his disconnect tab.

He stifled an impulse to turn off his phone. Lisa might call, and so would Lily, if she heard anything. But he simply could not face the shit-storm going on at home: the phone ringing every other minute but never the call you're waiting for, only neighbors, coworkers, the idle curious, people with so-called leads *(saw some boy had a little girl with him at a truck stop up in Oklahoma last night, must of been a little past midnight)* and the yakking goes on for twenty minutes before the caller realizes the missing kids are white, as widely advertised. A midmorning call from their lawyer, berserk, ballistic, raging and raving—Jesus Christ, you'd think Jason had pistol-whipped the guy's granny the way he acted all indignant, saying that Jason had screwed up his case with this, made him look like an idiot, and so forth. Burl, irritated, would explain to him, *We've got other problems right now besides how all this will play out Monday morning,* and the lawyer would insist, *You'd better hope he shows, that's all I've got to say, or his ass is grass, my friend. This little prank is gonna loop us into a ton more billable hours, I gotta warn you that,* followed by a rundown on the impending civil suit and how Jason's antics might affect this suit which Burl had yet to mention to Lily. Burl would finally snap, *Look, gotta go. Can't tie up the line. I'll get him there.*

Strangers strolling nonchalantly through the house from room to room blabbing on their cell phones, setting their crap down on tables and chairs, on the sofa, like they're all at a . . . a ballgame or a campout, and Burl's home was community space. That cameraman wearing the photo vest one-handing a kitchen cabinet door open and moving things about on the shelf with another, without asking, not diddly squat. *Can I help you?* Burl would reluctantly ask. *Uh, yeah,* he says, only the faintest bit sheepish, *like you got any sweetener?* The satellite vans from the TV stations pulling up, pulling away, going off, coming back, the ebb tide of the daily news, one event momentarily eclipsing another, their generators churning diesel fumes. Nigh onto impossible to drive down the street on this block because they're parked on both sides. Jesus, a frigging circus.

At the Bennigan's on Peachtree Road, he trekked grimly past the archway into the bar and moved on into the dining room, where a hostess led him to a table that was uncomfortably close to the bar. He took a seat with his back to it. He looked at the menu, noting a new item, a chipotle burger. Wouldn't that call for a margarita? Fajitas, enchiladas—a couple of Tecates? As if reading his mind, his waitress, Norma, a young Hispanic woman with highly arched brows clipped close and a hole for a nose ring, said, after he'd ordered the burger, "And what to drink? We've got a Happy Hour special on Cuervo Gold margaritas!"

Burl, rattled, said, "Uh, well . . . " and kept his eyes on the menu, but the girl, smiling, joshing him, cajoling, said, "On the rocks or like a Slurpee—your choice!"

"Like a Slurpee?" he asked, though he knew.

"Yeah, you know, frozen. Like a sno-cone. They're great! Lime and salt on the rim or not, whatever. Can I get you one?"

"Uh, okay, yeah." He was still staring at the menu and pretended that his answer had been to some other question asked earlier before his attention had been scattered by his growling stomach and the photos of food in the menu. He hadn't ordered a margarita. He'd ordered a Slurpee or a sno-cone, something cold and salty to drink, with a refreshing lime. It wasn't vodka, not a vodka drink of any kind.

"And—uh—Miss?" he spoke to her departing back. When she turned, he said, "I'd like some ice water, please."

"Sure thing!"

In a bit, a frosted fishbowl hoisted on a thick crystalline stem and disk appeared on the table before him.

"There you are!"

The waitress wheeled off before he could react. *I don't drink them. Oh. Oh, yeah. Your sorry ass son.* The doc's own offspring were nothing but sterling examples, of course. Must be superior genes, right? *Like I told the detective, I could make things easy for you and your boy or I can figure out a way to make you grovel and bow and kiss my ass, and of course that was the thing that popped to mind first. Thought I'd require your presence here at my almighty temple, where I could sit on my throne and make you feel like a worm there in the chair on the downside of that desk. Take out a restraining order. Pledge this, pledge that. Vow this, that. Promise. You're a sorry-ass excuse for a father, and your son is a sorry-ass product of your sorry-ass loins.*

*You know what, dickhead? Raising kids is a hell of a lot easier when their mother doesn't die on you.*

The margarita was like the very small heart of a glacier, so cold it gave off wisps of icy vapor, and its green tint, pale and hinting of the lime flavor and juice, was restful to his eyes. The ridge was ringed with rime, my boys. The ridge was ringed with rime. Anybody ever make a vodka margarita? Would any harm come of just bending over and sliding the tip of his tongue along the salted rim of the glass? What harm could that be? He'd been outside and sweating, no telling how much salt he'd lost in the past few hours between the heat and humidity and the nerve-wrenching interview and such. It seemed like the least they could do was to have brought the water first.

"Miss?" he hailed a passing waitress, not his own. "Could I get some water, here?"

"You bet!"

But the water didn't arrive. The contents of the fishbowl looked like a Slurpee or a sno-cone, sure enough, and the icy lower end of the straw, he saw after drawing it up from the deep bottom of the bowl, was shaped like a spade. So you wouldn't have to be *drinking* this concoction that was not vodka, would you? Spoon it. Like ice cream or sherbet. Yes, that was it—lime sherbet, with salt. Cooling to the throat, the tongue. You sip from this—what the effing eff was the size of this eff-er, anyway? A quart?—thing, it quenches, it cools the blood, the brain. Just one good swallow of this fruity iced refreshment would help no end to soothe your overheated skull, ease your jangled nerve endings, untie the knot between your shoulder blades. Cool and damp between your fingers as you grip the frosted belly of the bowl.

He uprooted his phone from his pants pocket and mashed number seven on his speed dial. Three rings cycled to voice mail: "Hey, this is Jack! Leave a message, and I'll get back!"

"Hey, Jack. It's Burl. I'm sitting here in Bennigan's with a huge margarita in front of me that I swear to God I did not order but I'm afraid I'm about to just toss the sucker down, like I'm telling myself it's a harmless fruity drink and it's not my own brand of poison, and I'm just messing with myself a dozen ways here. Get back to me if you can. I think I'm okay. But."

He hung up and stationed the phone on the table between himself and the drink. When his waitress arrived with the water, he took it from her hand before she could set it down, quaffed the glass in one chug, and handed it back to her.

"Thirsty. I'll have another just like it, please. And would you please take this?" He flipped his fingers toward the schooner.

"Oh, you didn't like it? Something wrong with it?"

"I don't know. No, it's okay. I just, my stomach's a little upset or something."

"Oh, I'm sorry. Something else?"

"Iced tea, please."

What he should've added in his call was that he'd driven a good piece out of the way to wind up here rather than, say, Denny's or Luby's Cafeteria. Chose it because they served the thing you wanted most and needed least. The drunk was planning the route and driving the truck while the sober fellow lolly-gagged and imagined all was well.

As he was finishing his burger, his phone rang. He jumped six inches. Lily.

"What? What is it?"

"Burl, Vinnie called!"

"Has he—"

"They came to his place but he said they ran away! He said he's been out of town and just got back earlier today and that Emily and Jason showed up and made some kind of scene. She was acting crazy, he said, and then they just took off again! Do you think it's possible she took some kind of drug?"

"What? What do you mean?"

"I mean the way she was acting."

"Are you asking me if Jason gave her some kind of drug, Lily?"

"No. No! I don't know what I mean! Did you see the news?"

"How could I? I was at Lisa's father's office!" Lily seemed unhinged. "Listen," he said as quietly and calmly as he could manage, "What's the point of the Amber Alert now, seeing as how they showed up at Vinnie's place? Did he say anything at all that sounded like Jason was making Emily stay with him?"

"Well, no. But she wasn't herself. I mean, if she went down there to be with Vinnie, why didn't she stay?"

"I don't know, but I think it's time to stop all this nonsense about an abduction!"

"I'm sorry, Burl."

When she didn't go on, he said, "You're sorry?"

"I'm sorry, but until Emily's right here beside me I just cannot do anything that will stand in the way of getting her back. They said the Austin police are on the case now really big. I just don't want to take any chances. I'm sorry if that means that Jason looks bad, honey, I really am, but you have to understand—"

"*Looks bad?* Do you have any idea what the police will do when they're hunting him down as a kidnapper? They're liable to shoot first and ask questions later, Lily."

"Channel 39's news is coming on, Burl!"

He twisted about and looked toward the bar, where a TV monitor hung over the counter. As he squinted, the screen drew into focus: white shoes, the head of a putter, a swatch of green somewhere. He imagined that just over the horizon in the video shot, over on the next green, a black-clad Austin SWAT squad, assault rifles at the ready, poured across the turf in hot pursuit of his son.

"Burl, you need to be here with me! I'm just worried sick about Emily. I just can't stand this waiting alone."

*You're not alone. The house is chock full of people on your side. Not a one of them worried sick about Jason.*

"Well," said Burl, "I think I better drive to Austin to try to salvage a very bad situation." Before he could hear her objection, he hung up. He'd been too lame too long. His boy needed him. His sorry-ass boy needed his sorry-ass dad, whether he knew it or not.

# Twelve

Emily had led Jason up several staircases and through a maze of rooms with shelved volumes, so that when they arrived at her secret spot, he had no idea what floor they were on and couldn't have found his way out of the building without asking for directions. The ceiling was low, and the room smelled musty, the air still, the shelves standing like walls in the dimness. Along one side were study cubbies, each with a fluorescent lamp dovecotted so that a bony light misted the marred tops of the desks. She ushered him to a space at the far end of the room opposite the entry door, behind the last free-standing shelf. The linoleum-tiled floor was dusty, the walls a faded institutional-green plaster.

"Nobody ever comes up here to study."

"I can see why. It's pretty spooky."

"Well, that's why it's safe!"

She left him with their gear and went off, saying, "I'll be right back. When I come in the door, I'll be trying to see if I can hear you or see you back here, so you'll want to pay attention, Jason."

Dusty or not, the floor looked inviting, so he stretched supine on it with his head on his bag. Good to be off his feet. Life was very weird. Not only was he unable to drop this kid on her father's doorstep, he was now following her around like a retard. She had taken to giving him orders, and, weirdest of all, he was taking them. Being in charge of yourself is a hard enough row to hoe, as Meemaw would say, let alone trying to steer a balky kid about from place to place while having to think about her comfort and safety. He'd never had a sibling to babysit, and these many hours since they left home had given him a bigger dose of caretaking than he'd ever dreamed he'd have to do. Sitting with Meemaw for an hour on a Sunday, as tedious as it seemed, was nothing next to worrying about whether an eleven-year-old would have a place to sleep or something to eat, or whether she'd find her certified genius daddy or get her damned cat back. Jesus! Why would anyone want to be a parent?

So if Emily wanted to take charge of their lodging, fine. It was quiet as a graveyard up here with all these dead authors, and, though the air was close and it could use a fan, it was cool enough. Somewhere around ten o'clock. Saturday night on Sixth Street, Lisa prowling with pals or on a date—ten was like just getting started. Jason would go up behind her, place his hands over her eyes—*Hey, guess who? Oh Jason! Gee, what a swell surprise!* Then, later, holding her hand in the dark, in a park, he'd gaze steadily into her eyes, singing, *I don't want to stand in your way / I hear what you say / I'll be there in the wings / while you dance on your stage. . . .* "Free to grow," she says. When he had told her back in May that he was writing a song for her, he had no idea this would be the theme. He sighed, slumped back against the wall and tried to settle in to relax but couldn't. He hadn't known what shape the song would take. Well, he hadn't known a lot of things about his future, a crap-load of things. "Jason, did you really break that man's collarbone?" Supposedly there'd been some kind of skull fracture, too, or maybe just a concussion. That stupid old fucker!

---

That Miata clung to the curves like a squirrel on a limb. He'd eased away from the house thinking he'd take it for a spin and slip it back into the pasture before anybody noticed, but soon as he pulled out onto Barnes Bridge Road and took the first hard turn at double the posted twenty-five and the rear tires scrawled a furrow in the shoulder, he'd had a yen to test the car's maneuverability. He'd give Lisa tips about handling it.

At Collins and Bobtown Road, he turned north and eventually took the access onto I-30, heading toward the interchange with LBJ 635. He swerved neatly like a NASCAR driver across six lanes, whipped hair shuttering his vision. Dodging the oldsters and pokey hooptys, he swung into the fast lane. Kicked the low little car up to seventy, then eighty and eighty-five. Trucks buffeted him with drag envelopes as he nosed in and out of them, and the steering was so tight he feared he'd sail right over the median if he moved the wheel more than a jig or a jog. At these speeds, the little car seemed not so much unstable as subject to wind shear or oversteering, and the smallest object lying in the road could send you flying, flip the thing. It was jittery, skittery, like a big skateboard screaming along at eighty.

He'd not bothered with the belt since he'd not been thinking of driving fast when he vaulted behind the wheel. Way too late to latch it now, with the median and guard rail and curb within arm's reach on his left and vehicles looming in front and beside him. A green Altima climbed his ass and blinked his headlights as if to say, *Move it out, motherfucker!* Jason wanted to brake-check him with the flasher but didn't know where it was. He was sailing along at eighty-two, but the asshole in the Altima wanted *more! more! more!* To Jason's right, a big truck with the blue word FISH on its broad white side churned past backward as Jason zipped by; as soon as he thought it was clear, he swerved into the lane in front of the truck. As the Altima blew by, Jason sat on the Miata's horn, but it only bleated like a wounded lamb. He couldn't resist swinging in behind the asshole and charging up to his rear bumper. Jason would've blinked his lights if he could've found the switch quick enough, but instead wound up flipping him off. The asshole brake-checked him when his bird was still flying, forcing Jason to slap that hand down and grab the wheel all at once as he hit the brakes. As the little car kissed the left hand curb and jolted and fishtailed momentarily into the next lane, he felt that chilling fear that comes when you unexpect-edly lose your footing on a roof that's steeper and more slip-pery than you'd thought. Luckily, a momentary hole in the adjacent lane opened for Jason to plunge into, but it took a wild few seconds to wrestle the car back safely on line.

He'd almost crashed.

He needed to get off, to exit, to slow down—he was not sharp enough, he realized now, not quick enough for this right now. He clamped the wheel and hung on, the way you do at a carnival ride, holding his breath, waiting for an opening so that he could climb down from this precarious perch and make his way to the access and find a place to pull over and catch his breath. He checked the rear and side mirrors for an opening, thought the way was clear but couldn't be sure be-cause his hair was slapping his eyelids. At last he could click right and fall into the far right lane soon enough to exit at Galloway.

Back at city speed—the car seemed to be hardly moving at forty mph—he turned south on Galloway and pulled into the lot at a BBQ place, slid the shifter into Park, took his foot off the accelerator. His heart was thumping wildly, and his head reeled. His hands trembled slightly in his lap. *Dr. J, you shouldn't let Lisa drive this car! It's a death trap! Give her something that puts heavy metal between her and the next guy. The Hummer. Dude, give her the Hummer.*

He had a headache now, probably from the vodka and the heat. He turned off the engine, slipped the key out, went into the restaurant's bathroom, washed his face in cold water. His hair was wild, wind-tossed and tangled, and his eyes showed a nest of red veins. He slicked it down with his fingers dipped in the faucet. On the way out, he stopped by the order counter and got a Styrofoam cup of black coffee whose heat stung the tip of his tongue numb, but it didn't seem to sober him any.

He sat in the Miata sipping the coffee. The implications of what he'd done crept slowly over him. He had not parked her car for the valet; he had taken it without permission and had been gone long enough that somebody had probably told her it was missing.

It got worse the longer he considered it. Lisa hadn't just withheld her permission; she'd said no when he asked. So, basically, he had stolen her new car, taken what old farts call a "joy ride."

He checked the dash clock: 9:06.

He was royally screwed. What could he possibly say? If Dr. J found the car missing, he would ask Lisa where it was. She wouldn't rat Jason out, probably. She'd say she let him drive it. Dr. J would be furious at her and at Jason. But when Jason returned, he'd say, "Dr. Johnson, I took that car without getting permission from Lisa. In fact, she told me I couldn't drive it." Because? Because? Never mind because. "But I know a bit about Miatas—" Yeah, really? Like, they're small? No, more than that! That kid in Duncanville, last year, street-racing one—it flipped, killed him and injured his girlfriend. (Or was that a Mini Cooper?) ". . . know a little about them, and I heard they weren't very stable, they weren't safe, and I was worried. I don't mean that you'd put her in harm's way on purpose or anything, just, you know, maybe you were too busy to really check it out, and I was like worried that she might not know how to handle it, and I was going to show her and everything, with her in the car with me, maybe coach her a little while she drove, but when we got back to the house, she had to go inside for something, and I just hated the idea that she might get out on the road without, you know, knowing enough about how that car handles and stuff."

How could Dr. J be pissed off about that? Maybe he'd even be grateful that Jason had cared for his daughter's safety.

A semi hauling a Home Depot trailer down Galloway blasted its air horn, and Jason was jolted back to Earth. He clicked the key over, eased out of the lot, driving carefully now, and cruised down Galloway, considering his options. He was sober enough now to realize he hadn't been when he and Lisa had driven to the park.

He drove aimlessly for several more minutes, wound up doing a pointless slow slalom around the light stanchions in one of the enormous parking lots at Town East Mall, which had emptied out for the most part, since the stores closed at nine P.M. on Saturday. Then he drove across the street to Denny's and went inside to the payphone.

He dialed Lisa's cell, and she picked it up on the first ring.

"Hello." Her tone was neutral—her caller ID wouldn't recognize this number.

"Leece—"

"Jason! Where are you?"

"At Denny's on Town East."

"I can't believe you just took my car!"

"Does your dad know?"

After a beat, she said, tightly, "I told him I said you could." Jason could tell she regretted covering for him.

"Thanks."

"It doesn't matter because he knew I was lying, and he said if you weren't back by ten, he's reporting the car stolen."

"Shit."

"I just can't believe you did that." Her voice trembled and the register shimmered, disintegrating. "You pretty well ruined my party, I guess you know."

"Aw, Leece . . . listen. I had to test drive the car, honest! Remember what happened to that kid in Duncanville last year in that Miata? I had to find out if it was safe for you to drive— please! Tell your dad that—"

"Oh my God, just listen to yourself! I cannot believe you would try to tell me such a . . . such a fucking lie!"

She disconnected. He was stung. It was maybe only the third time he'd ever heard her curse like that in the many years he'd known her.

The car clock showed 9:43. Time enough to get back for the deadline. There's her dad glowering; there's Lisa beside her dad, miserable and sick of Jason, disappointed to tears; there's the whole damn party spoiled, Chase and Destiny and everybody looking on, gloating as Jason crawls back in shame. He could slip the key under the mat and phone the house, leave the message that the car's here in the lot. Then call his dad or hitchhike or walk home. Burl wouldn't be happy to hear about all this, either.

He turned the key and the engine caught. He groped for the

light switch and quickly found it again. Weird how the new was already wearing off. Now the car was like a giant bobsled on which he'd taken a long, thrilling plunge down a mountain, and Jason faced the task of heave-ho-ing it back up to the summit on foot. With the top down this way, you couldn't even detect that "new car" smell of the interior. He no longer had any interest whatsoever in driving it. He'd had his fun. Now it was just another automobile.

The engine was idling. With the dash illuminated, the gauges were clearly visible. The tank was full. He could probably go four-fifty, five hundred miles before running out. Way down past San Antonio, maybe all the way to Nuevo Laredo. He had maybe ten bucks or so in his wallet. He could make Padre and sleep on the beach. *So what do you do, then, tomorrow morning when you wake up? Walk into the surf and drown yourself?*

*How pathetic can you get?*

Until his meeting with Lisa's father, Jason marked time mentally, not exactly dawdling or procrastinating. It wasn't just fear of facing the doctor that compelled him to keep cruising the streets at legal speed and making turns that put him farther away from the Johnson home; it was a need to solve the mystery of himself. How could he have dreamed that he was "test driving" the car? How could he have actually thought that? Why did he feel it was so goddamn important to drive it right then? She said she would let him, and no doubt she would have, eventually. Maybe tomorrow. Or the next day. What did it matter to him? Why was it so crucial that he had to drive this car here and now? Was it just that he couldn't stand being told he couldn't? Like she was cutting off his balls? He couldn't just take the car back without an explanation, and the test drive story—well, it was complete bullshit. So what could he answer if Lisa or her dad or her mother or his own dad or anybody else asked, *Jason, why did you take Lisa's car?*

*I thought she said it was okay.*

*I didn't think anybody would mind.*

*I didn't trust the valet.*

All these excuses sounded puny. Of course he knew it wasn't okay; of course he knew someone would mind; of course not one thought about the valet's driving had popped to mind at the time.

There had to be either a good story or a real reason. He just kept driving, trying to blank out the space in the dash where the clock was mounted. Jason felt a little as if he were on a scavenger hunt; his task was to find his reasons for ignoring Lisa's "no" and taking her car. *Don't come back until you've bagged it. It will be all your sorry ass has to show for the trouble you caused.*

The car found its way, as if by itself, to a park where local teens often gathered chiefly because of its heavy foliage and proximity to a convenience store where fake IDs often secured beer and cigarettes. Jason wheeled slowly through the parking lot. Scott McKee's red Jeep Cherokee, Sonny Jeter's old worn-out Audi with the torn headliner, Linda Redding's Tercel. Probably Carson Todd's sister Julie, too, and that girl with the butterfly tattoo above her thong strap who always hung with her. Slackers, dropouts, flunk-outs, dopers but no ropers: a crew you could feel comfortable around.

He pulled the Miata next to the Cherokee, unknotted and yanked his tie free of his collar, got out, stripped off the coat and threw it into the seat, undid the makeshift cuff links—this caused a faint ripple of regret as it briefly tipped him back to those moments in Lisa's living room that afternoon, when he'd been so excited, so hopeful that things would go okay— slipped the pairs of buttons that Lily had sewed back-to-back into his trouser pockets with the fleeting thought that since they were his mom's he shouldn't just toss them. He rolled up his sleeves.

He went down the path that curved behind a pecan grove choked with brambles and shrubs and eventually led to a cluster of playground equipment, where, as expected, orange arcs of held cigarettes and shrieking laughter told him they were here and they were stoned. Strolling closer, he measured how far gone they were by how they were treating the swings, the slide, the seesaw, the merry-go-round, the monkey bars. No doubt when they'd arrived, they'd plopped that case of Bud Light onto the picnic table and sat drinking and smoking weed, feeling they were above and beyond this childish environment, much too cool to show interest in the equipment. But now that they'd put away the first case and passed around the X or whatever the night's intoxicant might be, they'd all collectively agreed to pay homage to their former state, indulge in the nostalgia. They were draped across the monkey bars like just-fed snakes; they were sitting on the merry-go-round, screaming as someone pushed them about; they were idly swaying in the swings; they were trying to climb up the slide and into the tunnel.

"You're busted!" Jason yelled.

Someone screamed in fright, but everybody else laughed when they saw him. The roll call met his guess, though he hadn't thought of pairing Jennifer Santos with Scott and wondered what had happened to her banger boyfriend; Julie and her bud Becky were Xed out. "Kiss and dance, dance and kiss!" they kept screaming, like a song, running up to the guys and laying sloppy wet ones on their mouths then skipping off; Scott popped a Bud Light for Jason, then he had another, and when somebody put pills in his palm, he washed them down with a slug from the quart of Jack Black open on the table without even asking what they were.

Within the hour, they'd run out of beer and cigarettes, and Scott and Linda and a guy clad in hip-hop jeans whose back pockets slapped his calves said they'd go for more. When Linda said she was working steady as a "cosmologist" now and offered to treat everybody, Jason wondered if he had heard right and shook his head in confusion. He was getting messed up, all right. But he had a way to go, yet, since he was still aware of his surroundings.

They went across the street to the Pic-n-Pak, came back with two cases and several packs of smokes and a fistful of Slim Jims and said some ancient fucker behind the counter thought he was on CSI or something and like put Linda's license under a fucking microscope, which was funny, you know, she said, because she'd had it altered a long time ago but was actually over twenty-one now, and they all thought that was hilarious.

A while later, Scott and Linda and Becky were singing, at full drunken volume, "This jerky makes me urpy!" to the tune of "The Farmer in the Dell" when somebody saw red and blue lights flickering through the trees and shushed everybody. Jason had been stretched supine along the incline of a seesaw with his head lower than his feet, looking at the night sky and thinking that the ambient city light was like a cataract that kept you from seeing the stars and the planets. It kept you from getting off the Earth, like you were blind, sort of, and could never *apprehend the beauty* (the phrase rang in his skull like a portentous pronouncement of a guru). Then Sonny shook him and said, "Hey, dude, check it out. There's cops in the lot."

"I bet that fucker in the store called it in," someone said.

Jason did a sit-up, swung his legs down. He sat for a moment letting his head clear and watched them all creep off toward the pecan grove, giggling and thrashing about, making a racket, too stoned to be stealthy, sober enough to be aware of the danger but not enough to quietly slip away. He saw the lights, then, and had an instant and chilling snapshot in his head of the police car parked behind the Miata while they ran the plates.

Then the poles of light from their big handheld flashes arced and jutted through the trees just like on the old *X-Files,* and the crew who'd staggered into the woods scattered crashing through the undergrowth, stifling their laughter, calling out to one another. Jason hoisted himself upright and numbly stood, thinking that he was better off stock-still in the dimness under the swing than careening off into the shrubbery and tripping. Thinking he might safely scoot away, get across to the store and pose as a customer, he eased away from the playground, stumbling in the dark, not sure what was ahead but aiming his body toward the lighted storefront across the way, where there now seemed to be people standing around the door.

A light beam fell over his shoulders and a shout rang out, sharp, urgent, and angry, and he took off running, stumbling, light from the storefront making everything below his waist as hidden as the floor of the ocean under the surf, and he slogged, tripping, as they came on behind him, still yelling, then he reached the street and propelled himself forward over the curb, head out front, arms flailing, and a figure moved toward him from the doorway of the store, as if to intercept him, not a cop, and that confused him, and he tried feinting left and nearly fell but the man's gray head reflected the store light and Jason saw his arm coming up with something in it, and then he was yelling at Jason.

Flying on, Jason tried to dodge, but then the man reached to grab him, and Jason crashed into him, bowled him backward. Then Jason tripped over the sprawled form underneath, kicked wildly to be free of grasping hands, stepped on something squishy as he bolted up, pedaling frantically to get away, but then he was slammed hard by a flying tackle. It seemed to take only an instant for them to roll him on his stomach with his face scraping the asphalt. They jerked his hands behind his back and cuffed him.

---

Emily startled him by kicking the sole of his shoe. She was carrying books in her arms.

"Hey! You didn't even hear me come in, did you?"

"No. Were you being stealthy or something?"

"No. You weren't paying any attention! Jason, we have to be on guard! The library closes at midnight and they'll probably come around checking and stuff."

"All right."

"Were you crying?"

"No!"

"It sounded like it."

"Well, I wasn't, Emily! All the dust up here, it's clogging my nostrils."

She sat cross-legged on the floor and fanned the books in front of her. "Which do you want—*Le Petit Prince,* the new *Harry Potter,* or *Goodnight Moon?*"

"Don't you think we're both too old for *Goodnight Moon?*"

She shrugged. "Were you crying about Lisa or your mom? It's okay if you were. I've cried a lot today. It's only fair that you get to."

"I'll let you know when I want to take my turn."

He scooted up with his back to the wall, and she collapsed beside him, close enough to be hip-to-hip, handed him *Goodnight Moon.*

"Read this one to me."

"You sure?"

He opened the cover, and her cheek fell against his bicep. "'In the great green room, there was a telephone, a red balloon, and a picture of the cow jumping over the moon.' You must know this one by heart."

"Yeah. 'And there were three little bears sitting in chairs . . .' Jason, why do you think your daddy married my mom?"

"I think it's because they're both alkies, but he told me she reminded him that he could laugh."

"He doesn't laugh much."

"Not lately, that's for sure. Mostly barking. At me. If I'm not around maybe he'll be happier."

"Mom said she married him because he was always there."

"What'd she mean, like your dad travels all the time?"

"Maybe. But more like when she says something he looks at her and answers. Daddy sometimes has his head in the clouds. I hate that girl."

"She's just his assistant."

"Assistants don't take off their shirts in people's bedrooms."

"Maybe your dad hates her anyway and just can't wait to dump her."

"Could that happen?"

"Yeah. Sure. Happens all the time."

She scooted closer into him. "We have to be really quiet after midnight. The guard will stick his head in down at the end. They'll have a big buzzer go off in a minute to tell people to leave."

"How do you know all this?"

"My friend Stacy and I—her dad's a history professor—we each told our parents we were spending the night at the other's house, and we came up here and hid out until after midnight."

"Why?"

"We were going to write a mystery story together that takes place in a library after it's closed, and we needed to do research. We dared each other to do it."

"Wow! What happened?"

"We made too much noise when we were prowling around and a security guard caught us."

"Did you get into trouble?"

"Boy, I'll say! We can't ever play with each other again."

"When was this?"

"When we were in Miss Wilson's third-grade class. We still text each other with code names, though."

"What's yours?"

"I can't tell you—it's a secret! We swore!"

"I guess if I learned it, you'd have to kill me."

After a moment, she said, "We'll have to be really quiet now." She lay on her side again and yawned. "Aren't you sleepy?"

"Naw. Not yet. I'll stand guard. You can sleep."

"Okay." Then, after a minute, she said, "Jason, you know how I always say I hate living there and everything?"

"Yeah."

"There's *some* good things."

"Yeah?"

"I'm really really glad to have you as a brother. I always wanted a big sister, but you're the next best thing."

Jason laughed. "Story of my life." *Next Best Thing*. Song title.

"Didn't you ever want a sister or brother?"

"Oh, yeah. I guess."

She was quiet a good while, and in the silence he felt the tension of her yearning to hear more of his answer, to hear he was glad to have her as a little sister. The thing about Emily was that even though you might think she's complicated and tricky, in the end what she wanted was always pretty clear. But he wasn't sure, yet, that he was glad. The responsibilities he'd come to know quickly and unexpectedly were burdensome.

"When we get back home," he said, "maybe we can do stuff, you know."

"Really? Like what?"

"Maybe go to Hurricane Harbor or something like that. Hurricane Harbor's really cool—they've got this really humongous slide. It's great because you get going down it maybe a hundred miles an hour or something before you hit the water at the bottom. It about ripped my swim trunks off one time."

"I'd be too scared to go down that."

"Naw, you wouldn't. You'd go with me. You know, tandem. Like skydivers do it."

"I bet Mom wouldn't let me go."

"Hey, you and me, we're way past that, right?"

Her head, nodding, bumped against his arm. "Why don't you lie down and I'll sing you the Emily song?"

"You finished it?"

"Not yet. But I have a couple of verses."

She sank to the floor and lay curled on her side with her cheek propped by her hands, the top of her head against his thigh. He leaned to slide his case over, plucked up the snaps, lifted the guitar out. He'd set the words to a lullaby-like melody, folk-tune-ish.

"*I know a girl named Emm-a-lee,*" he sang softly, lightly strumming. "*She has to wear glasses 'cause she cannot see. . . .*"

"Jason!"

"Take it easy. Stay tuned. *But she's just so darned charming and so full of dare / That ponies and pigs give their tails for her hair.*"

"That's better." She yawned. He waited a bit, as if finished, strumming and humming, while her body seemed to ease, sinking, into itself. Then he went on, hardly a whisper. "*Where oh where, will Emm-a-lee go / when the dogs start their howlin' / and the moon's all aglow? / What oh what will Emm-a-lee see / when the cats have their kittens and the honey's from bees?"*

He sat stock-still for a long moment listening to her shallow, steady breathing. Trying not to jostle her, he reached into his pack and slowly drew out a sweatshirt, folded it, eased her head up off her hands, and wedged the makeshift pillow under her cheek. Then he sort of keeled over himself and fell into a fitful sleep while the building went on thrumming quietly and distantly like a machine on idle.

# Thirteen

Paige drove Lisa back into town, and Jorge went along for the ride. They tried to make her feel better by claiming that they wanted to swing by his place and pick up some CDs, anyway, that he'd forgotten to bring.

"If you need anything, please call," urged Paige as Lisa was getting out at the dorm. She appreciated that they'd been so-licitous and sensitive toward her feelings, but she ached to imagine that when they got back to Ashley's house, they'd spend half the night yakking about Lisa's trailer-trash soap opera.

It was close to seven o'clock, and Tera was sitting in her robe with a towel swathing her hair as she texted her boyfriend who went to Baylor. They often drove the hundred-mile stretch between cities on weekends alternately, so Lisa was a little surprised to find her in the room.

"You're not going to Waco?"

"Stevie's coming down here tomorrow. 'Sides, I thought maybe, you know. . . ."

Gal-pal solidarity or just another person itching to live in-side somebody else's high-voltage troubles? "Well, thanks. The police came out to interview me. They said —"

"I saw the Amber Alert," said Tera, nodding at their TV set perched on Tera's dresser. She spoke approvingly, as if it were a special program that Lisa had had a hand in produc-ing. On the set, presently muted, QVC beamed a special on

**205**

cubic zirconia earrings.

"I haven't seen the whole thing yet."

"Oh, I should've saved it for you! But I guess it'll show again."

"I'm sure it will make the reruns."

Lisa collapsed back on her bed. Tera wasn't her bosom-buddy or even a confidante, but it felt comfortable to be with her right now. She didn't know people at the party Lisa had just ostracized herself from. Though she'd been Lisa's room-mate since the start of school, Tera's attachment to her guy in Waco had made her inaccessible during leisure hours, and so they hadn't grown *really* close, but, in the present instance, she was like the person seated next to you on the plane that you wind up revealing things to that you'd never confess to friends.

"I love this guy but I'm sick of him."

"Lovesick?"

"No, definitely not. Sick of love."

"Didn't you just write him the 'let's be friends' note?"

"I'm afraid it didn't sink in or he just can't accept it and that he's coming here to badger me or beg or whatever."

"Maybe the police will get to him first."

"Maybe." She had mixed feelings about that—it would be a relief but would only put off a later encounter. And she'd feel guilty that he risked so much to see her but didn't get to.

"Well, if they don't—" Tera picked up a pair of scissors and brandished them. "Not to worry. We'll get a crew to cover your back, girl!"

"Oh, I don't think he'd . . ." But she didn't know for sure, did she? Maybe the Jason she knew eons ago could be trusted, but. . . .

"I guess you have to do something dire enough that he finally gets it." Tera grinned. "You know what I did to this nerd who kept bugging me in the tenth grade? I told him to think of us as Lancelot and Guinevere and that if he wanted to hook up with me, he was gonna have to perform some really cool stunt or retrieve something for me, and so I told him this bull-shit story about how this older guy I'd known had taken some thong panties he stole from my drawers and took them up to the top of the water tower in the middle of Lufkin, you know, and was gonna like fly them like a flag but where he put them it turned out nobody could see them—and I told this nerd he had to climb the tower and bring them back to me."

Tera laughed.

"That was inventive." Lisa was thinking that Tera had a mean streak she hadn't noticed before. Her major was fashion merchandising. "Did he buy it?"

"Well, he did go all the way up. That night. In the rain. And he called me from his cell. He wanted me to drive down there and stand at the bottom and he'd wave just so's I'd know he really did it. I just asked him, 'Well, did you find my panties?' He said he couldn't find them anywhere. I said, 'Well, you were *supposed to*. Maybe it was some other water tower. I forget.'"

She laughed again.

"And that was the end of that?"

"Uh-huh. Never called me again. Somebody did put sugar in my gas tank senior year, though. I bet it was him. It was just the kind of thing he'd do."

Safe in her dorm room and away from the scrutiny of her aspirant peers, Lisa listened to all her voice mails. Several had been superceded by the interview with the detectives; Alison wanted to know what was going on and could she help. There was a call from Jason's dad alerting her to Jason's plans to come to Austin and asking her to call him if Jason contacted her.

Apparently she was message central for this uproar.

"Do me a favor, okay?"

"Sure."

"Take my phone, and when it rings, go ahead and answer it and pretend you're me."

"Well, I'll be your executive assistant, how's that?"

"Whatever."

"Why not just turn it off?"

Lisa sighed. "He might call."

Tera had a stack of pirated DVDs that Stevie had burned for

her, so they ordered a pizza and watched *Bridget Jones's Diary* again. Tera said that it was comforting to see Renee Zellwegger so fat.

"Who do you think is hotter—Hugh Grant or Colin Firth?"

"In this movie? Or just in life?"

Tera shrugged. Either would do.

"Ugh. Hugh Grant had that disgusting thing with a skanky whore in L.A."

"Gosh, Lisa."

Lisa sighed. "Sorry to be such a sour puss. Reality's too much for me right now. Saps my imagination."

They played Uno on her bed while the movie went on. They'd seen it twice already. This time through, Lisa was acutely aware of the story's bad-boy/good-boy dichotomy, and knowing where and, even more, *how* the flips would come annoyed her.

Her phone rang several times, and Tera did a right proper job of screening, including two calls from her dad, and about a dozen from Mesquite classmates just now getting the news. Lisa did take another call at midnight from Jason's dad, who was at a Motel 6 out on I-35. All she could do to reassure him was to say that if Jason called her, she'd let him know.

"If you hear from him, just tell him I'm here, please," Mr. Sanborn said. "I'm not mad. I'm *worried*. I don't know what else to do but just stay close and hope he lets me know when he needs me. Please tell him that I'm here for him, you know?"

"Okay," Lisa told him. She added that he might want to go walk Sixth Street, that Jason might be busking there.

That Jason's father was in his corner gave her slack to worry less about him. She turned off the phone's ringer at one A.M. They turned out the lights and Tera went promptly to sleep. Lisa lay awake thinking about Colin Firth and Hugh Grant. *Those kinds of guys*, she thought. *Trouble is, life's not that simple. What if Hugh Grant used to be Colin Firth or Colin Firth turned into Hugh Grant or if Hugh had a lot of Colin in him and Colin had a bunch of Hugh?*

She wept silently for a while. What was the cheesy old country song? *I've got tears in my ears from crying over you?*

Thinking about Jason aroused a tumult of feelings that swept over her in passing waves—nostalgia, tenderness, irritation, and guilt being foremost in her heart but leap-frogging over one another in no particular order. Way back when, there'd been the sweet, note-passing junior high phase where he made up silly poems to her and about her ("you're a butterfly I want to flutter by . . .") and the night their church youth group went out to somebody's farm for an old-fashioned hayride in a horse-drawn wagon, he'd kissed her, on the mouth, his lips soft and parted a little, and she parted hers and felt his breath in her windpipe and thought *this is my first real grown-up kiss*, one kiss only, then he held her hand for the next hour, and they were both so . . . so *rattled* that it was all she could do to keep from swooning. Then, sure, it was writing his name all over everything—her notebooks, her inner arm, her ankle, her diary, doodling it and embellishing it, big, little, vari-colored. She'd felt as if she had a huge, delicious secret that she could relish keeping but was too big to contain. She'd felt as if he was a marvelous solution to a problem she hadn't known existed. Writing his name, over and over, retracing her own pen lines, was mysteriously incantatory, as if it might evoke or elicit his form out of the air like a bottle-bound genie. *Jason. Jason. Jason. Lisa Sanborn.* Once this kid named Todd Williams came up behind her in the hall and pulled her bra strap to snap it through her shirt but the catch broke, and Jason gave her his jacket to wear the rest of the day. She knew he said something to Todd about it because he apologized.

Tera murmured something indistinguishable in her sleep. Lisa raised her phone over her face in the darkness, cracked open the cover, feeling the cool blue light envelope her face, the glow shimmering in the gaze of her stunned pupils. No call. She shook her head. *Jason. Jason. Jason.* After junior high there'd been a wonderful honeymoon period sophomore year, the summer after she got her car, and fall of their junior year. Hours and hours on the phone, lunches at school together, head-to-head shots for the yearbook, the football and basketball games him in the bleachers or the stands while she was leading cheers, roller-skating, swimming, and there was that sweet time when he had the idea of getting a bunch of kids together during Thanksgiving and volunteering to bring a dinner to old people, shut-ins (one young guy had muscular dystrophy), and the two of them had given up their own Thanksgiving dinner so that they could load up her car from the kitchen of a downtown mission and drive to apartments in east Dallas to deliver these meals. And Jason was always so cheerful and kind to these people, joshing them, making them laugh—just the way he was with his grandmother, still—and at the end of that day she'd had just a great feeling about having done that, with him, the two of them doing something that nice together, the thing itself bringing out the best in them, and she'd had this really powerfully appealing idea that they could go on the mission trip in the summer together and help build a school in a Peruvian village, how great that would be, to do that together.

That was sort of the beginning of the end, she thought now. He kept balking and she'd thought it was because he'd thought he was too cool to do such a thing (now she knows it was that he didn't have the money and had too much pride to tell her or to ask her for any), and, well, Chase Putnam wound up going instead. Jason had gotten jealous and when they got back accused her of cheating on him, which she hadn't, but when they'd separated because of it, Chase had asked her out. The truth was Chase had been pretty worthless on the trip— it was clear he just wanted to hang out and not do any work.

Then when Jason's mom got sick they'd gotten back together. Maybe it was *because* his mom got sick, she couldn't say for sure. But it did seem that all the innocent fun of their early times together vanished or dissipated in the air. It was so sad to think back on it now, because, though the best feelings of love seemed to get shoved to the side or withered, it was hard to admit that then: when they're gone there's no more reason for the two of you to be together except—in their case—looking after him, worrying about him, helping him deal with his mom's death and his dad's drinking again. It was as if these new developments requiring her loyalty, her energy, and her time were the signs to herself of a truer kind of love, like an adult love, what it means when the vows say *through sickness and health*. So she'd told herself that just because it wasn't *fun* anymore to be with Jason, that didn't mean she could bolt: it meant that if she had real character, she'd stick by him. If you were with somebody just for the fun and deserted them when things got tough, then you had no grit, no perseverance, no value as a true human being.

Then when things got too much for him and he started acting out and acting up, getting into trouble, ignoring his classes and responsibilities, she had to add defending him to people who criticized and judged him to the list of her duties as a true-blue girlfriend.

The graduation party had brought it all to a head, and the negotiations leading up to it were so completely typical of how she was living with all that then. Thinking back on it made her stomach ache. Her mom told her that they wanted to give her a graduation party but "for grown-ups only. Our friends and family."

"I can't invite somebody to my own party?"

"Well, you could have your own party another time. This would be more of a party for the family to honor itself through you, you see?"

The distinction seemed legalistic to Lisa. She was not cynical enough (then) to suspect that her mother might've drafted the terms to exclude the one person Lisa automatically thought to invite. At this time, her parents had taken care not to arouse her protective instincts by being openly hostile to Jason. His infractions then could almost be wedged under the "boys will be boys" rubric, with one exception: the Johnsons couldn't countenance Jason's dropping out of school. They didn't understand it, and it made Lisa uncomfortable to talk about it. For one thing, his grades hadn't been so hopelessly low he couldn't have salvaged them with an honest effort. (This despite Lisa's tutoring him in Algebra II and keeping track of his homework assignments by talking to his teachers.)

Lisa acquiesced, and the date for the party was set for a Saturday night in mid-June. Since she thought of this as her mother's party where she'd be an indifferent honoree, she paid little attention to the plans. Jason found out that his musical hero, Pat Green, would be performing that night at the Yeager Coliseum in Wichita Falls, and he excitedly told Lisa that he'd buy tickets. Lisa then told him about the party. Her characterization was in keeping with her belief that it was for family, and she treated it as a dreary obligation that she couldn't duck out of.

Her father invited two partners at his clinic and their families, along with a longtime office manager and her daughter, and her mother invited her best friend from her book circle and her family, along with Lisa's uncle and aunt and their children. Thus it turned out that several young adults would be guests. Unbeknownst to Lisa, her mother invited two current and one former classmate of Lisa's as a surprise. Considering that her mother had supposedly restricted the invitees to "close grown-up friends and family," it seemed that her mother had cast her net wider than intended, but to Lisa it was just an incremental and accidental escalation. It happened when you sat with a couple friends in the cafeteria and you wound up with an ad hoc posse.

So to her, Jason should be invited. Someone else's daughter might've simply announced it as a *fait accompli,* but Lisa was a dutiful child. Though she didn't feel that she had to have her mother's permission, especially since the guest list had ballooned so, she did believe her mother should be notified as a courtesy.

Lisa drove her mother to her annual mammogram at the Women's Diagnostic and Breast Center at Presbyterian in Dallas. Because the test showed no abnormalities and her mother was relaxed, even jovial, Lisa said, "Mom, I think I'm gonna invite Jason to the party."

"Why sure, honey!" her mother said after a moment. "If you think he'd be comfortable."

"Comfortable?"

"Yes. So many folks he doesn't know."

This puzzled Lisa. "Mom, he knows almost as many as I do."

"I was just worried that he might feel out of place."

"Gosh, he's been at our house a million times!"

"Honey—" Her mother reached over to pat Lisa's thigh. "You know, all the other kids there will be either graduating or have graduated. It might be embarrassing for him, that's all."

Not having considered this shamed Lisa. She was pleased that her mother was thinking of Jason's feelings.

"We'll have to make him feel extra-welcome, then."

Lisa soon called Jason to invite him.

"Really? I thought it was just for family."

"You're family, Jason."

She was talking on her cell phone outside the clinic, standing in the shade on the wheelchair ramp. The traffic noise on Belt Line almost kept her from hearing him snicker. It bothered her that he imagined her family was against him. Yes, they didn't approve of his dropping out—and she didn't, either!—and if they knew how much he'd been drinking lately or about the misdemeanor marijuana charge, that would raise parental eyebrows as well. But she honestly believed that they felt his troubles were just a phase he was going through because of his mom's death.

"Come on. What's up with the attitude?"

"I guess I'm the black sheep, then."

It annoyed her that he didn't seem grateful to be invited.

"You don't have to come if you don't want to."

"Do you want me there?"

"Of course. Or I wouldn't have invited you."

Two days later, her mother proposed a trip to North Park Mall so that "you can buy something nice to wear for the party."

"Mom, I've got a whole closet full of clothes. I'll probably just wear shorts and a tank top."

"Lisa, this is a *garden party.*"

Lisa laughed. "Don't tell me I've got to get a hat!"

"Of course not. But I saw the cutest summer party dresses

at Neiman's, and I need you as an excuse to get myself something."

At the store, Lisa declined dresses suggested by her mother and said that she'd make do with maybe her sleeveless knit dress from L.L. Bean. Her mother bought a rose-colored strapless silk dress with a full skirt for an astonishing $1,100. Lisa considered that you might wear it to a "garden party" only if you arrived in a chauffeured Rolls Royce.

On the way home, her mother said, "Do you suppose Jason has a suit coat or a blazer?"

"Sure he does, Mom. Golly, is this a barbeque or what??" She wished that she'd never agreed to let her parents "give" this party. "Since when does a party in our backyard require a coat and tie?"

"For us it's a special occasion, whether you think so or not. We don't want it to be just like any old Saturday night. It's going to be catered, and there won't be brisket and beans and coleslaw. And nobody said anything about a tie. It's very common for men to wear blazers to garden parties, you know. Your father will be wearing one, believe me."

That was surprising, since her dad's usual outfit for a summer backyard barbeque even with guests who weren't family consisted of old Mexican tractor-tire sandals, golf shorts, and a polo shirt.

"Really? Mom, it'll be a hundred and two even after the sun goes down!"

"Well, you're going to have to indulge us. I'm sorry."

Her mother didn't sound a bit sorry.

---

Once Lisa fully understood her mother's plans, she'd worried about Jason's feelings. It would wound his dignity to tell him outright that he needed to take care in choosing an outfit or warn him that her parents would expect him to behave like the young gentlemen who were, say, presidents of their chapters of the National Honor Society or who went on Christian Youth weekend retreats and led the prayers, the kind of young gentlemen who normally provoked his contempt. She wasn't sure he had it in him to rise to the occasion, and she resented that in an unsettling way. That she might have to be a buffer between him and the world was a familiar expectation, but since this party was intended to honor her achievement, it irritated her to have to walk on eggshells about it. Automatically she caught herself apologizing for him (to herself): he's been poor all his life, he's almost an orphan, he probably has an undiagnosed learning disability, he's been depressed and is still grieving, etc., but the litany had the air of a favorite song heard too many times.

Why couldn't he have been pleased to be invited? Why did he have to act as if he'd just be doing her a favor? Why did Jason make things so hard for himself (and for her) all the time? Why couldn't he just grow up?

Back then they met often at the Starbucks in Town East, and later on that same night, while she found herself waiting for him, having already paid for both his iced café latte and her Tazo iced tea, she shocked herself by considering sabotage. She couldn't say, *believe me, you don't want to be there!* but she could rag on her mother's plans, make it seem like the garden party from hell for somebody like Jason, and maybe he'd back out.

She could just pick a fight about it, but she wouldn't allow herself to do that because she knew the snobbish part of her mother that was inside Lisa herself would push her to it.

All this subterfuge made her feel sneaky. Low as a snake. She sipped the tea through the straw with small, measured kisses, thinking somehow it would be rude to finish her drink before Jason got here, but then she checked herself: he was ten minutes late, goddammit!

In the opposite corner from their usual table, Robbie Baldwin and Carter Bledsoe were writing in spirals while referring to a text splayed between them. A silver-backed laptop was yawning open on the table and its wallpaper was a huge photo of wet-haired Carter grinning while standing on a beach in swimming trunks, so Lisa knew it was Robbie's. They'd been a couple since like forever, she thought. Probably wind up at

Duke together. Carter was a very white whiteboy—no wigger or rapper wannabe, for sure—in fact, Lisa recalled that both he and his longtime girlfriend played viola in the school orchestra. Robbie took a lot of heat from some black kids for not acting black enough, but, then again, her mother was Hispanic, and her enviably unblemished skin was a rich amber.

Lisa picked up her sweating cup, and, leaving Jason's, she struck out toward their table as if on her way out, and when she was alongside it, she feigned surprise. "Oh, hey! Hi, guys! What're you doing?"

Robbie groaned. "Summer project for Miz Wilson's AP World History next fall."

Lisa smirked. "Ah, those were the days."

Carter grinned. "Wise ass."

"I remember she had us working on Sudan and the rest of North Africa."

"We're all about Iraq now. We've got to summarize the history of the whole sucky region from the end of the First World War to Desert Storm and what's going on now."

"School's out. You're getting an early start."

Robbie said, "Carter's volunteered for a project in Atlanta this summer to help ghetto kids." Her inflection was a complicated mix of rue and pride. "I get his help now or not at all."

"And if I don't do it now I won't do it at all."

"What're you doing this summer?" Lisa asked Robbie, thinking surely she'd have lined up something equally meritorious.

"Back at Rio Vista again as a counselor."

"She's awesome," said Carter. "Eighth-grade boys fight to the death to get in her sailing class."

A peachy tint bloomed in the smooth cheek facing Lisa, and Robbie said, smiling, "I hope you do get jealous."

Carter asked Lisa about her summer plans and she answered, then they talked about UT Austin and what Lisa might major in—she told them "premed," and Carter said, That figures, and since she was still standing, Robbie said, why don't you help us? She waved toward the laptop and the empty chair that would put her at the keyboard.

She looked back to the table where Jason's drink was melting into an unpalatable solution.

"You waiting for somebody?" asked Carter.

"I bet it's Jason Sanborn," said Robbie, beating Lisa to the answer. Lisa went over every spike and dip in the wavelengths of Robbie's utterance like a forensics technician searching for the sign of a lie or an identifying characteristic. *I bet it's Jason Sanborn.* Was that *good ole Lisa—always faithful!* Or was it *foolish girl!* Was it teasing or accusatory? How Robbie spoke his name: what did it signify? That Jason was someone worth waiting for?

"It was," Lisa said finally, and scooted back the chair. They set her to work exploring the period of Iraq's independence from British control—1932 to the outbreak of World War II—and she quickly descended into a dense article in an online encyclopedia involving a flurry of competing interests (Arab nationalists, regional tribal leaders, monarchs, the army) who jockeyed for power once Britain had surrendered political authority. As she was cut-and-pasting several passages into a blank Word document for them to refer to later, Jason appeared at the table holding his watery latte. He had on cut-off jeans and a green Mavericks tank top with Dirk Nowitzki's 41 on it. Sweat glued his blond hair to his forehead, and grass clippings were pasted to his neck. She detected the odor of gasoline.

"Sorry I'm late, Lis," he spoke to the top of her head. "Dad made me do the lawn before he'd loan me his truck."

Robbie and Carter looked up, but when he didn't acknowledge them, they pretended his appearance wasn't their business. Lisa pointed at the couple across the table as if to call his attention to them. "I'm helping Robbie and Carter on their AP history project."

Hearing their names, they had to look up officially.

"S'up, dudes?"

Robbie said, "We're doing Iraq."

Carter put a little flourish on a bit of cursive and tossed his Bic onto the page as if he'd just signed a million-dollar check.

"Yeah. Know anything about it? We need all the help we can get."

"You know Toneekwah Jackson?"

"Uh, no, don't think so," said Carter.

"She graduated last year, and she works at Chick-fil-A?"

"Oh yeah," said Robbie brightly. "She's cute."

"Her uncle got killed last month."

"Wow. What happened?" asked Carter.

Jason shrugged. "Got shot. All I know."

"That's awful," said Lisa. Shouldn't she send a sympathy card? Working in Amy's Hallmark had inflamed a profligate card-sending that she'd vowed to curb, but this one seemed justified. Then she wondered how long Jason had known and if he'd been keeping it from her. As he and Carter fell to dueling with Rangers statistics, Lisa ran a news clip looped in her memory—a silent grainy video, US military vehicles moving on a Baghdad road, then the image jittered as shock waves rolled over the camera when in the distance a huge orange ball bloomed suddenly and fire and smoke swallowed half the convoy. No way out for anybody there. Jason joked that the local army recruiters were like a Whac-A-Mole game, and she hated it when he mentioned even casually that a lot of their arguments made sense to him. Her dad had chimed in one night to tell Jason that his own two years in the air force in Japan had been the best years of his bachelor days. Wink, wink. Multinational nookie or something. Join the army and whore your way around the globe.

She realized that she was idly scanning prose she'd lifted and splashed onto the Dell's LCD screen, still highlighted: *Without political parties to channel their activities through constitutional processes, politicians resorted to extraconstitutional, or violent, methods. One method was to embarrass those in power by press attacks, palace intrigues, or incidents that would cause Cabinet dissension and force the prime minister to resign. The first five governmental changes after independence, from 1932 to 1934, were produced by these methods.* She'd hardly paid attention when she'd snipped it— it was the inert lingo of ancient history, like the surnames on bridges, streets, and schools that belonged to the dead who were now unknown and whose importance was a matter of only the barest utility. Now, though, that Jason had interjected this cheery note of mortality into the subject, the passage rang with an ominous and prophetic determinism. That French phrase: *Plus ça change, plus la même chose.*

"Guys," said Lisa, breaking into the argument about whether Soriano was worth $5.5 million, "I think I know what your thesis statement of this summary should be." Jason cocked his head as if puzzled by her interruption, and Lisa, realizing her mistake, added, "the Iraq thing."

She and Jason left Starbucks, and she acted as if she wanted merely to stroll and window-shop. She took his hand—she always appreciated that unlike a lot of guys, he didn't mind holding hands in public—and, though his hands still smelled of gasoline, something left over from her grim thoughts about war casualties made her feel a special connection, and she sent her good thoughts down into the place where their palms were joined and warm. She was extemporizing, regrouping on her original plan to discourage him from going to the party, but, picturing him as a soldier in that exploded war machine, she felt tearful suddenly and, knowing she didn't have it in her to underhandedly manipulate him, said, "Jason, my mom's party's gonna be kind of fancy."

"Yeah?"

"Yeah. She bought an eleven-hundred-dollar dress for it."

Jason did a half-whistle "Whew!"

"My dad's wearing a blazer." She looked at his profile. He'd swung his head away and was gawking off. She wished he'd have showered before he came, but she knew he'd been worried about being late. He wasn't usually inconsiderate that way.

He turned to grin at her. "So I can't come like I am right now, right?"

"Probably not a good idea."

"Would it be okay if I wore like a suit?"

"Oh! You don't need to do that."

Jason chucked with relief. "That's good. The last time I

wore my suit was to Mom's funeral and the cuffs were like halfway to my elbows, remember?"

Lisa laughed. She one-arm hugged him from the side. He could surprise her sometimes with an effort to please. All that agonizing for nothing. But you never knew with him.

"I was thinking we could go to Sym's and find a good sport coat on sale. It could be an early Christmas present or something."

"I can pay for it," he said tightly. "I saved money for the Pat Green tickets."

That he was willing to spend it pleasing her sent a ripple of thrills along her spine. She hugged him again.

"You love me," she said.

"No kidding. Like my guitar loves its strings, like a bird loves its wings, like two hundred puppies, yeah, that's my love for you—two hundred puppies' worth. Two hundred puppies like rolling and jumping around on your bed while you're in its worth. Two hundred *really cuddly* puppies with big wet eyes and happy grins crawling over your feet's worth."

She grinned. A glimmer of the old funny Jason. "But what kind of puppies?"

"Cock-eared kind, a course. All mongrels and strays really eager to belong to you, but they all just had a bath."

They arm-and-armed on a circuit around the lower level, her cheek pressed to his bare bicep. But soon her relief gave way not to doubts or anxiety but rather, annoyingly, to ambition, a restless inability not to let well enough alone and be content with what she'd won. She experienced a greed to execute a wholesale makeover, including a short course in making a good impression. Look adults in the eye when you shake their hands. Tell Mom how nice she looks, how much you love the food, eat a little of everything no matter if you like it or not, use your best grammar, say please and thank you and pardon me when they're required, don't brag about stupid, dangerous, or illegal stuff you've done with other kids, ask my dad if he's been working out. Talk a little bit with each adult not about yourself but ask about what they do, and excuse yourself when you join or leave a conversation group. When it's time to go, tell my mom how much you appreciated being invited and what a wonderful time you had.

And how did she know to do these things? It's not as if either parent sat her down and told her to take notes while they lectured, was it? You picked them up by watching your role models and by wanting to emulate them. Jason's dad was a really good man despite having fallen off the wagon for those crucial months, and though he had some rough edges, he knew how to behave in social situations when he was sober. And Sue had been the sweetest! She was so dear that nobody would care if she made a *faux pas*. Jason's problem wasn't really that he didn't know deep down how to behave—it was more that he took a perverse pride in rebelling, showing his butt. She needed to get him to set that aside.

As they passed Master Cuts, she mentally tacked "haircut" onto the list.

"Jason?"

"Yeah?"

She took a deep breath, held it. Released it.

"Nothing."

"What?"

"Just, you know—thanks for being so understanding about Mom's party."

"No problem."

She slept fitfully until seven-thirty, when she arose and checked the phone again and saw that several people had called, including her dad, more classmates, and a clutch of unknowns, but when she opened them, Jason hadn't left a message.

In the cafeteria, she suddenly found herself the center of attention—Tera had apparently spread the word, and no sooner had she sat at a table with a half grapefruit and a cup of yogurt than a handful of other girls seemed somehow to "accidentally" wind up there as well.

"We saw the alert," one said.

Tera said, "We got a call from the guy's dad last night."

Since Tera seemed to have rounded up this posse, and since

she seemed to be enjoying the role as Lisa's spokesperson, Lisa didn't bother to contradict the mistakes of fact that popped out when Tera told the story of Lisa's conversations with various parties and her history with Jason, though when Tera described the "just friends" letter, Lisa burned and kept her gaze on her gutted grapefruit. She'd let Tera know for sure later that she didn't appreciate having all this broadcast about. The other four girls were vaguely sympathetic, but Lisa knew them by their first names only, and she also knew that most likely they seldom ate breakfast in the dorm cafeteria, and certainly not at this hour on a Sunday morning.

Tera retold her "panties up the water tower" story, and that set off a barrage of yarns about stalking nuisances, pestiferous suitors, scary dudes who hound you even after you've said no twice, scary dudes you finally go out with because you're scared not to, boyfriends of long standing who must be dumped—all that leading inevitably to how each had been cruelly dumped, humiliated, ignored, cheated on, stood up and stood *on*, ground under a heel, etc.

In the middle of which, Lisa's phone rang. Tera was holding it.

"No ID on the number," she said.

Lisa shrugged. Tera was eager to play her part, however, so she gave her audience a saucy, *we'll see about this!* look, pushed the talk button, said, "Hello."

Two seconds later, she grinned and stiff-armed the phone at her, mouthing, "It's him."

# Fourteen

Guadalupe on an early Sunday morning had a holiday-calm, the air cool, the sun out but not yet baking the macadam, with early worshippers disappearing into the little Catholic church across from the campus for Mass. Jason and Emily strolled up and down the avenue looking for a working pay phone, finally locating one at a coffee shop that boasted organically-grown teas and coffee and breads baked locally by, to judge from their hand-crafted labels, artisans who led lives based on a holy poverty and a whole-grain, close-to-nature goodness. He bought Emily a strawberry yogurt smoothie and a huge, carob-encrusted cookie and bought himself a large, plain, very caffeinated coffee. He was too anxious to eat anything. Emily had urged him not to put off his call any longer.

The pay phone was mounted in a hall leading to the shop's rear exit, and the wall had been well-used as a notepad by callers. The management had thoughtfully provided a bar stool. All of this attention and care to the pay phone was partly explained by a sign on the front door: *Please No Cell Phones!! Face-to-face conversations only!*

Emily was seated at a booth nearby. She watched him, as if monitoring him to make sure he made the call. He'd argued that it was too early, that Lisa had probably gone out last night and was sleeping in, but Emily insisted that it was *very* important to talk to her, right? And that he'd said they wouldn't go back to Mesquite until he'd seen her, right? So the call had to be made when there was a chance she wasn't doing something else. Right?

He lifted the receiver, slipped coins into the slot, dialed Lisa's cell number.

To his surprise, someone female, but maybe not Lisa, answered on the first ring.

"Hello."

"Lisa? It's Jason! Hey, sorry to call so early, but —"

There was a weird interval while the other end was muffled and he heard muted voices. Apparently the phone was being passed.

"Jason? Jason? Is this you?"

"Uh, yeah. Hey, listen, I'm at —"

"Where are you!!? Are you here in Austin?"

"Uh, yeah, and —"

"Is Emily with you?"

She sounded panicky, excited, stirred up, not at all like someone who'd stayed out late and was sleeping when her cell rang.

"Well, yeah." How would she know that?

"*Where* is she?"

"Right here. With me. We're like on Guadalupe, you know, right down the street from your dorm."

"Is she okay?"

"Yeah, sure. Why wouldn't she be?"

"Oh, Jason! You didn't *kidnap* her or anything?"

He laughed. "You kidding? Why would you say that?"

"It's what they're saying."

"Who?"

"The police. There's an Amber Alert out for her and you."

"Amber Alert!!? You're not serious!"

"I wish I *were* kidding. Jason, let me talk to her."

He waggled the phone at Emily. "She wants to talk to you."

Emily wiped her mouth with the back of her hand, climbed out of the booth, and took the receiver from him.

"Hello. This is Emily speaking. Am I speaking to Lisa?" Jason watched as Emily listened. She was rolling her eyes now. "No, I'm not in any danger, I'm *fine,* really! Nobody made me come here." She listened a moment, then turned to Jason with a smirk: "She wants me to use the word 'Saturday' if I'm in trouble and can't talk about it—isn't that cheesy?" Since she hadn't bothered to cover the mouthpiece, Jason knew Lisa had heard that, so he said, loud enough for Lisa to hear, "Well, you just said it, didn't you? Say it to her again if you want." Emily put the receiver back to her ear and said, "I will not be saying that word." She listened, but Jason impatiently grabbed the phone.

"Lisa, Jesus, tell me you're kidding about this crap! Kidnap? Man, I would've left her back home if she'd been the least willing to stay. She *blackmailed* me into bringing her along. She just *had* to see her dad. We saw him. Now she's ready to go back home, and I'm gonna take her. But I don't wanna go back without seeing you once and talking to you. Please!"

Lisa was silent, as if mulling this over, so he added, "I've finished the song for you. I've got my guitar."

"You don't mean right now, do you? It'll be a while."

"Oh, no—*whenever*! You say!"

A police cruiser went by on Guadalupe. He was suddenly aware of being a *wanted* person. It was all a big, big mistake, yes, but he sure didn't want to get netted and arrested no matter how briefly, interviewed and probed until he could prove his innocence and the absurdity of the idea that he was a kidnapper.

"Where are you right now?"

"We're on Guadalupe. Some place, I don't know the name."

"Come to the dorm lobby around eleven, okay?"

"Yes. And, listen—*thanks*, babe."

When they hung up, he slid into the booth opposite Emily.

Emily said, "Amber Alert! Wow! I wonder what pictures they're using. What do you think they're saying about what we look like and stuff?" Her gaze went flying about the shop as if she hoped to find a TV monitor. Jason could imagine that her next utterance would be *man, that's so cool*.

"Emily, you told me you left your mom a note. What'd you say in it?"

"Nothing."

"Whatta you mean *nothing*?"

"I didn't say anything."

"So you lied to me about the note?"

She dropped her gaze to her hands. She was busy origamiing her straw into a geometric shape. "Uh-huh."

"God DANG it! Why didn't you leave a note? Now they're all freaked out about you being gone and they think that I abducted you. This is a *federal* crime, Emily! They're going to arrest me and throw me in the penitentiary until it all gets sorted out! Thanks a lot! Just . . . thanks a *freaking* lot!"

She teared up and started sniffling. "I'm sorry. I wanted her to worry. I didn't know she'd get so crazy! I was just mad at her. I didn't even think about her calling the police and stuff. Really!"

"Quit crying! You don't have anything to cry about. *I'm* the one ought to be crying!"

"I'm sorrreee!"

"Just shut up!"

She wallowed in an abashed silence, head bowed, mouth downturned, lips pouty. He finished off the rest of the coffee. Cold now. It was only nine-thirty. He sighed. His brain was awhirl, thoughts scattered.

"What're we gonna do now?" she asked meekly.

"Well, pretty clear we have to get you to a police station so everybody'll know you're okay. And I have to call Dad and your mom and you have to talk to them and tell them that."

"But I don't want to go to the police station, Jason. Puh-leeze! If we go there, they'll lock you up and you won't get to see Lisa. They might call Child Protective Services and put me in *foster care*!"

"Don't be stupid. Besides, I wasn't planning to walk in there with you, believe me."

"I'll go back to Daddy's and get Trippy and they can tell everybody I'm okay. Then Mom can come get me or Daddy can drive me home."

That damn cat! He'd like *totally* forgotten it!

"Whatever."

He got up from the booth. "Come on. We're going to call home."

She stood with her arms folded while he slid one haunch up on the bar stool, fed the phone, dialed their home number after being connected to an operator.

Lily answered. The operator said, "I have a collect call for anyone at this number from a Jason."

"YES!" screamed Lily. Then, to someone else, "It's Jason! He's calling!" Then there seemed to be all kinds of clicking and rumbling and thumps, as if an army had suddenly been galvanized into action. "Jason, where are you! Where is Emily! I want to know RIGHT NOW!!"

"Uh, hey, Lily. We just heard you guys were pretty worried, you know, and we heard about the Amber Alert and I thought we better check in so you guys can call it off. We —"

"WHERE ARE YOU!!??" Lily screamed. "TELL ME RIGHT THIS INSTANT!"

"We're like in Austin, Lily. Calm down. Emily's fine. We just came down here to—"

"PUT HER ON THE LINE THIS INSTANT!"

Emily heard this without Jason's relaying the message and took the phone from him.

"Mom, I'm here. I'm okay, really. Jason and I wanted to come to see Daddy and Jason's girlfriend, and I really didn't think you'd mind. . . ." She listened, nodding, sheepish, "Uh-huh. I know. I should've left a note. I'm really, really sorry. We went to Daddy's, and I thought I could stay there, but Mom—he has a *girlfriend*! This girl who was sleeping there and she took off her shirt in his bedroom and was naked and I got so mad I kind of shoved her and I bit her and she HIT ME!!!, Mom, and Daddy got mad at me and I hate them both and he changed the lock on his door and I couldn't get into his house and this girl put all their stuff in my room and they lost my glass sea horsies and everything, and now they've got my kitten, and —" She burst into sobs. During the course of her tale to her mother, she seemed to have regressed about three years to Jason, all that piss and vinegar gone, just a broken-hearted child pouring out her woe to her mother. He gently took the receiver from her.

"Uh, hey, Lily. Like she's upset and all and —"

"She's upset? *She's* upset!! Jason I want you to take her right now to the nearest police station! Or just call 911! Everybody's out looking for the both of you, and I will not be responsible for what happens if they find you before you turn yourself in! Where are you *right now*?"

"Uh, like I said, we're in Austin. Near the campus."

"Where?"

He hesitated. "Look, she wants to go back to her dad's and get her cat."

"Her cat? Since *when* does she have a cat??"

"She's scared to go to the police station. I already mentioned it to her. She wants to go back to her dad's place."

"I do NOT want her going there, not after what she told me!"

Jason stalled, considering. "Where's my dad? I want to talk to him."

"As far as I know, he's there in Austin."

"Here? Why? When—"

"Jason! You can call his cell. I'm going to ask you one more time—where are you and Emily? I want a *street address*, young man! And I want the two of you to stand right there until a patrol car arrives!"

"I don't know. Thing is, there's something I have to do first."

"Jason, you —"

He hung up on her. After eleven o'clock, after he'd met with Lisa, he'd do anything they asked.

"So what'd she say?"

"We'll go to your dad's place."

"What if they make you stay?"

"All due respect, Emily, your daddy doesn't look like somebody who could do that to me."

"I meant the police! What if they're there, too?"

He sighed. "Why do you care? Why are you even asking? You're gonna get to be with your daddy and your dad-blasted kitty."

"I want to make sure you get to talk to Lisa."

"Don't worry about it."

He was thinking that they should probably leave by the rear exit to the shop. He poked his hand and arm through a loop of his backpack preparatory to suiting up for travel.

"Let's wait until after you see her, okay? I'd hate it if you didn't get to talk to her. It's only an hour from now. What if, you know, we got lost or something? Besides, if she doesn't see me, she might not believe I'm okay, right?"

She sat back down in the booth.

"I want another smoothie, this time blueberry and banana."

He sighed. "Okay."

He went to the counter, ordered for her and got himself the same and a chunk of bread that might serve equally well as a brick in the wall of a third-world habitat. While he waited for their orders, he decided against calling his dad's cell. No need to stir the hornet's nest any more than it was already. Couple more hours, then he'd turn himself in. If his dad was really here in town, Jason could maybe get him to walk in with him—if he would!

When he came back to the booth, she said, "I think we need outlaw names now that we're outlaws."

"Get serious."

"I am!"

She worked slowly on the new smoothie and he nibbled at the bread.

"Okay. What's yours?"

"Sadie Rae."

He laughed. "What's mine?"

"You have to give yourself one."

"Have to think about it."

"You can have Slim while you're thinking of another one."

"Oh. Okay. Thanks. A placeholder name, huh."

*Slim* was a tad better than *Dumb-ass. Dipshit. Loser.*

# Fifteen

The child tapped her shoulder blade, startling her, but Lisa, feigning calm, said, "Hello, Emily. It's nice to see you."

"Hello. Jason wanted to be sure you knew I was okay, so I'm here alone."

"And you're okay?"

"Don't I look okay?"

Emily's hair was in tangles and a pigtail had come unraveled so that the end was frazzled as an old paint brush; her t-shirt had stains on the chest, and her jeans sported knee patches of dust—she might've been camping.

Lisa smiled. "You look like you could use a shower."

Emily sneered. "I'll get one later at my daddy's house. Are you ready?"

"Ready?"

"To go see Jason."

Lisa's pulse flickered as her heart thumped up a notch. "Isn't he here?" She looked off toward Guadalupe, where the Sunday morning traffic had picked up. Hadn't Emily walked to the dorm from that direction? She wished now that she'd told the police eleven and not eleven-thirty. She wanted that grace time with him; she owed him that, at least, but she'd presumed he'd come to the dorm.

"But we were supposed to meet here."

Emily shrugged.

"Where is he?"

Emily waved vaguely toward the campus. "Come on. I'll show you."

"But Emily—we were supposed to meet here!"

Emily stamped her sneaker. "Do you wanna see him or not?"

In truth? Not. "Where will you take me?"

"Just over there." Her head dipped. "He's got a place where he's sitting. He's got his guitar. It's nice. Shady. You'll like it. There's grass and benches."

"Do you know what it's called?"

"Why do you need to know? You think he's gonna like *strangle* you or something?"

"Of course not."

"Well, I don't know what it's *called*. I call it a nice grassy shady spot with benches and stuff where a guy is sitting with a guitar and he's practicing a song he wrote that he wants to sing for this stupid girl he's in love with."

"You don't have to be so snotty, Emily." She wanted to add that she'd surrendered to the impulse to put on lipstick for this meeting and to brush her hair out. She rotated on her heel and glanced back into the lobby of the dorm. Tera was gazing pointedly off in another direction; she and her cohort of aspiring Nancy Drews would track them to wherever Emily led her, so no need to worry.

"Okay. But can we go now? He's really excited to see you." Emily smiled quite insincerely. She was apparently not a person who could apologize; her style of approximating an apology was to shift her mode of behavior to a more civil demeanor as a contrast to her rudeness.

"All right."

Emily struck off toward the heart of the campus, and Lisa followed; she was tempted to look back but didn't, trusting Tera's eagerness to be involved. Emily strode the walk between the HRC and Calhoun and then beside Parlin Hall, where Lisa's English class met, and—very logically—to the other side where the open sweep of the commons unrolled south of the main building. At this later hour on a Sunday morning, they shared the path with joggers, dog walkers, and skateboarders. As they approached beds of blooming flowers, Lisa saw Jason situated just as Emily had promised: on a bench, in the shade, his guitar across his thigh.

He jumped up from the bench before they'd reached him, held his guitar in one hand like a trophy fish, waved widely with the other. As always, he needed a haircut, but his boyish eagerness to see her snagged a reciprocal response in her heart that she'd not expected. She fought it back.

"Hi, babe!"

"Hello," she murmured as she stepped into his embrace. Her heart pounded—his size, the heat of this body, it had been so long, his neck sour with sweat and he was rank as a goat, but, still. . . .

"Gosh!" he burbled. "You're here! I'm here! How about that!"

"Yes."

He turned to Emily. "Why don't you go get us a Coke or something?"

"You don't actually think I want to hang around and *hear* this stuff, do you? You don't have to tell me to go or make a pretend suggestion. I'll be back in fifteen minutes then you better take me to my daddy's house."

She strode off. Jason sank to a crossed-legged lotus on the grass and couched his guitar in his lap. Watching Emily's sturdy back and her purposeful stride, Lisa smiled. "I pity the poor soul who *would* try to kidnap her."

"Tell me about it. She's not always this grouchy, though." He winked. "I think she may be jealous."

"Always the player."

Her light joke apparently jabbed deeply, though. He said, "You know, in all the time we've been together, I've never once cheated on you."

"I never said you did, Jason."

All this was a reference, she knew, to his tired old grievance about Chase. She had *not* cheated on Jason. She wasn't going to reargue all this now, but having to even think about it made her sullen and weary. Across the expanse of lawn, Tera and two of the girls from breakfast were idly lounging on the close-cropped turf. Tera was practicing tai chi moves she was learning in a wellness class. Lisa felt her knees quiver; her breath was shallow.

"Won't you at least sit down?"

She went to her knees, eased one hip down and propped herself with her arm stiff and her palm to the ground.

When she looked back at him, he had the letter between his hands. "This thing pretty much tore me up, Lisa."

She shrugged and looked away. He was going to guilt her, then? Shame her into reneging?

"I just said what I felt, you know. I thought it was something I needed to do."

"I understand, really."

She doubted it, but she nodded as if she agreed. "I only meant that, you know, we're in different *places*, and I, you know, didn't or don't mean just Austin and Dallas, but we're having such different experiences. You know?" she pleaded. The last thing she wanted was to chip away at the message of the letter, taking it back bit by bit, but she was afraid that this was exactly what would happen if she kept trying to explain the impulse behind it.

"No, I get it. You're in *college*. I'm . . . *nowhere*."

"That's not true, Jason!" She regretted it the instant she said it. It was her role in the old script: building him up, helping him deny what's real. She didn't want to do this kind of thing! And this was *exactly* why she'd written the letter! She steeled herself and added, "You're in Mesquite. It's a place. People live there. Work there. Get married and have families and careers. You dropped out of high school. It's up to you whether you stay there or go or whatever, you know?"

"But that's why —" he waved the letter. "Right?"

She sat upright. "Yes. That's part of it." It felt good to tell him the truth. She was tired of the old *it's not you, it's me* crap.

"You need to grow up."

"Just friends, huh?"

He wouldn't meet her eye. Bitter. She was sorry she'd agreed to meet with him. He was going to make it hard, twist her heart to extort a retraction of the letter here and now. Just friends? Maybe not even that. But there was so much history. . . .

"Doesn't that mean anything to you?" she asked.

He shrugged. A silence seeped in around them like a stench. The impulse to fill it with chatter or phony reminiscences burbled up inside, but she squelched it, recognizing it as part of the old pattern, too: Lisa the peacemaker, the pacifier. At the Lake Travis house right now, her friends would be crawling out of bed, drinking coffee on the deck, shaking off the hangovers, maybe fixing breakfast tacos, talking about school, Professor Lenz or Coffey, the war in Iraq, Phish or Coldplay, concerts they'd been to, movies and books they loved—*her*—they'd be talking about her, wondering how it's going.

It's like having food poisoning.

He lightly strummed the guitar and shot her a quick glance. "I wrote the song, finally. I mean I finished it. After I got your letter."

She didn't know what to say. Or, rather, what she wanted to say—"I don't want to hear it!"—seemed too cruel to utter.

"Do you wanna hear it?" He finally met her gaze, and she had to look away.

"Okay."

"It's called 'Stand in Your Way,'" he declared, then strummed an intro and began crooning softly, *"I don't want to stand in your way / I hear what you say / We're so far apart / I can't make you stay,"* and it went on, *he* went on, but the static in her brain roared much too loud for her to listen with any real attention, though she immediately saw the ironic contradiction between the title and the first line. He didn't want to stand in her way? He was standing in her way *right now*! He was keeping her from a long list of more desirable things to do, places to be, people to be with! He droned on. He kept his head down over his strings, like a preoccupied genius letting himself ostensibly be an object of appreciation and admiration—the soulful performer, ripping his guts out, knifing open his veins. He looked too scruffy this morning, like a homeless guy, and it pained her. Dozens of dudes walked around campus like old-time hippies or grunge fans, but Jason didn't look *clean*. The nails on the hand working the fretboard had slim moons of grime.

She surveyed her surroundings: this part of the campus was very familiar, as the Hogg Building just on the north side of the commons was home to the Plan II program, and everybody congregated around the longhorn statues and the fountain in front of Main: it was where you'd tell people to meet you. Aside from the tower made infamous by Charles Whitman and Memorial Stadium, the mall here was one of the best-known landmarks on campus. The window to the classroom in Parlin where her English course met was visible, as well. Jason didn't belong here, but she did. There were figures in their field of vision now that she knew well but he had no notion of. When Tera looked her way, Lisa bobbed her head to acknowledge her awareness of them.

Then he was winding it up, shifting to face her squarely; he looked up from the guitar as he sang, *"But I'll be there in the end / Just as a friend / Even growing apart / there'll be time for a start . . ."*

When the last chord drifted off out of hearing, he said, "Well, it's not quite finished, you know." He grinned. "There could be more to the story."

"It's nice. I like it." She didn't even try to pass him her "sweet cheerleader" smile because he knew her too well.

"*Nice,* huh."

She shrugged. She refused to let him extract a false compliment by acting hurt. "It's hard to concentrate on it right now, Jason. I'd have to hear it again under different circumstances, you know."

"Yeah, I guess. Like what circumstances?"

"Like when you're not the object of an Amber Alert, for one thing."

"That was all Emily's fault! She told me she was leaving a note!"

"And that was all you thought you and she needed to just hit the road without discussing it with your dad and her mom?"

"I guess I wasn't really thinking too clearly. I'd just read the letter."

"So it's my fault, too?"

"Oh, no."

Then the silence again. She was turning over various excuses she might give right now as to where she had to be or what she had to do, when he said, "Lisa, I need to know. Is there anything I can do to change your mind? I mean, I'll do anything. I just am not . . . able to, you know, get up every day knowing you don't want to be with me anymore."

Now he ducked his head, and she knew he was on the verge of tears. "Please. Just tell me! I'll do anything!"

Panties up the water tower. His pain was twisting her heart, wringing it out, tears swelling now in her eyes. But she vowed not to relent. *Keep it real*, she told herself. *Keep it real.*

She sighed. "Jason, do you realize that you never apologized to my dad for taking my car that night?"

"I told you —"

"I know what you told me! But you never said anything to him, like you were sorry. All that stuff you tried to tell him about wanting to make sure it was safe for me? God, that was *such* complete bullshit! And he knew that! And you never admitted that you took it because you were drunk and you were mad at me for not letting you drive it!"

"Is that what you want me to do?"

"No! It's not what I *want* you to do! It's what you should've done in the first place, and not for me. Because it's right. Because that's what grown-ups do."

Her voice was shrill suddenly, and she caught herself, took in a deep breath. She was being too harsh, she guessed, kicking him while he was down? Or was that just the old Lisa thinking, the one who was always afraid to tell him what was wrong?

"No, you're right. I do owe him an apology. I'm sorry I haven't done it. But I will! I swear to God I will!"

*Oh crap!* she thought. *He is just not getting the point.* "Well, it would be good if you did, Jason. But."

He waved the letter. "I know. It wouldn't change this, right?"

"I said what I said."

"Okay."

"Something else, Jason."

"What? Please tell me, babe. I mean, *anything*."

"Did you ever tell that old guy whose collarbone you broke and whose skull you fractured that you were sorry?"

Jason sighed. "No. It was a *concussion*, not a fracture. Anyway, I don't think our lawyer would —"

"I don't care what the lawyers say. I'm talking about what's right to do! That old guy was just doing his job and trying to keep you guys from boosting stuff, and he wound up with a broken collarbone and whatever else you want to call it. You *own* that, Jason!"

"Yeah, yeah. I see it." He sighed. He looked up and met her eyes; he smiled, sadly, "This is why I've always needed you, you know."

The clock on the tower bonged the half hour. He sighed again. "Look, I know that these are things I need to do and that you're not promising anything, okay? But I want to do them, not just to please you, but because I know deep down that it's right." He grinned suddenly. "The old guy—well, sure, that's a no-brainer. But your dad?" He shook his head. "I don't think he's gonna let me get the first word out before he boots my butt out the door. But I will try! I swear to God! And I know you're not saying that this will make everything all right, you know, but—"

"There is no *but*, Jason! You have to see that!"

Emily was trotting toward them, waving. Behind her, at some distance, a couple of uniformed Austin police were jogging their way, as well, one with a radio to his mouth.

"Did you call the police?"

Lisa looked away. "Yes. They found me yesterday afternoon and asked me to call them if I heard from you." She rose to her feet. "I didn't have any choice, Jason! But I lied about what time we were meeting."

The look he gave her was full of disbelief and betrayal.

"Okay." He held out his guitar for her. "Please tell Emily to take care of this, okay?"

Then he bolted, running full speed deeper into the campus.

---

He ran through the East Mall legs churning and lungs burning, snagging gazes as he galloped by. Since he was neither dressed as a jogger nor trotting, loping, or bounding along with an exercise runner's deliberate gait, everything about him spelled danger, warning, emergency, alarm; one look at his flying form and you were sure that behind him or at the end of this mad dash lay a disaster. People stopped chatting as they strolled to watch his feet slap the pavement past Rappaport and on toward the geology building; bicyclists quit pedaling and coasted with their heads a-twist. A bright and calm Sunday morning on the campus such as this was simply not the time or the setting for whatever catastrophe lurked at either end of his flight, and that piqued curiosity—what's that kid running from? Where's he running to?

Cops? A mugging victim? A chase requires a hunter and the prey, but which were they seeing?

Nobody'd guess you'd run that far that fast in street clothes to flee a humiliation, the sorrowful embarrassment of being arrested before the gawking eyes of the one person in the world you need to impress and whose approval you so dearly need; nobody'd guess you'd run that far that fast because you'd just had your dearest hopes dashed and you couldn't stand to face the one who'd shunned you; nobody'd guess that some instinct told you that to run would make you vulnerable and endangered in her eyes and so you'd eke out a bit of sorely needed sympathy.

You'd guess he ran because he was scared, and you wouldn't be wrong.

They watched as he shot past Winship and onto San Jacinto Street, where a caravan of sedans and SUVs bearing dressed-up citizens away toward lunch or church streamed by, and he had to lurch and dart between, back-step, side-step, slam a hand on a hood to vault out of the way, and now they knew this meant the kid was desperate. And only seconds later they heard a ruckus from the opposite side of their frame of vision and here came two uniformed Austin patrolmen slamming their hard soles on the concrete slabs while a third, dropping back, palms to his knees, seemingly about to puke, lifted one hand to unsnap his radio from its holster. Now these spectators knew—the kid was running *from*! It was a foot chase by cops as good as those on *Cops,* only live action, here, right in their Sunday morning, unexpected, uncharacteristic, and therefore doubly exciting.

*Hey!* The cops kept yelling. *Hey, you! Stop!*

Then the last officer, completing his call, switched his hand from the radio to the 9mm in his holster and went charging off after the other two and the boy. Now we're getting somewhere! Now everything's in place—a fugitive, maybe armed, chased by some cops just as it is on *Cops,* and it looks like he might draw his gun. Some perp pops a cap at him—he's ready, by God! And he wouldn't have that hand on his gun as he trotted on if the perp, the fugitive, the thug-on-the-run hadn't done something to earn the starring role all this live drama, right?

Where's the . . .? Ah, hey! Look up! A cop chopper whacking toward the scene and a news bird in hot pursuit! Dude! We're watching something big, really big! Cool!

Why's he running? What'd he do? What do you think? I dunno, says one spectator. Probably stole something. Or maybe tried to carjack somebody? Where's his gun? Maybe he used a knife? Could it be rape? You know we might oughta think about not standing here in the open in case he doubles back. Like Virginia Tech, man. Columbine—like, hey!—UT Austin!

Yes, you could ask: why is he running? Jason, breathless, panicky, blood pounding in his temples, hearing the shouting behind him, and now the pulsating *tok, tok, tok* of chopper rotors overhead—he couldn't tell you why right now. He doesn't even have the excuse of needing to be free long enough to pitch his case to Lisa, now, or needing to stay free so he can deliver Emily to her father. There's no excuse, no rationale, no reason for it except for the ancient, atavistic impulse in his blood to keep moving as prey because hunters are hot on your heels. He's not even thinking of how it would be better at this point to stop and give himself up—since Emily's safe, all this hyped-up, hopped-up crap about a kidnapping wouldn't be draped like a smothering blanket over his head, at least no longer than it would take to interview the kid, check her out, see that she's safe and sound, and when you get right down to it—happy to have been on the road with him. She fucking *blackmailed* him to do it! You want to press charges—get the kid as a blackmailer! Extortion, pure and simple!

Honked at! Almost got creamed there, dude, one more quick dart right here, and—whew! And now plunges into more of the campus (he doesn't know he's in the fine arts and law quad), taking a quick glimpse behind him, looks as if they've gotten wheeled reinforcements because now the screaming squad cars are charging up the street behind him to disgorge a new phalanx of armed, foot-chasing cops, they've got a round-robin relay deal going—not fair!—he's just one kid with two lungs like withered old balloons at the moment, one kid out of shape, scared shitless, pounding on through this grassy commons laced with sinuous concrete paths, running literally on adrenaline. Here, too, there are casual strollers and purposeful power-walkers and those ambling from car to a building or from a building to a car, and the form of this red-faced frantic kid barreling toward them shunts them off the path: they don't know what's wrong, but they know *something* is. He fairly radiates the condition of something having gone very wrong; if it were audible, it might be a screech or a howl as from an animal with its paw clamped between steel jaws just snapped shut.

He's not thinking, though his mind's like a too-fast slide show: night, a park, drunk—cops are here!—everybody running, he also, too dark to see, stumbling forward, clopping out to a street, lights across the way, a Pic-n-Pak, people out front of it yelling at him, but now that his feet are on solid pavement and he half-sees where he's going, he revs into overdrive, heading for the far side of the street and around a corner, safe maybe from being collared, but—what the fuck!—here's some dude kind of doing a hockey goalie deal or like the kicker who's unexpectedly the last dude between you and the goalpost after you've fielded the punt—and you crash onward, and—is he trying to jump out of the way? Or is he jumping into the way? . . .

Broad daylight now, though, and nobody's ahead, but they are sure behind and overhead. Jason barrels across Robert Dedman and into the LBJ Library complex, across the grounds toward Red River and the athletic fields and the elevated skyway of I-35 beyond. It dawns on him he can't outrun them all—his legs are giving out, his lungs sore and hot and aching.

He tries to stay under the cover of overhangs and trees and out of the sight-lines of the choppers, but now they've multiplied and circle overhead like a gaggle of buzzards.

# Sixteen

On Sunday morning Burl scoured the streets of downtown Austin, feeling hopeless in the face of nearly empty streets. Hopeless and useless, he didn't know what else to do but set himself onto the numbers grid, beginning of course with First Street and all the way up to Nineteenth or MLK just under the southern edge of the campus, one-way streets this way, the other way that. Navigating Austin's streets was frustrating enough for a casual tourist but maddening for someone agitated and worn to the bone. Across the numbers, using the river streets like steps up the ladder north. Burl didn't have a plan; his alternative was to sit somewhere and stew, tormented by dark possibilities of Jason being manhandled or, worse, shot at, or even worse, shot at and hit, or, worse, beaten or TASERed to death. These images seemed less persistent and potent when he had to assign at least a small part of his attention to driving.

Last night when he'd gotten into town, he'd immediately gone to the police to declare his presence and to offer his help, given his phone number to must have been a dozen different officers, trying to plead Jason's case, hoping to intercede, hoping that if they found Jason before he did that they'd at least let him know before something, something . . . bad happened. Yeah, hell yes! He'd stand in front of the fire if need be, of course! Then he'd gone to the motel, and, after he'd talked to Lisa last night, she'd given him hope with her suggestion about

Sixth Street, so he'd spent most of last night walking the street and going in and out of clubs, up and down a dozen times. He'd finally given up when the last club had closed just after two o'clock. He'd never seen so many drunk young people in one place in his life, and it weighed him down with worry and sadness.

He was driving about this morning with his cell in his lap, and when the phone rang, he almost flung it out the window in his spastic attempt to pick it up. It was Lisa—she'd heard from Jason. Both he and Emily were fine, according to Jason. (According to Jason. . . .) They'd come to Austin to see Emily's father. Emily was going to her father's house after Jason had met with Lisa at her dorm to talk to her at . . . at around eleven or so.

"Thank God!" Burl exclaimed, fairly shouting into the phone as his pickup drifted toward the curb, almost striking it, and he pulled to a stop for safety. Lisa promised she'd call Burl back as soon as she'd seen Jason, or she'd get him to call. Burl was so relieved he was too rattled to drive, so he sat for a minute of deep breathing, then slowly nosed the truck back into the street, went up San Antonio Street and pulled into the Wendy's at MLK Blvd for coffee, all loose and jangly now, feeling the loss of sleep, the adrenaline diet of the last forty-eight hours, just plain crashing. He needed food. He needed rest.

He'd just planted himself in a booth, thinking that as soon as he got the coffee down he'd check in with Lily, when his cell rang and the caller ID showed his own home phone number.

"Burl!" Lily shouted. "I talked to them. They're right there in Austin. Emily said she wanted to go to Vinnie's but I forbade it, and then Jason hung up on me when I tried to make him—"

"Calm down," Burl cut in. "I know they're here. I talked to Lisa. Have you called off the Amber Alert?"

"He hung up on me! Can you believe that? After all he's put us through?"

"But you've called off the search, right?"

"Burl, I will let the authorities know she's safe when I find out for sure that she is! And not a minute sooner!"

"Lily, that's insane! We know they're okay now. You can't
. . ." He squeezed the phone as if it were her neck. "Okay,
never mind! I'll do it!"

Then he hung up on her. Instantly he was back on the ride,
flung about, blood and brain dosed with his body's own speed,
frantic with worry and feeling the alarm rush through his system like nonstop static pops between your fingertips and all
the objects around you on a winter day. Once again, the night-
mare images: the chase, the guns, the kid, the shots fired; the
chase, the snare, the beating with batons and boots.

But, surely, once they found out that Emily was with Lisa,
the police will call off the alert regardless of what Lily said.
Timing was everything, though. Burl spent the next several
minutes frantically trying to contact the officer whose card
he'd taken at the Austin PD but only got his voice mail. He
fleetingly toyed with the idea of a 911 call but didn't know
what he'd say, where to send somebody. You couldn't call 911
to say there IS NO EMERGENCY. He could hope that a calm
patrolman would come upon the pair if Emily were still with
Jason or if Jason were alone, and, knowing the alert had been
called off and that Jason wasn't a fugitive, might coax him
into his patrol car. Jason might even be eager to get the kid off
his hands.

Burl got back into his pickup and went up Guadalupe toward the heart of the campus. When he heard the throaty
sound of helicopter rotors thrashing humid city air vibrate
through the cab of his truck as the chopper soared just overhead, his heart fell as he craned his head forward over the
wheel to see it zoom across countless city blocks that he'd
crawled over, whisking them off to the scene of a crime. If the
cops hadn't gotten the word. . . . A million things could go
wrong—the cell phone goes dead, the computer blinks, the
cop on the beat mishears the crackling static on his radio. Even
if Emily were "safe" in Lily's eyes and the officials in charge
had called off the dogs, there's always the lag, the gap between
conception and execution, between the order and the action.

Best he could hope for in that case would be a standoff between Jason and the police. Perhaps Burl could reach them before things went south, went sour, though so far as he knew, Jason had no tool to keep anybody at bay. If he were scared enough, he'd pick up a rock.

Burl wheeled the pickup into the first access into the campus off Guadalupe, quickly learning that the narrow traffic lanes inside the grounds were a labyrinth of dead ends, one-way-onlys, cul-de-sacs, or entrances to parking lots in which he couldn't even turn around because their gates prevented access. While he tried to negotiate this automotive maze, the air seemed to grow ever thicker with circling choppers belonging to TV stations.

Jason managed to reach East Thirty-second without being spotted and, ducking into a parking garage, he came to a halt to catch his breath, plopped onto a curb near an entrance to St. David's Medical Center. The cops who had been running after him seemed to have lost the scent, but, just to be safe, he stood from the curb and walked through the automatic doors trying to adopt the posture and attitude of a loved one coming to visit someone sick. *My mom is sick. Real sick. Ovarian cancer. No, I know the room number, believe me.*

He trod down the main hallway toward an information kiosk, walking rigid as if the walls were an inch outside his elbows and electrified, breathing shallow, eyes locked on a space before his face. This was sweeping him back, a claw from a grave clutching his ankle. Jason must've spent a hundred days and nights in hospitals, a whole fucking week at MD Anderson in Houston, he and his dad totally lost in the complex at first, but by the time she . . . by the time it was over, time to go home, they'd carved out their rat runs to and from the parking lots, the restrooms, the cafeteria. Jesus, how many sad, sorry-ass meals he and his dad shared sitting in plastic scoop chairs, eating something you wouldn't hardly recognize, something food-like from brown plastic trays, using clear plastic utensils, drinking from foam containers? Like living in an orbiting space station. Bringing Mom back senseless treats she couldn't possibly eat in her condition—doughnuts with white frosting and rainbow sprinkles, strawberry milkshakes. She couldn't even smell them without her eyes rolling back, but they brought the delicacies anyway because she always asked. It wasn't until later that Jason realized she asked for the desserts to give him and his dad something to do that supposedly helped. Creating this pretense of helping required Sue to pretend that she yearned to chomp that doughnut. She'd smell it and smile best she could, and at the time Jason just thought that maybe she'd really wanted the damn thing, but when it showed up on a foam plate before her chin, she'd had a sudden wave of nausea.

Recalling all this, he had a swoony little session all his own and had to duck into a chair near the hub where a volunteer receptionist was fielding phone calls and visitor questions. He figured out after his mom had . . . after she was gone . . . after it was time to go home . . . that she'd either wanted to get some space by sending them on an errand or she'd wanted them to feel less . . . less fucking helpless!

Here, now, he buried his face in his hands and gritted his teeth and clenched his jaw to keep his sobs from busting free. *Ah hummpt! A hmmpt!* he shouted to his palms. *Wow! Dude. You're like totally wiped out.* He tried to breathe. Lisa. His mom. Double whammy, the old one-two, one to the gut, the other to the chin and he's out for the count.

"Son, are you all right?" A hand lightly tapped his shoulder. He looked up. The receptionist, a gray-haired grandma with wireless glasses, hovered over him. Everything about her said homemade oatmeal cookies.

He sniffled, sucked back his snot, slid a forearm across his nostrils, nodded. "Yes, ma'am. It's my mom."

"Aw, hon, I'm sorry. Would you like for me to call the chaplain? We have a little chapel." She gave him a syrupy smile.

"No thanks, anyway. But could I like use your phone just for a minute?"

"Is it a local call?"

Apparently her compassion for his plight had some limits,

perhaps geographical.

"I don't know. I guess not. My dad's cell. We live in Dallas."

"Oh. Well, you can use my cell phone if you like!" She beamed." I have unlimited roaming!"

---

Before Burl could reach the hospital where Jason had called his cell phone and begged for his help, the Austin PD had found a very truculent and caustic Emily strolling on Guadalupe carrying her bag and a guitar; she was on her way to her father's house. That deflated the big news balloon, so the choppers were free to roar off to a burning multiple-vehicle wreck on I-35.

The officer at APD called Burl to let him know that Jason was still wanted for questioning, though he was no longer a suspect because apparently no crime outside of sheer stupidity had been committed.

Burl located the hospital north of the campus and found Jason skulking about just inside the sliding doors to the emergency entry.

"Thanks, Dad. I'm sorry."

"Emily's with the police, so nobody's after you now."

"I'm really sorry. Am I supposed to be interrogated or anything?"

"You have to talk to them."

"Can we do something else first?"

Burl said, "If you have some plan here, I'm gonna have to hear all about it before I say yay or nay."

---

It was going on twilight when Jason and his dad pulled into the long graveled driveway of a small-frame house set back from the highway on a couple of overgrown acres of crabgrass and volunteer hackberry near Seagoville. Burl idled the truck a moment, craning his head over the seat to look out Jason's window.

"Well, he's not standing on the porch with a shotgun, anyway."

"He said he'd be out back. Will you go with me?"

His dad shook his head. "Bad enough that we're here, son. It's best if I just wait. Far as I'm concerned, I'm not here at all. This is your row to hoe." He tapped the digital dash clock as if Jason had never seen it. "We got forty-five minutes to do this and get all the way across town to Sgt. Brookes's."

"Believe me, he's not going to care if I'm late." Jason exhaled, like a sigh. Then he climbed out of the cab and eased the door to quietly, thinking even as he did that it might be better to just slam the sucker to announce his arrival. No way to ease into this, that's for sure. He moved to the side of the house and walked one crumbling ribbon of the two concrete driveway runs that led to a garage in the back. The garage was an old-fashioned one-bay affair with one big swinging wooden door that was now cocked open on a tilt, a forward point buried in turf, no doubt stuck there permanently. In the bay facing him was an old Chevy pickup with the hood removed, a work light hung by its question-mark hook from a line strung over the engine. A man was bent over the engine. His right arm was nestled in a sling—that surprised Jason. It had been three months since he'd bowled this old fart over and broken his collarbone. Wouldn't it have healed by now? Was this just for show? Like an ambulance-chasing lawyer's whiplash client?

Jason stood several yards from the entrance to the garage, waiting to be noticed. *Thing is,* he thought, *I wouldn't be able to pick him out of a line-up, really. That night I didn't even get a good look, just slammed into him, and if he'd come up to me on the street since then with murder on his mind, I wouldn't even have known what he looked like.*

The memory lapse wasn't to his credit, Jason realized. If something you do causes somebody a shitload of grief, the least you can do is remember what he looks like. The least you can do is pay him the honor of acknowledging his existence, that much anyway.

"Mister Crawford?"

The man straightened up out of the engine and stood with a socket wrench gripped in his one good fist. His white hair was long around his ears, and he had a Colonel Sanders goatee and wire-rimmed reading glasses low on his nose. He was wearing denim overalls, a garment that conjured images of *Hee-Haw* reruns that Jason had flicked by while on the way to a better channel.

Instead of answering, the man expressed his undivided attention in a steady and distinctly unsmiling gaze that approached a glare. This look unnerved Jason, as it called for him to speak again as a response.

"Uh, Mister Crawford?" He took a couple of steps forward, and the man countered by stepping out in front of the bumper of the pickup, the socket shank silvery steel in the reflected light, held out from his body and waved, metronome-like, in the air between them.

"You got something to say, sonny boy, get it said and get on your way. And it's like I told you on the phone, nothing you got to say to me is gonna make no difference, you got that? And you best keep in mind, in case it comes up, that *you* come to *me*. You come to me. I didn't call you on no phone and tell you to come tell me jack shit. Maybe I'll hear what you got to say and maybe I won't." He took still another step toward Jason and lifted the socket wrench even higher so that it was now at eye level between them. "I tell you right now what I won't be hearing," he went on. "I *won't* be hearing no 'Please, Mister Crawford, don't be siccing your lawyer on me and my family.'"

He stood trembling, just out of Jason's reach, glaring. Jason was struck dumb momentarily, since, of course, that was exactly what he'd hoped to say. After a proper apology had been made.

The man's sling looked to be fashioned from an old tea towel, as it had roses and such printed against a green background.

"Why aren't you in jail?"

"I didn't break any laws."

"That's bullshit, I bet!" When Jason had nothing to say to

this, the man said, more calmly, "I seen on the TV where they got the girl back home."

"She and the kitty she picked up when I wasn't looking. I didn't kidnap her." Though he was tired of having to say this, he knew that eventually he'd have to say it a lot more when he finally showed up at the police station to answer questions. Not something to look forward to.

"She's my stepsister. She wanted to go live with her dad in Austin. She told me that if I didn't take her, she'd run away. I didn't want to see her do that. End of freakin' story, Mister Crawford."

"So you let a little girl drraaaaag you into all that trouble?" He smirked and shook his head.

Whatever his own motive for being here, Jason thought, Crawford's motive for receiving him was to scratch the itch to rag him to death. Something Jason could've easily foreseen. Maybe the best thing to do would be to just stand here and let him vent, spill over, maybe even tattoo the top of Jason's head with that socket wrench until Mr. Crawford felt they were even-steven.

"Sir, I got no excuse for it except stupidity."

"That ain't no excuse."

The old fellow's forward leg was trembling minutely, and Jason wondered if this was from anger—or fear of Jason. Did he imagine that Jason had come here to kick his ass? Scare him off from suing?

"No, sir." They had a silent face-off for several seconds during which they both looked everywhere but at each other.

"If you say you won't hear me ask you not to sue my dad and my stepmom for what I did, then I can't help it. But I wanna say that I *am* sorry for running into you that night and hurting you. I was running away and I guess I saw you zigging when I thought you were zagging, sir. Believe me, last thing I wanted to do right then was run into somebody or something that would slow me down. I wound up on the ground, too. With an officer's knee right smack in my back. I'm sorry we had a . . . had a wreck, sort of. If I had it to do all over again,

I sure as heck wouldn't, I guarantee you that."

"Well, that's a pretty speech all right. Kind of last-minute, though, don't you think? Kind of a day late and dollar short, you know? You're due in court tomorrow 'cause you're charged with assault with bodily injury. Now here the day before, you wanna come play kiss and make up? You think I'm an idiot, son? You think that's all you have to do to make up for this?" He heaved his bound elbow up like a shortened wing and waggled it in the air. "You ever try to wipe your ass with the wrong hand? You see anybody else around this place? You think it's easy just putting your damn clothes on and trying to make yourself a meal with just one hand? Did you know I lost that job?"

When Jason shook his head, the man said, "Did you?"

"No, sir."

"Well, I did. Who the hell's gonna hire somebody with an arm in a sling? You tell me that. You have any idea what it costs to have your collarbone and your skull broke and you got no damn insurance? Do you know?"

Jason shook his head again, but the man said, "Do you?"

"No, sir."

"You see that truck in there?" He dipped his head to the side. "Water pump's gone on it. You ever try to work on a car or a truck like that using just one hand?"

"No, sir."

"Well, let me tell you it ain't easy. Not at all. I got two cows out yonder in the pasture I gotta see to ever' day. You ever try to fix a barbed wire fence that's down with just one hand? Did you?"

"No, sir."

"I didn't think so. I got nobody helping me. I got no daddy standing by ready to bail my ass out of a jam night or day. My wife's been dead ten years, and my daughter's been dead five. From cancer. Both of 'em."

"I'm sorry, sir."

"You are. You are pretty damn sorry, all right. I don't hear jack shit from you for months and the day before you're due in court you come around wanting to make it all go away just by saying you're sorry you and me got into some kind of *accident?*"

"Well—"

"Do you think that's what it was?"

"Sir, I didn't mean to run into you, like I said."

"But you think it was an *accident*? Who was it put you on that street right then? Who was it set you down in that park with all those other worthless turds? Who was it made it so you thought you needed to run from the *poahleese*? Who was that? You say 'accident' like you had nothing to do with none of it." Crawford turned his head to the side and spat. "Damn! Naw, son. Too late for this."

"Sir, I'm not asking you to do anything. No kidding. And I'm not asking you to not do something. I'm here because it took me this long to see the need to apologize. I could tell you my dad's a working man and has been all his life, and about all he's got to his name is a five-year-old pickup that's not all paid for yet and a mortgage on a house. He—"

"Aww! You're breaking my heart now! Boo . . . fucking . . . hoo!"

"Okay, sir. Since you're not listening, I might as well go on. He's had his spell of rotten luck, too. His wife, my mom, she died a little over two years ago. Cancer, just like yours. And I know you're thinking I'm making all that up or trying to just use it to sway your mind, but he about died, too, when it happened."

"Appears to me like he's got over it. Got hitched again."

"He about drunk himself to death before that, though."

"So the whole bunch of you's a sorry lot. That what you're telling me?"

Jason watched the cloud-strewn sky overhead career momentarily. Dusk had settled into the yard, with the light over the truck engine glimmering in Mr. Crawford's eyes and backlighting the old man. His knees were rubbery and his vision went all gray for a moment.

"I gotta sit down," he whispered, and he sank to a squat and used his fingertips to balance himself. This old guy's resistance and rage made him implacable, a wall you bounced off when you tried to walk through it. He lost touch with the ground and wound up on his butt, hugging his knees with his forehead pressed to their caps.

"This is going to sound really stupid and lame," he offered after a moment of breathing had restored his equilibrium. "But the truth is, my biggest problem is I'm lovesick."

Crawford's surprised laugh was like a bark. Then he followed it with a nasty chuckle to make sure Jason knew he was disgusted. "You're shitting me, son. Lovesick! For crying out loud. You *are* a piece of work. I don't envy your daddy, I tell you that."

"You asked who put me in that park that night. Right? Okay, yeah, I did. I know that. But—and I'm not making excuses here, just trying to explain—earlier I'd been to my girlfriend's graduation party, and we had a fight about my driving her new car. Well, it wasn't about that, really. We've been together since middle school, and thing is, she was going away to UT, and I knew, I just knew, that it was over between us. For her, I mean. Not for me. I knew she was going to go away to school and forget me." He sighed. "And sure enough, she did."

To his surprise, Crawford had no insulting response to this. Jason shut his eyes and rocked on his haunches for a moment. A muted rustle caught his ear; he opened his eyes. Crawford was leaning one shoulder against the garage doorframe, and the hand holding the wrench was loose at his side.

"So I took her car, even though I knew she didn't want me to, because I had to get away from all the people at the party who knew us and probably knew my future better than I did. And I just drove it around for a while and wound up at the park and drank a bunch of shit and took some pills and got really messed up, and that's when the cops came and I ran. And ran over you."

"You think all this was her fault."

"No, sir. But I was really . . . hurt that night. I was afraid I'd lost her. I had, really. I mean I have. I know it now. I just couldn't face up to it and I was just kind of thrashing around.

So, anyway, she did go to Austin, and that's where she is now. And—what's today, Sunday?—just Friday I got a letter, you know—" he sighed, deeply, like a gasp. "Saying she thought it was, you know, best if . . ."

"Dear John."

"Yeah. So I still couldn't face it. Believe it. And that's why I decided to take off to go down there and try to talk her out of it, and Emily, my stepsister, wanted to go along to see her dad. And all I could think of was to get myself down there and try to talk to her about all the stuff that was in the letter. I couldn't think about anything else. Not the hearing tomorrow or anything. Or how much trouble I might be in for taking off with Emily. I mean, an Amber Alert! That about knocked us both off our feet."

After a minute, Crawford said, "So how did I finally come to your attention? How was it you had your head up your ass about your girlfriend and then all of a sudden you're thinking about how you owe me this visit?"

Jason considered pointing out that the lawyer his dad had hired had rigid instructions and rules that included, of course, having absolutely no contact with the old guy. It could pass as a credible reason for why his apology was so tardy, but since it wasn't the real reason, Jason was superstitious about playing that card, afraid his insincerity might backfire or cause the fates or gods to punish him.

"Well, I did get to see her down there. She made a special point of totting up all my flaws, in person, in really big print, in case I'd missed the main idea of the letter and all. One of the things on the list was how I'd never come here and apologized to you."

"So you think doing this will get you back together."

"Oh, no. No. Not at all. No chance. I see that now. She's got her future, and it's not mine. She laid all that out plain and simple. I could be the world's best Boy Scout from now on and it wouldn't make a speck of difference to her. I'm doing this now because it's right. Even if it's not, you know, advisable."

As if reading Jason's mind, Crawford said, "What's your

lawyer think of this?"

"He doesn't know about it. I don't think he'd like it very much."

"Mine neither."

Another silence eased over them. Under its weight, Jason sensed a minute shift between them. They were allied for a millisecond against the shiny-suited, $400-an-hour, Beamer-driving assholes who run the world way up over their heads, run it without regard for the wishes or needs of a high-school dropout from a blue-collar suburb and an unemployed widower with the use of only one arm. *Lawyers*. The gap between Jason and the guy whose collarbone he'd broken hadn't closed—that would be hard to say—but it seemed at least that the wind roaring down between the walls had died so that Jason might be heard if he called across it.

# Seventeen

"You look all beefed up."

"You look all tarted up."

"Tarted up?"

"It's what my mom used to say. It means, uh, like a ho or something."

"Well, thanks. I hate your haircut. You look like a skinhead."

"Skinheads shave their heads."

"I liked your hair a lot better long."

"I liked you better in pigtails and glasses."

"Shut up."

"I see you got your ears pierced."

"They've been pierced since I was a baby, dummy."

When Jason didn't respond, she said, "But they grew over because I didn't like wearing ear studs."

"Are those real diamonds?"

"Yeah. My daddy's mom gave them to me. So what? Is that a real tattoo?"

Jason swung his left forearm up between them like a classroom desktop on a hinge so he could admire the design and she could, possibly, be impressed.

"So are you all like riding horses or something?"

"Don't be stupid."

"There's a horse's head on the shield."

"Well, it was originally a cavalry unit."

"Do you all ride Vespas now?"

He grinned crookedly. "No. Tanks, Bradleys, Humvees."

"Oooo!" She backed away from the threshold in mock alarm, raised her palms at him. Her t-shirt peaked slightly at her chest, its fabric bunched under the small bulge. An impulse arose to tease Emily, but Jason thought better of it. She looked years older, like an altogether different person, an almost-teen, though in the several months since he'd seen her she'd only had one birthday, bringing the total to twelve. Her hair was shoulder length and loose, with bangs she kept sweeping out of her eyes with fingertips whose nails were painted black. She'd painted her toenails red.

She dipped her head as a mute invitation to follow and turned on her bare heels. He went through the front door and closed the aluminum screen behind him. The early March morning was mild and balmy, so the house was open.

"Where's your mom?" He spoke to her receding back as she padded through the rooms. The house was a small brick-and-siding ranch-style bungalow in an older neighborhood of Austin on a number street. It reminded him of their old house in Mesquite—you entered right into the living room, with an adjoining dining room and the kitchen straight through an archway. The scent of patchouli wafted through the air as he tracked her into the kitchen.

"At work."

"How come you're not at school?"

"Gee, you're so nosey!" She went to the counter beside the sink. On the sill were plants in small Mexican pots. A dishrack held plates and clean glasses. "You want some coffee?"

"You drink coffee now too?"

"Too? You mean like in addition to all the other wild ho stuff you seem to think I'm doing?"

"No, smartass. I meant like me."

"No. Hate the stuff. No caffeinated drinks, no meat. But here's some left over from breakfast." She lifted the glass pot from its station in the maker and sloshed its contents at him.

"Okay."

"Staff development."

"I thought maybe you were being home-schooled now."

Emily laughed. "Seriously? Who would do it? I'd have to do it myself."

He shrugged. She poured coffee into a blue ceramic mug. "You want cream and sugar?"

"Black is fine."

She passed him the mug, and he took it, standing, while she leaned her hips against the counter and crossed her arms over her chest. She'd grown a couple inches, it seemed, and Jason was astonished to think that she might wind up being a tall person. Taking the coffee was only a ceremonial act, and he sipped it once ritually. He'd already had a quart of it this morning back at the motel.

"I thought you'd be wearing a uniform."

"I'm not on duty. Dog tags only. Did you want to see me in it?"

"No."

He chuckled. "Uh-oh." Truth was he'd wanted to wear it, but Phillip would've ragged him to no end if he did.

They fell silent. He sipped again. The brew was bitter and tepid. They were self-conscious.

"Whose car is that?"

"My buddy Phillip's."

She grinned at him. "He knows you've got it, right?"

He laughed. "Yes. Not to worry."

"Are you going to see Lisa?"

"No. Absolutely not. Why would I do *that*?"

She turned at the sink, twisted a faucet, plucked the spray nozzle out of its socket, rinsed down the sink.

"Why would I do that?"

Then she turned with a grin, aimed the nozzle, squeezed the trigger once, and hit his gray t-shirt square in the ARMY logo, darkening his chest like a shotgun blast.

"Jesus!" He hopped backward, sloshing his wrist with the coffee, and she laughed. He swiped at his chest. She tossed him a tea towel, and he set the mug on the table to wipe his chin and arms with it.

"That was for lying."

"For God's sake, why do you think I'm lying? Lisa and I are history. I haven't seen her since that day on the campus."

"Have you called her?"

"No. No way."

"E-mail? Text?"

"No."

"Okay." She cocked her head, squinted, grinned out of one side of her mouth. "Tell me this—have you asked somebody who knows her how's she doing?"

He wiped his face with the towel. "Why are you giving me the third degree here?"

"So how's she doing?"

"I have no idea. I'd say she's probably on spring break down in Cancún or something, doing the rich college kid thing."

"So you did check? You know she's got a MySpace page. I'm her friend on there if you want to look."

His stomach lurched. Lisa at play. Lisa with pals. Lisa with leering apes. Lisa with drooling dudes like Chase.

"Emily, get off my back."

"Okay. My sensors say you pass inspection. You're clean."

After a moment, he grinned. "You look like you might have a boyfriend these days."

"What? Why? What do you mean I look like that? That's stupid, Jason, really stupid."

"Boy, I pushed a button that time."

"No, you didn't push a button! You just said something stupid, and I hate stupidity."

"The toenail polish, the bling, the contacts. Got your braces off too, and your hair is *styled*. You're like all those beauty pageant twerps who grow up to be sorority girls. So what's his name?"

She batted her eyes in mock flirtation. "So does this mean you think I'm beautiful?"

"It means I bet you're running around these days with mall rats who filch cosmetics at Foley's."

"I'm in a junior science exploration group and a chess club and an astronomy club."

"I bet he's a chess player."

"He—shut up!"

Jason chuckled. "I can't believe you fell for that. So is he coming over later since you're both out of school and mom's away at work? Have you figured that one out yet?"

"Not that it's any of your business, but he is coming over, and we're doing our algebra homework together. We study together. That's all."

A tsunami of sadness crashed over him suddenly, driving his gaze down to his sneakers. Studying algebra together! The flashcards on the lawn of the Eastfield campus, a thousand hours with Lisa patiently rehearsing formulas that went with word problems. A knot like a tumor next to his heart, a constant throbbing pain that waxed and waned throughout the night and day. Guys got their legs blasted off and said they still felt them, ghost pains. Lately this kind of involuntary recollection caught Jason off guard because he liked to think the army had made a new man of him, had shaken him loose of his old habits of being lazy, irresponsible, aimless, without a goal. He had pride in this new self and wanted someone who'd known the old one to see that the new Jason merited respect. He'd like to think the new man had no business carrying the boy's old sorrows around his neck, dragging him down. Guys in boot got those letters from girlfriends after they'd left town—he was lucky, maybe, knew going in he'd lost her. He'd arrived on the scene with the knife already sticking out of his back.

"That's fun, studying together," he said gently. "That's really a lot of fun."

"It's school work."

"Yes, but. But they are golden hours, believe me."

She snickered. "The oracle speaks."

He smiled, waved as if to dispel his portentous pronouncement. "You won't even know it had any value until it's all gone." He picked up the mug from the table and sniffed at its contents but didn't drink. "Is he hot?"

"Jaayyy-son!"

"Okay. Maybe I'll just stick around until he shows up. I

should check him out. Make sure he's on the up-and-up."

"You better not."

"Okay. But we're all even now, right?"

"Right."

The walls of her bedroom sported a big poster of Avril Lavigne giving what looked like a gang sign to the photographer, unsmiling, intense, almost glaring, another of Jessica Alba, another of a Goth-looking girl singer he'd not heard of. On her desk was a laptop clamshelled closed and a book with a strange title, *The Sisterhood of the Traveling Pants*. She caught him looking at a Kerry-Edwards bumper sticker pinned to the wall.

"John Kerry was in San Antonio last week. Me and Mom went with some other parents and kids from our school to hear him."

He nodded. But the response didn't suffice for her. "Are you voting for Bush in November?"

"I haven't registered."

"So?"

He shrugged. "I'm not sure but what my legal complications will stand in the way."

"You weren't convicted of anything, were you?"

"Deferred adjudication."

"What is that?"

"I guess in my case it meant my hiney belonged to Sgt. Brookes or Judge Adams, the army or jail, I had my choice."

"Really?"

"It's not like I'm getting off, you know. Crawford's got a cut of my pay for the next ten years or something."

"I'm glad you're not in jail."

"Me too."

His guitar was lying on her bed. He couldn't see its case. She picked it up—rather expertly and confidently, he saw—sat on the edge of the bed, set it in her lap across her bare legs, draped her right arm over its hip and strummed across the strings with the backs of her nails.

"Ah-hah! Did I give you permission to play my beloved instrument?"

"No, but you didn't ask me if I minded babysitting it, either, did you?"

"True."

"Like I oughta charge you for storage."

"No, if you've been messing around on it, I oughta charge *you* rent on it."

Her left hand crabbed around the fretboard so her finger-pads easily tapped A minor, he saw, without her even having to look. She picked a line with her thumb and fingers. She had the classical form, he knew. Lessons, even, most likely.

"Who are you listening to these days, Alanis Morisette?"

"Oh, puh-lease! Yuck. Are you kidding me?"

"Avril Lavigne?"

"You're getting warmer. Listen—"

She had a strong right hand and pretty good movement with her left on the chords, but her voice was a little thin and reedy, the words swamped by the instrument. He caught snatches: "*Wanderers true they* something something *the land / how do you like* something something." The thing was folksy bluesy sort of stuff, like what he did. It was clear Emily had talent, had taken hold of this guitar, and was well on her way to being passable. Twelve years old. He let his gaze click about the room while she went on, head bent, long black hair cascading over her playing arm and falling like a scrim through which he heard her steady rhythmic strumming and her voice rising and falling. In a chair against the wall opposite the bed was a Papa John's pizza box, lid cocked open to show two joined slices of plain cheese which he automatically, reflexively, was hungry for. Chess set on the floor in the corner, hard to tell if a game was in progress, and on her made bed, past where she sat, was a small petting zoo, including two sock monkeys and an old teddy he recalled from her room in Mesquite.

When she finished, she pitched her hair back over her shoulder with a flamboyant toss of her head.

"Who was that?"

She grinned. "Did you like it?"

"Yeah. It was cool. Who?"

She blushed. "Me. I mean it's kind of like something Melinda Blanke would do, but I wrote it!"

"Melinda Blanke?"

"She's part of the Austin thing."

He felt a pang of envy that Emily had somehow managed to come closer than he to the Austin music scene, by proximity and now by emulation, but he smoothed over the jagged edge of his jealousy. He had a mission, a man's job to do in the world, no time for busking and club-crawling. And, truth be known, the whole idea of Austin was now a slow poison in his gut, made him a little sick to his stomach the way drinking a giant glass of water just after waking up with a hangover does. Memories singed his brain with shame, regret. This was why he'd procrastinated so long to reclaim this guitar, and he might've stayed away longer had Phillip not ragged his ass to come along.

She jumped up, set the guitar on the spread, dropped to all fours, reached under her bed, agile as a monkey, bending far with her cheek to the floor to grab, lithe limber limbs (a sign that she was still a child, or at least had been one recently), dragged the case from the recess, put it on the bed, clicked open the latches, swung the cover upright disclosing the pale yellow plush of the lining. She set the guitar in the case, though not before giving it a once-over with a polish cloth he'd never seen before.

She closed the lid slowly, snapped each latch shut, lifted the case from the bed and set it on the floor, pointed toward him. She sighed. He almost laughed aloud.

"Look, I want you to keep it. I can see you've already put an Avril sticker on it."

"Oh, gosh, Jason! I couldn't keep it!"

"It's just a cheapo I picked up in a pawn shop, okay? I can see you're really good. You've taken care of it and made use of it. I know I said I was coming by to pick it up, but now I think you should probably keep it."

"What would you do? You haven't quit writing songs and playing, have you?"

"I've kind of put all that on furlough." He was like the laptop with its cover closed, the hardshell case latched shut—waiting, waiting, to be opened. "It's not much use to me where I'm going."

She looked stricken. He'd forgotten how sharp she was.

"We're deploying next week. We're relieving the First Armored. A lot of my unit's been in Iraq since January."

"Jason! Don't go!" She leapt and stood in front of where he'd settled into her desk chair. "It's a stupid war! And besides, Bush said it was all over, remember? 'Mission accomplished.' How come you have to go now? Can't you tell your colonel or general or whatever he is that you don't need to go? They don't need you?"

She darted off through the door, bare feet thudding on the hardwood, leaving him startled and puzzled, but after a moment he heard the thudding again and she thundered through the door, waving a newspaper at him.

"It's right here. Today. Look!"

She shoved the newspaper into his face, but he couldn't see anything with her waggling it about. She jerked it back down and pointed at a column. "It says 552 American soldiers have died just since he said that! Five hundred fifty-two!"

"Don't worry. We're well trained. I'll be fine. We'll just, you know, be there to keep the peace."

She jumped into his arms and hugged him ferociously, buried her face in his neck. She'd never hugged him this way. He reeled inwardly with the sense of himself as a brave soldier playing the departing hero, brow furrowed, jaw clenched, eyes planted on the far distance as he steels himself to march into the fire, his womenfolk clinging to his legs . . . though the fact that Emily was twelve and his would-have-been stepsister, not Lisa as his fianceé or wife, seriously undermined the romantic glory of the moment.

By the time they'd reached her front porch again, she had calmed down.

"You can get your guitar when you come back, okay?"

"Sure. That's good. You just take care of it for me."

"I can get Daddy to buy me one, then. I'm thinking electric."

"Sell out."

She laughed. They fell silent. There was nothing keeping him from leaving now except the desire to stay. For which there didn't seem to be any excuse. But there was a reason, one that needed to be revealed: he owed her an acknowledgment that they'd shared an adventure that neither would forget, no matter who or what they became.

"I wish my dad and your mom could've made it," Jason said.

"Really?"

"Yeah. It was great fun having you as a stepling. And I'm really glad you came along on my trip here. I'm sorry we're not going to get a chance to do more stuff. If I was going to have a sister, I'd want her to be exactly like you."

Jason's confronting her so directly sent Emily into paroxysms of self-conscious embarrassment. She bit her lip and turned her head and kicked at a porch post lightly with her bare big toe.

"When you get over there, will you e-mail me?"

"Sure! Same one as now?"

She nodded. "And I'll write back! Keep you up with everything."

In case she imagined he wanted news about Lisa's comings and goings, he said, "Well, not everything. Some things are off-limits."

"I get it."

She went back inside when he stepped off the porch, for which he was grateful since it relieved them of a protracted waving bye-bye, the kind of exchange he always dreaded and only endured with an inward shudder. It felt right to be empty-handed, leaving her this souvenir of their time together, passing on a musical torch, and he smiled to recall that morning with the Africans when she had wanted him to smash the guitar over a fence post.

---

Phillip's old Neon fired up on the second crank, and Jason

notched the shift into D but didn't take his foot off the brake. He was afraid that the car of its own volition might take a notion to head over several blocks away to Forty-sixth and Ramsey. Just as it had done last night when he wasn't keeping close track and thinking. Well, it had been destiny, right, to run into Destiny at Town East, and, sure, she'd heard that Lisa had moved out of the dorm second semester and was with other kids in a rent house. A house with overgrown shrubbery, a little rundown, with cars at the curb but no Miata at that hour last night. What was he supposed to do, hang around the motel room while Phillip banged his old high school squeeze, who'd slipped away from her mom's house in Lockhart to spend the night with Phillip? Jason had left the room around midnight when they persisted in making out under a blanket while they all ostensibly watched *Real World*. The pretense was absurd, since they had the blanket pulled over their heads and Jason hated the show anyway, so he said, "I'm going out to catch some tunes," and somebody grunted back. Jesus, why hadn't they just asked him to take off in the first place?

So he'd cruised Sixth Street, but the weeknight scene was dead, and he just kept driving until the next thing he knew he was gliding past that house on Ramsey. Just seeing it and thinking that Lisa was behind the walls made his head ache and his heart massage itself like a sore muscle. If she'd come out onto the stoop, swear to God he wouldn't have stopped. He had nothing to say, though of course he'd have liked for her to know that he and the US Army had molded a soldier out of a slacker, loser, witless, and aimless kid. Driving by the house where she supposedly now lived aroused so many contradictory emotions he thought his head would explode, and he just kept gliding on, not even looking in the rearview mirror, feeling that he had a big load to carry and no place to put it down. He had a powerful sense of himself as a fool, a deluded fool, who, like an alkie, had convinced himself he was over her but was now glug, glug, glugging. He felt lost and alone; he'd fled from a room that wasn't his own and was driving a car not his own through the night streets of a town not his own looking or not looking for a girl who was not his own. Fucking pathetic.

She was an addiction. He was, like, sniffing the cork here today just to entertain the memory of shaming himself by driving by last night. And when he'd returned to the motel around three last night, the blissful couple had worn themselves out, he guessed, because they were inert, had moved between the sheets, cuddled, asleep, and he'd dropped like a bag of wet sand onto the other bed, just digging his toes into the heels of his shoes to shuck them. Finally, maybe about four, he'd fallen asleep only to be awakened about eight-thirty when the girl, Jessie, was slurping.

He wheeled away from the curb. Since it was full daylight and he wasn't presently afflicted so much with the hopelessness and melancholy that leads to doing things such as driving by your former girlfriend's new house, he might as well head on back to the motel. Phillip and Jessie would probably still be celebrating their fuckathon, or maybe they'd gone in her car to eat or were sated by the pool. If it were the first, Jason would just take the second or third options.

But, since it was full daylight, there was no real danger, right, in driving by her house? A guy could do it without losing his cool, since it was late morning, near lunch time, and at such an hour any emotional shenanigans he might play on himself wouldn't work. That house on Ramsey was on his way back to I-35, anyway.

He almost puked when he saw the Miata in the driveway. And he just blinked and jerked his head back and shot the Neon up to fifty momentarily, speeding away from the scene as if the Miata itself might spot him and give chase. His heart was pounding, and it took a full ten minutes for him to stop shaking.

This whole trip had completely unhinged him. Except for seeing Emily, all it had done was shower him with doubt that he'd been retooled, revamped, transformed. He'd have to count on the future to take another shot at the job. Well, at least now he had a fervent hope for change, a deep desire to be someone he himself could respect. He longed for the experience that he was about to enter to be so engrossing, so overwhelming, so harrowing, that it would burn out every thought of Lisa; he yearned for a future in Iraq where every space in his skull would be filled with the day's necessities, and he'd be stripped down lean and clean, without memory, with each moment requiring such intense concentration that no nanosecond would be left open for his past to creep in like a finger of gas under a door.

He yearned to be consumed, yearned to walk through the fire to be tempered like a samurai sword. To be forged through the flame into hardened steel.